FUGITIVE PRINCESS

"I should have guessed," Carig said, using his free hand to peel off her skullcap and reveal her silver hair. "I should have known. *Thou!*" The malice in that single word struck her like a spray of acid poison, but she didn't flinch. Instead she struggled all the harder, which only made him laugh.

"Poor little Princess," he mocked as he shook loose a tanglefoot web to bind her tight. "Who's this, thy savior?" He lashed out sideways with his foot, striking the fallen warrior hard enough to break ribs. "Sorry, my lad, I have first claim on 'er."

"You have nothing."

"Beg t' differ, Sacred Highness. Pity, really. It's almost a shame to end thy story when it's only just begun. Hopes as high as thine, a soul as noble, should be destroyed slowly."

"Go to hell."

"Dare I say, ladies first?" He stole a glance toward the Gate, which coated the grotto in a sickly radiance that washed away all color and flattened all figures, so that everything appeared to be two-dimensional, without depth or reality.

"*Never!*" she cried.

In that same moment, crossing every mental finge̶̶̶̶̶̶̶̶̶ since she last tried thi̶̶̶̶̶̶̶̶̶̶̶̶ nder Thorn's direct su̶̶̶̶̶̶̶̶̶̶̶̶ a deep breath and ca̶̶̶̶̶̶̶̶̶̶̶̶ e very fabric of the ro̶̶̶̶

PUBLISHED BY BANTAM BOOKS

SHADOW MOON
First in the Chronicles of the Shadow War
SHADOW DAWN
Second in the Chronicles of the Shadow War
SHADOW STAR
Third in the Chronicles of the Shadow War*

*coming soon

Shadow Dawn

Second in the Chronicles of the Shadow War

BY
Chris Claremont

STORY BY
George Lucas

BANTAM BOOKS
New York Toronto London Sydney Auckland

SHADOW DAWN
A Bantam Spectra Book

Publishing History
Bantam hardcover edition published January 1997
Bantam paperback edition / March 1998

Library of Congress Catalog Card Number: 96-45148.

ISBN 0-553-57289-X

Published simultaneously in the United States and Canada

Bantam Books are published by Bantam Books, a division of Bantam
Doubleday Dell Publishing Group, Inc. Its trademark, consisting of the
words "Bantam Books" and the portrayal of a rooster, is Registered in
U.S. Patent and Trademark Office and in other countries. Marca
Registrada. Bantam Books, 1540 Broadway, New York, New York
10036.

PRINTED IN THE UNITED STATES OF AMERICA

OPM · 10 9 8 7 6 5 4 3 2 1

To
THE GREY LADY

who nourished my soul,
without whom this book would not have been possible

&

Black-Eyed Susan's
Finn & Pam
Donald & Yoshi
Who sustained my body

And thanks as well and most of all to
Diane & Peter
for Edgewater
A home away from home

THE TWELVE GREAT REALMS

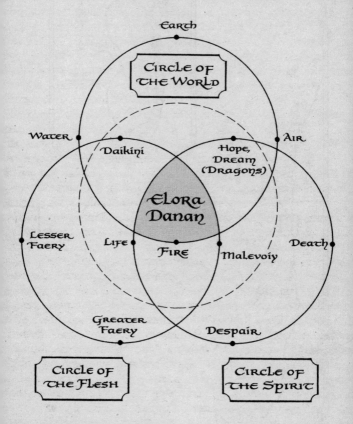

Earth

CIRCLE OF
THE WORLD

Water · Air

Daikini · Hope,
Dream
(Dragons)

Elora
Danan

Lesser
Faery · Death

Life · Fire · Malevoiy

Greater
Faery · Despair

CIRCLE OF
THE FLESH

CIRCLE OF
THE SPIRIT

© A·Karl/J·Kemp, 1996

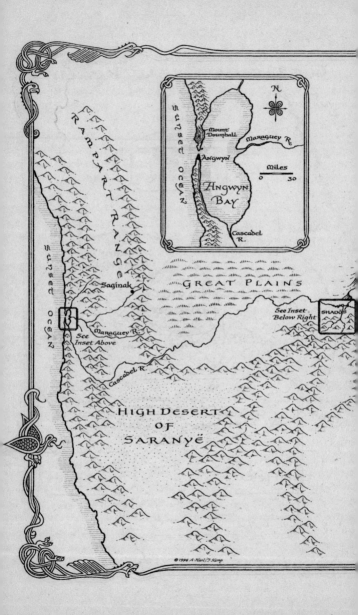

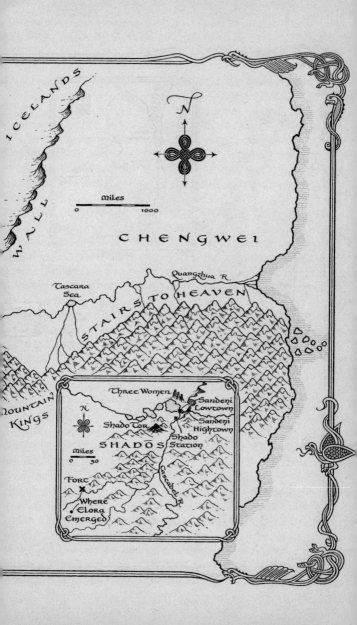

Shadow
Dawn

Chapter
1

With a grin of purest delight, Elora Danan summoned fire.

It burst from the ground as though she'd simply opened a tap, a tiny geyser of raw incandescence drawn straight from the molten heart of the world. In a heartbeat, every aspect of physical sensation within the forge was transformed. Each breath tasted sulfurous on her tongue, the furnace heat baking the air so fiercely that sweat evaporated the instant it formed on her skin. Phosphorescent lichen had been gathered in wall sconces to provide illumination, but the fountain's radiance made them instantly redundant, dominating the modest chamber as the noonday sun would a cloudless summer sky. The room's many shadows had been utterly banished. Instead the dark face of the chiseled stone was painted now in wild hues of scarlet and gold that never stayed the same from one moment to the next, but moved and changed with such madcap abandon the stone seemed alive. Impressive as those colorations were, they paled in comparison to the appearance of Elora herself, as the fireglow danced across skin the shade of purest polished silver.

She'd spent the better part of a week preparing the kiln for her examination, scrubbing it clean both physically and mystically. She'd gone over her notes until the order and structure of the requisite spells were engraved as deeply in her consciousness as the house sigils were in the mantelstone above the family hearth. She knew what to expect when she began the summoning, but wasn't sure what would actually happen. It was one thing to watch, no matter how intently, when Torquil or his apprentices worked their special brand of magic. It was another altogether to try it herself.

She was dressed for work in ironcloth trousers, padded at the knees and tucked into stout-soled moccasin boots that laced to the tops of her calves. A sleeveless cotton undershirt hugged her torso. Over that went a proper shirt of soft brushed cotton, proof against the natural damp and chill of the tunnels. Last, a tunic of the same battered ironcloth as her trousers, padded at elbows and shoulders. The tunic hung to her knees, slit up both side seams to the waist to allow her legs total freedom of movement. It was cut big in the body, too, which she found a cause for some annoyance, as it made her appear far heftier than she actually was. She was proud of her physique; she'd worked hard and long burning off the excess pounds that had been a part of her all through childhood and didn't care for any reminders of the way she used to look.

As she crouched before the firespout her face split in a grin of irrepressible delight. She was determined to fix every aspect of this, her first conjuration, in memory, the better to transcribe it later into her journal. The molten rock, she observed, was of a thicker consistency than water, heavier even than oil. Tiny sparks flashed all along its length as the intense heat ignited any stray and wayward scraps of dust in the air that swirled too close. Elora could feel prickles across the small patches of exposed skin and she had to narrow her eyes against the glare, even through the dark glasses the Rock Nelwyns used whenever they channeled lava.

Unexpectedly, and with a small pop, something wrestled its way through the fissure and slithered up the interior of the small fountain, to burst into full view at its summit. Elora beheld a figure that, in broadest brush strokes, consisted of a central torso, a pair of arms, a head. She could see no legs. The lower half of the creature was one with the pillar of molten rock. Its head began as a featureless orb, but the longer she stared at it, the more features and definition appeared: eyes where human eyes should be, a nose bisecting the face, a proper mouth above a strong chin. Streams of russet flame poured back from a sharp widow's peak to form a thick single plait that reached all the way down the figure's back until it flowed into the molten rock.

Elora thought it was a most attractive creature. She hadn't realized she was looking at a vision of herself.

"Hello," she said. The elemental cocked head and eyebrow together in a gesture that was a match for hers, as if each were the reflection in the other's mirror.

Its mouth worked to form a similar reply, grew teeth and tongue behind the lips to follow Elora's template. Lines formed between the brows, in an all-too-human expression of puzzlement, as the elemental measured the gap between form and function and attempted to divine where it was lacking.

Elora took another, more obvious breath, to demonstrate that speech came from the outrush of air over her vocal cords.

"Hello," she tried again.

The elemental's chest swelled as it drew in air for speech. Elora smiled, so did it, both in anticipation of what was to come.

A hand near the size of her head snagged her by the scruff of the neck, and just as the elemental began to reply Elora found herself yanked bodily behind one of the massive shield walls that ringed the furnace.

"**Hello,**" was what she heard, in a voice strangely like and yet unlike her own. What she saw was an outrush of raw flame powerful enough to put a dragon to shame. What she felt was the last awful glory of a moth in the face of the candleflame that consumes it. For a span of heartbeats that seemed an eternity—and which for Elora Danan, very nearly was—her forge was engulfed in elemental fire, to scorch walls and floor and ceiling, to sear the very surface on the opposite side of the barrier behind which she and her savior lay huddled.

Then, just as suddenly, the fire was gone, the forge plunged into comparative darkness as her eyes struggled to adapt to the light shift. The lichen had been consumed by the miniature holocaust and the elemental itself had vanished that same instant. The vision that remained in Elora's memory, like an afterimage imprinted on the eye, was of a creature as startled by what happened as the young woman herself, who'd done harm where none was meant and had fled in shame of the deed and terror of the consequences.

"Wow" was what she tried to say, though the air in the chamber was too hot for any proper breaths and far too dry to make the act of speech practicable. Neither lips nor tongue felt flexible enough to form the words. There was precious little sensation to them and she wondered if her skin was as cracked as earth after a drought.

She was set roughly on her feet and propelled out the door into the main forge beyond, the plunge in temperature so sudden and extreme that, despite her protective clothing, she couldn't help a brutal attack of shakes.

Water was offered. Elora took a shallow sip from the flask, her eyes remaining downcast while she sagged against the wall behind her. She assumed that stone would be as cool as the air, but it was actually warm to the touch, as the shell of even a well-insulated oven would be after a day's hard cooking.

She was shakier than she'd first realized, as both the efforts required in casting her summons and the shock of the encounter with the elemental took their fierce toll. She found her legs suddenly unable to support the rest of her. She folded in on herself, barely aware of running feet in the distance and harsh-voiced cries of alarm and concern.

Manya, as always, led the way, donning the last of her own protective gear as she burst through the entrance to the forge with a mix of siblings and senior apprentices close on her heels.

"Torquil," she cried, searching the vaulting chamber for a sight of her husband, "*Torquil!*"

"I'm here, woman," was his reply, sounding hoarse and stressed from a throat as parched as Elora's. "I'm all right. Everything's all right."

"The devil you say." She had a broadhead ax in one hand that could cut through stone as naturally as wood. In the other was a sealed flask, which held the strongest sending the Nelwyn shamans were able to cast, to be used only in the most dire of circumstances.

"Peace, Manya," Torquil said again, adding enough force of command to his voice to bring both his wife and her companions to a stop. "The danger's passed, of that, you have my oath."

"You look like hell," she told him gruffly, making a face as she flicked char from his hood.

He grinned, teeth gleaming against a sooty visage. "It was only a brief visit."

"Damn near gave Rakel a seizure, Torquil," she said seriously, and made a gesture with her head toward the household shaman, whose drawn features with lines of pain and stress etched deep around eyes and nose and mouth provided eloquent proof of how severe a shock it had been.

"It won't happen again," he assured her.

"Please the Maker, let that be so," was her response. She flipped the flask end over end in her hand, ignoring the shaman's swift intake of breath as she caught it and handed it to him in the same swift gesture. "It came through our wards as if they didn't exist. If things had gone bad in here, husband, I'm not sure this would have made a difference."

He sighed. "Rakel, was the phenomenon localized?"

The shaman's reply was terse, each phrase making clear how painful it was for him to speak. "Manifestation, yes. Effects . . . ?" He shrugged his shoulders.

"There'll be queries from the other forges, then."

It was Manya's turn to chuckle. "Shrieks of outrage and fury, more likely, if their shamans were hit anywhere near as hard as Rakel here. No fear, though, I'll deal with 'em." She shook her head as if to clear it, and said in her pragmatic way, "Back to business. Got a message from the Factor. If you've consignments on order, the sooner they're filled, the better for all. Seems pretty certain the bazaar won't last the full season. May not even see the next full moon."

"That's today's task."

"All right, you lot," she began, directing her attention to the clutch of apprentices strung out behind her, but Torquil stopped her with an upraised palm and the shake of his head.

"The child and I will handle things," he said.

"Don't be ridiculous."

"The forge is my domain, wife," he told her formally. "Trust my judgment in this, as I do yours in other things."

Manya considered the better part of a minute before replying. As she watched from her seat against the wall, Elora could tell that Manya was of a mind to overrule her husband, for while the forge was his, theirs was a marriage of equal partners. To the girl's surprise, Manya reached forward with her free hand and caught her husband around the neck, gathering him not into a kiss but a close embrace that in its own way was even more passionate. Fear was as strong in both of them as relief and that realization made Elora's heart pound painfully in her chest. The elemental had come and gone so quickly, the moment of its manifestation had seemed so wonderful to her, that she hadn't given a thought to the danger.

"Nothing to say for yourself, then?" Torquil demanded.

The question caught her by surprise. She hadn't expected to be challenged.

"I meant no harm."

That response won her a dismissive snort from the forgemaster.

"Neither did the elemental!" she protested further.

"Fat lot of good that would've done you. It'd be sorry, you'd be ash, an' where'd the fate of the world be then, I ask you, eh?"

She lifted her gaze in what started as defiance but just as quickly turned to something else before the unflinching glare she found facing her.

She was small for her age, she'd hardly grown at all these past three years, but that still made her a head and more taller than the average Nelwyn. In Daikini like herself, height was determined mainly in the length of the legs; not so for the Nelwyns. They were mostly torso, and that was packed with a ferocious strength out of proportion to what one might expect from a being their size. Big shoulders, powerful arms made them born farmers and born miners. Among their number, working in wood or stone or metal, were counted some of the finest artisans in all the Twelve Great Realms on either side of the Veil.

Torquil was an elder of the Rock Nelwyns, which put him a few turns past the prime of his life. Even so, he hefted with ease hammers Elora couldn't lift from the ground, and was as renowned for the delicacy of his work as for the purity of his ore. His age made itself plain in the salt and pepper of his hair, and in the deep creases and textures of his face. His beard was a throwback to younger days, composed of fire colors only lightly scattered with snow, and he wore it close-cropped to emphasize the strong line of his jaw. His eyes were gray as primal stone, as cold and unyielding now as the granite on which the two of them, child and guardian, stood.

"I thought," Elora conceded, after drawing out the silence as long as she dared, "I'd taken the proper precautions," which was true.

"Elora . . ." His exasperation was plain. "I should box your ears. And worse. It's no less than you deserve for such foolishness. By the Maker," he continued, the words tumbling from him like a flash flood from a dam that had just burst, his tone making plain that his ire grew mainly from fear for her safety, "what were you thinking?"

He tore his padded skullcap from his head and turned this way and that, wanting a physical release for his wrath but unable to find one that was suitable.

"What am I saying? If you'd thought a whit, the smallest jot and tittle, we wouldn't be standing here in the first place. Whatever brought you here, *thought* had nothing to do with it." He rounded on her suddenly and thrust a finger straight to the end of her nose.

"And don't you dare cry on me, girl!"

"I'm not crying," she said as she used the heel of her free hand to wipe away her tears.

"Have you learned *nothing* since you came among us?"

She had no answer that wouldn't make things worse, so she kept silent.

"What's the first rule of the forge?" he demanded of her.

" 'Fire is our tool and we, its master.' "

"And the second?"

" 'Above all else, see to the safety of the forge.' "

"Which means?"

" 'When faced by the unexpected, stop. Everything. At once.' "

"At least you know the words."

"That isn't fair!"

"Thorn Drumheller placed you in my care. 'For all that she is the Sacred Princess Elora Danan,' he told me, 'she is as dear to me as if she was my own. And I charge you, cousin, to care for her as if she was *your* own.' By blood and blade are we kin, yet in all our years he's never asked a favor of me, nor called in the debts between our houses. How am I to say to him, then, forgive me, cousin, but the Sacred Princess Elora got herself burned to a crisp?"

"I'm sorry."

"Well, that makes everything all right, then. I feel much better already."

The Nelwyns she'd known of had been a small village of farmers, half the world away in a lovely vale off the River Freen. They kept mostly to themselves, and seemed happiest when they interacted least with their neighbors, be they Daikini or the various races and creatures among the Veil Folk. Their credo was modesty in all things. The key to their survival was simply to stay unnoticed by those who might do them harm.

These Nelwyns were altogether different. They made no attempt to hide, quite the opposite. They took their cue from the great peaks where they made their home: here we are, they proclaimed to the world, here we stand. They mined and worked metals, base and precious, as skilled in the art of crafting fine jewelry as they were renowned for the quality of their weapons.

"Sacred Princess you may be, Elora Danan," Torquil continued as he led her back around the shield walls to examine the furnace for any damage from the elemental's manifestation. "Blessed by fate. Protected against all manner of magic. But still flesh, still blood."

"Spare me," she said, and thought, with all the asperity only a fifteen-year-old can muster, *because I've heard this lecture before, Uncle. I know it by heart.* She spoke with an unconscious hauteur left over from childhood, when all her days had been spent in a tower in the city of Angwyn, capital of the westlands kingdom of the same name, waited on hand and foot, her every whim someone's pleasure to fulfill.

He let her rudeness pass, to bring the lesson home. *"I will. Others might not be so forgiving. Special as you are, Elora Danan, you're still mortal. You can bleed and you can burn."*

Torquil frowned as he ran experienced hands over the

face of the massive slabs of stone that ringed the pit. They had been quarried from primordial rock, as thick as the Nelwyn's own body, and had withstood the abuse of years protecting the training forge without showing significant wear. The tiny elemental had changed all that. Although the exposure to its flame had only been a matter of seconds, the phenomenal heat had cracked and pitted the surface of the stone, exposing the most minute flaws and in some spots leaving the stone itself so brittle it powdered at the slightest touch. One massive slab had cracked right through.

"Torquil, why are you so angry?" Elora asked quietly, watching him. "I was just trying to raise fire, as you taught me. I've worked alongside your apprentices for months, learned as they learned."

"And done well," he conceded.

"You thought I was ready, you said so yourself."

"My error. Bless the Maker, neither of us had to pay the price for my foolishness."

"That isn't fair!" she said again.

"Elora, you were to Summon fire on this exercise, not an elemental. The instant it manifested, you should have aborted the spell."

"It was such a little thing, Uncle. I didn't think it could do any harm. I'm certain it meant none."

"Sometimes, child, there's a world of difference between intent and execution." He waved a hand dismissively. "It's not you I'm furious with, Elora, but myself. I'm the one who's supposed to know better."

"What do you mean?"

He cocked a quizzical eyebrow. "Did Drumheller teach you nothing before he brought you here?"

"Thorn did the best he could." She chuckled at the memory as she took the wire brush he handed her and began scraping at the char on the furnace, to see if any of it was salvageable. "Considering we were pretty much always on the run. And that I was about as ignorant as a girl could be."

"You know there are four Great Realms to the Circle

of the World, as there are four also to those of the Flesh and of the Spirit."

"Of course," she replied, slipping easily into the role of pupil to schoolmaster. Before continuing her reply, though, she frowned and shook her head. The damage here was worse than to the shield walls. The furnace was ruined. The walls of the chamber itself, where the fire had struck, hadn't fared any better. She and Torquil may have emerged unscathed, but the forge was a total loss. She recited, "The Realms of the Circle of the World are Earth and Air and Fire and Water."

"We Nelwyns are of the Earth."

"I know that, too. You resonate to its power the same way the Wyrrn do to the Realm of Water."

"But it's *fire,* Elora, that forms the heart and core of Creation. All was void until that first fateful spark was struck."

He was paraphrasing the Nelwyn catechism, their story of the origins of the world and of themselves. In the Beginning was Nothing, until the Celestial Fire was lit, to cast the Universe into the defining duality of Light and Shadow. From that fire came all the aspects of being, and, as importantly, of life.

"Fire made us," he went on. "Its warmth sustains us. Its passion inspires us. Its fury consumes us. It can take a solid and melt it into liquid, that liquid into gas, and ultimately flash even that gas into nothingness."

"Earth to Water to Air," she said, completing the litany of transition for him.

Torquil nodded. "Nothing in our lives is so essential, or so deadly. As this lesson has shown us both."

"I'm sorry."

"So am I," he agreed, and he furrowed his brow, pursed his lower lip between his thumbs in thought. "Shouldn't have happened, this. The wards were set right and proper, as you've been taught. The songs of making were performed likewise. This was as fine an examination as I've seen. . . ."

"Until the elemental came."

11

"Aye."

"Proof positive maybe, Torquil, that the enchantment or whatever it is that makes me immune to magic also makes it impossible for me to *work* magic?"

"This isn't magic, Elora, any more than striking flint to steel makes a spark, or applying sufficient heat to a pot of water can bring it to a boil."

"Then how come everyone in the world can't do it?"

"Climb to the top of the Stairs to Heaven, try boiling water. You can't, no matter how much heat is applied. Try striking your spark to a log instead of tinder, or soaking wet scraps instead of dry, where's your fire then? You need the proper interaction of natural forces for the processes to work, same here as there. To draw molten rock from the heart of the world, as we do, what's needed is a place where the stones are receptive to our songs, as our farmer cousins seek fertile land and sweet water for their crops."

"So what happened here, Uncle, with me?"

"As nearly as I can gauge it, child, you must be like some beacon on a cliff. Or perhaps the pole to a lodestone. You draw things to you simply by *being*. Especially fire. Grown elementals have sense enough to know you for what you are. . . ."

"Sacred?" She cast forth a joke. Torquil didn't bite.

"Human. So they keep away. But that was a youngster, the barest wee bit of a thing, probably only just coalesced to awareness. All curiosity, no sense. You've that in common, the pair of you."

"Are you going to keep hammering at me about this, Torquil, till I'm flat?"

He tried to look stern, but then grinned, which made him look surprisingly handsome. Elora could easily see why his wife loved him so. There was a fair measure of imp in that smile, a roguish coloration to his character that reminded her of friends she hadn't seen in far too long.

"I'd as soon try to crack a diamond with my teeth, thank you very much, and no doubt have about as much success. I tell you truth, Elora Danan, because you need to

12

hear it, and tell you often in hopes that someday you'll actually listen."

She stuck out her tongue at him and made a rude face to go with it, and he laughed.

"Strange, though," he mused when his chuckles subsided, more like thoughts spoken aloud than words actually meant for her ears.

"I beg your pardon?"

"That wee bit. It was *too* young. wouldn't have thought to see one without its mam being close at hand. And no mam worth the name would've let her bit come near the likes of you unattended. Too dangerous by far for both."

She stuck out her tongue again and crossed her eyes in the bargain and Torquil laughed all the harder.

"Should we do anything about that?" she wondered aloud. "I mean, if it's lost . . ." She spoke with more passion than she realized, the elemental's plight striking too strong a resonance to the experiences of her own young life.

"Not much we can, to help. And we're in enough trouble already, the pair of us."

He was trying to deflect her from her purpose with humor but she wouldn't have it.

"That's cruel, Uncle."

"We *work* with fire, Elora. But there are creatures who dwell amongst it, as we do the air or the Wyrrn the oceans of the world."

"I know, I've met them."

Torquil shook his head in wonderment, and no little awe. Thorn's tale of his and Elora's encounter with a school of firedrakes still had the power to thread the older Nelwyn's heart with ice. "So I recall. You saw just now what the smallest one of them can do. Our magicks were no proof against it, only good, solid rock saved us. And that by a margin so slim I don't care to think about it. Imagine one of full growth, perhaps of a mind to do us harm. Even stone burns, child, and I've no desire to see our mountain home turn into a bonfire."

She allowed herself to be convinced, but she didn't much like it.

Each household had its own smelter, linked to the mine by broad tunnels that snaked outward from the vertical shafts sunk deep into the earth. The shafts themselves plunged a mile and more through the heart of the mountain, from well below ground level to near the summit, with a new mining level every fifty feet or so. Excavations followed the veins of ore, some petering out after a few hundred feet, while others plunged ever onward, sprouting offshoots along the way just like the roots of a tree. The effort was communal, the work and the profit shared equally among the entire clan. For the most part, the refined ore was sold in great blocks and slabs and sheets of metal, to be transported by caravan or keelboat to various Daikini strongholds, where it would be put to its final shape and purpose. Each household was entitled to claim a portion of ore to do with as they pleased. Some chose iron, to shape into steel and from there to weapons. Others, Torquil foremost among them, preferred to work with stones and precious metals.

Payment was by barter, goods for goods. There was no sense offering gold to those who made their living liberating it from the rock. In terms of absolute wealth, the Mountain Kings could probably beggar an empire, so they used that fortune to acquire materials and possessions that didn't come so easily to hand. Fine woods, for one, both as raw material and finished product, to furnish their habitats. Tapestries to decorate the home, cloth to adorn the body. Delicacies of both food and drink to delight the palate. Manuscripts of both fact and fiction to intrigue the mind. Rock Nelwyns worked hard; to live well, they felt, was no more than their just reward.

During her travels Elora had seen termite mounds better than twice the height of a tall Daikini. One had been broken open, as though cleaved from top to bottom by an ax, revealing an intricate network of tunnels and chambers. It was an image that often came to her when thinking about the Mountain Kings, who made their own home in a similar kind of honeycomb labyrinth. To these Nelwyns, this was paradise—but Elora missed the sun, and the star-scattered sky at night.

Torquil set himself in a crouch beside where the ore would be melted, one hand resting lightly on the cool stone, his head cocked slightly to the side in an aspect of rapt attention.

"Uncle," Elora prompted, after he'd remained there unmoving for what seemed to her the longest while. "Is anything the matter?"

He didn't appear to hear at first, but before she could repeat herself he forestalled her with a shake of his head.

"Just deciding to accept Dame Nature's suggestion that we fulfill our commitment the old-fashioned way," he told her with a grin, to be answered with a heartfelt groan, for that meant *much* more work for the apprentice.

"Couldn't you sing the songs of Shaping?" she asked.

"I could, but I won't. Fire's a chaos to deal with at the best of times, an' right now, child, the patterns feel too wild and unpredictable."

"This has never happened before. I mean, I've helped you lots of times. . . ." She caught herself as she heard a whine creep into her voice.

"All the more reason to be cautious. One surprise like that is enough for any man, thank you, an' fate's been tempted enough for any day. Besides, as the first part of your exam was, shall we say, inconclusive, I want to see how much you've *really* learned at my side."

First, Elora had to load the coal to fuel the furnace. The fire was perpetually lit, but since most of the actual smelting was done in concert with a sophisticated network of manipulative enchantments, those flames were maintained at a fairly low intensity. Now they had to be stoked until the kiln blazed white-hot. Elora lost track of how many shovelfuls she pitched through the grate and had even less idea whether the sweat that poured off her was from the tremendous and sustained effort required for this task or the raw heat barely two body lengths from her masked and goggled face.

Normally this was a job for the entire crew of apprentices, and even then it was backbreaking labor. She had no words to describe what it meant to do it by herself and no strength to spare for any emotional response. Quite the contrary. She didn't dare indulge in any resentment because it was simply too dangerous. The smallest misstep, the most minor of misjudgments, could have catastrophic consequences. Like all the apprentices, and Torquil himself, Elora had the bumps and bruises and burns to prove it.

"That'll do, Elora," Torquil said at long last. But there was no rest for the weary.

He called her to his side and allowed her a moment to marvel at the sight of what had been a pile of rocks better than twice her height reduced now to a pool of glowing liquid. Then, to her amazement, he passed off responsibility for the pour to her.

The normal means of production was to sing to the liquid rock in the language of stone and gradually reshape both melody and lyrics to that of metal. In the process—and with great care, because even in a liquid state stone could be notoriously stubborn and hard to move—impurities and lesser metals would be cajoled from the mix and directed into drainage channels where they were allowed to pool to hardness. Some of these castoffs would be recycled into later pours, others used by the apprentices for practice. One way or another, everything that came through the foundry had its purpose. At the same time streams of different ores would be blended to create alloys that were far stronger than their component parts.

Unfortunately Torquil made plain that today's pour would be a manual operation from start to finish, completed without the benefit of magic of any kind.

The equipment and tools were designed for Nelwyn hands and Nelwyn strength. Neither they nor Torquil made the slightest concession to Elora in terms of gender or size or race. She was expected to pull her own weight, just like the other apprentices, no matter how much greater the effort. Heavy protective clothing was an absolute necessity, for despite everyone's care, there were always splashes and overruns, and the ferocious heat emanating from the melt sometimes seemed enough to ignite the very air they breathed. Elora had seen, and survived, far worse, but on that occasion she'd had the benefit of one of the most intense defensive wards Thorn Drumheller had ever cast. As her encounter with the elemental had brought home, she had no such armor here. At the same time she was manhandling ingots and beams whose standard size was twice hers and weight better than triple. Even with the inventive arrangement of slings and counterweighted pulleys that Torquil had rigged, each workday left her aching and breathless as she pushed and pulled and hammered and chiseled her way from slab to slab. Where a Nelwyn used one hand to wield a hammer, she used two. Where a fellow apprentice might maneuver his piece with an application of brute force, she finessed it with Torquil's rigging. She gave little thought to the fact that she was managing loads today that would have been impossible when she arrived, and doing so with an ease and relaxed confidence in her body and its capabilities that she'd never before known. All that mattered was that the job be done and done well. That was the core of her pride.

Torquil's was in seeing her do so.

Their consignment for the day was a dozen ingots, a full load for the wagon waiting beneath the crane station at the far end of Torquil's cavern. He was rare among Rock Nelwyns—*in that,* Elora thought, *I bet he takes after Thorn*—he liked space. Most forges were cramped into the smallest space practicable. This was a cave that dwarfed the High King's throne room in Angwyn. Better than a hundred yards from end to end, a bit less than a hundred feet across, a level floor for the most part, with a network of ducts that diverted water from the household spring for the use of the forge. Others sent jets of air rushing through the furnace to keep the ore properly oxygenated as it was reduced to pig iron and later refined to various grades of steel. The walls came together high overhead in an off-center arch, like a letter *A* that was curved on one side but slashed straight down the other, with ledges that Torquil used to hold the crosspieces of his hoists and cranes. If necessary, he and Manya could run the entire forge by themselves.

With a dull, metallic *thunk,* the last ingot dropped into place atop its fellows. Elora clambered aboard the wagon and wrestled free the restraining clamps, putting her shoulder against the crane arm to shove it back against its safety stops. Then she folded at every joint—knees, hips, vertebrae, shoulders, skull—and took on the aspect of a stone herself, too exhausted to do more than breathe as she dropped to her rump. She didn't budge when the dray horses were harnessed into place on either side of the wagon tongue, and only cracked an eyelid when the wagon itself began to move.

"You're taking me along?" she asked Torquil.

"You've earned the treat" was his reply. He knew how difficult it was for her to live underground. "From what the Cascani Factor told Manya, this may be your last chance this season. Keep your hood on and your wits about you outside, you'll be fine."

"Wits," she snorted, in a fair approximation of Torquil himself. "I'm so tired I'm lucky I can string two coherent words together!"

"So I notice," he agreed, his tone dry as her throat.

She clambered forward to take the seat beside him and gratefully accepted the proffered water bottle. She drank as she'd been taught, slow and shallow sips at first, to remind mouth and throat what cool liquid tasted like. Then, in a matter of swallows, she drained half the flask. The only greater pleasure, she decided, would be a swim.

Perhaps later, she promised herself.

Torquil was right. There was little chance of her being recognized, even by those who knew her. For one, given the passage of time, both enemies and friends would be expecting someone taller. And while her silver skin and hair were dead giveaways, there was precious

18

little of either to be seen beneath her own clothes. She wore gauntlets that touched her elbows and a hood that fastened across the front of her face so that only her eyes were visible. All she needed to do to cover those was slip her goggles into place. The lenses were smoked so dark as to be nearly opaque and the frames had blinders attached to either side to protect her sight from any wayward sparks. Under the flap of the hood was a scarf, usually worn tucked up over the nose, one more added layer to shield her from backflashes. This was far heavier clothing than an adult Daikini could comfortably wear, let alone an adolescent, but Elora was stronger than she looked. More so, stronger than she gave herself credit for. The last piece of camouflage was the soot and dust raised from the forge that always managed to work its way beneath all those layers of clothes to darken cheeks and chin more effectively than any cosmetic.

As the wagon emerged from the outer cavern Elora's eyes swept the encampment beyond with an eager gaze. Normally, this deep into the trading season, the bazaar had the appearance of a small, portable city, home to a score of trading houses, hundreds of tents, and at any given instance a thousand inhabitants. There were merchants, of course, dealing in every conceivable article of commerce, the bankers that financed them, the roustabouts and joy houses that hoped to separate much money from many people, the constabulary that tried to keep such transactions within acceptable bounds of propriety. There was a hospice for the sick and a ministry for those poor souls who failed to recover. No boneyard, though, that was an unbreachable stipulation of the master trading agreement: no bodies to be laid to rest within a ten-day march of the bazaar. The dead didn't just draw flies and corruption, they attracted ghouls, who generally attracted trolls, and the only taste trolls savored more than carrion was that of Nelwyns.

There'd been few caravans this season, none at all since solstice, and even a cursory glance revealed the bazaar as little more than a shadow of its true self.

Hardly a surprise, Elora thought sourly, *given what's happening in the world.* It seemed that everywhere she looked, she beheld shadows where once had stood healthy substance. The forms of reality, but little more.

Dominating the campground was the Cascani pavilion, the largest tent on the highest rise of rock and earth. The Cascani were wanderers and explorers, and considered themselves traders to the world. They'd travel anywhere by land or sea, and it was said they even ventured beyond the Veil for the sheer fun of it and as often as not found a way to turn a tidy profit from the trip. They hailed from an archipelago of seamount islands scattered along the coast above Angwyn that reached as far as the northern Ice Lands. In spirit and occasionally blood they claimed kinship with the seaborn Wyrrn, whose race dominated the Great Deeps as the Daikini did the land. The one guaranteed safe passage over the waves, the other an equivalent access to the land, to the benefit of both.

The Cascani were a rough-hewn breed, their character shaped by the harsh physicality of their home, forever presenting themselves to outsiders as the quintessential country cousins. One small step removed from bumpkinhood. They were the kind of folk most would expect in the role of pirate and freebooter, more comfortable muleskinning a wagon train than in the halls of political power or courtyards of high finance. This was a foolish, fatal assumption which generally cost those who made it dearly. It was no accident that Cascani letters of credit were honored virtually everywhere, or that their word was the hallmark of trust throughout the Great Realms. They drove hard bargains, but kept every one they made. They were true to their friends, allies, and especially customers, grim death to whosoever was dimwit enough to cross them. They weren't the only traders in the world, but they set the standard the others found themselves forced to live by.

In happier times, Elora remembered a half dozen more pavilions of rival trading houses, trying their best to eclipse the Cascani in size and opulence. Smaller boutique firms offered a less comprehensive selection of wares or sought to purchase something equally specific. On the road, each caravan looked after itself. The Cascani assumed responsibility for the bazaar, ensuring their claim by establishing a permanent residence for their Factor and a modest contingent of cavalry. Each spring, it was the Factor's responsibility to block out the configuration of the encampment, with space for every tent and sufficient access to freshwater and forage.

This season, it was clear from the outset, there would be no need for such an effort or much precision. The plain should have been crowded for the better part of a mile, fanning outward from the entrance to the Nelwyn stronghold. What Elora saw in addition to the Cascani pavilion was a second of like size, a handful belonging to lesser firms, and a sad scattering of household and individual tents, clustered as close as they dared to the larger encampments, like children snuggling up to a parent in a desperate attempt to keep warm. Normally there was a separate paddock for the livestock, but with few exceptions both horses and draft animals were picketed within the arc formed by the dominant pavilions. In the distance Elora could see outriders, in patrols of four, ranging the approaches to the bazaar, complementing the constantly manned observation posts whose locations on the distant heights gave commanding views of well-worn trails.

"Have you ever seen the bazaar so empty, Uncle?"

"So deep into season." Torquil shook his head. "Not like this. Not ever. And d'you see the way the stock is set?"

"As if they expect a raid."

"More than that, starskin." That was the nickname he'd given her, at their first meeting. She didn't mind. Torquil meant it as a term of affection and endearment. From others, though, she'd heard it as a curse. "Usually, the animals are all grouped together in a common herd. Folks trust to brands and truthtellers to tell them apart."

"These are tethered in discrete groups," she finished, nodding in comprehension. "Close by their owners. D'you see, Uncle—the household tents have their animals staked right outside. How long do you think it would take everyone to leave?" she asked suddenly.

"Start your strike at first light, be an empty valley by sundown. This lot isn't just ready to go, they're eager."

"Do you need me at the tally station?"

"Itching for a stroll?"

"Curiosity."

"Have a care, child. And don't dally. The mood here is catching. I'm of a mind to be back under my own roof quick as I'm able."

"Is there anything that's needed at home?"

"Here's Manya's list, and the household chit as well. Give both to the Cascani Factor, let him and his staff do the work. I'll meet you at his pavilion within the hour. Agreed?" Tone notwithstanding, this wasn't a suggestion. He said an hour, he meant an hour, not an instant more.

She could have hopped from her perch but she descended to the ground in Nelwyn fashion, a careful, questing step at a time, bearing the whole of her weight on her arms and shoulders until she was sure of her footing. She walked as they did, with a slight side-to-side waddle, and took the easy path upslope to the Cascani pavilion.

"From Torquil Ufgood," she said to the sentry, holding out both chit and list.

"Ahhhhh," she heard from within, and cranked her neck back a notch as the Factor himself came out to welcome her, "the Master Smith's apprentice."

"One of many, lord," she protested humbly as he looked over the two slates.

"Aye. Tha's true. But t' my mind, as there's but one among the Rock Nelwyns worth that title, there's also only one among his helpers worth calling a true apprentice."

She was glad he couldn't see her blush but also thrilled to his praise.

"How could you possibly know the difference in our work?" she wondered.

"Whose ingots're those y're jus' deliverin', hey? Trust an old man's eyes, lad. Quality tells."

"I thank my lord for his generosity."

"An' a diplomat in the bargain. 'Strewth, y're a wonder, y'are."

Hanray Rutherwood wasn't as big as the pure-blooded Cascani she'd known, but there was a solidity of spirit that more than made up for the lack. He was an odd mix of color and features. His skin was fair, yet the almond shape of the eyes, the structure of the bones, came from the people of the Spice Lands well to the east. They were mostly dark-eyed and dark-haired. His eyes were green, and as age had stripped the mahogany from his hair it had left behind the russet undercoat, with an end result that appeared more salt and paprika than the salt and pepper she was familiar with.

At a glance, the fitments of the pavilion seemed far less impressive than one would expect of a merchant of the Factor's rank and responsibility. In the main, the other trading houses had more lavish presentations, as though each was trying to create a palace in small out here in the wilderness. To Elora, whose upbringing had been in the grandest palace on the continent, if not the world, the end result appeared far better than she suspected it actually was, pretty without being practical. The Cascani hallmark, by stark contrast, was function over form. The traders had no objection to their movables looking good, but they had to travel well and serve their purpose; those were the paramount considerations. They didn't come all this way merely to impress, they were here to do business.

The Factor liked to eat on the run, so a table had been set in buffet style with baskets of breads and platters of sliced meats, trays of cheese and bowls of fruit. There were decanters of wine for guests, but the Cascani contented themselves with carafes of springwater. They enjoyed their drink as much as anyone but never allowed it to interfere with the job at hand. Called from Elora's side by the sudden entrance of a subordinate, the Factor snatched up a crisp apple as he passed and flipped it underhand back to her, indicating with a wave that his bounty was hers to enjoy. She caught the apple easily, and snatched up some cheese and a couple of boiled eggs and a small sausage pie as well, wrapping her booty in a napkin and snugging the whole lot into the belly pouch she wore beneath her smock as she slipped out a side entrance to the pavilion. The Factor was busy and she was of a mind for a stroll. If the season was to be cut short, as seemed more and more likely, she had some shopping of her own to do. Moreover, she was intensely curious as to the reasons why. The Rock Nelwyns delighted in the fact that the world came to their doorstep, but that also meant news of that world came only with their clients. In that regard, this year's pickings had been fearfully lean.

She quartered the apple blind, and fed the bits of core to a nearby horse. Her hood was oversized and even with the flaps unfastened she decided it left her features sufficiently in shadow that no one would notice her unique coloration, especially with her face as smudged as it was. The fruit was tartly sweet, the cheese sharp, their conflicting tastes quickly exciting her palate. She was starving, she hadn't eaten since breakfast, but she forced herself to be as deliberate with her snack as she had been earlier with Torquil's flask. She needed to be more than the sum of her appetites, that was another lesson she was still learning the hard way. She should be their mistress, not the other way 'round.

In Elora's tower, servants had cringed at the flick of her eyelid, and no doubt cursed her when her back was turned. In the bazaar, no one spared her a second glance. She preferred the anonymity. She enjoyed watching the faces of those around her, which represented races she knew, others she'd heard of, still more that were wholly and utterly strange to her. No two were alike, and every moment brought a new adventure, in endless fascination.

She also liked to listen. What she didn't like was what she heard.

"Soon as deal's done, I'm gone," a trader said in passing, his bluff tones a fit complement to the solid construction of Cascani trade tongue, which had long since established itself as the standard language of commerce. "Ye've half the sense Cherlindrea gave a rock," he continued to his companion, who walked less heavily, as befit a warrior, "ye'll follow my lead. C'd use a good bow wi' my train."

"Fair offer."

"Better'n ye'll see from the likes o' them," outthrust thumb in the direction of the Chengwei pavilion, the only one to rival the Cascani, who'd made the trek all the way from the continent's eastern shore. "Slit y'r throat as soon as look at ye, those slant eyes, so I've heard."

Grunt of agreement but the spoken reply took the discussion in a different direction.

"Is't bad?" the warrior asked. "In the west, I mean?"

She never heard the answer as the pair passed beyond earshot. Instead she found her attention drawn by the tavern across the way. Without moving from where she sat, Elora tightened the focus of her OutSight to bring both men and conversation into sharp clarity.

"What's the old saying"—rumination from a smoker, each phrase broken by a meditative puff on his pipe—"wherever a Maizani rides, the Maizan rule. They take it seriously."

"That's daft, wha'cher sayin'," protested a drover. "They can't conquer *everything!*"

"Givin' it a fair country try, way I sees it. Spent a year or so consolidatin' their hold on Angwyn . . ."

"What really happened there, does anyone know?"

Elora blinked her eyes and held herself close as a skirl of ice twisted outward from her soul to remind her of that awful night. Her thirteenth birthday, when the rulers of all the Great Realms gathered in Angwyn to celebrate her Ascension, the fulfillment of the age-old prophecy that proclaimed her as the savior of this world and those beyond the Veil who would bind together all those disparate domains and peoples in a lasting era of peace and harmony. Among the Daikini, since it was generally assumed that she was one of them, this had been popularly proclaimed as the Age of Man. At long last the youngest race would have its chance to stand beside the other Realms as an equal.

Instead an evil sorcerer—known to her only by the name Thorn Drumheller had given him that fateful night, the Deceiver—had struck down the ruling heads of those domains and, in trying to seize her soul as well, cast a dread enchantment over the entire city. He had reached out to everything in Angwyn that lived and had stolen the warmth from their hearts, the joy from their eyes, the light from their souls. It was as if, in one terrible instant, winter had come to the city in the guise of a spider, to encase it within a cocoon of the most delicate ice crystal. Nothing was said to be more beautiful to behold, nor likewise more deadly.

She and her companions had barely escaped with their lives that fateful night. They'd been running, one way or another, ever since.

"Who's to say for sure? Cursed, the city is, tha's certes."

"I hear it's like the Ice Lands. Unbearably cold."

" 'Unbearably cold,' " mocked the pipe smoker. "The city is ice, the bay is ice, any fool enough to come within a day's travel of the place is turned to ice. In a word, pure an' simple, Angwyn is hell. And all within are damned."

"The Maizan did that?"

"Elora Danan did that." A new voice, to more mutters of agreement than protest.

"The Sacred Princess?"

"Hers is a blessing I can live without." More rough chuckles, a popular sentiment evidently, followed by the sound of spitting to ward off evil and the sight of hands making signs to do the same. Different cultures, different traditions, the same intent.

"What's that y'say, dog?" Surprisingly one among the group stood to her defense. He was in a minority.

"Dinna get'cherself in such a twist, man," cautioned the pipe smoker, waving the protester back to his stool and further attempting to mollify him with a fresh tankard of ale. "But look to the plain truth of it. The gal's supposed to be the world's savior, am I right? Yet you've heard the stories, have yeh not? Tir Asleen—"

"Where?"

"Some damn city or other," groused one of the merchants, "on the far side of the damn world, so the Cascani say. Shut'cher gob, willya, an' let folk listen."

"—was her home," continued the first speaker, unheeding of any interruption, "an' it was smashed t' dust, so the tale goes."

"Your pardon," said a voice she knew to speak in her favor, the Factor himself, "but I've heard tha' tale told a mite differently. Were a battle with a Demon Queen tha' came before, some sorceress name of Bavmorda."

"With respect, milord Factor, what of it?"

"Y' canna have it both ways. Which is truth?"

"Could be *lies,*" her first defender exclaimed in final protest, though his tone suggested he knew full well the ears he addressed were mostly closed. "Unless any of you have actually been there t' see for yourself."

"Fine, they're lies," agreed the smoker, without conceding the point in the slightest. "What *is* known for *fact* is that Angwyn took her in, an' it's been rightwise cursed. Were up t' me, I'd think twice about offering sanctuary, that's all I'm sayin'."

Elora blinked back a sudden rush of tears, and concentrated on silently peeling the shell off an egg. She wanted to cry a protest of her own, to tell them they were wrong, but she had no arguments to marshal against them. Somehow, even though it was through no fault of her own, save perhaps the simple fact of her existence, she'd brought doom to both cities. Despite all the faith invested in her, she'd been unable to save them. Without the aid and sacrifice of valiant friends, she'd have been unable to save herself.

What was I supposed to do? she thought miserably. *I was a baby when Tir Asleen was destroyed and all of thirteen when the Deceiver came for Angwyn!*

"Does the child stand for good or ill?" she heard asked.

"Bein' a child," commented one of the others, "can she stand for anything?"

"How old is she," came the question, "anyone rightly know?"

"Does it matter?" said the smoker. "Should we care? If she *is* a child, dancing to the tune of others while they pull her strings, do we have any business paying her heed?" Murmurs of agreement. They knew, either directly or through histories, of crowns worn by those who'd not yet come of age, mere figureheads all, with the true governance of the realm held by regents and powers behind that throne. "An' if a woman grown," the smoker continued, "then she must take responsibility for what's done in her name an' for her cause. The suffering as well as the joy."

"Sod the girl, tell more of the Maizan."

"Sweepin' 'cross the land like a tidal race, they are," muttered the Factor.

"A what?"

"Like locusts then, like a herd o' buffalo, like the flamin' light o' day!"

"Heard tell," came a surprise interjection, "the lord o' them Maizan, their Castellan what'sisname—?"

"Mohdri," said Hanray.

"Aye, that's the one. Heard tell he set his pet hunters on the girl's tail."

"The Black Rose?" the Factor asked.

"Aye." And with that acknowledgment, a ripple of nervous commentary made its way around the small assemblage. Everyone had an opinion, none was comfortable voicing it aloud, almost as though they feared one of the Maizan might be hidden nearby, listening. Or worse, lurking among them.

"Ain't they killers, belike?" someone else inquired.

"Can be, if it's needful. As assassins, they're s'posed to give even the Chengwei a decent run for their money."

"Get out!"

"I swear! The gods' honest truth."

"They are reputedly," Hanray nodded agreement, "as good as their reputation, which is considerable."

"An' now, gentles," the pipe smoker announced, "they seek the Sacred Princess."

"How's this madness to be stopped, can anyone tell me that?"

Elora's ears perked up slightly. The exchange, the undertones that often belied the actual dialogue, crystallized the feelings she'd had since she started eavesdropping. These were merchants who made their living in the wildlands, who thrived on risk and viewed the unknown as merely another challenge, or a market to be opened. She'd never heard such fatalism from them before, nor even imagined such an attitude possible. In their souls, many in the tavern had already conceded victory to the Maizan.

"Who's to say it's madness?" offered the smoker. "The tales I've heard from those who've been conquered, they're not so bad."

"Somethin' else," scoffed Hanray, "y' know for *fact*?"

A ripple of laughter swept the gathering, but faded quickly.

"I get around, Factor. I see things."

"I didna' know the borders were tha' open."

The smoker chuckled. "It's a big country. Most times, I didn't know there *were* borders." That provoked another round of laughter.

"Hardly likely to talk ill o' them tha' rule 'em, are they, these folk y' speak of?"

"They speak of fair treatment and just laws. And in truth, I've seen little evidence to the contrary."

"Take up arms against the Maizan," another interjected, "they'll kill you fast an' that's no error."

"Chengwei out east do worse."

For the next few exchanges, the men compared notes

29

on which state was the more brutal. Some of the group excused themselves and returned to their businesses while others drifted in to take their place.

"I've also heard," again from that pipe smoker as he brought the discussion back to his baseline topic in tones of absolute certainty, "that where the Maizan rule, there is no sorcery. That the Veil Folk no longer dictate to the Daikini. That the World Gates to the realms beyond the Veil are shut and sealed, and the earth left for humankind alone."

"Not possible," snapped Hanray, in an equally flat and absolute dismissal. "The Veil Folk, they'd ne'er allow it."

"Mayhap, that's what this war is all about?"

"That's why I'm for hearth an' home," a new voice piped up, "to defend what's mine."

"*Think,* will y'! If what he says is true—blessed martyrs, who's to say you, or *any* of us, will have hearth or home to return to? To throw down the gauntlet to the Veil Folk!" Hanray sounded aghast at the thought.

"Ain't'cha bin lis'nin', Factor? The Maizan, he says they're *winnin'!*"

"Consider tha' a breath or two, my friends?" Hanray challenged them. "The Veil Folk are part of the fabric of the world, we depend on them in more ways than we can number."

"Is that a good thing?" the smoker wondered. "We depend on them for so much. It's *they* who define the form and fabric of our world. And our lives. Because we allow it. I mean, look at the lot of you, listen to what you've been saying, arguing over whether or not a *girl* who's not seen even a score of summers is the rightful savior of the world. Simply because some *prophecy*"—and there was no hiding the contempt invested in that single word—"names her so? Pardon my bluntness, gentles, I say the devil take that. Mayhap the time's come we stood for ourselves. Held destiny in *our* hands."

The man was a spellbinder. There was no need to raise his voice or pound the table, the others listened because it seemed the right and natural thing to do. He was the kind of man who'd make himself heard in the heat of battle or the madcap din of a parliament. Elora wanted a look at him, but she'd angled herself the wrong way. The pipe smoker was just out of eyeshot and all her own instincts were screaming at her that this was not the time to draw attention to herself.

Desperation proved the sire to inspiration. Without conscious thought, she cast her awareness free of her physical body, to flow into the being of the nearest animal to hand. This was another skill Thorn had taught her, how to tap the power of her InSight, allowing her to see the world through the eyes of another, in this instance one of the mares corralled behind her. It was a clumsy transition, the animal recognized an intrusion and reacted by dancing on all four feet, pounding her forehooves against the earth as though she was striking out at a foe. Quickly, praying none of the merchants—and especially the pipe smoker—noticed what was happening, Elora tried to gentle the mare, but her own agitation fueled the horse's. She wouldn't calm down.

Elora was on the brink of casting herself loose and returning to her own body when she felt a hand on the mare's neck, another on her broad forehead, heard soothing words from the mouth of the very man she sought.

In her own mind, the girl cursed to high heaven, certain that her deception would be discovered. On another level of herself, though, she had to admire his skill with animals, as she did his skill with his own kind. A few words, a few more caresses, restored the mare to a state of tranquillity, and he closed the moment with an apple for the animal to munch on, which she took with eager gratitude.

His hands were callused, that Elora could feel through the mare's skin. A confirmation of his trade that was just as soundly belied by his appearance. A handsome man, but not exceptionally so, half again her height and surprisingly thicker about the middle than she would have expected, until she realized that much of the bulk was

31

padding. His clothes were a masterpiece of design, the robes of a middling successful merchant making the transition to middle age. Broad of chest, thick of gut, with the air of a man for whom the road held less and less allure. Power going to seed.

An artful deception, on a par with her own, one of the best she'd ever seen short of an actual magical glamour. His eyes looked sleepy but they missed nothing, and lingered on the mare's for a fraction of a look longer than Elora would have liked. She felt no probe, though, nor any manifestation of either Greater or Lesser Art. If the man had sorcerous abilities, they were beyond her ability to detect. Given his skill with disguise, he didn't much need them. She came away with a strong sense of his features, coupled with the absolute certainty that they were all wrong. She might know him from his voice, the next time their paths crossed, or more likely from the seductively commanding way he used it. But not from his face.

As soon as he turned his back to rejoin his fellows, Elora slipped free of the mare. She stayed seated where she was, though her hour was very nearly up. She would not leave until the merchants had, and especially not before the warrior—for that was the smoker's true occupation, regardless of his outward seeming—was long departed.

"Which side's Elora Danan on, I wonder?"

"Should we care?" came from the pipe smoker. "Whichever, it's the likes of us most likely to get crunched in the jaws of the nutcracker."

The mare started her dance again but this time it was none of Elora's doing. The breeze was off the plain and through the animal's ears and nostrils came double confirmation of the approach of other horses, racing flat out. Something in their scent, the pattern of their hoofbeats across the smooth terrain, transmitted agitation to the mare, which in turn registered to her as a potential, onrushing threat, to which there was but one acceptable response: flight.

Elora didn't try to calm the mare, her panic was almost more than the young woman herself could handle. Instead she broke contact, tucking her senses once more firmly within the confines of her own body, and waited to see what happened next.

She could hear the horses with her own ears as their riders brought them across the face of the encampment without the slightest moderation of their headlong charge. It was one of the Cascani patrols. To judge from the sight and sound of their mounts as their officer reined them to a halt before the tavern, they must have galloped the entire length of the plain. The horses were heavily lathered, sweat thick as foam on their necks and shoulders. Their heads bowed as they stopped, lungs pumping like bellows in the furnace, nostrils flaring visibly with every great breath.

The officer tossed his reins to his sergeant, with the command that the mounts be walked around the paddock until they'd calmed down, then fed and watered and put to bed. The undertone to those orders was an injunction that they'd surely be needed in the morning, if not sooner. The man's features were equally grim.

"Courier, milord, from Testeverde," he told Hanray.

"It were a caravan I was expecting, Alyn."

"Not this season, mayhap not ever again. The city's fallen."

"Damnation." There was an air of rote to the factor's profanity, though. This news wasn't altogether unexpected. "When?"

"A fortnight past." Hanray cocked an eyebrow in sharp and silent query, prompting his officer to come to the courier's defense. "He had no remounts, milord. He came as fast as he was able."

"And the Maizan? How fast did they follow?"

"Not at all, he says. He's told me already and I think it's a report best made in private."

"Tha' bad?" The officer replied with a curt and shallow nod. "Sound officers' call, then. Boots and saddles for all our troopers."

"Done and done, milord."

"Ahead o' me as always, Captain?"

"With respect, milord, this strikes me as more of occasion for speed than deliberation."

"One man's dispatch is another's panic. Damnation and bloody hell, word's running through the camp already, like a bloody wildfire!"

All around Elora the air began to fill with the sounds of outcries, hurried voices, and scurrying feet, some hearing the news with a studied air of nonchalance while others lit off like field mice stampeded by a pouncing cat. Everyone had somewhere to go and things that needed doing. For those in a sudden panic to break camp there were others who saw that haste as an opportunity for profit. Wranglers dashed for the paddocks to claim their stock while a delegation of merchants struck out for the Cascani pavilion, to demand further news from the Factor. Freelance teamsters found themselves suddenly in a seller's market as every trader in the bazaar decided to strike their tents at once. Bidding for their services quickly shot out of hand and more than a few negotiations exploded into outright battles as hard feelings found their expression more in fists than words. Hanray's troops did their best to keep order but the lunacy was too widespread to be completely contained.

Elora lost her hiding place behind one of the dray wagons right at the start, and from then on she was forced into a madcap scramble that had her dodging every which way to avoid Daikini, horses, mules, trucks, merchandise, tents, and cordage as the bazaar was deconstructed before her eyes. There was short-term purpose: get packed. There was an immediate goal: get out and away from here. But no one stopped to think whether either made the slightest sense. It was as though the enemy was just over the horizon, when for all anyone knew they were still hundreds of miles away and not even coming this way at all. This was the reputation of the Maizan.

Elora took a wrong turn somewhere, heard the thunder of hooves, found herself in the path of a charging picket line of horses. All the activity had churned the ground to mud beneath her feet, deep as her ankle, but even on solid ground there was nowhere to go for cover before they reached her. The wrangler on the lead mount saw her but there was precious little he could do. Instead Elora remembered something Thorn had told her, a wayward scrap of Nelwyn knowledge, gleaned from his own encounters with Daikini on horseback: when confronted with an obstacle in their path, horses will do almost anything to avoid trampling it. Thought and execution came in that single flash. She stood stock-still and presented her back to the horses and prayed her mentor had known what he was talking about.

To her amazement, he had.

She caught a couple of blows but they were accidents, a horse not quite picking its feet up high enough to miss her. Soreness today, a possibly spectacular set of bruises on the morrow, nothing lasting much beyond that. Otherwise she emerged unscathed as the charge flowed around her or leaped over her and continued on its way.

She screamed as the horses thundered past, a bellow of primal defiance with only the smallest scrap of fear, as though she was daring the animals to do her harm. There was an instant of tumultuous noise and then she was spitting grit from her mouth, wiping it from her eyes, amazed to find herself still in one piece, delighted to discover that the pieces all still worked.

She knew she should get up and out of the way. This was evidently a major thoroughfare and she might not be so fortunate a second time. She found, though, that she couldn't move. The sheer exhilaration of survival had turned her into a statue that was grinning like an idiot and trying to manage coughs and laughter with every breath.

Both Torquil and Hanray reached her at the same moment.

"Elora," cried the forgemaster in his bull voice, the need for secrecy swept away by concern for her.

"By my oath," returned the Factor, equally upset, equally relieved.

"What the *hell* was that all about!" Torquil raged.

"Are y' determined t' make us all ancient b'fore our time, then?" demanded Hanray.

She had no answers for either of them, nor wit to form them or breath enough to give them voice. She could only smile and hope that charm would win her the engagement.

"How far . . ." she managed as they yanked her to her feet and frog-marched her between them up the slope toward the Cascani pavilion. ". . . Testeverde?"

"Far enough," was Hanray's terse reply.

His pavilion and the Chengwei were the only oases of calm and relative sanity in the entire bazaar. All around them, tents were collapsing, men groaning under the burdens they had to hump aboard their wagons, the wagons themselves compressing their springs flat as they were fully loaded. Every man and woman Elora could see wore arms, regardless of whether or not that was their profession, and those who had no transport were starting to look increasingly desperate.

"Alyn," called the Factor to his captain as they crested the mount and came up to Torquil's wagon. "Pass the word, we'll look after all of those who require safe passage. And we'll charge no more than the standard fare."

"Some down there'll bless you for that, milord. And others curse you."

"I'll live with both. Just see to it, will y', lad."

"With Testeverde gone," the Captain said, "there's no through road to the west."

"The east is open."

"I think most here would rather leap down the tiger's gullet than trust their fates to the Chengwei."

"North, then. For those who can't afford pathfinders, offer them maps. But keep our own people close and secure."

"Lord Hanray," Elora asked, managing to squeeze in a question, "are the Maizan coming?"

"So everyone believes," was his terse reply, but the bulk of his attention was on Torquil. "We need to talk, Master Smith."

"Manya can convene the council. You'll join us for dinner."

"Perfect. That might even give me time to try to sort out this lot." He waved a hand across the encampment.

"Good luck there, Hanray."

"I'm Cascani, Torquil. Don't believe in it."

"You believe most will travel north?"

"It's the harder trail but in the eyes of most, the safer destination. Not a few down there, though, might choose the Maizan over the Chengwei."

"And Sandeni's caught between them both."

"Not for the first time."

"Will the Republic fight?"

The Factor shook his head as he helped Elora clamber up beside Torquil on the wagon seat.

"If the report out of Testeverde is true, all bets are off. One way or t'other, though, they have t' be next on the Maizan list. Move east or west across the continent, eventually y' have t' face the Wall, an' tha' means dealin' wi' the Republic of Sandeni."

"Can they win?"

The Daikini shrugged. "They have till now. But so had Angwyn. From what I've heard, Sandeni's given sanctuary to the Sacred Princess and her protector. An' acclaimed her as their talisman."

"Like Angwyn and Tir Asleen before them?" asked the Captain as Torquil flicked the reins to stir the team into motion.

"Aye."

The Captain had the last word as the wagon trundled back toward the cavern mouth, with the offhand finality of a knife to the heart.

"God help 'em, poor bastards."

Chapter 2

Dinner at Torquil's that night was formal. It wasn't pleasant.

The children were sent off to bed early, and Elora with them, ostensibly to make sure they were all tucked in safe and sound. It didn't take much insight on her part to figure it was also to get her well out of the way.

The whole mountain was on edge, as though every surface of every stone was a jagged crystal; the same applied to those who dwelled within. Elora got backtalk from kids whose usual nature was sweet as sugar, tantrums for no reason, and a couple of siblings who clung to her with the leechlike desperation of rescued kittens. Hearth fires blazed as big and bright as ever but they seemed to cast no warmth as the youngsters crowded together, as many to a bed as would fit, clutching down comforters snug about them and piling blankets and pillows high as though sheer desire could transform their bedspreads into mighty redoubts capable of repelling any onslaught.

"What's all this, then?" Elora asked, upon discovering that all the massive beds had been shoved together before the fire and arranged so the taller headboards faced the doorway.

Nobody replied at first, as everyone feigned sleep and waited to see if she'd make them set the room to rights.

She lifted the end of one quilt and raised questioning eyebrows as a half-dozen anxious faces peered up at her from the shadows beneath.

"Expecting an invasion, Paj?" she wondered in a casual and conversational tone, adding a reassuring smile that in truth she didn't feel. Part of her wanted to crawl right in and join them.

"The stones aren't happy," he said. He was Torquil's blood son—as opposed to the children fostered to his care, since child rearing among the Mountain Kings was very much a communal responsibility—on the cusp of adolescence, that transition defined to his intense annoyance by a voice that chose to splinter at the most awkward of moments.

"Your mam and dada have seen bad days before. They passed, so will this." The confidence in her voice surprised her.

"It's a time of change," she told them, casting about the room for a chair to sit on. Instead a section of quilt was drawn up and back from the corner of the bed nearest her. With a nod and chuckle she accepted the invitation and snuggled beneath the crisply ironed sheets, shifting a couple of plush pillows against the headboard to support her back. There wasn't room to stretch fulllength, so she folded her legs close to her body and luxuriated with closed eyes in the basking heat of the fire.

She loved to be warm, probably because her first and most basic memories were of the opposite. She was born to the damp, achy, desolate chill of a Nockmaar dungeon, to be followed almost immediately by the bitter winds that howled across the mountaintops of the Nockmaar Range as she was carried from that awful place. Harsh and horrible as those ordeals may have seemed, they paled in comparison to what lay ahead: an awful cold she couldn't easily describe, even in memory, because it touched her soul rather than her flesh, as the Demon Queen Bavmorda tried to cast the Rite of Oblivion and hurl Elora's spirit forever into the Outer Darkness, beyond all hope of rescue or redemption.

Bards told the story better, but they were supposed to, that was their profession. Each time she heard it, there was some new twist, an even more fantastical adventure to add spice to the retelling. Much more romance, for example, between Madmartigan and Sorsha, the wayward warrior and the princess who turned from evil to good for love. And Elora's guardian, her godfather, the Nelwyn sorcerer Willow Ufgood, assumed a majesty of bearing, a force of command that would have done a Daikini warlord proud.

The story she chose to remember was much simpler, almost a chaos from start to finish, a cascade of seemingly happy accidents that cast the infant Elora Danan into the arms of one decent man after another, whose only real thoughts were to do her a kindness, which led to them being acclaimed as heroes.

It ended originally where such stories should, with battles won and villains vanquished. The final images were those she held closest to her heart, of her friends and companions as she remembered them best, with smiles on their faces, fearlessly facing a future as bright with promise as a spring sunrise.

They'd all forgotten that dawn does not banish shadows. Quite the contrary, it makes them that much sharper and more intense. The war they'd won had not been the last.

Elora slipped from the bed and made sure everyone was tucked in snugly, pausing a moment to brush some unruly clumps of hair from Paj's face. The fire had reduced itself to banked coals, no more open flames, but these would continue to throw off heat until well into the following day. Yet, as Elora released her breath in a long, deep sigh that flushed her lungs to the very dregs, she saw a cloud of condensation form in the air before her, as though the air itself was freezing.

It had been cold as well the night of Tir Asleen's destruction, a year to the day past Bavmorda's defeat. Elora had fallen asleep in her own bed, all as well around her as any child could wish, waking from the most terrible of nightmares to find herself transported halfway around the world, naked, scorched as though she'd been scoured by the fiery breath of a dragon.

That night a cataclysm struck the globe, whose effects were felt across the whole of the Twelve Great Realms. Tir Asleen was destroyed, along with better than a score of other sites where the natural lines of force and energy intersected to form the principal loci of magical power. Elora found herself utterly alone, a stranger in a strange land, with no one to answer her cries for comfort in the night. When the King in Angwyn, in whose palace courtyard she'd suddenly appeared, and his advisers realized who she was, they immediately made her an object of veneration. At the same time, though, they had to face the very real fear that whatever had destroyed Tir Asleen might in turn come for them.

A decade later, on the night of Elora's Ascension, when the rulers of the Great Realms gathered in Angwyn to witness and celebrate her coming of age, it did.

An ingenious network of ducts and flues kept the household hallways comfortably warm, but Elora reflexively gathered her nightcloak close about her as she made her way to the dining hall. The main courses had long since been served and eaten, the last remnants were just now being cleared away, host and guests left to relax over brandy and hot spiced wine, cheese, and sweets. Manya was serving coffee and the rich aroma poked Elora's belly like a stiff finger. With a rueful twist of the lips, nothing nearly that might be called a smile, Elora recalled how she'd planned to eat once the children were seen to. Then, as she concentrated on what was being said within, that twist turned downward into a frown and even the pretense of humor left her eyes.

The passageways and antechambers abutting the dining room were still bustling with activity. The only way she could approach unseen would be to enshroud herself in a magical Cloak, a basic spell that made the mind ignore whatever its senses perceived. People might see her, smell her, even touch her. The reality of the moment simply would not register on their consciousness. Or if it did, they would see only what was right and appropriate to the occasion. For example, instead of Elora Danan, the silver-skinned Daikini Sacred Princess, a scullery maid, as good as forgotten the moment she passed by. It was one of the first bits of magic Thorn tried to teach her before realizing it was no use.

Right then, Elora thought, rising to the challenge, *since spells are out, what's the alternative?*

This time, when she answered herself, her grin was true.

The mountain was as much a living thing as those who made it their home, though the cycles of its life were measured in geologic ages rather than years. In its way, it breathed and even moved. A change in pressure within the planetary mantle miles below the surface would manifest itself in the shift of a reef, in layers of stone moving apart or closer together. For those brave enough—or fool enough, to hear their parents talk—to look, there were always new nooks and crannies to explore. One such circled up and behind the dining hall, forming a tiny gallery that was a close fit for Nelwyn children. The wall that overlooked the hall itself was pockmarked and eaten through, as though the stone had fallen prey to a madcap variety of moth, with a taste for something a bit more substantial than wool. If she twisted her head until it felt like it was about to pop off her shoulders, Elora could gain herself a marginal and one-eyed view of the proceedings below. Regardless, she was still able to hear.

Someone hammered fist on table, to emphasize the passion in his voice. The clan echoed the structure of the Great Realms themselves: it was divided into a dozen primary houses, the titular head of each serving as representative to the council. From their number, one was chosen on a rotating basis to officiate at meetings and speak for the clan as a whole. According to Thorn, Elora was apparently to play a similar role in the greater scheme of things. Only her Twelve Realms encompassed the domains of Earth and Faery, of this world and those beyond the Veil, who'd been crash-banging together harder and more frequently over the generations, with less resilience to cushion the impacts as time went on and far less willingness to compromise. Unable to live apart, unwilling to live together, the Great Realms and their component races were rapidly approaching the flash point where irritation would become outright enmity and disputes would be settled only by blood.

Elora had seen three different Nelwyns head the council during her stay. Over the course of a score of formal assemblies, plus countless informal gatherings in Manya's kitchen or Torquil's study, she'd long since come to the conclusion that Manya was the best. Patience was one of the keys to that success, she decided, as Ragnor's fist thumped the table again and his gravelly voice pitched words like thunderstones. He had a tendency to treat opposing opinions like battlements to be smashed to rubble and from thence to dust. Usually, once he started this rhetorical bombardment, he'd keep on going until he won the day, unswayed or undeterred by anything short of outright surrender.

"Impossible, is what I say," he bellowed.

In reply, she heard the Factor's voice, calm on the surface but with anger percolating just beneath, the way bubbles do in a pot that's close to boiling. Hanray was a proud man, he didn't like having either word or honor questioned. "These days, my friend, that's a word wi' less and less meaning."

"You believe this report then, Hanray?" Manya asked.

"I tell y', lady, wha' the courier told me. And as well tha' my truthtellers can find no evidence of deception in him. Can y' offer any confirmation?"

"Regarding Testeverde, no. But as nearly as we've been able to determine, the World Gates closest to Angwyn have been sealed, as if they'd never been. We've been unable to establish contact with any of the Houses of Lesser Faery who reside within Maizan-controlled territory, in the vicinity of those closed World Gates. Not fairies, nor dryads and naiads, not even any of the carrion eaters, ghouls, trolls, and the like. What we have heard are rumors of mass migrations."

"Dryads leaving their groves?"

"It can be done. They cast an offshoot of their essence into the seed pod of their MotherTree, and let wind or bird take it to hopefully safer soil, where they can plant themselves and grow anew. The land itself has been stripmined of every scrap of magic. Nothing remains," Manya finished, sorrow and denial mingling in her voice, as though she dared not accept what she was saying. "Not even the potential for power."

"And I say again, Manya," hammered Ragnor, *"impossible!"*

"Will the Veil Folk fight that?" asked another of the council.

A shrug in Manya's voice to echo the shrug of her shoulders. "There is an opinion among them that if the Daikini desire absolute dominion over this world so badly, let them have it and be damned. A rival opinion posits that the Daikini, already being damned, should be put out of their misery."

"And us along with them, Manya? We are of the Veil but we dwell upon the world. What's to become of us?"

"I wish I could say, Simon," she told the much older man. "All the Great Realms are in a tumult still, have been ever since they lost their monarchs in Angwyn. Unfortunately politics, like nature, abhors a vacuum. And the easiest way to consolidate power, once you've seized it, is to take arms against a foreign foe."

44

"What, does Greater Faery think to do some conquering of its own?"

"The High Elves want war?"

"Do the Daikini?"

"Many of Lesser Faery have already made their choice," she said, "fleeing to the far side of the Veil as desperately as the merchants quit the bazaar this eventide."

"Bugger that," spat Ragnor. "We draw sustenance from the world's soul as much as its substance. Damn Daikini do the same, 'ceptin' they're too damn dumb to realize it. Sever that bond, we're all of us doomed."

"What of Greater Faery?"

"Testeverde's y'r answer, I suspect," noted Hanray quietly. "It was the polar opposite of Sandeni, a location thick with magic, where the other is totally devoid of it, built around a World Gate, where Sandeni stands about as far from one as a body can get. Of all the cities in this part of the globe, Testeverde was where Daikini and Veil Folk could interact most easily, even those of Greater Faery. Tha' point of contact was considered its greatest defense."

"But the Maizan attacked regardless."

"Made plain they could," Hanray told the council. "Made plain tha', if necessary, they would. Made plain the consequences if they did. An' then, they offered honorable surrender. Which was accepted. Tha's when the local Factor sent out his couriers."

"What went wrong?" Manya asked gently.

"Damned if I know. Courier said he an' his mates'd been riding the best part of the night, pushing hard to put as much distance as possible between them an' any pursuit b'fore first light. He was up ahead, walkin' his animal along a switchback canyon. Said the others saw witch fires punching t' the top of the heavens, climbed the ridge for a look-see. He hung back. There was a terrible light, so bright it seemed t' turn the ground itself transparent. There musta been sound as well, but nothin' tha' stuck in memory. He didn't have much wit t' spare for lookin' because the flash had driven his horse near t' madness. Took all his strength t' keep it from bolting. Other animals in his string, they weren't so fortunate. Ran themselves right off the trail, as though death was preferable t' whatever they had to endure right then."

He paused and the room fell absolutely still, broken only by the occasional pop and crackle of coal in the hearth.

"The other couriers, Hanray," Manya prompted, "what of them?"

"Wouldn't say in detail," was his reply. "Nor much of what he saw beyond where he found them, save that the city was gone and the land scourged. He spoke of shapes an' colors too awful t' behold, that made the insides ache to look upon them. Then he fled, an' never looked back."

"Is that what the Maizan do?"

"Hardly. Some force or other among them apparently steals magic."

The room grew deathly silent as each Nelwyn assessed what that would mean.

Finally a cautious voice broke the silence. "And the Maizan? How did they benefit from this?"

"They didn't," the Factor answered grimly. "Whatever army they sent to seize the city, they lost."

From there, voices rose fast and furious, some she recognized, others she didn't, lines overlapping or chasing each other like a pack of dogs each other's tail.

"What do *our* shamans say, can you answer me that, Manya?"

"Something as big as that should have made *some* impact."

"It did not," she said.

"That isn't quite true," Elora heard quietly from behind where she couldn't see, as Torquil spoke in the most casual and conversational of tones, responding to his wife in terms meant for the young woman's ears alone.

With an effort, she wriggled free of her hiding place.

"You're supposed to be in bed," he noted amiably.

"The stones have been twitchy," she said. "I told you

46

that days ago, as if the substance of the very earth had changed."

Hastily, she tugged herself into a semblance of order and decorum, drawing her cloak all the way across her body so she was completely enclosed. She stood straight to her full height, but Torquil was lounging across the way on an outcrop of rock, so he retained the advantage on her.

"But why," she continued, "could I sense something that the shamans didn't?"

"Or couldn't. That, lass, is a question."

In the distance they could both hear the heated voices of the council, batting opinions back and forth as though they were playing tennis with thunderstones.

"You sayin', then, we should take a stand with the Daikini against the Maizan?"

"Look what's happened to those who've tried already."

"Who's to say they'll even *want* our help?"

"Can you see us standin' against a charge of armored horses? Ride us down, they would, trample us to bits, without even knowin' we was even *there*!"

"We chose long ago to live apart and alone, from the other races as much as from our fellow clans," Manya said quietly, stilling the arguments battling before her. "Now we behold the price. There are precious few who know us well enough, or care enough, to stand by our side. None to ask our aid, and none from whom we can ask the same in return."

"So what're you sayin', Manya," challenged Ragnor, "that we're done?"

"She's wrong," Elora said. "Thorn Drumheller offered help from the start, without being asked."

"That he did," agreed Torquil.

"They need to be told."

"Trust Manya, child. She'll make the point."

"Why can't I—?"

"It's better all concerned remain ignorant of your presence."

"Why?"

"Clan business. You're an honored guest. . . ."

"But I'm not 'clan,'" she finished, to a nod of acknowledgment from Torquil. "Terrific," she growled, waving her hands beneath her cloak in a moderately helpless gesture. She wanted them free, to help her express herself better, but they got tangled in the overlapping layers of cloth. "I'm supposed to be the solution here, Torquil. But how can I do that if nobody'll let me?"

"Do you have a clue what needs doing, Sacred Princess?"

She had no answer, and instead vented her frustration against an increasingly common target.

"Damn Drumheller, *damn* him!"

"He did what he thought was best, Elora."

"He dumped me, Torquil. He left me behind! Without a word of explanation."

"You were ill."

"I got better!"

"He had responsibilities. And I think you needed what we have to offer. A stable environment, a place to learn and grow among—"

"A family," she finished for him, and couldn't help the edge that turned those words into a slash keen enough to draw blood.

"There is that, yes. Is it so bad a thing to have?"

"Torquil, it's something I've wanted my whole life," she cried, "more than anything. But kind as you are, generous as you've all been, I'm not. You just said so. Not clan, not family, not really. I have no family, Master Smith. My mother died in Bavmorda's dungeon, I don't know *who* my father was. All my life I've been passed from hand to hand and mostly brought doom and disaster to everyone who ever offered me a kindness. Sometimes I think I'm better off alone!"

"That's not true."

"Then why did Thorn leave me?" As the echo of her cry faded she became aware of a burning in the back of her throat from vocal cords pushed past their limits, and of a sudden silence in the dining hall beyond.

"I told you, he felt it was for the best."

Her reply was an obscenity that took them both aback, both the word itself and the uncontrolled ferocity of its utterance. Elora knew this, too, had been heard by the others and her face flushed argent rose with shame. Before anything more could be said—ignoring the hand that Torquil reached out to catch her arm, and the look of sympathetic anguish on his face as he snared a flash of her pain instead—she bulled past him, letting her feet take her as fast as she was able to the sanctuary of her own room.

With every step along the way, a terrible hollowness grew within her, right beneath her breastbone, as though heart and soul were being scooped right out of her. Each beat of her pulse summoned forth another image, of someone loved and someone lost, from the nurse who'd given her life to smuggle her out of Nockmaar, to the wandering warrior Madmartigan and his beloved Sorsha who'd fought beside Thorn to save her. All the folk of Tir Asleen and later of Angwyn, too many of them faces she'd seen only in passing, that had still become indelibly imprinted in the vaults of her memory. There were countless more, she knew, who'd fallen before Maizan steel, or perished from disease, from hunger, from the savage collapse of the world that had sustained them all their lives.

Everyone said she was supposed to put a stop to that. No one told her how.

She was sobbing when she pitched herself full length on her bed, caught up in grief so primal she had to give it physical release or else be utterly consumed. So she struck at her pillows, punch after punch after punch, hammering at the plush down with more force than she'd use to shape raw steel on an anvil, thankful that the outburst was so extreme that it left her no lasting recollection of whose images appeared to serve as objects of her fury.

Too much passion, too much intensity, far beyond what her body was willing to sustain for long. The sobs quickly became simple tears, the pounding arm too heavy to lift, red rage gave way to more coherent thoughts, which in turn toppled into a deep and blessedly dreamless sleep.

When she awoke, she wondered if this was what it was like to have a hangover. None of the pieces of her body seemed to fit together and all felt as clumsy as her thoughts, which had never come with more reluctance. Her cheeks were stiff with dried tears and her mouth tasted foul as she struggled to make herself comfortable amidst a wild tangle of bedclothes.

She wasn't happy with her conduct, she was ashamed of the way she'd lost her temper with Torquil, thankful that the worst of the outburst had occurred in the solitude of her room. She hadn't behaved so badly since Angwyn, and thought she'd grown beyond such rotten behavior.

"Old habits die hard," she told herself in the merest whisper.

With her next breath, she smelled smoke.

She followed her nose, and poked an eye out through a crack on her pillow pile to behold the tiny fire elemental crouched on the footboard of her bed. It balanced sinuously on a stalk of molten fire that rose up through the core of the thick timber planking. That was the source of the smell, as the heat of the creature's body charred the wood. Elora leaned her head over the side of the mattress, to see where the creature emerged from the bed, linked to a similar hole in the slate floor by the thinnest thread of iridescence.

The elemental had refined its imitation of human shape since their last encounter and Elora had the disconcerting sense of looking at her own self in miniature. The main difference was that her tiny double possessed a truly boneless grace that no being with a skeleton could ever hope to match. Its body didn't bend at the joints so much as flow through a succession of gentle curves and its facsimile of hair, possessing a length and texture that made Elora groan with envy, stirred as though the liquid mass was imbued with a life and sentience of its own. The elemental looked at her with an expression of such profound earnestness that Elora had to stifle a chuckle in response. It reminded her too much of a puppy trying its level best to look grown-up.

She saw the elemental's chest rise as it drew in a breath.

"*No!*" she cried, raising a hand before the creature in a desperate attempt to stop it before it could speak and torch the entire room. It was between her and the door, and there was nothing in reach even marginally capable of surviving that intense a blast of flame.

"**Help,**" was what it said, in a very small and tinny voice, but Elora didn't hear. The elemental's voice had been drowned out by a yelp from the girl that represented a healthy mix of startlement and pain as her palm was fractionally scored by its breath. The noise was mainly surprise. The actual experience wasn't so bad, like being stabbed by the hot tip of a just-extinguished match.

Elora blew on her palm to ease the pain, then gathered herself to her knees at the midpoint of the bed, using her other hand to pull her hair out of her eyes and into some rude semblance of order.

The elemental watched her wide-eyed, with a stricken expression on its features. Whatever its intent, it wasn't to do Elora harm.

"What did you say?" Elora asked.

"**Help,**" it tried again, and the young woman saw what had happened before. The outrush of breath needed to project that single word brought forth in addition a modest gout of superheated air, laced with flame.

"Offer or request?" Even as she spoke, the submissive curves of the elemental's body provided the answer. It was a plea, as heartfelt and desperate as any Elora had seen.

"**Help help help help help,**" it repeated in a wild torrent of words, as if this was the only one it knew and it wanted to use it to best advantage.

Wouldn't have thought to see one without its mam being close at hand, Elora remembered Torquil telling her. *And no mam worth the name would've let her bit come near the likes of you unattended. Too dangerous by far for both.*

As quickly as she could, Elora exchanged nightgown for a fresh undershirt and shorts of cotton, followed that with a pullover shirt, a wool tunic, and her buckskins. Thick socks and her boots took care of her feet, gloves she tucked through her belt, making sure at the same time that both of her traveling pouches were securely attached. She gathered her hair into a thick ponytail and fastened it in place with a chased silver barrette. Lastly she grabbed her journey cloak, patterned wool that felt like it weighed almost as much as she did herself. The weave was as tight as looms could manage, to proof it against both wind and water. The cloak itself was so long she had to wrap it one full turn across her torso before anchoring it over her left shoulder with a brooch the width of her fist.

She was out the door and well on her way before she gave any thought to what she was doing, or where the elemental was leading her. It seared a tiny rivulet through the rock ahead of her, sometimes along the floor, sometimes the walls, sometimes the ceiling, always remaining close enough to the surface for Elora to follow its trail. She tried to keep track of the route herself, but soon discovered that she dared not take her eyes off her guide. The signs it left her lasted barely a heartbeat and the elemental never looked back to make sure she was there.

The foundries were sited mainly for convenience to the mines and the bazaar. The community itself was a fair distance removed, one entire peak over in fact, linked by an intricate labyrinth of tunnels. Some were wide enough to allow a wagon to pass—that was how goods were transported—but most of the rest were scaled down to Nelwyn proportions.

Hurrying along channels she'd never seen before, sometimes twisting through narrow spaces she was sure were designed to break her bones, sometimes crawling on hands and (thankfully) padded knees, Elora soon found herself without room to stand upright, much less the opportunity to draw a proper breath. She quickly left the familiar confines of the Nelwyn community and descended through the mine itself, into a darkness so profound that she had only the brief and transitory flash of the elemental's passage to show her whatever perils lay ahead. She tried to reach the elemental with her InSight, at the very least to persuade the creature to slow down, only to discover that it had no true consciousness in any terms she could relate to. No thought, no mind, no awareness of anything beyond a fundamental terror, bonded to an equally basic certainty that Elora was the only entity capable of putting things to right.

Again, as her skull glanced off a nasty outcropping of rock, she blessed the common sense she'd learned from Thorn and Torquil that had prompted her to bring and wear her skullcap so that its padding would absorb the shock of every collision. She had no idea where she was, save that she stood well within a mountain. She suspected she'd traveled as far beyond the mine as it was from the Nelwyn community and had the further sense that without the elemental she'd be hard-pressed to find her way safely home. None of the tunnels she'd passed through were artificial, she'd been scrambling and slipping through natural cracks in the fabric of the rock itself, and drew analogies to the gullies and arroyos and valleys scattered across the surface. It stood to reason they'd find their echoes in the land below.

The elemental finally came to a halt, flitting back and forth beneath her feet like a firefly trapped in a jar, casting enough light to illuminate the hollow in which Elora stood. There was nothing pretty about the rock jumbled close about her. The weight of eons had compressed all delicacy from its substance, so that what remained was harder than anything she'd touched before. The seams between the strata were so tight there wasn't even a trace of water, and the air possessed a mustiness that told her it hadn't been stirred by any movement in the longest time.

"What is this place?" she muttered, more to herself than her companion. She felt a sudden twinge of apprehension at the thought the elemental might reply, even a single spoken word might warm the air enough to make it difficult for her to breathe.

The mountain groaned.

Elora felt it initially as a tremble beneath her feet, and her heart skipped a beat or three as panic labeled the sensation as the beginnings of an earthquake. Those were hard enough to face in the open. She had no desire to meet one with the whole of the world sitting atop her head. Then came a basso tearing sound that transmitted itself directly from rock to bones, making her bare her teeth in sudden, silent, sympathetic pain as phantom spikeblossoms bloomed along the currents of her marrow, from one end of her to the other. She'd beheld a thunderstorm from a mountaintop and always believed that to be the most majestic noise in nature, painting it in her imagination with the vision of a god striking out with his hammer, crushing utterly whatever it struck.

That was air, this was earth. There was no comparison.

The shock left her weak in the knees, but fortunately there was too little room for her to collapse. Her body folded until she found herself wedged tight against the rock. There she rested until breath and wits came back to her. She placed bare hands flat on stone, and forehead as well, and in that passive, receptive state, she heard the cries.

Wails of fear and torment. Rage at what had been done, was being done, would be done. Passion enchained, bound tight by spells so dark the stygian cavity where Elora lurked might as well be lit by the noonday sun, so fetid that an abattoir would smell sweet by comparison.

She blinked, and realized she'd bared her teeth again, only this time in a snarl. A stir of air tickled her cheek and with it a strand of heat, a scent of sweat. Elora levered herself up on an outcrop of rock, then another, found a side channel barely sufficient to admit her. She shimmied herself inside without allowing a thought of what might happen should she get stuck. She made her awkward way along and the gallery's orientation rolled from vertical to horizontal. At the same time she also refused to consider stripping herself of any of her gear. Every piece had its purpose and she wasn't willing to risk doing without.

Suddenly the stone beneath her fingertips lost all definition. For the barest instant it skibbled, as though every particle had become a separate entity like grains of sand on a beach, and each of those supercharged with energy. It crackled to the touch, the same as fur on a long-haired cat would when stroked. She snatched her hands away as best she could, and rubbed them together. They'd gone numb, she initially thought with cold, yet the skin felt coated with some oily substance that struck her as unutterably foul.

She could hear chanting, so distorted by the breaks and hollows and twisting byways of the rock that she couldn't place its direction or its distance. Whatever the ceremony being performed, the mountain clearly wasn't happy. If the earth's reaction was anything like hers, this was no place to be.

Withdrawal, unfortunately, wasn't an option. Even if retreat was possible, she doubted the hollow would prove a place of safety. The only route open to her was to forge ahead.

She sensed a distant *thrum,* a gathering of forces, and stretched herself to full extension, ignoring the pain of her back where it joined her pelvic girdle as she pulled her knees up flat to the rock on either side of her as far as she was able, fighting for purchase with toes and nails, hooking them into the most subtle flaws in the stone and praying nothing would slip loose.

There was a rumble in the distance, a grinding of stone on stone that quickly became a monstrous tearing sound, the tectonic spasm gathering force and volume as it rushed toward her. Once more, memory served her ill with a vision of the terrible wave that had almost drowned her and her companions in the Sunset Ocean during their flight from Angwyn. As then, she felt her senses battered and overwhelmed by a noise and an unstoppable power that beggared her comprehension. She heard herself scream, not the high-pitched shriek of a girl but a bellow that began from the deepest point of her gut and met the mountain's fury like an emplaced spearpoint would a foe's onrushing charge.

The battle was joined and ended in a single instant. As the earth shook, Elora Danan found herself propelled forcefully into open space. It was an utterly graceless landing, the kind of belly flop that would have raised an impressive splash in water. Since this was rock, it merely drove every scrap of air from her lungs and bestrew her vision with all manner of garishly colored dots and slashes and swirls.

The chanting was louder, taking form on a multitude of levels, both as sounds cohering into words and as expressions of sorcerous energy.

The elemental glowed beneath Elora's nose, heedless of the gimlet glare she cast its way. It had drawn itself into a little ball, a marble with a vaguely human face, shining as faintly as possible for fear of being seen. Elora knew this was as far as the little creature would go.

The oily quality to the stone she'd felt in the gallery had transferred itself to the very air, leaving her with the unpleasant feeling that she'd been coated all over with slime. Whether clothes or skin, she was slippery to the touch, and that forced her to move with exaggerated care, in case the slickness applied equally to the soles of her shoes and the rocks she walked on. She wasn't so much worried about falling but rather, like the elemental, she didn't want to be detected.

The closer she came to the source of the chanting, the more intense that concern grew. Even when he saw she had no talent for the Arts Arcane, Thorn continued teaching her all he'd learned himself, of magic, of sorcery, even of necromancy. He taught her to recognize spells and enchantments the way a hunter might "read" a trail, and all the ways he knew to counteract them. She confessed more than once that she didn't see the sense of it; she couldn't battle any sort of mage on his terms any more than she could face a warrior like Khory Bannefin with a sword.

He'd smiled, as though she'd just stumbled over some great, transcendent truth. "That's the point," he told her gently, though she didn't really understand. Neither had he, in the beginning. "You don't face someone like Khory with a sword, you find another way to win. *You* don't fight a magus with magic, because you can't. But you *can* use your knowledge to pick his own apart, to assess its strengths and flaws the way Torquil might a rock face to determine where best to cut. Like expects like, Elora. Warriors fight with blades, because that's how they're taught. Sorcerers the same, with spells. You find another way, you blindside them—the way the Deceiver did at Angwyn—and the day is yours."

There was a definite beat to the incantation, built around what she recognized as the form of a standard spell of Binding: *one* and *two* and *three* and FOUR and *one* and *two* and *three* and *FOUR*. . . .

The culmination of each verse was a fraction louder than the one before, and the speed of recitation increased as well, like an engine slowly but steadily building in force and momentum to craft chains that were barbed and unbreakable. It wasn't the spell alone that frightened Elora, but whatever being it was designed to restrain.

She snaked herself carefully up a slanting tier of rock, her mouth working of its own accord to expel the taste of each breath. There was nothing organic about it, but still she had the unshakable sense that something was dead and rotting around her, and to her horror, she wondered if it might be the mountain itself.

Beyond was a cavern of modest size, average for a Nelwyn forge. Some work had been done to regularize the floor and provide a comparatively flat and even surface. Similarly a pool had been opened at one end, filled to the brim with liquid firegold. At first, Elora thought it was no more than molten rock, but then a gleaming, sinuous shape broke the surface and she bit down hard on a gloved fist to smother a gasp of shock and recognition.

The grotto was hot as any working forge, but in that instant Elora felt herself flooded by an arctic chill that left her shaking.

Three years ago was when she'd seen them last, on a ridge in Cherlindrea's Grove, half a continent to the west, when the Deceiver had cast them loose to consume the forest that could not be burned. They were firedrakes.

For most of the inhabitants of the Great Realms on either side of the Veil, these were creatures out of legend. Some stories labeled them as one of the core forces of the cosmos, who made their homes in the molten hearts of the stars themselves, while others held it was they who burned holes in the velvet fabric of the sky that allowed the light of heaven to fall upon the waking world. They were kin to dragons or kin to demons, no one knew for sure. The one constant thread through every story was that they were beings of raw and untamed passion, whose quicksilver spirits were a match for their protean substance. If they were intelligent, their minds raced along paths neither Daikini nor Veil Folk could easily follow, and those who tried were quite often driven mad by the encounter.

They were powerful beyond measure, so much so that only the most absolute and all-encompassing of wards could have even a hope of restraining them. Without exception, they were considered the bear best left sleeping in its den, to be ever avoided and never disturbed. Yet some mage had taken this whole clutch captive and even now was working further magicks on them.

She saw five figures, four cloaked in robes as well as shadows, moving in ritual unison a fair distance behind their companion, who stood at the very edge of the pool. He was the celebrant of this obscene rite. As Elora watched he swept a spearlike pole through the depths of the molten pond and up into the air. From the angle where she lay, it appeared that the man was etching sigils on the surface of the wall before him, but Elora knew different. Each swipe of the javelin's needle point seemed to leave its mark on her nerve endings as symbols of raw fire were cut into the fabric of the very air, a Nelwyn body length outward from the rock.

The celebrant was masked beneath a fantastical demon's head helm of leather and iron, accented with gems and sprouting a double curve of ram's horns from each temple. The mask's face would be a horror to behold, she knew, designed to confuse whatever entity was being Summoned into believing it stood before one of its own. At a glance, the gems themselves might be mistaken for rubies, since they glowed with the dark radiance of rich wine, but here again Elora knew better. These were bloodstars, she remembered from what Thorn had taught her on the road, mystically charged crystals that focused and amplified the user's magical talent. In their natural state they most resembled diamonds and were often mistaken for them. They could be energized, and their malefic power unleashed, only by the execution of a blood sacrifice.

Elora tasted a metallic liquid on her tongue and found teeth marks leaking blood from the pad beneath her thumb. Using the tip of the pinkie of her other hand, she daubed a set of sigils of her own on the rock beneath her in small, precise strokes. If she was the beacon Torquil described, the combination of the summoning sigil and her own blood to mark it should bring the elemental back to her. The others in their prison wouldn't hear the Call and the celebrants were too caught up in their own frenzy to notice something this small and focused. Or so she hoped. A heartbeat later the elemental came in answer to her Call, spreading its essence along the tracings Elora had drawn until the entire design began to glow.

"I should have known you from the start," she said softly, but there was no reason why. She'd never seen a young firedrake much less a newborn, and at this stage of their existence it seemed deceptively like the lesser elementals she and the Rock Nelwyn had often encountered.

Quickly, but without hurry, for this was *not* a time for carelessness, she covered the sigil with her right hand. Then she took a breath so deep she thought her ribs might burst. The infant's warmth spread throughout her body, casting tendrils of itself along the threads of her nervous system. At the same time Elora released an aspect of her own spirit, flowing into the firedrake as it did into her, until the two of them shared a conjoined corporeality.

Thinking became an effort. The firedrake simply wasn't old enough. This was still a creature of instinct, for whom desires were instantly gratified or as quickly forgotten. Almost nothing could be stored or remembered, and it lived totally and absolutely in the present and for the moment. That it had returned to her, and with a definitive purpose, was all the more remarkable.

She'd be of no use to anyone if she let its nature overwhelm her own, but that added a regrettable delay to her actions, as every thought and response had first to be processed through her human consciousness and then manifested through her elemental being. As the infant slithered through the rock Elora understood the anguish that drove it to seek her out, and the pain that was surging ever more forcefully through the heart of the mountains themselves. The other firedrakes were screaming, hurling themselves with furious and futile desperation against the bindings that imprisoned them, wriggling themselves into a frenzy as they tried to avoid the spear point that was claiming their lives and power with ever-increasing frequency.

Elora had seen World Gates before, the doorways that allowed transit through the Veil that separated the Realm of the World from that of the Spirit, allowing those who inhabited the Realm of the Flesh to pass from one to the other. So far as she had been taught, which she was beginning to suspect was precious little, they could only be located at the intersection points of arcane energy that the Cascani called ley lines. Supposedly there were none of those near the Rock Nelwyn holdings.

Yet here was a sorcerer building one out of thin air.

That has to be why he's using firedrakes, she thought. *What else in nature could be powerful enough to form a Gate and then maintain it?*

She'd given little consideration to what was actually happening here, the purpose behind the enslavement of the firedrakes and the Gate that was being constructed. She really didn't care. These were creatures she knew, to whom she had offered friendship and received it in return. They were in danger and there was no question in either mind or soul that the threat to them was evil. Nor was there the slightest doubt that she would try to save them.

The question was, in the face of such a formidable foe, how?

From that need came an inspiration.

The four chanters were responsible for maintaining the bindings about the pool. They also helped sustain the Gate. The closer the spell came to completion, the more effort and concentration would be demanded of them. That made them vulnerable.

Using her InSight, Elora cajoled the infant firedrake to do as she asked, wrapping her wits tight about them both as she came up right beneath the chanters. Through its eyes, she saw the scene, noted how the acolytes' footsteps struck the rock like hammers, each one sending streamers of malefic energy outward through the very fabric of the mountain. If there was a flaw in the substance of the rock, they would find it and, once found, make it a fraction worse, until the solidity of the mountain was reduced to a cruel deception. The stone that the Rock Nelwyn depended on for their protection would instead guarantee their destruction.

The infant firedrake had the power to incinerate the quartet. A part of Elora yearned to yield to that temptation, but so sharp and sudden a disruption of the spell would be as catastrophic for Elora and the infant both and very likely the adult firedrakes as well. Frustrating as it seemed to her, subtlety was the better way.

So she asked the firedrake to overcome its instinctual fear and prick one with a needle of white-hot flame, straight through his boot to the sole of his foot. The fastest possible jab, here and gone so quickly it could

61

hardly be noticed. In response, the acolyte fell the merest fraction out of sync with his fellows.

She struck again, one of the others, and then the next. A succession of random pokes that barely registered on their conscious awareness, just enough to tease the nerve endings and put all four fractionally off stride.

When she slid back into the comforting mass of the basal rock and felt the rhythms thundering from above, she couldn't help a grin. She'd broken their pattern, and they hadn't noticed.

In and of itself, this didn't change a thing. The bindings still held, apparently as firm as ever, renewed with every repetition of the chant. Only now those repetitions carried within them the tiniest flaw, which with every cycle became increasingly pronounced. And, glory of glories, with the Summoning building to its own crescendo and the chief celebrant caught up in the equally demanding rhythm of his own responsibilities, he hadn't yet realized that anything was wrong.

Such good fortune wouldn't last, of course. Moreover, the moment the flaw was noticed, it would also be recognized that this was no accident. Even if Elora went undiscovered, the chamber would immediately be laced thick with protective wards so tight she'd never break back in. Or worse, she might find herself trapped outside her body, with no way of returning home.

Back to the pool she flashed, to strike at it with even more care and accuracy than she used against the chanters. She couldn't afford to let the other firedrakes even suspect what was happening, because in their panic they'd be sure to reveal her activities to the celebrant. The hardest part for her was to force herself to take her time, to work as fast as she was able but always stay within the rhythm of the deed, which meant ignoring the thrashing cries of the firedrakes in their increasingly futile attempts to evade the celebrant's lance. Paradoxically, as their numbers lessened and the survivors gained more room to maneuver, his accuracy improved to match. Each stab found its target, each wriggling eel of flame found its life force added to the construct overhead. The little creature Elora had bonded herself to was no less affected by the ongoing massacre, which forced her to devote a portion of concentration, that she could ill afford to spare to restrain it from hurling itself against the wards in a wasted attempt to blunderbuss a hole in the prison they formed.

To those whose senses are acute enough to perceive them, wards initially appear as solid objects, walls or globes of shimmering translucence that can range from nearly invisible to wholly opaque. That appearance is dangerously misleading. In reality, they're a woven lattice of energy, whose strength derives from the density of the "thread" count and the complexity of the weave. A coarsely loomed network is surprisingly porous, while its opposite is virtually unbreachable, depending on the strength of will of the sorcerer who casts and maintains it.

These wards were near solid, which was why Elora struck at the chanters first. That attack established a flaw in the maintenance matrix. As the surface strata of the ward structure were worn away by the constant assault of the imprisoned firedrakes, the layers that replaced them incorporated that flaw into the core structure of the energy field.

Elora scooted right up to the field and began to weave the most minute strands of the infant's essence into those imperfect threads. This close, she had no effective buffers against what was happening above. Each stab of the lance struck an equivalent sympathetic resonance in her—*like what I did to the chanters,* she thought ironically, *only worse*—in a succession of razor cuts that drew no blood, did no physical damage, but hurt nonetheless. She ignored the pain, choosing to focus on the task and the goal.

Her stitching finished, she gathered her strength into herself and smiled wickedly, for this was something she alone could do and no one else in the world or the Realms. For reasons she or Thorn had yet to divine, she was immune to magic; spells rolled off her like water off a duck.

And wards had no power to hold her.

She sent a minute charge of her essence along the string of fire she had laid, and—*poof*—the section of ward she had attacked shriveled at its touch. She poured a dollop more of self into the infant as it hurled itself into the breach, combining her strength with its form to keep the way clear while calling out to the others that the route to freedom was open.

The firedrakes rushed her in a stampede, the brute force of buffalo mixed in with the slip-wriggle sensation of being caught in a salmon run as more bodies than Elora could count hurtled past, enveloping her in a radiant tide of cascading firegold. There was no way to hide what was happening; the chanters knew instantly that their containment had been ruptured and struck back with all their own considerable strength. Strands of energy tried to leap the gap across her body, to restitch the lattice closed. She grew as many hands as needed from the substance of her elemental to ash them in mid-flight, flexing her eldritch muscles at the same time to force the opening even wider.

Those natural gifts weren't enough. She had strength, she had knowledge, she had courage; they had more. First one, then a second, then a third strand made a successful leap, to form the beginnings of a cocoon she suspected she could not easily break, and she knew she'd soon have to run herself.

She never got the chance.

Without the slightest warning, Elora's material body folded in on itself in its hiding place above the grotto with a hoarse cry that couldn't be bitten back as the barbed and gleaming point of the celebrant's lance punched straight through the slim form of her firedrake.

The shock of contact was so blinding, it broke her hold on the wards. Before she knew what was happening Elora found herself being scooped up through the now empty pool and into open air. Like so many others before it, the infant tried to wriggle free, to no avail. Elora could offer no help. This was primarily a physical assault, her special gifts were useless against it.

"Bless my damned soul," she heard the celebrant say in wonderment as he held the infant firedrake aloft like a trophy, "what've we got ourselves here?"

The small creature spat flame at him but the celebrant merely laughed as its flame skittered harmlessly off his vestments. With the firedrake, Elora struggled to reassert a measure of control, to redefine the input of its senses in terms she could comprehend. First and foremost, that meant manifesting eyes to see with, but the image that loomed before them when she did was one she outright refused to believe.

The celebrant of this unholy rite was a Nelwyn.

In that same flash of time he realized he held far more than a simple elemental.

"Well well *well*," he repeated, "what *have* we here?"

"Carig," called one of his acolytes, and to her horror Elora recognized them as Nelwyns, too, "the 'drakes are away."

"No matter. They've served their purpose an' this'un I'm thinkin', best of all."

"But they're sure to come back!"

"If thou'rt so concerned, Samel, thou'd best maintain the wards. They can't fry what they can't touch, remember. 'Course," he said to the infant and Elora, in a more quietly conspiratorial tone, "wouldn't be any call for such an upset if he'd done his job square. That was a neat little scheme, I'll grant thee that, shoulda spotted it myself. Serves me right for depending on lesser souls. Serve *them* right if I let 'em burn."

Who are *you?* Elora demanded wordlessly, although she knew he could not hear. *Why are you doing this, how can you betray your own kind?*

"Think themselves safe, they do, snugabed in their rock holes, in their rock spells. Be a revelation when that selfsame rock crushes 'em, burns 'em, makes of them and their precious community naught but a memory. So *sure* they was, that a Gate could be built only where the laws of nature permit. Branded me outcast for sayin' different, that with the proper alignment o' forces y' could generate

65

a Gate matrix *any* damn place. Manya, she believed, say that right off. Took one look at my calculations, knew I was right, had me banished straight—because, she said, the *means* o' sustaining my construct were an abomination."

He smiled, and Elora beheld in his eyes an expression she'd never seen before, a hunger that was insatiable mated to a spirit more dead than ashes. They were eyes whose gaze might have given even Bavmorda pause, possessing a cruelty she could not comprehend.

"The plan," he continued, "is to corrupt the fabric of the mountains. The opening of this Gate will breach the pool here an' the wards like a broken dam. The Ancient One I Summon will drive the firedrakes before it. They'll follow the paths of least resistance, through the flaws an' fissures my folk bin opening in the rock, an' tear into the mine an' the community beyond like a flash flood. They'll burn, those who cast me out, an' their precious mountains with them. And all will assume that they'd brought this doom upon themselves. None will look past the obvious to note the true purpose of the exercise, none will realize till it's far too late what dread power now haunts the waking world.

"That's the idea," he said, with a mad smile to his tone.

Suddenly a flick of the wrist launched his spear. The haft exploded as it struck, casting forth a shower of metal that struck only the frame of the World Gate, acting as a fixative to seal all the sigils firmly in place. The elemental howled, and Elora with it, as their merged body was shaped and twisted to fit the mold laid down for it and then saturated in a substance that dulled both flesh and spirit. In less time than a single human heartbeat, the elemental grew cold as dead stone and as its fires dimmed, so, too, faded the link between Elora and her own body. At a moment when she needed her thoughts to race, they staggered, fell, found themselves drowning in tar.

The Gate was complete. The Summoning had begun.

Elora heard music. It was the only word that came to

mind even though the sounds she applied it to had no connection to any composition she'd ever heard. The melody swept out of the darkness beyond the World Gate and wormed its way into a dark place she never knew existed within her soul, drawing forth a vision of herself that spun and pranced and preened before her with a delight that made her ache to embrace the cause. This was the Elora of her dreams, when she took the duckling she saw every day in the mirror and imagined herself a swan, with a lush beauty she knew she'd never possess, with skin the warm and pale hue it was meant to be and hair the color of sungold. It was the kind of face and body that drew men's eyes, one fit for a proper Princess, the Elora that should have been in a world that never was.

As she watched, ever more entranced, the vision of herself began to dance. There were no physical limitations or inhibitions to this Elora, nor the slightest restraint. It embodied all the whimsical license of the elemental, where conception and execution were as one, and the wild grace of the human girl herself. With every movement the dance grew more complex, more passionate, more enticing. The images within her mind's eye splintered. She didn't know where she was anymore—trapped on the Gate in the form of the infant firedrake, trapped in her human body, slumped and helpless where she'd left it, or prancing with madcap abandon in the air before the Gate, drawing forth whatever lurked within.

She didn't know where she belonged, but as the illusion became tangible, the lines blurring between what was real and what was not, she felt the links with her true body dissolve.

Another shape was emerging from the darkness, reaching out for the Gate from across an abyss. Elora had a sense of something taller and broader than she, and the sense that here was a masculine ideal to match her feminine. She stayed on her side of the boundary, it on the other, so close she thought she might touch it with just a little stretch of her arm, yet somehow it managed to stay far beyond the limits of her sight. Its every move seemed a match for hers and as the dance progressed it became clear that this newcomer was taking the lead, initiating steps that Elora willingly, eagerly followed. The culmination of their duet would be when it revealed its face to her.

When that happened, she knew she was done.

How can this be happening? she cried to herself. *No spell can hold me!* A moment later she provided her own answer, one part of her mind holding fast to rationality even as the rest of her was overwhelmed. *It isn't me that's being held, not altogether. I bound myself to the firedrake, I'm trapped by the bindings that hold it prisoner!*

The music called to her, the dance tried to sweep her away, and she found too much of herself too eager to yield.

"No," Elora said, a statement as implacable as it was still-voiced. "I deny this, I deny *you!*"

She called for help, with every fiber of her being.

Something broke open, deep inside herself. There was a rush of heat, so intense it should have consumed her utterly, reduced her to ash before she was even aware of her doom. Flesh rippled, stretched, grew, arms reaching forth to encompass horizons yet undreamed of, body rearing up to embrace the stars. She was giddy with disorientation, as though she'd been spun like a top and suddenly cast loose to stagger drunkenly about while her wits and perceptions went haring off along pathways of their own.

Then, as they had before, in Angwyn, the mountains answered her.

Far beneath Elora's feet, fire stirred, flashing solid stone to incandescent gas in a passing instant before shunting that expanding bubble of pressure into cracks and fissures within the world's crust. Massive plates of primordial rock that had remained still for eons shifted, throwing off powerful shock waves that shook the cavern so hard that all the Nelwyns, celebrant and acolytes, were thrown from their feet. Stone cracked, boulders fell, the necessity of maintaining the Summoning spell hurriedly cast aside in favor of simple survival.

The fixative crazed, its surface marred by scores of spiderweb cracks as the frame of the World Gate was twisted past the limit of its tolerances.

Neither dancer paid the slightest heed.

With a fierce effort, Elora wrenched a portion of will back from her vision self, and in the process drew the newcomer's gaze toward her. She didn't dare look, she saved herself by throwing herself completely back into the substance of the firedrake, flooding it with her own absolute need to escape.

The creature ignited like a newborn star, but nothing happened. Despite all the damage done to the Gate, all the passion and will and desire they could manifest, the pair of them could not break free. Carig would not let them.

Elora had never seen such hatred, it made her own emotions seem like such puny, half-formed things. All the strengths and virtues she admired in Torquil, as in Thorn, were present in Carig as well. Only they had twisted in upon themselves, laced through with a feral rage reminiscent of an animal gone mad, until all the light had been squeezed out of them, or crushed, or simply smashed to bits. His soul was shadow, his desire to make the world pay for the harms and insults he believed had been done him. Pain would beget pain, and his joy would be to bring forth greater horror.

In her own body this would have been a hard and brutal fight, with no guarantee of her success. Sharing forms with the infant firedrake, she was shackled by too many limitations. She lacked the skill to finesse an escape, the strength to smash her way free, the time to think of what next to try.

Through all of that, she gave hardly any thought to herself. It was the tiny firedrake she grieved for. The ache within her heart was that she was unable to save it.

Carig staggered, the expression of rage on his face taking on a measure of confusion as one hand plucked aimlessly at something behind his back. He couldn't reach the first arrow that struck him. He was turning as the second hit home, its shaft ablaze from the scorching ambient temperature of the grotto. The narrow, armor-piercing head buried itself into the breast of his smock, the impact driving him back a step. The renegade Nelwyn stared stupidly at the flames rising right beneath his bearded chin before reflexes acted of their own accord to slap the arrow aside.

He wasn't hurt, his ironcloth smock had seen to that, but he had been distracted. For Elora, that was all the opportunity she needed.

The firedrake erupted from the apex of the Gate with a fiery joy that shattered its hold and set every other sigil blazing in its turn as the other firedrakes regained their true form. Simultaneously Elora cast her own essence through the firedrake into every particle of the Gate's substance, to make herself one with it. The Gate was a creation of magic, held in place by spells, the core nature of her being could not be leashed by magic. Two contrary absolutes. A paradox that could not be resolved. The Gate was the one to buckle.

With a hoarse yell, Elora found herself back in her body, the force of her reentry propelling her up off the slab on which she lay to butt the crown of her head full into the belly of a Daikini looming over her. He went down in a breathless *whoosh* of air, she following, the pair tumbling together to the bottom of the slope. As they fell she recognized him as the pipe smoker from the bazaar, the one she'd decided was a warrior in disguise. There was nothing of the merchant about him here. He was dressed for war in burgundy leather, broadsword on his hip, quiver of arrows slung across his back, bow in hand with another shaft nocked for firing. They landed awkwardly, more or less side by side, though he managed to retain hold of his bow. His nose and lip were bloody and she thought that without the services of a qualified physician, and a *very* good cosmetic shapemaker, his profile would never be the same again.

"Blessed *be*!" he exclaimed, at his first full sight of the World Gate.

Elora didn't look, she didn't dare. The entity Carig had Summoned was too close. Breaking the sigils might not stop its manifestation, shattering the Gate itself might not either. Her great terror was that if she looked it in the eye, if it reached out its hand, she would take it. Embrace damnation, joyously.

"Forget about that," she screamed at her savior as the frame of the grotto twisted around them like a box of paper being crushed, "we've got to *go*!"

She'd forgotten about Carig. Even as a fresh temblor calved the rock on which they lay and dropped a piece close beside her the size of a modest house—she heard a scream that started in terror, spiraled to something beyond, was suddenly cut off, and knew that at least one among the acolytes had paid the price for his crimes—she was yanked off her back and thrown against a wall hard enough to stun. She struck at the Nelwyn with hands and feet as he held her one-handed in place, but her best efforts only made Carig laugh. She might as well have been hitting a man made of steel.

The Daikini lay stunned atop a swiftly growing pool of blood. Carig hadn't been as gentle with him as with Elora, taking just a single blow to smash his face.

"I should have guessed," Carig said, using his free hand to peel off her skullcap and reveal silver hair above silver skin. "I should have known. *Thou!*" The malice in that single word struck her like a spray of acid poison, but she didn't flinch. Instead she bared her teeth and struggled all the harder, which only made him laugh out loud.

"Poor little Princess," he told her as he shook loose a tanglefoot web to bind her tight. "Who's this, thy savior?" He lashed out sideways with his foot in what seemed like the most casual of gestures, yet Elora knew he'd struck the fallen warrior hard enough to break ribs, complementing the blow with a disparaging snort. "Full marks for bravery, I suppose, an' skill, got to grant him that for making his way through the Nelwyn stronghold wi'out

71

bein' detected. Hardly salvation, though. His colors mark him as Maizan, prob'ly seekin' t' make his name by bringin' you hog-tied to his castellan.

"Sorry, my lad, I have first claim on 'er."

"You have nothing."

"Beg t' differ, Sacred Highness. Pity, really. It's almost a shame to end thy story when it's only just begun. Hopes as high as thine, a soul as noble, should be destroyed slowly."

"Sorry to disappoint you."

"And most definitely, such a spirit should be broken with care."

"Go to hell."

"Dare I say, ladies first?" He stole a glance toward the Gate, which coated the grotto in a sickly radiance that washed away all color and flattened all the figures, so that everything appeared to be two-dimensional, without depth or reality. "For thy bride, most dread and puissant lord, I offer thee the heart and hope of the world!"

"*Never!*" she cried, with all her strength.

He cast the web, but he was too late. In that same moment, crossing every mental finger because it had been years since last she tried this stunt, and even then only under Thorn's direct supervision, Elora Danan took a deep breath and cast her body backward, into the very fabric of the rock.

Chapter
3

WHEN ELORA WAS VERY SMALL, THORN TOLD HER A story of a young girl who'd chased a brownie down one of its barrow holes. It was a tight fit because while Daikini are giants compared to Nelwyns, Nelwyns have much the same relationship to brownies, the height of the greatest among the Wee Folk being measured in inches. However, what they lack in size, brownies have always made up for in raw cunning. Few are the races on either side of the Veil who can match them in that regard. There's nothing in the world, so their reputation goes, that's too big for them to steal, nor any foe so large they can't somehow cut him down to size.

The girl had popped through the entrance only to find herself in a sheer drop of quite some distance. You see, when a brownie enters his barrow, it's along paths and handholds set off to the side. Anyone else tumbles headlong into a pit that won't be easily escaped. Nothing bad happened to the girl, of course—it wasn't that kind of story. She had a series of wonderful adventures in a succession of fantastic lands, looked after all the way through by a pair of irreverent brownie companions who saw her safely home before her parents even became aware she was missing.

That was the image that came to Elora, of falling down the brownie barrow, as she tumbled backward head over heels in a succession of slow rolls down through the solid substance of the mountain. She'd sat attentively by Thorn's side as he explained to her what a demon had once told him, how everything in existence was composed of incredibly tiny dots of matter, bound together by interlocking, invisible strands of energy. This combination of forces was overlaid one upon the other like a lattice, on a larger and larger scale until they manifested themselves as the forms and shapes of the world she knew. From the faint quavers she heard at the back of his voice, though, Elora couldn't help wondering if he *really* believed all this. She certainly had a hard enough time comprehending it. He pointed to the stars in the sky and told her to imagine them as the foundation of creation, minute dots of brightness with incredibly vast spaces between them. Of course he was talking rubbish, she protested; anyone with half a brain and a single eye could see that solid was solid, period, exclamation point. End of story.

He laughed at her in genuine amusement, and related that he'd said much the same himself. Then he took a picture from his own traveling pouch, a perfectly adequate forest scene he'd collected from somewhere or other as a gift, and held it before her, asking what she saw. She told him: a forest glade, a pond, trees, a mating pair of swans, a stag and doe. As she spoke he brought the painting ever closer and gradually her voice trailed off, for what appeared to be solid blocks of color at a distance discorporated before her eyes, until finally she beheld an almost incomprehensible jumble of small colored dots. The subtleties and gradations of hue that she had seen were illusions, tricks of the eye brought about by all those separate and individual dots blurring together in her vision.

"It's a matter of perception, really," Thorn said, "and I suspect, a matter of faith. Reality *is* because we believe in it."

"Bollocks," was her reply, which earned her a modest glare and a spoken reprimand at such an unladylike comment.

The fact was, there *were* comparatively vast gaps in the fabric of what she preferred to think of as rock-solid matter, because Thorn could move through them. He'd taken her with him, more than once, and taught her the trick as well. She hadn't practiced much since for fear of losing her concentration and finding herself trapped forever, like a fly in amber, only with the horrible thought that she might somehow remain alive and aware throughout that awful eternity.

So, earlier tonight, when she cast her consciousness into the physicality of the infant firedrake, she also passed along a message to the mountains themselves, apprising them of her intent and asking their aid. Now, in addition, she prayed for safe passage.

She let herself free-fall because that was the fastest and most effective means that came to mind of getting clear of Carig's Gate. She didn't know all that much about them, she'd been running mostly on instinct the whole time. As a result she wasn't sure whether she'd disrupted the framing matrix, or if the temblors had shattered the lintels themselves, in time to prevent the emergence of the being Carig was Summoning. She refused to think of that entity, she thrust all recollection violently from the forefront of her mind, afraid that even the merest conception of it might reestablish the link between them. Impossibly, her body tingled with the energies it had wrapped about her, ached to complete the dance they'd begun, wondered about the shape of its face and the feel of its flesh against hers.

Stop it, she cried in silence, taking refuge in the vehemence of her denial, even though she knew it was a lie.

She thrust out arms and legs to regain some measure of control over her descent in much the same way she'd perform underwater, the main difference being the density of the medium. She had no idea how long she'd been falling, or how far, but she had only the one breath to draw on, which meant there was no time to waste in returning to the surface.

Another tremor snapped past, sending ripples through the earth nearby. The movements appeared slow and lazy to her perceptions, which made the end result even more impressive. With due deliberation, strata were compressed and rock crushed to powder. Then, after the wave had moved on and the dynamic pressure relaxed, the incredible weight of the world above once more settled down upon it and squashed the seams even more flat than before.

Without warning, the structure of the crust around her collapsed, the state of the rock transformed in that blink of a moment from solid to molten liquid, and Elora found herself immersed in a current of fast-flowing lava. Somehow, though she remained blessedly impervious to harm, she was tangible enough to be acted upon.

She'd seen such floods on the surface, making their stately progress down volcanic slopes. Visually impressive but not a ferocious danger provided a body could maintain a fair walking pace, and at some point manage to get out of its way. However, there was another product of such eruptions that Thorn had shown her which was an altogether different magnitude of threat. Essentially, the molten rock superheated the air and water of the mass until it became a virtually frictionless surface. Instead of creeping, this type of flow took off at speeds a thoroughbred horse couldn't match, roaring down mountainsides with the force of a tidal wave, consuming everything in its path.

This underworld river acted much the same, sweeping Elora helplessly along with such violence that it was all she could do just to keep from drowning. She knew she couldn't stay, she could already feel the beginnings of a burn beneath her breastbone as her lungs protested the absence of a fresh breath of air. At the same time she also knew she'd only have one good chance at escape. The force of the current was too strong, it would take a supreme effort to work free, with no reserves left if she failed.

The joy of no alternative, she thought, *it* so *focuses the concentration.*

And, she hoped, the will.

She sidled herself as close as possible to the edge of the flow and then, before she could think anymore about the cost of failure and thereby lose all her nerve, tried to throw herself clear.

It was the strangest sensation, battling through total darkness, her imagination applying arbitrary values of color and sound to the unworldly perceptions passed along by her InSight. The lava flow she painted in varying gradations of red, dull scarlet at the edges to gold-edged white in the center. The layers of rock likewise had their appropriate shades, much cooler in aspect and exhibiting considerably more variety. At the same time there was a tremendous roaring, akin to an entire ocean's worth of water plunging through an equally impressive cataract, highlighted by grumps and groans and tweaks and tears from the world about her. All her senses were involved— the stench of sulfur, the taste of pumice leavened by iron, a touch that struck an eerie chord with the memory of fingers struggling to grip a plate of ice—but she was well beyond the limit of what her mind would accept.

Making her way to the boundary of the flow was comparatively easy, but try as she might she couldn't get any farther. She was caught in the geologic equivalent of a rapids, with no handholds on the bank she could use to pull herself free, or even simply anchor herself. Her final attempt almost brought her to disaster as the current folded her body over and in on itself, slamming her into the boundary wall where she was deflected back into midstream. Only quick reactions and the wit to tuck herself into a ball proved her salvation.

A pyrrhic victory, she feared, as the burn within grew to match that without, and her temples throbbed with her brain's and heart's mutual need for oxygen.

Brighter lights appeared within the body of the stream, but she gave them no thought at first, assuming them to be a product of ongoing delirium as they moved around and past her with the lithe and careless ease of serpents. It wasn't until her infant companion put its version of her face in front of Elora's own, and stuck its tongue out at her to tickle her nose and thereby get her attention, that she realized who had joined her.

As she watched, the firedrakes gamboled to the boundary and, arching along the whole length of their entrancingly sinuous bodies, with a kick of the tail end for good measure, slipped free. They almost immediately returned, and here Elora finally got a tangible sense of the flow's velocity, for even the briefest of excursions left the elementals far behind. The speed was a revelation. Elora never imagined it was possible to move so fast.

She wished there were a way to harness the firedrakes so they could pull her free, but feared that doing so meant becoming more substantial, and along that road led catastrophe. Her only hope was to follow their example.

She stopped swimming as a person, with arms and legs, and instead tucked all her limbs in a line along her body. The firedrakes moved with a sinuous undulation from top to toe and so did she. It was awkward at first, since she had a spine to deal with and they did not. She doubted they had a skeletal structure of any sort and in this instance envied them for it. Her lungs were frantic in their demand for air, triggering all manner of backbrain images of panic and doom and despair. She thrust them vehemently aside, she knew she was dying, she didn't need these herald pronouncements as confirmation. But in the past too many others had fought and sacrificed to save her, and more than a few had died. The least she could do was fight for herself as hard as they had.

She flexed and rolled and couldn't help glorying in the sensations as she slipped with surprising ease through the folds and layers of the stream.

Hello, she heard from that well-remembered chorus of melodious voices, caressing her with warmth and affection.

In this cauldron she had neither air nor voice to speak with, she didn't know how to answer. They didn't appear to mind.

Hello hello hello hello.

With each greeting, a new shape slipped close beside her as each member of the school came forth to welcome her and, by extension, thank her for their rescue. Her hands stretched out of their own accord, but the firedrakes wouldn't let her touch them. They treated this as some delightful new game, arching their bodies, twisting *just* fractionally out of reach, then flicking so close she could feel crackles of energy from their flesh to hers.

The infant took station right in front of her face, its tiny form transmuting yet again into its version of her own. Then, with a suddenness that made Elora gasp, it went straight for her, passing through human flesh and bone as if both were as intangible as air. That must have been some signal for the others because they all leaped at her, through her, filling her for those brief moments of contact with the most delicious of flames. They moved, she followed, only now there seemed to be no skeleton to limit the possibilities of her movements.

She understood where they were now, and where the firedrakes wished to lead her. This was the heart of the world, the fiery core that warmed and nurtured this globe from within as the sun did from the sky above. It spun with a life of its own, far faster than the shell that encased it, and sustained a blaze whose life span stretched far beyond Elora's ability to comprehend. She could apply numbers to the years but those numbers were meaningless to her. The essence was that here was another living thing, as finite in its way as she and as full of passion.

She remembered the Nelwyn catechism: *The first realm is Fire.*

It burns, the firedrakes cried, as though they'd sensed her thought. Perhaps they had, as their forms became more and more alike. **We burn. All things burn.**

Their existence was as simple as it was primal and the image came to her of them as the sparks that ignited the first celestial fires.

But who strikes those flames? she wondered.

Follow us. Follow follow follow. And see!

They broke from her, singly and in groups, to dive into the world's core. From her vantage point, Elora could somehow see them burst out the other side. The substance of her perceptions was stretching along with that of her body, right the way around the center until it seemed that the firedrakes were swimming in and out of *her.* That *she* was in small measure the heart and soul of things.

Her eyes, such as they were by then, turned upward, and the thought came to her of the second verse: *The second realm is Earth.* Because earth restrains fire and gives it purpose. From the interaction of those two come the final realms of the Circle of the World: Air and Water. For without the blend of all four primal elements, the second circle, that of the Flesh, has no hope of existence.

Without her, according to prophecy, that circle—and the other two bound to it—has no hope of survival.

This is wrong, she said, unaware that she spoke aloud and that her voice was much like the firedrakes', as was her body. **I would love to stay, I'm happy here. But I cannot.**

Wrong, they cried, turning her own words into a protest. **Here is safety. Here is family. Here is joy.**

It was true. It didn't matter.

Her whole life she'd been in hiding. People who loved her were afraid for her, and some she knew afraid *of* her. Somehow that fear had transmitted itself to her like a sickness. She was too precious, too important, too young, too fragile; a whole host of reasons not to act, all of them sound and logical as they led her inexorably to disaster.

She found the infant pacing her again, wearing her visage a final time, only the face Elora beheld wasn't entirely human, as though the reflection presented a version of Elora Danan that was defined more by spirit than flesh. She tried to fix the physical details in memory but the images dissolved like quicksilver. They could be seen but not retained. Only the eyes held her, pools of cobalt gazing into her own with a gravitas and maturity the infant could not possibly possess. Nor Elora herself.

And yet she knew, this face was hers.

I must go, she said. And then, to anchor the decision, she spoke it to herself in her own voice. "I must go."

She popped out of the ground like a projectile, burped straight up well past the nearest treetops. Habit and momentum kept her wriggling right to the moment gravity reasserted its hold on her and brought her back down into water.

She flailed like a soul accursed, forced suddenly to deal with the presence of arms and legs as she beat them every which way to no purpose whatsoever and decided after the fact that it was a modest miracle she didn't end up properly drowned. Fatigue helped, she was too exhausted to sustain so much activity.

A residue of common sense prompted her to roll over on her back, at least long enough to gather in a brace of decent breaths. The air was wondrous sweet, the water deliciously cool, tempting her to stay immersed until she shriveled. The corner of her gaze revealed a bank not too far distant and she began to propel herself in that direction with clumsy paddles of the hands and feet. She'd have attempted something better but the weight of her waterlogged clothes was more than her muscles could overcome.

She knew she'd reached shore when her head bumped into it. The ground fell into the pond along a gentle slope, which allowed her to lie still awhile and gradually recover. Her lungs pumped like a bellows, a faintish *hah* sound on the inbreath, a hoarse and flat-sided *hunh* when she exhaled. All her might was required to draw the air in, but letting it go felt like an anvil was dropping on her diaphragm as she excavated her lungs to their very dregs. Each pulse was so violent she half feared she'd pop her ribs out through her skin, like a too worn piece of hide stretched too tight on its rack, finally giving way from the endless, unendurable strain. Her heart was going so fast she couldn't keep count of its beats and the phantom spikeblossoms that had taken root within her chest underground had decided to migrate north to her skull, refusing to take her hint that, since they'd traveled so far already, why not complete the journey and depart her body entirely?

Yet, for all the upset, each breath was a victory, trumpeted in the loudest and most majestic of fanfares.

I'm alive, she thought, and the realization made her as giddy as a firedrake. *I'm alive! I'm alive!*

When at last her eyes were open and functioning as they should, she wondered if some kind of mist was occluding the surface of the pond, before realizing with raised eyebrows of genuine amazement that it was steam. Her body was throwing off as much heat as a well-stoked furnace and was acting on the cooler mountain springwater accordingly. A cockeyed glance down at herself reassured Elora that her clothes had survived their ordeal none the worse for wear. Apparently, the same could be said for her.

She needed food, she'd never felt so hungry, but sleep refused to be denied. She tried to elbow herself all the way onshore but the best she could achieve was to heave her shoulders clear. That, she decided, would have to do.

The sun didn't appear to have moved much across the sky when she awoke, but the chill stiffness of her limbs, the pressure of her bladder, told Elora that some considerable time had passed.

At least the leaves are still green, she thought, and then giggled, *unless I've slept the year through, from one summer to the next.*

Doubtful, she decided upon inspection, since her hair hadn't grown, nor her nails. A day then, perhaps a few.

She unlaced boots and trousers where she lay and slid herself out of them. Pulling them after proved to be a small struggle. Sodden as they were, saturated through and through with water, they were as heavy as she, if not more so. Her cloak, once she'd squirmed her way free, she was certain weighed more. She unfolded it to its fullest expanse on the ground and hoped it would dry out in less than her lifetime. As for the rest, she checked the angle of the sun, found a fallen tree trunk whose broken limbs would support her clothes, and stripping to her skin, hung them out to dry. This was one practical advantage of having a magician for a mentor: A housekeeping spell Thorn cast about her possessions not only made her outfits proof against most extremes of weather but ensured they would keep their shape. Normally, leather wet as this would shrink to nothing as it dried. Not hers.

That taken care of, she basked in the sun and rummaged through her pouches, another gift from Thorn, both for something fresh to wear and something good to eat. A sleeveless shift fulfilled the one ambition, but all she could find to satisfy the other were a couple of sandwiches and what remained of her pickings from the bazaar. Plus, thankfully, a flask of water to wash them down. Bread on a dry throat was bad enough, but sharp cheese was murder.

She didn't eat it all, much as she wanted to stuff herself until she was sick. She had no real idea where she was, and caution prompted her to husband what resources she possessed.

The sun was intense and she let its warmth and light fill her until she was sure she was glowing. In the two years she'd spent with Torquil, her trips outside had been few and far between, none of them beyond the confines of the valley that held the bazaar. She hadn't realized how easily she'd fallen into the rhythms of the Nelwyns' lives, accepted their values and their limits. Their tunnels were their haven, where they were safe. Beyond lay danger, and doubly so for Elora herself if she were ever recognized. Also, theirs wasn't that hospitable a land, possessing little to make it attractive beyond its stark and primal beauty and the richness of its ore.

A breeze stirred the trees, setting a grove of aspens across the pond to rustling with that *shhhhhh* sound she loved, and wafting the scent of a meadow of high-country honeysuckle over her. She'd already concluded she was still in the highlands. The problem, she feared, was *which* highlands. The shape of the mountains, the lay of the land, told her she was nowhere close to the Rock Nelwyn caverns. Beyond that, she had no idea. She could be anywhere.

Her clothes were still damp, so she decided to give her legs a stretch and some exercise with a brief stroll. She followed her ears, clambering up the jumble of rocks that formed a small waterfall at the head of the pond and making her way to the meadow beyond. The golden flowers cut a long slash along the field, the field interspersed with enough fallen logs and stumps to tell her that a terrible fire had raged here in the recent past. There were hills on every side, some with gentle slopes, a couple at her back formidable enough that she wouldn't attempt a climb without specialized equipment.

With apologies to the flowers, Elora gathered a few handfuls of blossoms as she walked and idly began to braid them into a crown. It was a lazy afternoon, utterly without complications. While she knew she should be making plans for her survival—finding food and a place to sleep tonight—she relished the sudden and absolute lack of household obligations.

The crown didn't fit quite right, she'd made it a tad too big, it kept slipping down irreverently over one eye. She had a mirror in her pouch, on impulse decided she wanted to see what she looked like, and quickened her step back to the pond.

It was such a careless, carefree moment, one of a rare

few in her life, that she didn't watch her step bounding off the rocks. She put her right foot into something viscous and yellow brown in color. It had the consistency of mud and gave off the most incredible stench.

Momentum carried her a couple of steps farther on, which she managed as a succession of left-footed hops while she made a face and an even more horrid noise of dismay at the sludge that enveloped her past the ankle. She didn't want to touch it, but when sluicing her foot in the pond didn't wash the mess clean, she had to crouch over and scrub. Only when she was done did the smell fully register.

Troll dung.

It was a fresh pie. Just how much so became shockingly clear as a scabrous, dun-colored form rose from its hiding place in the brush and bushes. By sight, trolls were disgusting enough, with skin that looked baked and blistered, as though the creature had been hosed down by a stream-of flame. Hair sprouted from its body like a lawn haphazardly planted, in tangled clumps and sprouts. Additionally, they seemed to attract filth. As a species, trolls possessed not even the slightest sense of personal hygiene.

This one stood head and shoulders taller than Elora, broader in the shoulders, with long, lanky arms and legs. Beneath a heavy brow was a face more disgusting than fearsome, especially when it opened its mouth to reveal teeth so discolored and worn the mere sight of them turned the stomach. But Elora had seen folk ripped and torn by troll bites, and slashed by the equally jagged and hooked claws that tipped every finger and toe. The creatures were almost naturally septic and consequently there was a certainty of infection, which often proved as deadly as the initial attack.

Worst of all, that description didn't even begin to take into account their smell. Like ghouls, trolls ate their fill of carrion, and at some point in their history the stench of rot grafted itself permanently into their bloodline. Unlike ghouls, however, trolls eat the dead by choice, because they are basically lazy. Deprived of that particular source of sustenance, a ghoul will starve. Trolls, however reluctantly, go hunting. And despite their appearance, trolls are neither stupid nor are they poor hunters.

This one stood between Elora and her clothes. She thought of diving into the pond, but she had little faith in her own ability to tread water for very long. Worse, now that the troll had identified her as prey, it wouldn't leave so long as she remained in sight. Nor would it mind waiting until she drowned. She considered casting herself back into the ground, escaping the troll as she had Carig, but rejected the thought almost as quickly. Magic took a fearsome toll on the body, she could move faster and farther on her feet.

She feinted for the pond, and when the troll followed her lead she broke for the treeline as fast as she was able.

Behind her sounded a hollow *halloowoowoo* and then the crash of a body through thickets as it gave chase. Size and agility were her advantages as she skated around every obstacle, but they were quickly negated by the troll's tremendous strength as it simply bulled its way through everything in its path. She put some distance between them at the start but time would soon take away that edge as the troll's endurance overcame her sprinter's speed. She needed a weapon, and when nothing presented itself to her questing eyes, she began to search for somewhere to hide.

She almost missed the barrow.

It was framed by a guardian grove of oaks, so impressive a scattering of ancient trees that Elora's first instinct had been to take to their branches, an opening tucked between a tangle of massive roots of such a size they could have been tree trunks in their own right reaching outward from the base of the senior member of the copse.

The angle and distance were all wrong. Realization and response came as one as she put a trunk between herself and the troll and pivoted to stand her ground. It thundered around the tree, to discover that she'd danced back the other way, keeping the massive trunk between them. It caught on quickly, though, matching her feint with a pretty good one of its own. It didn't seem to mind missing her, content to use the momentary stalemate as an opportunity to catch its breath. As far as she could tell, the troll was actually enjoying the chase. Every element of its body language proclaimed its confidence in the eventual outcome of the hunt.

Wonderful! she thought, as the absurdity of the situation struck her. *Elora Danan, Sacred Princess, savior of the Great Realms, and today's lunch meat.*

While moving back and forth, Elora scooped up a handful of fair-sized pebbles. She tossed the stones behind and away from her, making an intentional clatter as she scattered them down the boulder-strewn slope. They sounded just like a running figure losing her footing and starting a minor avalanche.

The troll fell for the deception and burst around the trunk to her right in the direction of the sound. She broke left. It caught her movement in its peripheral vision, but the lay of the ground wasn't conducive to that kind of sudden stop. It staggered, tripped, should have fallen, but did an incredible forward flip that twisted its body all the way around in midair and put it on both feet facing her. By then, she'd reached the branches above, though the audacity of the troll's acrobatics stopped her in her tracks, mouth forming a perfect O of astonishment and no little envy.

She had to leap a body length into the air and then haul herself up onto the branch. The troll reached it from where it stood in a single bound. Elora hadn't waited. The branches of the trees had long ago grown in and around each other, forming a comprehensive canopy over the glade. The larger ones were broader across than her own body, which made it easy to run from one to the next. She changed levels as well, scampering monkeylike into the higher reaches of the tree. The troll eagerly accepted her challenge, supremely confident of its own ability to catch her no matter where she fled.

That was when she let him have it, right in the chops, with a branch she'd bent nearly double, a strain so great she was sure her joints would pop. The branch whipped around with the force of a catapult. It swept the troll right off its perch and out of the tree entirely. The creature looked almost comical, seeming to hang suspended in the air for a brief moment before it began its fall, so stunned by the impact that its feline reflexes didn't begin to react to this new situation until just before it struck the ground. As Elora had planned, it landed on the slope and this time didn't stop tumbling until it reached the bottom of the arroyo. The troll regained its feet immediately, of course, and put all its formidable strength into the scramble back to the top.

Elora dropped to the ground the moment her pursuer took flight, landing right in front of the barrow entrance. She cried an apology to the residents within and pitched herself forward just like the heroine of the story Thorn had told her, arms extended full-length as though she was diving into a pool of water. Right then, she thought all her stratagems had gone for naught as her shoulder caught a corner of root just within the portal and she found herself stuck fast. The sound of the troll's hunting cry, the sight in her mind's eye of her being yanked unceremoniously backward into its grasp, was all the impetus she needed for a wrench of upper body, coupled with a tremendous heave of her legs, to pop her past the obstruction and completely through the entry passage. As she pitched into darkness her hands stabbed out to either side to try to find the safety lines strung along the paths the brownies used. One line held, the other crumbled in her grasp, and with a yelp of fright, she suddenly found herself dangling by three fingers over a pit big enough to swallow a full-grown Daikini with room to spare.

She tried to close her fingers around the line, at the same time scrabbling for purchase with her other hand and toes.

The troll's breath gusting through the entryway almost finished her as surely as its wildly flailing hand. The stench made her stomach heave, she barely managed to hold on to lunch and blessed the fates she hadn't had that much to eat. Fortunately brownies planned their barrows well, keeping in mind every kind of predator that might pit itself against them, be it snake, badger, mountain lion—or troll. The access was too narrow to admit the creature and the passage itself was longer than its arm, even at its fullest and most painful extension.

The troll tried tearing at the portal to enlarge it, but again brownie engineering proved more than its match. The entrance was framed by the oak's roots. Any decent excavation would have to involve removing them. The troll may have had the wit to realize that, and the will to give it a try, but it didn't possess the tools. Its strength was of little use—this oak was too old, its body too massive—and the troll's claws would break in fairly short order against bark weathered to the consistency of metal.

After a time, wherein it subjected Elora to an endless succession of cacophonous howls that left her as deafened as its breath had left her nauseated, there was no more scrabbling at the entry, no more shrieking, no more smell. The barrow lost even the pretense of light and the air took on a damp and earthen chill that made her wish for something more substantial than her shift.

Over the course of her impromptu incarceration, she'd succeeded in catching hold of the line with her other hand and finding an uncomfortable purchase on the narrow ledges that ringed the top of the pit. Like Thorn, she possessed a wizard's NightSight, the ability to see in absolute darkness, but that proved no help whatsoever. Around her, along the track etched in the wall of the pit, were revealed the main tunnels of the barrow, a half dozen to her count: all had been intentionally blocked. Worse, when she looked down she saw that the floor of the pit had been filled with stakes, branches mostly, firmly emplaced in the ground, their tips sharpened to barbed and wicked points. She wouldn't be the first to fall victim to the trap, either. There was a collection of bones piled at the bottom, and a carcass still impaled that would likely join them before the next spring.

"That's *very* nasty," she said to herself, brow furrowing as she considered the implications. She wasn't surprised at the pitfall. Brownies fought like demons to defend their homes and loved ones and were rarely inclined to show mercy to those who threatened them. For all that ferocity, however, they weren't by nature killers. Given the choice, they would much rather strip a foe of pride and dignity than of life.

Actually, she thought—remembering the many occasions when she'd seen Rool and Franjean double-team some poor benighted soul, occasionally herself, more often Thorn—*they don't just enjoy tormenting and humiliating their enemies, they pretty much love tormenting and humiliating their* friends.

To the brownies, life was the greatest comedy ever staged, and their role in it to delightfully butcher every sacred cow that wandered across their path. The more pompous the pretension, the more delight they took in cutting it down to size.

This deadfall wasn't in character, it was the kind of snare a Daikini would set. And that disturbed her far more than the burrow's evident abandonment.

Her fingers hurt, her arms hurt, her shoulders hurt, which she decided was a good thing. The moment to worry was when everything went numb. She put any concerns about the condition of the safety line firmly and irrevocably from her mind. If it held, it held. If not, there was precious little she could do about it.

She couldn't stay where she was. The question was, how to go? And which way?

Elora reached out with her InSight, praying for the response of a sympathetic thought anywhere within mindshot, a pair of eyes and ears she might briefly "borrow" to make certain the coast was clear. She made a sour face at the response. Nothing in the way of higher-order animal life, she had to content herself with insects and small lizards.

The bugs were the worst. Not only were their thought patterns rudimentary, their actions defined by the biological cues of scent and taste rather than any voluntary decision, but the construction of their bodies was frighteningly unlike anything Elora was used to. When she tried to gaze through their faceted eyes, it was akin to peering through a wildly distorted fun-house lens. More frighteningly, her attempts to meld perceptions so that she might properly interpret those images immediately stretched the link with her human consciousness nearly to the breaking point.

The link was possible, she knew that even as she sprang desperately back to her own mind, as daredevil and potentially deadly a feat as her tumble down the barrow's entrance. She had the knowledge, she possessed the basic skill. What was lacking was practice.

"Serve me right," she told herself over and over again, clocking her head back against the wall behind her, each gentle thump giving physical emphasis to her spoken rebukes, "serve me right, serve me right."

Thorn had made himself plain from the start.

"Talent is a wondrous thing, Elora Danan," he told her. "But it's only raw material. Much like the molten ore in Torquil's furnace. It has to be refined, then shaped into its ultimate form before it can serve its proper purpose as a tool. As you master the craft and art of iron, the same applies to that of sorcery."

"Except I'm not a sorcerer," she retorted sharply. It hadn't been one of her better moods, nor their better days.

"Sorcery," he said with a gentle implacability that made her suddenly think of Torquil, "at bedrock is the imposition of will on one power or entity by another. It is an exercise of might. The way given you to access magic—and make no mistake here, young lady, you *can* access magic—is different. In its own way, far more difficult. Even humbling. You must ask the powers involved, the entities involved, for help. Charm them, cajole them, inspire them, terrify them, whatever; there *must* be a give-

and-take, whereas a sorcerer need only take. The tools you are given to work with are not sigils or spells or wands or any of the paraphernalia the likes of me take for granted. You have to work with things that live, and have a free will of their own. So, for your own survival, you treat them with respect. You're bound together, like the Circles of Creation. Your survival is theirs is yours."

He'd given her a list of exercises, and the creatures he expected her to work with. She'd always felt she'd done her best. There was just so much to do around the forge and the home, she found it easier to let herself be distracted.

She found a skink foraging through the empty tunnels, and her delight at the discovery of something she could work with almost brought disaster to them both. She forgot, until it was nearly too late, how small the lizard's mind was compared with hers and in her eagerness to take control almost poured more energy into the tiny creature than it could safely withstand.

Her next approach was far more cautious, and attempted only after she'd sung a gentle song of healing to ease the shock of that brief contact.

The tunnels were empty, stripped bare, and not in any hurried or frantic evacuation either. Great care had been taken to leave nothing behind and then to seal the burrow by collapsing formidable stretches of passageway.

Likewise, she discovered after exchanging her underground companion for one scampering among the grass and flowers above, the dryads who would normally inhabit the hearts of trees as ancient and venerable as these had also fled. That couldn't have been an easy decision on their part, Elora knew, because wood nymphs mated with their trees for life. Separation could only be accomplished with many spells and much preparation.

She took heart from the fact that she'd found a lizard on the surface. None would have shown itself if the troll was still lurking.

When she finally emerged from the barrow, the only

sign of the troll was a lingering scent, the noisome residue of its presence.

It was still dusk, the air suffused with a magnificent twilight that would last well into the evening.

Her clothes and gear were gone, she discovered upon her return to the pond. She wasn't surprised. Trolls understood the concept of possessions and, more important, the value of those possessions to their owners. More than one unfortunate wayfarer had met an untimely demise following the trail left by a stolen pack or garments.

Find the troll, find her stuff. But what then?

Her stomach growled, reminding her it had been a long and very active day. She'd lost her garland crown within a few steps of beginning her mad dash from the pool, but a breath of honeysuckle on the breeze led her quickly to where it fell. She plucked a brace of petals and sucked them dry, savoring the rich taste of their nectar.

Tired as she was, she still moved with a lithe and near-boneless grace as she closed on the troll's den, so silent in every aspect she would put a ghost to shame. She recalled the sensation of her body melting and re-forming as she swam among the firedrakes and raised her hands before her to where she could see them. She took hold of a forearm, to find the flesh still firm to her touch, the bones comfortingly solid. She thought she looked the way she'd always been, at least since Angwyn, and yet she was just as positive that she'd changed.

She'd always measured herself against her companions, and chafed in silent frustration because every time she came up wanting.

Khory Bannefin was human, at least in form. Her soul, if the term even applied, was that of a demon. Ryn Taksemanyin was of the sea-dwelling Wyrrn. He was poetry to watch, on land as in the water. Khory was a warrior, with a grace to her movements that came from years of study. She was very close to a match for Ryn. Elora had never been so gifted.

Even though Ryn was extraordinarily patient with her as he demonstrated patterns of movement over and over again, Elora always hated the way her body tripped her up short. No matter how much she desired, how hard she thought she tried, she never came close. Thorn's kind and understanding explanation—that she was still a child who hadn't yet begun to properly grow, and moreover a child whose whole life to that point had been one of sloth and indulgence—provided no comfort. She wanted results and in those days was used to having every desire instantly gratified.

Perhaps, she thought amusedly, *that, too, is one of the hurdles of my old life I had to overcome. Certainly one of the first things Torquil taught me.*

She looked across her shoulders from east to west, wondering which direction would take her back to the halls of the Rock Nelwyns. She shuddered, just a little, with a flash of fear that if she undertook that journey, she'd find the Nelwyn stronghold as abandoned and desolate as this brownie barrow.

The world felt no different to her, and she wondered if she would notice if all its magic was stripped away?

I'm supposed to be bound to all the Realms, she worried. *If the World Gates are sealed shut, if the Deceiver steals all that power for himself, what happens then to me? Or is that maybe why I'm so important to the Deceiver—because through me he can reach all the Realms? Am I the battering ram he'll use to force the Gates open again? Was that what Carig was doing with me? Only he didn't know it was me at first, he was genuinely surprised when he found out.* She shook her head violently.

Stop thinking like that, she demanded of herself. *This isn't about you—not all of it anyway. If the Deceiver wins, what happens to everything? Maybe Carig was Summoning some force or other to fight him? From the way he talked, that would make sense. But it also sounded like he was ready to destroy his own people in the process. I've never heard of any Nelwyn acting like that.*

She shook her head, only this time more gently and out of weariness. *Folks always talk about fighting fire with fire,* she thought. *Can you defeat one evil with another?*

A question for Thorn. Only there was no Thorn at hand, and precious few letters since he'd left her.

Focus, she told herself sternly, deliberately quashing the surge of anger she felt at her so-called protector, *on the task at hand.*

Troll dens were generally easy to find, you just had to be able to stand the awful stench. No rubbish tip could match it, nor any abattoir she'd seen.

In this instance, she found herself clambering over a jumbled pile of gigantic stones, ranging in size from a large Daikini to that large Daikini's equally large house. This reminded her of a construction of building blocks, that might originally have formed a most impressive tower until some malicious devil had yanked loose just the right one to bring the entire edifice crashing down.

Here was the opposite of the brownie barrow. Instead of a single inviting entrance, she found a score of possibilities formed by the cracks and hollows where stone was piled awkwardly upon stone. The surface of the rock was dangerously smooth, with no easy handholds, and even in direct sunlight it would be difficult to see within to tell which way was safe.

Elora descended one crevasse by stretching her legs to full extension across the gap and bracing her back against the wall behind her, wishing all the while as she crabbed carefully downward that she wore something more substantial than a linen shift. Her skin burned by the time she reached bottom, though there was no sense of the wetness that would mean she'd drawn blood rather than given herself some nasty scrapes. Regrettably, this seemed the only way out as well, not a route she'd care to take in a hurry, with an angry troll close on her heels.

Her breath hissed with her first step and she picked a chunk of bone from the ball of her bare foot. Again, thankfully, no blood, but her heart sank with dismay as she beheld the cause of her discomfort. A Daikini, by the size of the skeleton, his bones long since picked clean and broken to bits so the trolls could suck out the marrow. Clothes and armor had been shredded in eagerness to get to the meat, there was nothing left of either that would be any use to her. Off in a corner, however, she caught the merest flash of reflection that led her to what must have been the slain warrior's primary weapon, a double-headed war ax. Short-handled, for use in close quarters, it actually weighed less than the Nelwyn hammers she was used to and was better balanced. The haft ended in a five-edged spike extending out from between the blades, which allowed the ax to be used as a stabbing weapon as well.

An empty keening coursed suddenly through the stones; it set Elora's hair so quickly and stiffly on end she knew at once it was nothing to do with the wind. She'd never heard such a sound from any troll and couldn't help the pang her heart felt at the disturbingly human quality of the lament.

Holding the ax before her, she made careful progress along the passage, thankful she had her MageSight to reveal the way as clearly as if she walked in sunlight, and was soon rewarded by a gradual widening of the path. Beyond was the den itself.

The troll had its back to her, apparently so preoccupied that it wasn't the slightest bit aware of her approach. Elora had had little practice at this sort of thing, but Torquil spent the better part of two years teaching her to take phenomenally exact measurements solely by eye. Three long strides would take her to where the troll sat and one swing of the ax would finish the job. The deed had to be done at once, before she lost the element of surprise.

Yet Elora hesitated.

Something about the noise the troll was making, about the way it sat and rocked back and forth, struck resonances within her that could not be denied. That, and the same sense of primal desolation she felt within the brownie barrow and the glade. A perception of the world rolling upside down, like a boat capsizing, to pitch everything that wasn't nailed down over the side. A sudden certainty that here sat no true foe for her but one of the lost souls.

The troll turned its head around and bared its fangs in a perfunctory snarl, and Elora caught sight of the bundle in its arms.

For the longest moment troll and girl locked eyes. Then, unexpectedly, it was the troll that looked away, putting its back once more to Elora, almost as if it was inviting her fatal blow.

Every scrap of learning, every piece of societal imprinting, told Elora to take the proffered gift and strike. At the very least she'd be putting the poor creature out of its obvious misery. She'd be doing what it had as much as asked.

She couldn't.

This was no enemy, no threat—though at another time and place she conceded that it might very well be both—but a creature in need. Mercy she could give, but not murder.

She set aside the ax and crossed around the periphery of the awkwardly circular space, noting her clothes and gear piled haphazardly by a sleeping pallet. The troll had searched the pouches thoroughly—finding them empty, of course, as would any who looked within save for Elora herself—and the pockets of her clothes as well, but it had done no damage.

There were three babies, small and helpless as any newborn, and she didn't need any of the enhanced aspects of her senses to see how near death they all were.

Elora crouched before the troll but the comforting hand she reached out was met by another ritual baring of the fangs, a warning to keep her distance.

Is it so far gone, she wondered, *that it can't see me for what I am? Daikinis have hunted trolls as long as our race can remember, just as they've fed on us.* Much the same relationship, she recalled, as Ryn Taksemanyin described between the Wyrrn and their ancient rivals, the sharks. *Or is that it just doesn't care anymore?*

"No problem," she said aloud, the troll taking no notice of her voice. "Maybe I'm here to care for us both!"

Not a second thought about the impulse or where it

came from. Conception begat execution in the same natural sequence as waking up meant getting out of bed.

The first requirement was warmth. While summer would remain in the lowlands for another month or more, here on the high meadows night brought with it the first crisp hints of approaching fall. The cave was chill and dank and in their weakened state the trolls' fur afforded little protection.

Elora decided against a fire, since that was one of the weapons used to ward off these creatures. Instead she gathered up her traveling pouches and fished out a quartet of smooth, egg-shaped rocks each the size of a clenched fist. She set them in a square on the ground so their ends were touching. She'd cooked them in the forge in anticipation of just such a need and now spread her hands over them, letting her eyes drift out of focus as she cast forth a Call to the powers of the earth below, once more asking their aid.

Next, she addressed the four stones directly, as Thorn had taught her, crooning a song as ancient as the world itself, gently reminding them of what it had felt like to be flushed full with heat, taking that memory and fanning it brighter just as she would the embers of a faded hearth with her breath. She couldn't see her own eyes or the expression on her face, how the one sparkled and the other grinned ear to ear with inexpressible delight to feel energy crackle down the surface nerves just beneath her skin and burst out from her splayed fingertips to play with the rising energies of the stones themselves. As she began to glow, so did they, silver casting forth gold, and in a matter of moments the stones were merrily giving off the required amount of heat.

Elora turned to the troll with a smile, reminding herself as she did so not to bare her teeth because that might be interpreted as a challenge. She wondered if trolls responded to eye blinks the way cats did, as a gesture of peace and friendship, deciding she'd hold off on that for a while, most probably would be pushing her luck a bit *too* far. The troll was staring at the stones, at her, at the stones, at her, only its eyes moving, back and forth, one to the other, the rest of its body still as a statue. There was a recognizable expression on its face, of utter confusion. Something utterly strange and wholly beyond its comprehension was happening. By rights, it should be terrified, yet it wasn't. Somewhere in that mind all Daikini assumed was irredeemably bestial was the capacity to accept the event, without fear or question, and marvel at it as well.

Elora had tied up the hem of her shift on one side to improvise a pocket, into which she'd stuffed the remaining honeysuckle blossoms. She pulled out a handful and sucked a petal dry, then another in demonstration to the troll of what she was doing. She offered it a blossom of its own. It made a face, as if to say, *What, you think I'm stupid or something?*—snatched the flower from Elora's hand, and proceeded to duplicate Elora's actions with an eager ease that suggested it knew full well how tasty honeysuckle could be.

Elora left the flowers in reach and returned to her hearthstones. From one pouch came a metal flask, a small pot, and a pair of mugs, from the other a selection of plants and herbs, together with some cubes of dried bouillon. One mug for her, one for the troll, as she quickly mixed what she hoped would prove a hearty broth. Her own preference was for spices, hot enough to provoke tears, but she kept this soup fairly bland, as the smell of the den had so totally overwhelmed her own nose and tongue that neither seemed to work any longer as a sensory organ.

When the mixture had simmered awhile, Elora hazarded a sip. She'd gotten the heat just right, the broth warm enough to send a glow surging right out through her body but not so blistering that the merest swallow burned the tongue. She mimed the act of drinking from the cup for the troll's benefit, then held out some soup. There was a good minute of puzzlement as the troll thoroughly examined the mug, carefully gauging its temperature before concluding apparently that comfortable to the

99

touch meant comfortable to taste. Next, it tested the cup itself with lips and teeth to determine it if could be eaten as well. At last, its copy of Elora so picture-perfect the girl had to choke back a laugh, the troll tossed back mug and head and swallowed the whole of its contents.

The broth was evidently to its liking, for it let forth a low trill—another sound Elora had never heard before from these creatures—and allowed another level of wariness to fall away from its features. Elora refilled the cup, only not so full, and indicated that the troll try to feed its baby. The troll caught on at once but tried to pour the contents down its child's throat in the same all-encompassing gulp it had used, which left the little thing sputtering and choking and howling its distress at being nearly drowned. Its agitation transferred totally to its parent and came close to undoing all the bridges that Elora had so patiently and laboriously built between them. This was no perfunctory baring of teeth, but a full-fledged snarl with a squalling growl to match.

Elora held her ground and kept what fear she felt at the sudden turn of events well hidden from her face. Her response to the challenge was to pour herself another mug of soup and savor each and every swallow.

A duckwalk sidestep took her to the other two babies, tucked snug about with rags and brush and scraps of flower to form a kind of nest. She gathered one close to her breast, in a pose that echoed the troll's, dipped a finger in the broth, and touched it to the baby's lips. Immediately, the little creature began to suck, finding strength within itself to cry out demands for more as Elora returned to the cup again and again until she felt secure enough to raise the lip of the mug itself to the baby's mouth. As the baby fed, Elora was ever conscious of the troll's eyes observing every move, cause and effect.

When the one baby burped to announce it was full, she turned her attention to the other.

She felt a touch on her bare arm, found that the troll had sidled up beside her so silently Elora hadn't been the slightest bit aware. A last bundle was handed to her by the mother, the troll's way of acknowledging that Elora could do what it could not.

There was no sense of time passing. The cave was so well hidden within the rock pile that no outside light penetrated, which meant Elora could only guess what was day and what night. She was kept so busy caring for the trolls that she soon lost track of which was which, or how many had passed. Their condition was as desperate as their need, demanding so total a commitment that she simply stopped thinking about any other obligations. She fed the trolls when they were hungry—which turned out to be quite often, once they set out on the road to recovery—and kept them warm while they slept, which was whenever they weren't eating. More than once she blessed the time Thorn had spent making her traveling pouches. To the eye, they appeared to be ordinary leather bags, albeit well tanned and tooled, that were slung from loops threaded through a stout leather belt. The magic of them was that the available space within bore absolutely no relationship to their exterior dimensions. Whatever fit through the opening of the bag would fit inside and another aspect of the spell brought immediately to hand whatever Elora required when she reached inside. Food remained fresh and nothing ever spilled. Indeed, since Elora was of the habit of absently depositing items into the pouches, she had no real idea of what they contained.

"This is no fit place for you," she told the troll without the slightest hope of being understood. "It may appear safe but the hunting's gone, can't you see? When you and the babies are better, you've got to move on. There must be other trolls," she continued, "somewhere. You'll have to find them, if that's the way of your kind"—for in truth she had no idea—"just as I have to find *my* friends."

Finally came the day when Elora was woken from her own sleep by the sensations of three rambunctious little terrors using her as an all-purpose play toy, chasing themselves over her with madcap abandon in a game of hide-and-seek that was their way of learning the rudiments of hunting.

That night, the troll returned with fresh kill and the three babies leaped on the carcass with an eager abandon that told Elora they'd take no more broth. She was offered a bloody haunch but demurred, preferring to finish her soup and record her observations of all that had happened here in her journal. Afterward, when the babies demanded attention, she was invited once more to join the family group. This time, however, it was the troll who offered lessons, in grooming, as it meticulously worked its fingers through the scalp of one baby, picking loose whatever grubs and scabby little bugs she found there and sharing them with the baby, squashing them between its teeth with a satisfying crunch. Elora did the same, only she gave all her bounty to the babies.

There was a curious formality to the troll's behavior, a solemnity of stance and manner that told Elora they were nearing the end of their time together. No troll had ever accepted a Daikini into its den, no Daikini had ever faced a troll he hadn't tried his level best to kill. Circumstance had sent the pair of them skating far out on a sheet of glistening ice, without a clue to where it was safe, and offered a way back that could only be traveled together.

Old patterns, Elora mused, *would have doomed at least one of us. So maybe all this change isn't such a bad thing after all.*

The problem was, she wasn't sure she believed a word of it.

The next morning, when she awoke, Elora was alone in the cave.

Chapter
4

With a wild war whoop she hoped would be heard all the way to the summit of the Stairs to Heaven, Elora Danan leaped from the top of the rock pile.

Her original notion was to enter the pool in a nice dive, but she changed her mind the instant she kicked off into the air, folding her body into as tight a ball as she could manage, knees tucked under chin and arms wrapped around legs to hold them in place. She struck the water like a thunderstone shot from a catapult and was rewarded by an appropriately spectacular splash.

She broke the surface in time to see her poor shift float gently after her to settle on the water with far more propriety. Her clothes, evidently, had more of a sense of dignity than the Sacred Princess who wore them.

She dove again, twisting and rolling through the pond as though born to it, in her best imitation of Ryn. The sun was near zenith, on the morning side of noon, and she was thankful that the warmest part of the day lay ahead. Plenty of time to scrub her clothes clean as well as her body. Both were in desperate need.

To wash, she planted herself beneath the waterfall and for the first few minutes simply let the spray pummel her silly. It was mountain water, just the liquid side of ice, and after the initial shock left her gasping, she stoked the inner fires of her body to counteract the cold. She had soap aplenty, but decided in a moment of madness that her hair would have to go.

It'll be easier to take care of short, she told herself quite sensibly. Then, in an unexpected but sensible coda: *and easier to disguise. Everything else seems to be changing, why not me, too?*

So, with awkward but enthusiastic swipes of her knife, she reduced her childhood pride and joy to a very serviceable cut barely the length of her pinkie. Her polished metal mirror revealed the result, a shorter fringe than many boys her age wore and not attractive to her eyes in the slightest.

Of course, the sight of her newly shorn scalp turned all her determination to dust and she very nearly burst into tears, wondering if there was some spell or power she might call upon to restore the lot.

That was when she decided to launch herself off the top of the rock pile.

She thought of throwing away the shift, despairing of ever removing the taint left by the troll's den even if she managed to scrub it outwardly clean. But the very thought seemed churlish to her, after the yeoman service the garment had performed. In addition, she wanted the shift as a reminder of what she'd done here, of how the hand of friendship had been accepted between two species who'd never offered each other anything but hatred and terror in the past.

Elora treated herself to a final swim, working the last

104

of the kinks from her muscles with a set of fast laps across the width of the pond, and when she once more reached the shore where she'd stashed her clothes, she gladly took the towel Rool held out to her.

She was so wrapped up in herself, the moment didn't properly register. When it did, she let out a screech that easily topped her previous outcry as startlement kicked her desperately away from the bank and toward deep water.

The towel flew up into the air as she toppled, but unlike her it never struck the water. A pair of claws descended from a set of golden wings whose span matched Elora's height with the better part of a foot to spare and snatched it up before it began to fall. She had that barest sight of an eagle, a moment to recognize it as Bastian, the sound of his bubbling laughter in her mind, before her body slapped itself noisily beneath the surface. Shock drove all sense from her head, and she forgot to close her mouth and nose. When she pitched herself back into the air, broaching with a forceful leap that would have done Ryn proud, the physical glory of the moment was immediately undercut by her collapse to hands and knees with a succession of watery sneezes and choking coughs that appeared to stumble all over each other in their eagerness to get out.

She felt the backwash of Bastian's wings scooping the air to brake his descent, followed by the touch of the towel across her back as the eagle let it fall.

Her heartbeat slowed and she found once more the ability to take a full and unbroken breath. Likewise, her vision gradually sharpened to reveal a small man-form standing before her in woodland attire. Rool was beside himself with laughter, clutching hands to his sides as though the force of each guffaw would pop his rib cage, rolling on his back because he no longer had strength enough or desire to keep his feet.

"Very"—she gasped, and had to take a few more breaths before she could finish the sentence—". . . funny."

"Yes, it is, actually," Rool agreed, even more uproariously. "Very!"

"Pest."

She kept her lines short, she didn't trust her voice to handle constructions of more complexity.

"Elora Danan, I am so hurt! Say not so, I beg you!"

"I'm going to be sick now."

She didn't recall blinking, but in that brief segment of time Rool shifted position well back out of reach.

"Don't you dare!" he cried.

"Fair warning."

"That isn't funny!"

"Neither is the way I feel!" And with that, she sprawled full-length on her belly.

"Life *is* tough."

She cocked a baleful eye in the brownie's general direction and stuck out her tongue at him for good measure.

Rool stood barely half as high as her knee, a perfectly formed figure of a man whose weathered features were matched to a body as lithe and limber as any youth's. For all the mirth of minutes past, his was a sober soul, as unassuming and practical as his outward appearance. He wore two swords, wickedly hooked blades carved from the fangs of a Death Dog he'd slain, and who in the process had very nearly slain him, leaving a cruel network of scars across his chest and a pale slash that ran from chin over right cheek to well beyond his hairline. His hair was chestnut, though the summer sun had given it more of a tawny cast, and he'd pulled it into a thick queue fastened at the nape of his neck with a forged silver knot. His eyes strangely were a match, flecked with gold in summer, a dark and mysterious brown when snow fell.

When Elora first met him, he wore the head of a mouse as a hood and its skin as a cloak, the rest of him covered by a loincloth and an intricate crazy quilt of painted tattoos, but he'd roamed the greater part of the world since then—a journey no sane brownie would contemplate in his most horrific nightmares—and expanded his wardrobe along with his horizons. His preference remained for leather, a taste Elora had adopted for herself, finely tanned hides that fit so well they might have been a second skin, as comfortable to wear as cloth yet far more hardy. His trousers were tucked into knee-high boots whose soles were firm enough for walking while allowing him the freedom of movement to climb. There was a shirt of finely woven cotton, and over it a high-collared jerkin of long-sleeved leather, most notable for big bellows pockets at either hip. Rool, and his companion Franjean, were thieves by profession as well as nature (since all brownies are, to some extent or other, packrats) and the pockets were useful places to stash both tools and loot. Topping his ensemble was an ankle-length coat of oiled canvas, also constructed with pockets aplenty, slit to the backside to allow easy riding on the back of an eagle. The air might be summer hot on the ground but at the altitudes Bastian soared and the speeds he favored such protection was a necessity.

It had been far too long since she'd seen her friends. She wanted to hug the brownie until he begged for mercy, but he was too small. Instead she contented herself by padding her towel on one shoulder for Bastian to use as a perch. When the great eagle landed, balancing himself with such precision that his cruelly pointed claws didn't even prick her skin, she worked her fingers beneath his thick coat of feathers to scratch his chest where he loved it best. In return, Bastian turned his head around to stroke her cheekbones with his beak, the same gesture of greeting and affection he used with his mate, Anele.

"How'd you find me?" Elora asked as Bastian hopped from her shoulder to a nearby log and she began rummaging through her clothes for something to wear. When no answer was forthcoming, she cast about for Rool, spying him close by the bulrushes, his arm draped with strands of her hair. He was examining shore and shallows in as intent a search as she'd ever seen, making sure to gather every shorn lock.

"Rool?" she called, donning her shift. "What're you doing?"

"What d'you think else, child, but savin' you from your own folly. As always."

She rolled her eyes, in the mistaken assumption that he was making more fun, until a flash of his own gaze back toward her made her reconsider.

"I don't understand," she said as she hunkered close by him to offer help.

"A blinding revelation, if ever there was."

"Don't be mean."

"Don't be stupid."

He shook a handful of tufts at her.

"This is a part of you," he told her. "Find the right sorcerer, there are spells aplenty to give him influence over your body. P'rhaps even control. Claim the flesh, you maybe gain access to the soul. You want to wake up one morning, find yourself marching clump-clump quickstep back into the Deceiver's arms?"

"I thought I'm supposed to be immune to spells."

"Look in a mirror, starskin."

She didn't have to. She knew full well what she looked like, the strain was in remembering what had been before. The words came easily to mind: hair like spun gold shot through with streaks of autumnal fire, skin as fair with the flush of ripe apples on her cheeks, eyes the rich blue of cornflowers. Plump baby, plump girl, easy to laugh in the cradle, easy to pout when she came of age to walk. Disturbingly, though, when she tried to match descriptions to the images of memory, nothing would fit. It was like gazing on a stranger.

The moon had been at its zenith the night of her Ascension, and as its radiance leached all color from the scene, casting every aspect of the ceremony of her Ascension in shades of absolute light and shadow, so did the Deceiver steal away the same from her. The gold was stripped from Elora's hair, the warmth from her skin, leaving a figure that might have been cast of purest silver. Over the years since, more than one person she met had to touch her to believe she was composed of flesh and blood rather than some form of animate metal. Only her eyes flashed color, and even they had paled to the blue of forged steel.

She'd heard the events of that awful night retold so many times in stories, around Highlander cookfires and Nelwyn tables and bazaar ale houses, of how the gods had reached out that fateful night and laid their mark on the Sacred Princess Elora Danan. What no one seemed sure of was whether this was a sign of good fortune or ill, though she wasn't apparently alone in coming to suspect more and more the latter.

She was immune to magic, that had been proven time and again. No spell appeared to have a lasting effect on her.

Save this one. Where the Deceiver was concerned, she had no special defenses. The only consolation was that in return she seemed able to hurt her foe where others could not.

Unfortunately the shape he'd settled on, when she finally slipped through his grasp, was that of the Castellan Mohdri, leader of the Maizan Thunder Riders. It was hard to do your enemy damage when he rode in command of the most formidable fighting force the Daikini world had ever seen.

"Point taken," Elora conceded grudgingly.

"At long last," was Rool's riposte.

"Spare me."

"Earn it."

Like Thorn, she'd learned the hard way when to engage the brownies in verbal combat and when the wiser course was to concede the field. In this instance, she backed off to where she'd left her clothes.

She decided to leave her legs bare, the better to cope with the heat of the day. If more cover was required, against brush or bugs, she'd sling on her leggings. Above the waist, she chose a cotton shirt beneath her buckskin tunic. Her boots ended at the bottom of her thighs, tied above and below the knee to keep them from slipping, with the joint itself well padded in case she either fell or had to do some crawling. She kept one weapon visible, her short-sword, which she tucked into her belt behind her. A much smaller dirk was hidden deep within the folds of her cloak. Lastly, she slipped a dagger into its boot sheath.

"Where's my hair?" she asked Rool when the brownie returned to her side.

"You have your places to hide things, I have mine."

"Just don't use it for anything mean."

To her amazement, he looked genuinely shocked.

"Elora *Danan*," he protested. "I would *never*—!"

His distress was so genuine and so intense that she couldn't help tumbling down beside him in the soft grass, to gaze at him with a hand outheld in comfort.

"I know you wouldn't, Rool. I'm sorry. But what brought you here?" she asked, gambling on changing the mood by changing the subject. "How did you find me?"

"The one is so obvious it doesn't merit an answer. The other—?" He paused for thought. "Brownies know when strangers enter their burrows."

"All brownies? All burrows? Even the ones that have been abandoned?"

"Well . . ." He temporized. "You let out a pretty wild cry when you dropped into that lava stream. Shot Drumheller from his sleep like a shaft from a longbow."

"How is he?"

"Cranky, all things considered. He doesn't get much sleep lately."

"Why aren't you looking after him?"

"We do our best. He's stubborn." The flash of his eyes, the way his mouth twisted at the memories, told her their best represented a considerable effort, and the brownies weren't at all pleased with their ongoing lack of success. "Mostly, he's well." A last, grudging concession. As evident was Rool's belief that condition wouldn't last.

"He sent you."

"As fast as Bastian could fly. Figured if he could hear your cry, so could the Deceiver."

"Has he been in contact with Torquil?" she demanded urgently, happiness at this reunion quickly giving way to concern for her foster home. "Does he have any news of the Rock Nelwyns?"

"Scared the demon out of everyone, you did. Made Franjean jealous. It was the sort of thing he'd have liked to do himself. Proper little frightener, he is."

"I'm serious."

"As am I, in my way."

"One of their own was trying to open a World Gate."

"I believe they know that, lass. From the telling, shaman to shaman, them to Drumheller, they had themselves a wild night of things. But they survived. Their mountain's whole. They'll be glad to have you back safe as well."

"What are you talking about?"

"We're to escort you home, Elora Danan. Back to Torquil."

"Bollocks!"

"What's that chy' say?"

"Bollocks!"

"I know the word, where'd *you* learn it?"

"It's common enough among drovers."

"You're not a drover, you're the Sacred Princess!"

"BOLLOCKS!"

"Will you stop saying that!" Rool sounded well and truly scandalized, which Elora hadn't thought was possible.

"I'm not going back."

To emphasize the point, she rolled to her feet in a single smooth motion, gathering up the last remaining piece of her kit, her cloak, and slinging it across her body. The suddenness of her action startled Bastian aloft and he beat the air with his great wings to establish both altitude and control. Elora immediately set forth in the longest strides she could manage and put a fair distance between herself and the others before they recovered enough to come after her.

Bastian swept low overhead. She ignored him, leaving it to the eagle to avoid any collision, which he did quite artfully. As he passed by, Rool leaped from his perch on Bastian's shoulders to Elora's, quickly anchoring himself amidst the folds of her cloak.

"This is foolishness, girl," the brownie said in her ear.

She said nothing and maintained a steady stride around the pond to the stream that flowed out from it. There were no obvious trails but the bank was mainly clear of brush and obstructions, so she chose to follow it.

"Stop being so willful!" Rool told her.

"Why?"

"Because you'll get yourself into trouble!"

"I mean, why must I go back?"

"You're safe there, Elora."

"I'm not, you know. But that isn't the point."

"You have a point?"

"If it hadn't been for this, I'd have left anyway, with the Cascani Factor if he'd've had me, or one of the other merchants."

"That's daft, girl."

"So *you* say. My whole life in Angwyn, Rool, I was a puppet in a dollhouse, a bright and shining object to be trotted out for state occasions and otherwise put out on display. I was their holy talisman, they would do whatever was necessary to keep me safe and secure in their possession, and if that meant making me a prisoner in a gilded cage, so be it. God forbid I should be allowed to take an interest in the affairs of that state, to grab hold of the reins of my own life and take it in what directions *I* might choose.

"Who knows, if I'd been properly taught, Angwyn might have escaped its doom."

"What's done is done, Elora. You can't blame yourself!"

"Can't I? Tir Asleen, destroyed because of me. Angwyn, cursed because of me. And how many more cities conquered since, how many people slain?"

"That's the Deceiver's doing, child."

"It's *me* he wants, Rool."

"Why else d'you think Drumheller wants you where you're safe?"

"Trust me, there's no such place. Even if there was, it'd be wrong. Don't you see, it's the same as in Angwyn, only the set dressings have been changed. Thorn's making the same mistake. Before, I was a pampered pet; now I'm an apprentice at Torquil's forge.

"Five years ago my every whim was catered to and my security guaranteed by a corps of Vizards culled from the finest families in Angwyn. Today I help Torquil's wife mind the house and baby-sit the kids. I was fat, I got muscles. But I'm never without supervision, and I'm never allowed out. Wherein is there any substantial difference, Rool?

"When comes the moment I take a hand in my own destiny?"

"You don't know the dangers."

"I think I do. More, I know the price this war's exacting. Harmony is the Nelwyn way, yet I saw a Nelwyn openly betray everything his people believe in to bring forth some power so ancient Carig didn't even have a name for it. He was working against his own community, Rool. They were to be the blood sacrifice that sealed the bargain with this creature."

"Impossible."

"I was part of the Summoning spell, I had a taste of its dimensions. Don't tell me what's not possible. So are brownies abandoning their burrow. And dryads their glade."

"There's no sustenance for them." Rool was temporizing, but there was neither heart nor heat to his arguments. "Food aplenty for the body, aye, but for their spirit, naught but starvation. The magic has left the land. Franjean and I, we might survive here but we'd not prosper. This isn't good land any longer for the likes of us."

"Exactly. And what happens, my friend, when you can say that about the whole entire world?"

She stopped and turned her head around to face him, unaware that her body had settled into a spread-legged fighting stance that left her totally balanced.

"I'm *not* a talisman, Rool. Nor some standard fit only to be waved as an inspiration to battle. I'm alive. I'm a person. If this fight's because of me, if I am to be anything like what the legends and prophecies foretell, I can't stand passively by and watch others shed their blood on my behalf. I'm sorry, Rool, I'm not worthy to die for. Not yet."

"Where will you go then, Highness?"

"To Thorn."

"Make my fortune sure selling tickets to *that* scrap."

"Feel free, my friend, and to bet on the outcome if you've a mind."

"You don't know where he is."

"I'll find him. Though it would be easier, were some kind soul to show the way. Less likelihood of accidentally walking into a Maizan camp, that's sure."

"You bargain like a Cascani."

"I've been taking lessons. Who knows, maybe I can learn to be a sneak thief like you?"

That pronouncement won her a disparaging snort, which she answered with a grin that promised their conversation was far from finished.

Though she never raised her pace beyond a steady walk, Elora made fair progress along the stream as it wound its way through the hollows at the base of this gathering of hills and baby mountains. Before half the afternoon had passed, trees and meadow gave way to bracken and heather and the ground grew perilously uneven, scarred at random intervals by channels created from rain running off the slopes above. That same water left the ground largely saturated, not quite solid underfoot, not quite marshland either. Elora had to pick her way with care or run the risk of a sprain or, worse, a broken bone. She could handle either but she'd rather not have to.

Bastian provided eyes, scouting out the path ahead. As the sun coursed below the western horizon Elora used InSight to join her perceptions to the eagle's in a search for somewhere decent to spend the night.

Fortune smiled on someone else that evening. The best that could be arranged was a moderately dry plot where Elora improvised a lean-to with her cloak, taking the opportunity to bless its unwieldy size and bulk as fervently as on other occasions she'd complained about it to high heaven. Bastian scrounged some stout, short branches that she used as tent poles. The sharp angle between roof and floor left no room to crouch, much less stand upright, but the final result allowed for some decent snuggling.

There was no convenient fuel for a fire but Elora didn't mind. In this bleak and open country, flames and smoke were too glaring a set of signposts for any pursuers. Better to once more lay hands on her firestones and call on them for warmth. Being a quiet sort of magic, no more really than an enhancement of nature, it could be easily hidden from questing scanspells.

Rool made a sour face when she passed him a mug of leftover soup.

"Tastes of troll," he groused. Then: "Smells of troll." And finally, what she knew had been coming all along: "So do you."

"Stepped in dung right after I arrived," she related, memory making the moment far lighter than it felt at the time. She even chuckled at the sight of herself hobble-hopping into the pond. "There was a den up under the rock pile, a ways beyond the waterfall."

"And . . . ?" the brownie prompted.

"It chased me into the burrow. It took my stuff. I went after."

"No blood smell."

"No, Rool, I didn't kill it. The troll had babies. They were hungry and sick. That was why she attacked, she was afraid for her young."

"With good reason. Only good troll's a dead one."

"I've heard the same said about brownies."

"And I, about Daikinis," he flared right back at her. "You *are* daft, to follow a troll to its den."

"It needed help."

"And if you found a Night Heron with a broken wing, I suppose you'd nurse it, too? Or better yet, a Death Dog!"

That brought a chirruping cough of protest from Bastian, who up till then had contented himself with the field mice and plump voles he'd claimed for his own dinner. To make his point, the eagle balanced with fine delicacy on one wickedly sharp set of claws, while holding his limp and lifeless prey in the other. A snap of the beak severed the corpse neatly in half and Elora tried not to hear the crunch of tiny bones as Bastian chewed and swallowed. The point was deftly made: where herons and hounds were concerned, the eagle offered neither quarter nor mercy.

"They're not the same," Elora explained patiently, trying to work out the concepts in her own head even as she spoke them aloud. It was quite an effort, to find explanations for acts she'd committed solely on instinct, and truth be told, she still wasn't altogether sure what impulse had prompted her. Her only comfort was the eerie certainty that she had done right.

"But if there existed the same spark, the same . . . potential . . . for decency and kindness in those creatures as I sensed from that troll"—she took a breath—"yes, I think I would offer the help. Remember Angwyn, Rool. You were there in my tower. You saw. A rookery of Night Herons, yet none of them ever did me harm."

"Doing the Deceiver's bidding, most likely." He spat, to put a period to his opinion.

She shrugged. "Quite likely. But I don't care."

"Madness. The whole world's gone so totally daft *nothing* makes sense anymore!"

"Can't argue with that. Thorn's in Sandeni, yes?"

The suddenness of the question caught the brownie off guard. Rool nodded before he could catch himself.

"Which is where?"

He gestured downstream with his chin. "Off thereaway. That was very neatly done, Elora Danan. I didn't even see it coming."

"Told you I was getting better. To the north of here, then."

"And a bit east, aye. This water'll lead us."

"That's a relief, anyway. I was half-afraid to discover myself on the opposite side of the world or something."

"Were that so, we'd be near Tir Asleen."

"Do you miss it, Rool? The lands of home?"

"Do you, lass?"

She shrugged. "How can you miss what you hardly remember? Angwyn should have more of a claim on me, considering how long I lived there. But to be honest, none of those places feel exactly . . . right. Is that strange, to think that home is somewhere I've never been?" She didn't give him the opportunity to answer that question but posed a more practical one instead: "And how far to Sandeni?"

The brownie looked to Bastian for the answer.

"Longer for Daikinis afoot," was the eagle's reply, "than myself aloft. Quicker for Daikinis than brownie."

"Some great thumping bloody help *you* are," groused Rool as he returned his attention to Elora. "But it'll be a fair walk, sure, an' that's a fact."

"The Maizan are riding out of the west," she said thoughtfully, and drew her body tighter, wriggling a touch or two closer to her heated stones, hooding her eyes beneath their lids to hide her growing apprehension. "Which puts us between them and the city, am I right?"

"Too right by half, my girl," Rool agreed unhappily. He sat with his back mainly to Elora, eyes sweeping the darkness beyond the open wedge of their lean-to. If she'd taken the effort to look for herself, Elora would have seen Bastian striking the same vigilant posture outside. She would sleep the night through. They would not, as each alternated a stint of sentry duty.

"I'm not a girl," was her rote protest. "I do think, though, I am in a whole lot of trouble. And, my friend," she continued, in a tone that the brownie hadn't heard from her before (as he hadn't been around for the two years she'd been growing into it), "it is Thorn Drumheller's fault."

"Blame him for all the faults of the world, do you?" Rool's tone made plain what he thought of that.

"No," was Elora's flatly rational reply. "I blame him for leaving me vulnerable. I can't defend myself without the proper tools. Without the proper *knowledge,* Rool."

"Defending you is our job, Elora Danan."

"Then where is he? Where were you?"

Rool didn't even try to meet her eyes.

"Told him," he said, staring out into the misty midnight darkness. "Me, Franjean, the eagles, talked ourselves stupid. But he wanted you safe. That meant, he figured, sending you away, keeping you distant. He had to establish himself in Sandeni; that meant taking risks, making enemies. His thought, an' you can't fault his courage, child, nor his love for you, nor his devotion to your cause—!"

"Have I ever?"

"Nah." That came forth as a sigh. "Anyroad, he hoped, if he made himself a target, too big, too important, to resist, you'd get lost an' forgotten on the sidelines."

"You believe the Deceiver would fall for that?"

"Think it through, Elora Danan. Polar forces you two may be, but you're not head-to-head in battle yet. Maybe not for a while. Have to work through surrogates. He uses the Maizan, while you've got us. If the Deceiver was all-powerful, we'd have lost an age ago. So, we confuse his cat's-paws, best we can, until you're a match for him."

"So tell me, O small sage, how's that ever going to happen if I spend all my time in hiding? I'm sorry, Rool, but those cat's-paws you mentioned, they flushed me out. I'm in the open now, I can't go back."

Bastian had stalked beneath the shelter during the conversation, and when Elora was finished, he leaned forward and bopped the little man on the crown of his head with the knob of his beak. Rool was of a good height for a brownie, but the eagle topped him with considerable room to spare and used that stature to good advantage. True to form, Rool squawked, so Bastian clocked him again.

"Told you so," the eagle said, with rare enjoyment.

"You never did!"

"Our bet. My win. You pay."

"Under protest! This isn't what we wagered on at all!"

"You'd rather feel the tip of my beak again?"

"Threats, is it?"

Bastian shook his head, and even if his face wasn't shaped to muster a smile, his voice did it for him, as broad as could be.

"Not in the slightest. I'm merely considering removing a dishonorable little wretch who refuses to pay debts freely—I might even say, eagerly—entered into from the collective food chain of Dame Nature."

Rool hunched his head deep between his shoulders, taking a stance that dared the eagle to try. Their confrontation was so serious to the outward eye that Elora had a sudden burst of unease that these two old friends might actually come to blows.

Then Rool growled, "Who you calling 'little,' feather-head?"

"Excuse me?" Elora prompted.

"All fledglings have to leave the nest sometime," Bastian said quite companionably. "They fly or they drop, but we don't carry them back."

"That's hard, Bastian."

"We don't abandon our chicks, Elora Danan. We protect them as best we can. But the air is our element. The nest is home, but never a sanctuary; our wings are that. Whatever the reason for leaving your nest, you've chosen to fly, and I salute you for it."

"You disagree, Rool?" Elora asked the brownie, with an expression of such dangerous innocence he considered a fair while before offering his reply.

"You're not a bird, and I've come to trust Drumheller's instincts."

"Bravo for him," she said. "But I have to learn some of my own."

Unbidden then came the thought, which she didn't bother hiding from either of her companions, *if it isn't already too late.*

They breakfasted with the dawn and were packed and on their way before the sun cleared the distant peaks. Elora started at a military pace that she'd learned from, of all people, Ryn Taksemanyin, a long-legged stride that made the miles pass at a surprisingly natural rate. Though where one of the sea-dwelling Wyrrn had mastered such a ground-pounding cadence she had no idea, nor was Ryn, ordinarily the most talkative and gregarious of souls, at all forthcoming himself on the subject.

She continued to follow the stream because it was the most comfortable route, again using Bastian high overhead as her pathfinder and lookout. Whatever moved within the eagle's eyeshot, she'd know about it.

"What do you know of the Realms Beyond?" she asked Rool. He was riding her left shoulder, snugged deep into the folds of her cloak with a spare blade thrust through her brooch as a companion to Elora's own fibula spike that held it fastened in place.

"I'm a brownie," he said, and she didn't need a sight of him to know he'd spoken with an all-encompassing yet dismissive shrug.

"Who know all," she chided gently, "but never tell."

"That's our reputation, right enough."

"Covers a multitude of sins, that does," she agreed, "especially on those occasions when you *don't* know anything."

She heard him snort, a sound that carried with it a fair portion of admiration.

"You *are* learning," he conceded. "Don't think Franjean'll like that. Nor Drumheller, neither," he finished with a grin, but her thoughts were too somber for these volleys of humor to have any lasting effect.

"I'm serious, I'm afraid," Elora said a while later. "How much do you know?"

"We watch the way the world works."

"So you told Thorn. Is the world all there is?"

He looked sharply at her.

"What makes you ask such a thing?" he demanded.

Now it was Elora's turn to shrug. "Too many things I

120

don't have definitions for, I suppose. Or explanations. How do you describe what isn't there?"

"Isn't that why the gods gave us speech?"

She looked back over her shoulder.

"Nothing's there, Elora," Rool told her.

"Are you sure, Rool?"

"If there was, Bastian would see. He's good like that."

She nodded, but plainly wasn't convinced as she picked up the pace again.

"You ever have the feeling, Rool, that you were being stalked?"

"Every time I see a cat. Or worse, don't see one. Stalked by what?"

"I wish I knew." Then, in the same rushed breath: "I'm glad I don't. If I call its name, I think I make it easier for it to find me. Assuming there's an 'it' that's looking."

Rool nodded agreement. Learning the true name of an arcane being, or a person, was the most effective means a sorcerer could use to gain power over them, but that knowledge could be a double-edged sword. There were some beings so powerful that no wards were proof against them. Worse, merely saying their name aloud might be all the invocation necessary to attract their attention. The consequences of such foolishness were often deadly.

"I keep drifting back in my head to the grotto and Carig's World Gate," Elora said softly, following a fair pause wherein she let her mind go still as she worked up the courage to confront her experiences of that fateful night. She remained vaguely aware of her surroundings as they passed but otherwise ignored the landscape as she would the background noise of a crowd. She spoke in a halting, musing tone, guardedly giving voice to her memories only after carefully vetting them to make certain they were safe. It was a kind of caution that didn't come naturally to her, or easily.

"It's like floating on what you think is a still pond, only there's an undercurrent you're not aware of. It doesn't seem that strong but it never goes away. You have to actively fight it just to hold your place and whenever you relax it takes hold of you again. Pulling you where it wants you to go.

"That ceremony's the same. It keeps calling to me. In that memory, I'm the only light but I illuminate nothing. The Gate frames nothing but darkness. Nothing to see, nothing to touch. I'm there to function as a beacon, for whatever Carig was Summoning. Just thinking about it makes me want to dance again. I can't fix the music in my head but my feet know the steps. Does nothing for you, my story?" she asked him sharply, glaring along her shoulder at his uncharacteristically hawklike mien.

"What you're talkin', Elora Danan, should be spoken to a sage. Franjean an' me, we're hunters."

"Great warriors, so I've heard." She took her cue from him and offered banter as a bulwark to a growing anxiety.

"Captured Nelwyns and Daikinis in our time, we have. And shared a tree with a captive princess.

"Anyway, sage would know, maybe, what you're asking," he told her, returning to the original subject.

"Can we contact one?"

"Where've you *been,* girl—?" He started to exclaim, then realized how absurd that sounded in the circumstances. "The burrows are closin' all across the continent. Maybe across the world entire."

"But surely, farther east, we could find one?"

"The burrows are closed," he repeated.

"All of them?" she persisted.

"To us." He nodded. "To you. More'n a few among the Veil Folk name you 'Cherlindrea's Bane.' Some have even branded you with a death mark. No appeal, no mercy."

He was speaking to deaf ears, she'd stopped listening after the first two words.

"You and Franjean, you can't go home," she said, mingling such sorrow and sympathy in her voice that the brownie couldn't help but respond with his bravest smile.

"In victory, Elora Danan, when we've won this war, that's when we'll return. An' if, in pride an' foolishness, they'll not have us, then the hell with 'em, we'll stay with you. More fun anyways."

She gave him a kiss atop his head, right where the eagle had bopped him, and quickened her pace. There was still fear deep within her eyes but also determination, backed by a force of will whose strength would surprise her.

Chapter 5

B IG MOUNTAINS GAVE WAY TO SMALL ONES, WHICH IN
turn gave way to rolling hills. Soggy moor grew
firm underfoot, then came more meadows
banked by spectacular forests that abruptly
ended in the first stretch of cultivated land Elora
had seen in years. Technically, by this point, the
stream had grown into a river. It was still ford-
able in places and not terribly wide, mainly because its course took it over rock more than
soil. However, its current was still severe
enough to gouge out the earth around those
stones, thereby creating some treacherous rills
and sinkholes, not to mention *very* wicked currents. The land close by its steep-sided banks
bore evidence of the occasional flood. Soon,
Elora knew, she'd have to choose which side to
journey on, and live with that decision until she
found a ferry or a boat.

Both she and Rool heard a keening cry from so far on high that the eagle who uttered it couldn't easily be spotted among the big-belly puffballs of cumulus that dotted the afternoon sky.

To the watching eye, Elora looked casual, just a slip of a thing, a gangly collection of limbs that didn't fit quite so well together as they had a month before.

"What?" Rool prompted.

She completed a slow pivot, turning right the way around, her gaze lingering a fraction back along the way they'd come before returning at last to the road ahead, sweeping the surrounding heights as she did. Every sense was preternaturally alert, from the feel of mingled grains of dirt and stone through both socks and the soles of her boots, to the faintest *shrush* of a breeze ruffling the topmost branches overhead and the burbling rill of the stream as it rushed beneath the bridge, to the taste of fruit starting to hang heavy on untended orchards. As for smells, they were as rich and varied as they were fundamentally *wrong* for such a setting. The scent of burned things, wood and plaster, cloth and flesh, mixed with the metallic flavor of blood.

Death had visited this place, and not so long ago.

Elora let out her breath in an outrushing sigh, a little nonplussed to discover she'd been holding it so long a while that her chest ached, her surprise deepening with the discovery that she held an ax.

"My-oh-my," she said, taking the measure of the tension across her body as she did of the weapon itself. "What do we have here?"

"You drew as you turned," Rool told her. "Reached into your pouch and there it was."

"Comforting to know my gear always seems to know what I need."

She worked her hand on the hilt to make the grip that much more comfortable, but did not return the ax to its scabbard. It was the one she'd found outside the troll's den and taken off the slain Daikini warrior. As she did with so many things she gathered up along the road, she'd simply stuffed it into a traveling pouch and forgotten all about it.

"What can you see?" Rool asked quietly, meaning through the eagle's eyes.

A blink of the eye was all it took for InSight to join Elora's consciousness with Bastian's. With another, she was back in herself, shaken by what lay ahead.

Rool, bless him, didn't ask for details.

"Go around, maybe?" he suggested, but Elora shook her head.

"Can't." That had been her hope as well until Bastian's perspective dashed it stillborn.

"Why not?"

"There's a natural flow to the trail, that's why the village was built here, this is the only way. Bastian can't see any other path through the hills. They either dead-end in some blind canyon or other, or wind back on themselves so a body spends more time going sideways than ahead. And while the summits aren't ferociously high, the slopes are murder, without an easy climb to the lot."

"What did you both see, Elora?"

"Someone got real mad here, Rool. And then they got even."

With that, she crossed the bridge, to discover in part the reason why.

Gibbets had been erected along the road at the far end of the structure, three on either side, with a crow cage hanging from each. Thankfully, their contents had long since yielded up their lives. Elora didn't need a close examination to tell what they were. A family of trolls, by the tatters of skin left on their collapsed and vermin-savaged bones, who in the ancient way of their kind had attempted to make a home beneath the bridge. Or perhaps, since this looked to be a natural ford, they'd been here all along, with a den tucked into the bank.

The reason for their being didn't matter, their mere presence sealed their fate. Trolls were here, they were in the way, they were removed. Hung like scarecrows, to scare away others of their kind.

"Is that all we can do, Rool? Hate and murder?"

"You're asking me? You're the Daikini, Elora Danan."

"I'm not very proud of that right now."

"Would you be so charitable if it was your lambs been stolen, or your baby grabbed for dinner?"

"You tell me. Those are naiads in the last two cages, and I think the pens hung up top inside, they were made for something smaller."

Water nymphs could be as changeable as the streams they called their home; the more wild the environment, the more wild the naiad who protected it. Two of them meant either siblings or a mating pair. One had died curled up in as tight a ball as possible, while the other's arm was stretched to full extension in a desperate attempt to reach across the gulf between the cages.

InSight had given Elora a spectacular overhead view of the setting, a modestly sized village numbering a couple of dozen houses whose construction mixed wood and stone, arrayed in scattered clusters along the slopes that reached up from this bank of the stream. They were solid, substantial structures that, in more than a few cases, were designed to be extensions of the hillside on which they rested. Elora suspected additional rooms had been hollowed out of the earth behind them. Each cluster of homes was arranged so that it formed a substantial defensive position, with interlocking fields of fire. Very much like other frontier communities she'd seen on her travels, and that Thorn had told her of.

An altogether sensible scheme.

It hadn't saved them.

The first house she came to proved the pattern for the rest. After the first cluster she lost all desire to see more. The assault had been as brutal as it was thorough, the stout stone walls breached by a massive succession of hammer blows, the rooms within consumed by balls of dragonfire. The heat of those magical flames was so intense, especially concentrated in so small and enclosed a space, that the inside walls crumbled to powder at

Elora's touch, reminding her of Torquil's training forge after their encounter with the infant firedrake. For all within the outer chambers, death came as a moment of blazing agony before oblivion. They were the lucky ones. Farther in, Elora found slaughter enough to sicken the most hardened of butchers.

The sun was still a presence overhead but not for much longer as it lowered toward the western ridges. This was the heat of the day but all she could do was tremble as a dank draft wound its clammy way about her head. She seemed to have lost all sensation in the outer parts of her body, while her inner self had never felt more delicate, almost as if she was at war with herself. Her mouth was dry, yet her skin felt slick and queasy on her frame, as though it had been coated underneath by a layer of slime. She forced herself to breathe in a regular rhythm, keeping it slow but shallow, to counteract the growing queasiness in her belly. She wanted to be sick. She didn't dare.

Strangely she also found she couldn't cry.

"No sign of siege engines," she remarked to Rool as he strode in her direction, "nothing powerful enough to make these holes anyway. Nor any residue of spells."

"No need for either when you can whistle up a crew of ogres to do your dirty work."

"I don't believe it. Ogres are like bears, territorial and solitary. One might claim this land, two at the most, but then they'd be more interested in fighting each other than any settlers. And even if you're right, attacking a village like this isn't their way."

"Who's the one been sayin' the old ways are changing?"

"That isn't funny, Rool."

"Signs are plain, Elora. Ogres and elves, working in concert. Ogres breach the walls, elves conjure the dragonfire. Ogres get to make a meal of whatever doesn't get too badly cooked."

Elora swallowed convulsively, her eyes blinking rapidly in a vain attempt to generate tears. She'd suspected the truth from the moment she stepped across the scorched and broken threshold. Hearing it from Rool's lips, in the brownie's matter-of-fact tone, struck her like a blow to the belly. Ghouls ate carrion, as did trolls for the most part. Ogres, however, liked their food fresh, preferably alive, and had a reputation as loathsome as their appetite. What made them all the more horrific was their physical resemblance to Daikini, and the fact that they possessed a keen intelligence. Ghouls and trolls could be thought of as mostly animal by nature; ogres seemed uncomfortably human.

"What do the elves get?" she asked at last.

"No more Daikini," he said. "Here'bouts, anyroad."

Rool held up an arrow as long as he was tall. Its barbed head was marked with stains of dried copper.

"Folk here didn't go quiet," he said. "They put up a fair fight for their homes, made their killers pay."

"How dearly?"

"Can't say for sure. Attackers took away their wounded an' their dead, but there's blood on the ground all about here. And the aftertaste of dying."

"Good."

He gave her a sharp and searching look.

"What's that you're holding, Elora Danan?"

It was a mess, a poor semblance of the stuffed toy it once had been. In one of the back bedrooms, snugged beneath the surface of the hill where the householders intended their safest and final refuge, she'd found a set of shelves, below which lay a collection of dolls and other toys. Some were hard, carved and painted wood, while others were stuffed cloth. All had been handcarved or stitched. All had been savaged.

"I think this was the child's favorite," she said, as her legs slowly gave way at the knees and she sat back on her heels. Reflexively, she set her ax by her side, never allowing her hand to stray far from its hilt. She spoke haltingly, finding it difficult to translate what she'd seen into words. "The poor dear must have thought it would keep her safe, same as I believed my bear would me."

When Elora was barely a year old, Thorn Drumheller had come to her on the night before the Cataclysm that destroyed her home and changed the shape of the world entire. He'd thought it a dream, because he'd ridden to her on the back of a dragon. Only much later did he discover that the dragon had been as real as the moment. He'd made her a stuffed bear for her birthday, and when he left it with her he charged it to keep her safe from any and all harm. It was the kind of wish any parent might make, but since he was a sorcerer it turned out to be the kind of wish that came true.

Somehow, when the night exploded into flame, she had emerged unscathed, with her bear held so tightly in her infant arms that even grown men couldn't pry it loose.

"There was nothing you could do, Elora," Rool told her, laying a hand on hers where she clutched the child's doll.

"I know, Rool. Doesn't make this hurt any the less. It shouldn't have happened at all! For as long as anyone can remember, there's been *peace* between the Realms!"

"Uneasy peace. Imperfect peace. There've always been outlaws."

"This was a deliberate massacre, Rool. Nothing was taken here except lives, and those as brutally as possible." She took a deep, shuddering breath in an attempt to master her emotions, to tame her rising fury. "I didn't tell you what else Bastian saw. Lining the road downstream of the town. Heads on pikes. Scores of them."

"What's the old saying, 'turnabout is fair play.' "

"*Rool!*" she snapped at him in horror.

"It's a warning, Elora, meant to be as plain to Daikini as those crow cages were for trolls and naiads and the like." Then his tone gentled slightly and turned a bit more sad. "Yours aren't the only kind with a claim to this land, you know. If Daikini won't share with the Veil Folk, why should any of the Veil Folk share in return?"

"Is that the future for us all then? We slaughter each other until the last one left standing claims title to whatever's left. Assuming it's even worth having? Can't we be *better* than that?"

"I think, Royal Highness, that's where you're meant to fit in."

"Well, right now I don't feel very up to the job."

Abruptly she sniffed, a furrow of concentration appearing between her brows as she cocked her head a little to one side and muttered a quiet curse. In that same brief span of time she gathered her ax once more into her hand. The doll was set aside, with a last loving finger-stroke caress farewell.

The river wound around a modest headland, a knob of rock on which had been constructed the town's most impressive building, rearing a full three stories above the road that passed beside it. The tower was stone, intended to provide a place of refuge and defense from any attack.

There was smoke rising from its chimney.

The sky high overhead was still blue but the valley itself was mostly shadow, peaks behind Elora splashed with light that mixed gold and rose, while those ahead had lost much of their definition. The evening breeze flowed the length of the valley, from darkness toward light, the tower to her, and she chose not to think about the other scents mixed in with that of wood smoke. Torches, as well as the cookfire itself, illuminated the interior of the modest keep, but nobody inside stepped out or passed by any of the narrow embrasures that passed for windows. She had no idea who might be present, or how many. Rool, however, was certain that she wanted no part of them.

"Hook around the backside of these ridges," he suggested to Elora and Bastian, tracing their route with a stick onto the dirt. "Bypass the tower to catch up with the road on the far end of town. Then walk straight through the night, get ourselves as far away from here as fast as possible."

"Suppose they come after?"

"Run."

"I don't see the sense of it."

"What, you'd rather they catch us? Or would you prefer simply hiding?"

"Of that, I mean," and Elora gestured toward the tower with her chin from where she lay beside a jumble of stones atop the ridgeline, so flat to the ground only eyes and forehead were visible. She'd blackened her face with soot from one of the burned houses to dull her argent skin and draped her cloak across her head to hide her hair. It was a simple camouflage, but effective. Even Bastian had a hard time marking her position amidst the gathering dusk.

"They raze the town, murder the inhabitants, carry off their own dead and wounded. . . ."

"Classic hit-and-run tactics," said Rool.

"Whatever. I defer to superior experience." Franjean would have preened at the compliment, Rool merely made a grimace of dismissal. "So who is it got themselves left behind?" Elora continued. "Or chose to stay? And why?"

"I have no great love for cats, Elora Danan," Rool told her, catching her drift and not liking it in the slightest, "but I caution you to remember what happened to the curious ones."

"Isn't that why they have nine lives?"

"Bully for them. You're no cat."

"So help me out, Rool. The breeze is in our favor, what can you tell me about the scents from inside?"

"What do you need me for? Can't you use your precious InSight to merge with some beastie or other within the tower for a look-see?"

"Already thought of. Already tried. The interior's barren. Birds, vermin, bugs, the lot. What's alive has long since fled. What remains isn't alive. There are wards up as well. I push too hard, I run the risk of tripping over one. Which none of us want."

The brownie nodded grim but heartfelt agreement.

"Two ogres," he said, flat-toned, pushing his tongue out across his lips, sluicing them clean of the foul taste of those monstrous creatures. "One of Lesser Faery, two of Greater."

"High Elves," Elora sounded shocked. "On *this* side of the Veil?"

"They don't cross over often and they don't much like it when they do, but they can survive as easily here as the likes of you or I can in their domains. They talk like they'd die before admitting it but all our races are bound by common threads. That's why the Great Realms are always portrayed as a sequence of circles."

"Is that 'hunter' knowledge?" Elora asked innocently.

"Franjean and I, we watch the way the world works," he said, as he had often before, as if the phrase was a sufficient answer in and of itself.

"I wonder what they're doing?"

"None of our damn business. An' even if it was, a *single* ogre is reason enough for us to keep our distance, much less a pair. Let's go."

She remained where she was, totally focused on the tower, chewing absently on a square of dried beef.

"Heed me, Elora Danan," the brownie repeated. "Let us *go!*"

"Something else is down there," she said in so still and offhand a tone she might well have been talking to herself.

"It's none of our concern. What's done here is done. If we interfere, all we'll do is add our own corpses to the boneyard."

"I can't turn my back."

"On *what?*"

"My instincts."

Rool was so upset, at her obstinacy as much as at the situation, that he spoke with far more heat than he'd intended, his words emerging almost as a snarl.

"Spare me," he lashed out at her. "Cloistered as you've been your whole life, when have you ever needed instincts? Or had much chance to develop any?"

"I know what I know." Her voice quavered ever so

slightly but she held her emotions on tight rein. That was the only indication of how deeply his insult had cut her. "I feel what I feel. And I'll no more ignore it than I will deny you as my friend. No matter how foolish that may sound."

She gave him no opportunity to reply. Before she'd finished speaking she'd levered herself up and over the ridgeline, spilling her cloak to its full extension and draping it over herself as she made her way in a cautious sideways crab scuttle down the slope toward the tower. Rool sprang after her but her long legs were more than he could catch. For all that she had no training in the arts of the hunt or war, her innate common sense proved more than adequate to the task at hand. She took advantage of the lay of the land, the dark weave of her cloak making her a shadow among shadows as she slipped from cover to cover.

"What have you *done*?" Bastian cried, using mind-speech to make himself heard by both brownie and girl.

"The hell with that," Rool howled back at him, the same way. "What is *she* doing?"

"Shut up, the pair of you!" came Elora's commanding response, with such intensity that both eagle and brownie were instantly cowed. "If you won't help, the least you can do is not make things worse for me. I can't concentrate with you shrieking inside my skull."

"What do you plan?" Rool asked, ruthlessly quelling his anxiety.

"The lights are on the second floor."

"Doesn't mean anything. Stay clear of the ground floor. Ogres like the dark and they don't like heights. Odds are that's where you'll find one or both. Can't magic yourself inside, either, those three of Faery would be sure to sense it."

"Come down from above, then?"

He snorted derisively. "You plan on climbing near forty feet?"

"The walls aren't so smooth, Rool. There are hand-holds."

"Daft daft daft. Child, is there no end to your fool-ishness? Give this up, I beg you, while there's still time."

"Bastian," she called with mindspeech, "I've at-tached a line to something that should stand in for a grapnel. Can you fly it to the top of the tower?"

"Say no," Rool cried. "Refuse her, for all our sakes."

"I've circled the tower twice, Rool," the eagle said. "In this, I side with Elora. There is more within than you could sense. I think they have a prisoner."

"If it's no one we know, why should we care?"

"If you have to ask," Elora replied primly, "why bother to explain?"

The eagle's wings set up a furious backwash as Bas-tian swooped down to catch the proffered rope and carry it to its destination. Elora crouched in a huddle against the base of the tower, where cut stone merged with the natural substance of the modest bluff on which it stood. She didn't feel anywhere near as confident as she made herself sound. Her heart pounded, her skin was chill with sweat, from top to toe she felt taut as a full-drawn bow.

She didn't want to be here. She'd love more than anything to accede to Rool's wishes and scamper pell-mell for safety. She knew she'd never be able to live with herself if she did.

She put weight on the rope to test how well it was anchored. No slippage. That was good. She'd have to walk the wall, taking consummate care to make no sound of footsteps. At the same time her arms and shoulders would bear the total strain of her climb.

She donned a pair of buckskin gloves, took a breath in a vain attempt to settle stomach and nerves, and lifted herself off the ground.

In fairly short order, she reached the parapet, sliding over it and onto the roof with smooth silence only a cat could best appreciate. She folded herself down by the seam where floor met wall and stayed very small and still, eyes open wide as they stared into the even deeper darkness of the stairwell. There were flickers of light and color from the illuminations farther below, and a mix of sounds that grated on her soul, not so much because of what was being said but from the underlying emotions. She'd never felt hatred in such a measure, nor so eager an anticipation to inflict pain and suffering on another.

Quietly she divested herself of her cloak and took her ax once more in hand, keeping her back flat to the wall as she crept down the curved steps. The darkness was no problem for her MageSight, which allowed her to see the room as clear as broad daylight.

All these aspects of myself I take for granted, she thought suddenly, *MageSight, InSight, the ability to speak to the creatures and forces of the world, and to understand them in return—what happens to them once the Deceiver steals away the magic that sustains them?*

She made a face at how automatically she had fallen into the trap of assuming that his ultimate triumph was foreordained. It was the tone she'd heard from so many others in talking about the Maizan and their leader, she'd simply followed their lead and assumed it for her own. *If that's how I feel,* she told herself acidly, *why even bother with a fight? Might as well give in and get things over with. The Deceiver surely wouldn't mind.*

She thrust the thoughts from her, to deal with another time, and picked her way across the floor with consummate care, trusting her feet to avoid any squeaky planks.

The tower had been ransacked as thoroughly as the town beyond had been destroyed. All that could be smashed, had been, the wreckage strewn about in helter-skelter fashion.

From the top of this landing she had a moderate view of the next level. No need for MageSight here, torches and a roaring blaze in the hearth cast more than enough light. Unfortunately for Elora, she couldn't find all that much to see. She plucked her mirror from its pouch and lay herself flat to the floor, dangling the polished rectangle over the lip of the floor.

Four figures came immediately to view. Two were

of Greater Faery, as Rool had told her, tall and lean in the manner of their race, whose outward delicacy of form and feature masked a strength of body that far surpassed the most formidable of Daikini. Their faces possessed an unearthly beauty that would never be mistaken for human, as though the concept itself had been pared to its purest essence. The High Elves, who made up the whole of Greater Faery, carried themselves with a natural hauteur that derived from their opinion of themselves as the greatest of the Realms that composed the Circle of the Flesh. In these two, that aristocratic mien manifested itself as a cruel contempt for the figure that lay bound before them. The irony, Elora could see plainly on their faces, was that they were no less disdainful of the denizen of Lesser Faery who stood with them as their ally.

As glorious as the two elves appeared, the goblin was their opposite. They dressed in fabric so sheer it might have been painted on their bodies. The goblin wore rags, stripped joyously from the corpses of the slain. Goblins were half as tall as Daikini, and were often mistaken because of size and manner for lost children, casting malefic glamours to make them appear to be exceptionally angelic in appearance. Only close up did they reveal the truth about themselves, faces so hideous that even trolls didn't suffer by comparison. Mouths stuffed more full than any shark's with teeth, and claws atop every finger and toe. They liked to braid their hair with shards of stone and crystal, honed to razor sharpness, so that they could flay a face to the bone with a sweeping turn of the head.

This one couldn't hold its glamour, or possibly wasn't trying very hard, as its countenance tumbled wildly from angel to monster and back again, sometimes presenting itself as a mixture of both. The prisoner endured both presentations without changing his own expression of defiance. He was bent back upon himself over an anvil, bound wrists to ankles so that his body was arched like a bow, with lines about his throat so that the only way he could draw breath was to hold that murderous position. Any attempt to ease the extreme pressure on his spine would strangle him.

He was naked save for a loincloth and Elora could see he hadn't had an easy time of his captivity. Part of his face was swollen, one eye almost completely shut, and he was covered with a generous scattering of bruises and abrasions, painted with filth and blood. Some of the cuts were fresh, the goblin's doing, as it casually flicked a hand across a stretch of skin to draw forth more.

"First he fry," the goblin cackled, "then he die!"

"At the proper time," one of the elves chided her, "in the proper manner."

The goblin made a foul noise.

"His sacrifice will place our seal on this land and cast it for all time beyond the Veil. You may toy with him all you wish, so long as you do not disfigure him or inflict any mortal harm. Defy us in this, and his ordeal will pale in comparison to your own."

For all the expression on the High Elf's face, he might have been ordering toast for breakfast, yet the goblin cringed as though he'd used a lash to lay her open to the bone.

Elora had seen and heard enough. This had to be stopped, she had no idea how. She was just asking herself where the ogres had gotten to when a hand the size of her head rose into view before her to close on her arm and yank her from her perch.

It let her go as she fell. There was no chance of recovery before she crashed onto the steps, taking the impact mainly across her shoulders, the edge of a step catching her right in the gap between two vertebrae and making a portion of her body go tingly and stiff. Momentum kept her going, but she managed to kick herself forward so that she landed on the floor, close by the anvil where the Daikini lay bound. It wasn't a gracious entrance, she ended up sprawled on her belly, with more shooting stars before her eyes than she'd ever seen in the heavens.

The ogre closed its massive hand about her head and yanked her up while the goblin waggled her claws in eager anticipation.

Neither creature was a great intellect, they hadn't a clue whom they'd just captured. The High Elves, however, recognized her instantly.

One cried, *"Kill her!"*

The other, *"No!"*

That's when Rool started shooting from the embrasure where Bastian had dropped him. It's easy to scoff at brownie arrows, for those shafts are as diminutive as their archers. No one, however, sneers at their poisons, which can be so formidable that the merest pinprick can render a full-grown Daikini quite unconscious. Moreover, in extreme circumstances, brownies can imbue their arrows with a portion of their own life force, which in turn allows them to strike with the force of thunderstones.

Where an ogre was concerned, especially when a squeeze of the hand could crush Elora's skull like a grape, Rool took no chances.

Faster than any eye could follow, three shafts were nocked and released, backed by all the fury the brownie hunter could muster. They left streaks of fire in their wake as they shot across the room. One struck the ogre at the top of his spine, one in the middle, one at the base, and in that instant his great body seemed no more than a rag doll as Rool's terrible rage swept him the rest of the way to the far wall. He was dead before he struck.

That selfsame moment Elora used her own mastery over fire to smother every flame in the room. Torch, candles, hearth, all went out, right down to the palest coal in the firebox, leaving the room suddenly as black as the deepest Nelwyn mine. She lunged forward, arms rising to block the goblin's attack with her elbows, Elora moving in too close for the smaller creature to lash at her with its spiked hair. She brought her leg forward in as hard a kick as she could manage and shoved the goblin aside, throwing herself toward the prisoner. The ropes were thick but the knife she yanked from its boot sheath was sharp and parted them with ease. She wasn't gentle about the rescue. As soon as she could, she hauled the Daikini from the anvil and along the floor to tuck him into the woodbox built into the wall beside the hearth. He made no sound, for which she was grateful, even though it was a rough and bumpy trip. She prayed that didn't mean she was too late and the Daikini dead.

MageSight was her salvation. She could see. The others, even though their eyesight was generally far superior to Daikini's, couldn't make the transition from light to darkness as readily as she. For a few precious moments their blindness was absolute.

She stuffed the handle of her knife into the prisoner's hand, closed his fingers about it, then pitched herself back into the fray toward where her ax had fallen. The goblin snagged a foot in passing, dropping Elora in an ungainly sprawl that left her limbs tangled or pinned beneath her in a way that prevented a quick recovery. The girl sensed the *swish* of air as the goblin snapped her head around, hissed in pain as some of the shards sliced through clothes to skin. The goblin's intent was to stab Elora right through from behind but she never got the chance as another of Rool's arrows hammered her to the wall. With a hoarse cry, the prisoner reared out of his hidey-hole to plunge the blade she'd left him hilt-deep in the goblin's breast.

Elora lunged once more for the ax, heard a tumult to the side, yelped in startlement as a pair of struggling bodies descended on her. The two High Elves were at each other's throat, one as intent on slaying Elora as his companion was in stopping him. Sadly, her defender was the inferior of the pair at a knife fight. Even as the girl caught up her ax, the other elf's bone dagger brought their battle to an end. The victor was off balance as he turned toward her, poorly placed to parry her attack as she brought the ax around like a mallet, swinging with both hands off her shoulder to strike across the leading edge of his face. She didn't want him dead, she had far too many questions, and so hit him with the flat of the blade. He bounced once off the floor and didn't move again.

Elora was on her knees, lungs pumping as hard as her heart, the beginnings of a grin on her face as the realization dawned that she and her friends had won. She'd quite forgotten about the last ogre.

It didn't bother with the stairs, nor was it the slightest bit fazed by the stone flooring. One breath, all was well. The next, two massive fists punched their way into view, filling the air with pieces of shattered rock of all sizes that sprayed the room as shrapnel. Its roar sounded loud enough to smash the tower itself to bits, and a single sideswipe of its arm was enough to blast the anvil off its mountings and right through the tower's wall.

Panic nearly drove Elora up the stairs to the parapet, but she couldn't abandon the life she'd just fought so hard to save. The ogre levered one leg free of the hole it made, pivoting its massive body to keep her in view, marking her as the paramount threat. Rool had not yet responded to its attack and Elora suddenly feared that he might have been hurt by all the flying masonry. The ogre grinned, flashing huge teeth in anticipation of how she'd taste.

All she could think of then was the back room she'd seen under the hill, and what this creature, or another of his kind, had left behind. A stillness settled over her in that moment, a calm such as she had never known. She had lost none of her fear, she'd simply set it aside for the duration. She held the haft easily in her two hands, the ax itself at the ready, cocked over her shoulder, her body centered on the balls of her feet.

Come what may, the ogre would know it had been in a fight.

Bastian got to him first, swooping down the stairway from the roof with his distinctive hunting cry, so loud and piercing in this confined space that it actually hurt to hear it. Even the ogre was distracted. It turned toward the sound but Bastian was too quick for it, and

141

the monster never saw the claws that stripped it of its sight. It screamed, arms flailing in a vain attempt to catch and crush its tormentor. Bastian was already moving clear, with an incredible twist of wings and body, but there was too little room to maneuver. The eagle swerved to avoid a wall, wings beating hard to maintain altitude, generating such a backwash of air that the ogre had no trouble following it to him. A slap caught Bastian square across the breast, only the tips of the ogre's fingers but more than sufficient to leave the eagle stunned and helpless before it.

One hand marked the eagle's position by touch, the other rose clenched into a fist to hammer it to a pulp. With a cry of her own, Elora sprang forward, sweeping the ax around to hook the back of the ogre's knee. She heaved with all her might and tumbled the creature onto its back, but she knew that wouldn't be enough.

She didn't consider what had to be done, she merely did it. Muscles conditioned by hours upon hours of pounding iron into steel brought the ax up and over her head, and as the ogre hit the floor she brought its gleaming, well-honed edge down onto its neck.

Now she knew the battle was truly over, well and truly won.

No grin, though, as she released her hold on the ax. There was too much yet to do.

"Rool," she cried, exertion making her voice sound more husky than normal. "Damn you, brownie, answer when I call—*Rool!*"

She denied the silence, rushed instead to Bastian's side, to discover that the eagle had suffered no lasting damage. Bruised, he was, but not broken. The Daikini prisoner wasn't so fortunate. His knife blow to the goblin's heart had taken the last of his strength. When Elora tried to find a pulse, his skin was so cold beneath her touch that she was sure he'd perished. To her surprise, though, she found a heartbeat and the ghost of a breath.

Lastly she approached the High Elf.

"Take care, Royal Highness," Rool cautioned. There

was blood on the brownie's face and tunic, but no weakness to the way he held himself, or to the bow drawn and leveled at the elf.

Hearing the honorific, the elf spat.

"He's some piece of work, this one is," Rool continued.

"He doesn't look so well, Rool."

"He's dying."

"You have slain me," the elf said, his voice thready, "Cherlindrea's Bane."

"Don't call me that," Elora replied sharply, before demanding of Rool, "What are you talking about, I hardly touched him."

"You drew blood."

"So what if I did? It couldn't have been more than a scratch."

"That blade is forged steel, Elora, anathema to such as he."

"Truly," the elf told her, "you are the destroyer."

"No!"

"You are the Deceiver, who promises salvation yet will bring about the end of us."

"No!"

"Compared to such as you, Bavmorda was a blessing."

With each phrase, the light in his eyes grew more faint. Those last words took his last breath.

Elora didn't seem to notice. She stood before him, just beyond his reach, glaring at him with such furious intensity that it was as if she could bring him back to life by sheer force of will so he could hear her one last denial. So she could make him believe it.

Rool lowered his bow, cast about for a way off the step he was standing on, to cross over to the elf and close his eyes. Elora was there first, and when she had seen to that elf she did the same for his companion, offering a quiet thanks for his sacrifice on her behalf.

"I told you," Rool said when she found his gaze.

He'd allowed himself to slump into the seam formed where step met wall and stifled a monstrous yawn as his body began to demand payback for the strain he'd put on it.

"He called *me* the Deceiver. And that other thing, about Bavmorda—!"

"Her rule was harsh, Elora Danan, but there was a structure to her world. Rules that ensured a measure of survival and, for some, prosperity. It wasn't pleasant, but it was dependable. By comparison, the world we now inhabit is nothing but a chaos."

"We're trying to make things better, Rool!"

"I know. So did that poor soul." And he indicated the other elf, lying at Elora's feet.

"This is so wrong," she said fiercely. "This is not what I thought things were supposed to be. This is not how the world should be!"

"But it's how it is."

She took a deep breath. "And it is what we have to deal with. No good complaining about a lousy pour, Torquil said. One way or another, find a way to make it right."

"Rare wisdom, for a Nelwyn."

Rool's small attempt at wit won him a ghost of a grin from Elora, that faded as she turned full circle to survey the carnage.

"I've never fought like this before, Rool," she said. "I've never . . ."

"I know that, too, child."

"I want to be sick."

She stood in the center of the room, wishing the darkness could blind her as powerfully as any ordinary Daikini. The floor was awash with the ogre's blood, she could smell its bitter scent on her own skin and clothes. She felt an aching hollowness deep inside, an awful sense of loss had been with her since she'd entered the first of the ruined homesteads. This combat hadn't lessened it in the slightest. By one reckoning, the scales of this massacre had been somewhat balanced, the dead a little bit avenged. Yet to Elora, these deaths didn't offset the others.

She picked her way with care around the bodies to gather Bastian gently into her arms, taking the greatest care to make sure his wings were properly folded against his body, grateful to see that they moved easily, without strain or break. She held out her left arm so he could use it as a resting post, and felt his claws close about her forearm while the rest of him sagged against her breast. For all the size and power of the great golden eagle, it was always a marvel to her how comparatively little he weighed, thanks to his hollow-boned skeleton.

On the way out she picked up Rool as well, before making her way down the final flight of steps to the ground floor and from there out into open air. Neither brownie nor eagle asked what her MageSight revealed to her in that close and fetid space, nor did she volunteer the information.

She found a resting place for them on a hump of rock upslope of the tower and the road that passed it by, then returned inside for the prisoner. A last trip was to collect her cloak and what could be found of the Daikini's belongings.

"Do we carry him?" Rool asked, when she rejoined them.

"He won't last an hour."

"What then? Wait till it's no longer an issue?"

"I can try to help."

She began by making the man as comfortable as possible, scrounging bedding from the ruins to improvise a pallet on the bluff, with enough left over for Bastian and Rool as well. True to form, the brownie insisted that he was fine and needed no such special treatment. Elora pointedly ignored him and continued on about her business.

Once more her cloak did double duty as the covering of a lean-to, although this time there were proper poles to serve as the frame. Again she set out her stones and sang warmth back into them, tucking them close about the Daikini and Bastian to combat the growing evening chill.

"Summer's fading fast," she noted conversationally as she set out kindling for a fire. "Even in highlands, I wouldn't have expected a chill like this for another month or so, at least."

"Speaking from experience, are you?"

"You're not the only one who watches the way the world works, I'll have you know. And listens to what folks say. Traders and drovers have been complaining the whole of this season's bazaar. Late spring, cool summer, less forage than they're used to, less game as well. Everyone talked about the weather, almost as much as about the Maizan. Nobody wanted to travel either. A lot of those who came did so because they felt they had no choice. They couldn't wait to be away, and didn't expect ever to be back. Why are they so scared, Rool?"

"You ask a brownie about Daikini?"

"The only Daikini available doesn't appear much in the mood for conversation."

She made broth for herself and Rool and the Daikini, found meat in her pouch for Bastian. She didn't feel terribly hungry, though, and sat cross-legged across the fire from the Daikini, staring intently at him.

"You're going to do something foolish, aren't you?"

She offered Rool a lopsided quirk of the mouth that made him shake his head in dismay.

"Elora, Elora," he repeated.

"I can't do spells."

"Bless Cherlindrea for that godsend."

"But I've learned from Thorn and Torquil to draw forth the inborn power of all natural things. If I can remind stones of what it was like to be warm, why not a body of when it was whole and healthy?"

"A rock is not a person. Its essence is simple, as is the task required of it."

"I can't think of any other way to help him, Rool."

"Not everybody *can* be helped, Elora. Sometimes you have to let go."

She nodded her head one way, then the other, agreeing with him yet at the same time objecting passionately. This time passion won out.

She sat close by the Daikini, letting an uncharacteristic calmness flow out from the center of her being to wrap herself in a blanket of serenity. The fire blazed high, sending a whirlwind cascade of sparks skyward, its behavior a stark contrast to her own, becoming increasingly wild as she grew more calm. Her skin gleamed in its light, as ideal a reflecting surface as the polished metal she resembled, painted in flickering shades of scarlet and rose. To Elora, there was no longer any sensation of being apart from the earth on which she sat. Her flesh and the world were growing one, the heat of blood rushing through her veins resonating in kind with the heat of the lava that raced beneath the planetary crust. Gradually, wondrously, the world's strength became her own.

Without a physical move, she reached out to the Daikini, seeking to establish a similar rhythm with him. His heartbeat was significantly faster, yet the force of each pulsation was fading markedly. No wound was mortal in and of itself but the cumulative effect was deadly. Too many insults to the body, too many demands on resources already stretched thin.

So she offered him a measure of hers.

She made her pulsebeat his, had her own heart bear the load of pumping his blood. At the same time she tempered his breathing so that each came more slowly and deeply. With his basic condition stabilized, she turned to each of his wounds in turn, reminding the torn flesh of what it was like to be whole. What the man's body would have done in days, given the chance, she charmed it into accomplishing over the passage of this single night. The energy to sustain the effort came from her, as the strength she required was drawn from the earth itself.

The healing was easier for her than for Thorn, because his essence was linked to the earth, while hers was to the primal fire at its core. The forces she could manifest were more intense and volatile, they responded more quickly than their more settled counterparts. By the same token, though, they took a fiercer toll.

Especially of one not so practiced as her mentor in shielding herself from those negative effects.

She heard her name called but couldn't find the wherewithal to respond.

"Good thing we're in a valley," noted Bastian. "Put her on a mountaintop, she'd be mistaken for a star."

"Whuzzat?" she wondered, her attempt to speak coherently forestalled by a yawn so huge it threatened to crack her jawbone loose. The Daikini matched her from his pallet, move for move.

"You're glowing," Rool said simply.

She wished she could see herself through their eyes but lacked the strength to cast forth her InSight. It took all her focus to laboriously make her way along all the connections she'd established between herself and the Daikini and pull them loose, a task that proved as exhaustive as saving him had been. No less necessary, though, if she was to keep herself safe.

"Elora," Rool called to her again, the wonder in his voice giving way to thin-edged urgency, "by the living host, what have you done here?"

A mist had grown off the river while she worked to coat the slopes and hollows of the town, shrouding the brutal remnants of the massacre and giving the scene a false seeming of peace and tranquillity. Cruel realities were blurred and softened, the boundaries erased between what was and should have been.

"Something moves in that fog," Rool reported.

"I see it. Put up your bow, Rool, they mean us no harm."

"You'll wager your soul on that?"

"It's what I'm here for."

She rose to her feet with a sleek grace that was totally at odds with a body that moments before felt as though it had been cast from lead. There were lights visible through the mist, a scattering across the hillsides that corresponded with the locations of all the houses. The structures themselves took on a more coherent form, trampled gardens resumed a vestige of their former beauty.

Figures appeared. Ghosts at first, for that was what they were, discernible by the way they stirred the mist with their movements. They were spots of darker gray against the lighter background that gradually assumed a tangible form.

At the sight of them, Rool groaned. For all their bad behavior and the grief they gave races other than themselves, brownies always considered themselves creatures of honor and decency. To torment their fellows was a joy and a delight. Murder was an abomination.

Here was murder.

The figures that wandered before them all bore the signature marks of the wounds that took their lives. Great slashes across the body, torn limbs, crushed bones, burned flesh, they formed a presentation of outright horror. Nor was this barbarity confined to the Daikini inhabitants of the village. Among the gathering, Elora made out denizens of Lesser Faery who'd also made this place their home. They had been slaughtered with no less savagery than the Daikini.

"They're coming closer, Elora," Rool said. "They should not be here, *we* shouldn't be here."

"Bastian," she called softly to the eagle, "can you fly?"

"Far enough."

"Take Rool, get out of here."

"Forgive me, Elora Danan, but I cannot carry you away."

"I'm not asking for me. Just take Rool."

"The devil you say, girl," the brownie protested. "I'm goin' nowhere without you."

"Nor I," echoed the eagle.

"They keep looking at me," she said. "Why do they keep looking at me?"

"You're the beacon," Bastian told her.

"They're lost," Rool echoed. "Cut loose from their earthly lives, unable to claim the peace of whatever lies beyond."

"There must be a way to release them."

"Don't turn to me, girl. Dead is dead, a fate to be devoutly avoided for as long as possible, that's the brownie way. We have no truck with necromancers, not those who speak to the dead, nor those who wield power over 'em."

"I'm sorry to hear that, my friend," she said, "because I think I'm about to try both."

"*What?*" Rool squawked incredulously.

She didn't mean that quite the way it sounded. She knew nothing of the spells required to perform either feat, and had no interest in learning. It was their wounds that sparked an inspiration in her. The ghosts were in pain, that much was clear. As she had found a way to heal the Daikini's wounds, she had the hope now of trying the same with them.

"Once, Rool, this was a place of peace and joy," she told him as she stepped beyond the firelight, haunted eyes and bodies turning to follow as she did. "There should be dancing."

Voices curled at her from the mist, a litany of resentment building to outright hatred: a Daikini, *The cursed naiads tore our fish traps*; the naiad, *The cursed Daikini befouled our water.* Another Daikini, *The dryads spelled our orchards so the fruit rotted on the stem;* a dryad, *They clear-cut whole groves!*

Good neighbors they had been, the Daikini who tilled the soil and shaped this rich land to their liking, and those of Lesser Faery who had resided here for as long as there was memory. There were resources in abundance and all the various races had long ago learned to share the wealth of this valley to the benefit of all.

Then came a change. A growing uneasiness that dated from the Cataclysm, open hostility following the debacle of Elora's Ascension. The culmination was an incident at midsummer. Children went missing and suddenly all the old stories about kidnapped babies and changelings didn't seem so fanciful anymore. By the time the youngsters had been found and the truth made known—that they'd run off because of a beating and stayed hidden for fear of a worse one—the damage had been done. A family of trolls had been discovered and locked in a crow cage, together with any of the other races that could be found. The village had its vengeance on all it thought had done it harm.

Not so long after, the slain got their own back. As they were murdered they cried out to their own kindred beyond the Veil, the High Elves of Greater Faery, who retaliated in kind.

The blood of too many innocents had been spilled, each drop tainting the ground on which it fell, poisoning the earth as thoroughly and lastingly as these souls had been.

For what seemed the longest while, Elora stood with shoulders hunched, back curved, head bowed, as if she'd suddenly been burdened with an impossible weight. Her hands hung straight at her side, half curled toward a fist. To Rool and Bastian, watching from the campsite, it appeared as though her inner radiance had dimmed to the point where she was no more noticeable than any of the ghosts. As wisps of fog curled and flowed about her, she too often reached the brink of vanishing. Far from healing these crippled souls, Elora looked more in danger of being consumed by them.

Then, as if in answer to some cue that only she could hear, the young woman's head came up, her body straightening to its full height. In absolute stature, there were many among the gathering who stood taller than she, yet her presence had become so forceful, her manner so commanding, that she seemed a match and more for them all.

She stepped back into a graceful pirouette, one arm and leg languidly extending with a sweeping elegance that bespoke endless hours of practice in flowing, floor-length formal gowns. It was the engagement used to open every grand cotillion in Angwyn and it ended with her standing before a wizened elder of the town, whose leather apron marked him as the publican of the tavern and sutler's store that had in happier times occupied the ground floor of the tower.

She led, he followed. Her invitation was too gracious, her smile too irresistibly winning, to be refused.

They weren't together for long before their dance segued smoothly into the more elemental and rustic steps favored out along the frontier. The publican began to prance and kick and whirl with an abandon he probably hadn't seen in himself in a fair while, and the smile that gradually swept out across his face was a wonder to behold. With a whoop that caught Elora by surprise, he spun her around in a fast pirouette that flung her to the full extension of both their arms. Before she had even a moment to collect wits or breath, he snapped her back against his body. He held one arm upraised and lifted her off her feet with the other, embarking on a succession of snap turns that ended with a dip and finally a release that placed each of them just out of reach of the other. They both looked ready and eager to start the whole joyous sequence all over again.

Instead, with an ease that suggested the entire dance was choreographed, Elora swirled into the arms of a lad half her size and age. The beat in this instance was sharper and more peremptory, in keeping with the boy's character. From one soul to the next she passed among the crowd, offering as much of herself as was needed, freely and without reservation, trusting to her own inner resources to sustain her. The only constant was that she led, her partner—regardless of age or gender or race or inclination—followed.

"D'you see, Rool," Bastian called softly, as though a normal tone of voice might shatter the crystalline delicacy of the moment, "what's happening?"

"Better to ask, do I credit it?"

"Your soul no more plays you false, runt, than does hers."

"What is she doing, Bastian?"

"No more, no less, than your eyes reveal. She's healing them, one and all."

Suddenly both bird and brownie were startled by the sound of fingertips on drumhead. Rool was still edgy from the battle in the tower, he had arrow nocked to bow in a twinkling as he spun around to behold the Daikini they'd rescued sitting up in the lean-to with a bodhran drum in his lap, fingers and dumbbell-shaped clapper tapping out a fast and fluid tempo.

Elora didn't acknowledge the unexpected insertion of music to her dance as the Daikini set aside his drums for a set of bellows pipes, to fill the air with sound as infectiously wild as the dance itself. Faster he played and faster she danced from partner to partner, as though each was trying to outdo the other, raising the stakes, consequences be damned, until finally and simultaneously, they reached a crescendo.

There were two figures left with her at the last, a little girl who Elora knew was the owner of the doll she'd found. And a naiad, a mother who'd reached in futile, heartsick desperation from her crow cage to her mate's as the sun broiled them both.

There was silence on the ridge, a hush and stillness that transcended the concept of sound. The three watching who could still breathe did so sparingly, so as not to mar the delicate purity of the moment. Elora swayed, moving between the two figures, alike in form and stature though they stood at opposite ends of a generation. Mother and child, both wrongly done to death, their afterlife tainted by a fear neither comprehended.

Elora set a gentle rhythm, the child matched it, so charmed by this argent vision that a smile broke her features for a moment. Elora did the same for the naiad, turning back and forth, from one to the other, bringing them ever closer until they were face-to-face.

They stopped. They stared. The little girl blinked

her eyes rapidly, casting about for somewhere to run and hide. Elora's lips tightened at the blossoming of a dark stain on the girl's breast, the reanimation of the wound that Elora had thought was healed.

The naiad was searching, too, but not for sanctuary. Her eyes marked the gathering beyond, the faces so bright with wonder and joy they might have been alive, only lightly dusted here and there with apprehension as the gossamer mood began to fray. Daikini held Faery in comfort and friendship, as those of Faery did in return.

With a smile of her own, the naiad spun herself into a slow and languorous pirouette that was a match for the engagement Elora herself had used at the very beginning. She held out her hands to the child with the same gentleness and generosity she would have used for her own offspring, all the while swaying in tune to Elora's waltz cadence.

Shyly the girl tried a smile of her own in return and lifted a hand to the naiad's. As delicately as if she was grasping the most fragile piece of porcelain, the most evanescent of soap bubbles, the naiad gathered the child into her loving embrace.

On the far side of the river, a gusting breeze set the treetops into motion with their characteristic *shushush* sound. It swept past the watchers with a chill harbinger of fast-approaching fall and cast the mist into instant chaos. The campfire blazed as though it had been fed oxygen through a bellows pump and a magnificent shower of sparks spiraled their way toward the heavens.

On the boundary where firelight blended with darkness, Elora stood alone. Of the townsfolk, the Veil Folk, there was no sign, save perhaps for some fast-fading sparkles that might be mistaken for wayward sparks from the fire. The spirits were gone. Only the living remained atop the knoll.

Elora was breathing hard and her skin gleamed with the exertions of the night. She had to be exhausted but in no way did she look tired. Rool started toward her, a query poised on the tip of his tongue to ask if she was all right, if there was anything he could do, only to realize that she was looking past him and that the night had suddenly grown far more bright and warm.

On its bluff, the tower burned. The stout stone battlements acted like a chimney, air being drawn in through the open doorway and the various embrasures to superheat the flames beyond white-hot. From the intensity, Rool knew that it would consume everything within its walls and very likely the walls themselves.

Whatever the High Elves had planned for this valley had perished with them. Now every vestige of their presence was being erased.

The land, the village, its people, were healed.

The valley was whole again.

Chapter
6

"Duguay Faralorn," the Daikini said by way of introduction, accompanied by an elegant bow far more suitable for an imperial court than this frontier lean-to.

"I'm Elora," she told him, returning his smile with a somewhat more weary one of her own.

He had height on her, which was nothing new among Daikini, but his shoulders weren't that much broader. His body was slim-hipped, lean as a rapier, and he moved with such a lazy ease that she suspected he possessed a formidable strength as well. His features were no more classically handsome than his body, yet the overall effect was quite pleasing to the eye. His mouth was wide, the nose above had been broken, and Elora couldn't help wondering what had happened to the fellow responsible because this was a man who didn't suffer such assaults lightly. His face was textured, especially around the eyes, in ways that told her he laughed easily and well. A level gaze, directed now on her, that saw far more than the man let on. A broad brow, topped by an unruly stirring of curly brown hair, a pair of piercing holes in the lobe of his left ear, one in the right.

He was a very nice man, but in many ways wholly unmemorable—which made the announcement of his occupation all the more remarkable.

"I'm a troubadour," he told her, fishing in his kit bag for clothes and other adornments, among them a set of plain gold rings for his ears.

Strangely Elora found it almost impossible to meet his eyes. When she looked at him, her gaze fixed itself on the tip of his nose, an ear, the hollow of his throat, whatever stood just beyond his shoulder. By contrast, his stare was disconcertingly level as he surveyed her from head to toe, cataloging her in a way that turned her hot and cold all at the same time and left her skin a mass of shivery goose bumps.

"I am in your debt, Elora," he said. Then he cocked his head a little sideways, to consider a new thought. "Famous name, that."

"Popular, too, so I'm told. Was a time when every newborn girl seemed to be gifted with that name."

"And the skin?"

"How about your silence for your life, Master Duguay, in any way that relates to me, and we'll call our debt square?"

"Bargain like a Cascani, you say." Rool sounded disappointed as he muttered in her ear a small while later, the bulk of his attention focused warily on their new companion while Elora busied herself with final preparations for their journey. "I think *not!*"

"Forgive me," she pleaded as she finished her packing, "I'm tired."

"That's when traders should be at their most dangerous, my girl!"

"My work here is done, Rool," she said, then brightened as the trill of a birdsong resounded from the trees across the river. It was the first she'd heard since their arrival. Off to the east, the velvet sky was taking on a faint roseate sheen in herald of the coming dawn. Mist had given way to morning dew, the air brisk enough to make every exhalation visible, and even the smell of smoke off the remnants of the tower didn't seem out of place.

"I don't want to think for a while, I just want to enjoy the moment."

"Walking alone?" Duguay wondered as they left the village behind.

She made no audible reply, but swung her eyes to the brownie riding her shoulder and from there to the eagle soaring just above the treetops.

"Apparently not," he acknowledged.

They'd lingered at the campsite one day more while Elora regained her strength, at the same time growing increasingly concerned about their supplies as she wolfed down every scrap of food that came to hand in her traveling pouches. Most of Duguay's instruments had survived his captivity. His clothes proved less fortunate, making the man cluck with dismay at the mismatched garments he was left with. He prided himself on his fashion sense and had no truck with ragamuffins. Rool's wound turned out to be mostly cosmetic, requiring a poultice instead of Elora's gifts as well as a bandage, which gave him a raffish, piratical air. Bastian, too, was well on the path to recovery, though both strength and endurance were limited until the soreness passed. His flights were of short duration and he didn't stray far.

Ironically the healthiest among them was the one who'd nearly died and he made the most of it, taking on himself the bulk of the chores with a solicitude and charm they all found irresistible.

"I can find another road, Elora, if that's your wish," he offered in that same vein. "It's nothing to me which way I go."

She slid a skeptical gaze his way, making an obvious show of looking past him at the steep ridge that rose up from the road on one side, then swiveled her head toward the widening race of water that paced them on the other.

Duguay chuckled.

"Fine," he said, waving his hands in a concession of defeat. "Shall I retire to some forest hollow to wait a day or three until you're too far ahead to catch?"

Elora responded with another dumbshow, cocking her head, raising her eyebrows, pursing her lips, making all manner of obscure sounds in mock consideration of his offer. In fact, a part of her deep inside was doing precisely the same in all seriousness. For different reasons, both aspects came to the same conclusion.

"You . . ."—she strung the word well past the point of decency, and let it trail off into a pause that lasted even longer, gleefully taking the opportunity to keep the troubadour dangling in suspense—"can stay."

"I am so honored."

She made him a face and threw a punch to his nearside shoulder that was meant to thump but only provoked a laugh when she ended up shaking the numbness from her knuckles. For all the man's lack of bulk, he was solid as forged steel. The only softness about him was the clothes on his back.

"I've never seen skin like yours," he noted.

One of a kind, that's me was her silent retort. Aloud, she was more circumspect. "It's a wide, wonderful world," she told him. "You'd be amazed at what you'll find in it."

"Considering my present company, I already am."

She rolled her eyes, shutting her mental ears against Rool's hoots of derision, but secretly she was smiling with an awkward shyness she'd never before felt.

His answers proved as vague as hers. He was from somewhere, en route to somewhere else, the clear impression being that his departure was hasty and involved some flagrant breaches of hospitality and etiquette, not to mention propriety. Troubadours had notorious reputations but in Duguay's case it appeared to be wholly deserved. His capture was deftly explained away as a case of being in the wrong place at the wrong time. Of the spell the elves planned to cast, he professed total ignorance. All that mattered to him was that he was to be the sacrifice that activated it.

For all his mysteries—and who was she to throw those stones, who kept tightly shuttered the doors and windows of her own past?—Duguay proved himself the ideal partner for the road. He was good company, silent when needed, always ready with a story to make her laugh or a witty, occasionally wicked observation, and a song to lift her spirits or make the miles go that much faster. When they broke for lunch and later found a place to pass the night, he pulled forth an instrument from his pack and spent some time in practice with it. Over the course of the days that followed, she saw a bodhran, a tiompan, a set of bellows pipes, and a pennywhistle, a fiddle, and a guitar, and had she not seen how artfully he arranged his kit—and tried hefting the load onto her own back—she was ready to swear he used a variation of her own traveling pouches and stored everything in a hidey-hole of magic.

For all that she came to like him, though, she still found herself unable to look him in the eye.

They were proceeding through highland country, and would be until they reached Sandeni, where the continent dropped literally off a cliff toward the west and ultimately to Angwyn. Mile after endless mile of rolling hills that passed through the most impressive forest Elora had beheld since Angwyn. Old-growth conifers, pointed crowns stabbing skyward like lancers at attention, the smallest of their trunks broad enough for a stout man to hide behind unseen.

Bastian was their primary hunter, providing them with a fresh kill for every dinner, rabbit one day, trout or salmon another. Responsibility for cooking was shared between Elora and Duguay, while Rool took himself into the woods for greens and vegetables, Elora producing condiments from her pouch to add spice to the meal. For drinks, they had to make do with mountain springwater, filling their flasks as required from the river.

There was no end to Duguay's repertoire and he needed no excuse to break into song, whether around their nighttime fire or during each day's trek. He had tunes for every occasion and could make Elora laugh as easily as cry. What she loved best, she discovered with an incendiary passion that was altogether new to her, were the ones that made her dance. She'd never had such simple, pure fun: Duguay would establish a beat on his bodhran before shifting to pipes or tin whistle and Elora would let her body take things from there. There were no inhibitions when she danced, no restrictions, she found in it the way to claim the full measure of freedom she'd been denied most of her life.

"You never danced at court?" Duguay asked as he ran through a series of paradiddles on his guitar. The word made her giggle to hear it, even after his patient explanation that it was a sequence of staccato, four-element beats, alternating between the strings and his fingers tapping the face of the instrument like a drum.

The question caught her off guard, as much as the casual way he asked. Her reply was automatic.

"That wasn't dancing," she scoffed, realizing too late what she'd just revealed about herself but deciding to plunge on regardless. To hear her name and see her argent skin told him all he needed to know about who she truly was, anything more was window dressing. "I've seen soldiers have more fun during close-order drill."

"That's harsh."

"Step-two-three-four-step-two-three-four," she continued in that same derisive tone, mocking court behavior with the same joyous enthusiasm as a brownie. "Wrapped so tight in gowns you can hardly move, face your partner just so, hold your body thus, such a touch is permitted while this other is most definitely *not*! See what the others are wearing and never let on that any look more glorious than you."

"I can see a lovely time was had by all."

"I wouldn't know. I was only ever allowed to watch."

She folded her body in on itself and dropped like a puppet whose strings had just been cut, loose-limbed and without the slightest stiffness to her joints as she planted her bottom on the ground and flopped full-length onto her back to stare at what stars were visible through the treetops.

"Enjoy that, my girl," Duguay told her.

"Enjoy what?" she wondered, bridling ever so slightly at the possessive reference.

"How easily your body obeys you. We take it for granted when it's ours, and lose it all too quickly."

"You move well enough, Master Faralorn."

"And greet the morning with groans to prove it." He strummed some random chords on his guitar. "Have you ever tried singing, Elora?"

"By myself," she confessed.

"I'd like to hear."

She shook her head, grateful the nighttime shadows hid the flush that warmed her cheeks. She wasn't used to compliments, and even when they came, a part of her always feared they were offered because of who she was rather than what she'd done. Reverence was hers almost as a matter of right. Respect, she had to earn. And once gained, it was something she was loath to place at risk. She didn't want to seem foolish in front of him.

"What's wrong?" he prodded gently.

She made a weak gesture in the general direction of her throat.

"You've heard my voice."

"I like it."

"Don't be mean, Duguay. It's deeper than most girls' and broken besides. Audiences like their girls to sing clear as crystal, sweet as May wine."

"That they do."

"You have a broader range and you're a wonder to hear. I'd just be a joke."

"You're too hard on yourself. Trust me, Elora, I've heard the others. Everyone sounds the same, where you'd be unique. Especially if we can find a way for you to sing the way you dance."

"Make things up as I go along?"

"With passion. The way you move, when the light flashes off your skin, it's like watching fire come to life, a radiance so intense it hurts. Yet one can't look away."

"Rool," she called, "help! The man's demented."

"Can't argue with you there," the brownie agreed, polishing off the last of a sprig of wild blackberries, each one of which was bigger than his head. "But he's right nonetheless."

"Traitor," she cried, plucking a couple of berries from his grasp to pop one in her own mouth and toss the other across the fire into Duguay's. "Score," she said proudly, savoring the tart juice as she swallowed.

"Where's the harm to try, Elora?" chided Duguay. "There's none but us to hear."

Her first inclination was to fake going asleep until they lost interest, but they all knew her too well to fall for that old ploy.

Duguay started a round, pitched the refrain to Rool, who caught it with ease, carrying the tune with a strong, mid-range tenor that brought Elora over onto her belly, chin resting in cradled palms as she listened and enjoyed.

Then it was her turn. She caught the refrain well enough but her position denied her decent breath or voice. Rool pinched her hard enough to make her yelp and the look on his face prompted her to sit straight up, promising far more inventive torments if she didn't at least make a credible effort.

"I thought you were *my* friend," she hissed at him.

"I am. I happen to think this'll do some good."

"Wretch!"

"Never in the history of the world, of *any* world, has there ever been a being so stubbornly determined to make herself utterly and eternally *miserable*!"

"Not so!"

"Really." He wasn't convinced.

Again the round came to her. This time she tried her best.

She was right on both counts. Her voice was low and husky, described by Duguay as a "whiskey contralto." The term meant nothing to Elora, who didn't drink beyond the occasional glass of wine. To her it seemed the poorest of tools, the weakest of her body's assets.

"An asset is what you make of it," Duguay told her. "And more often than not, it's the presentation of a song that makes the difference to the audience, more than the tune itself. Keep at it, you'll see."

Within a week they came to their first fork in the road, the other path branching off to their left to disappear into the deep woods, no doubt leading to some other remote settlement. Elora considered sending Bastian in that direction, to see if things there were all right. The problem was, what then? She didn't know these folk, nor how to use the golden eagle to convey a warning to them. If she went herself, who knew how long the journey might take or what might happen along the way?

Bastian spiraled as high as he could but saw no sign of any Daikini habitation. There were too many folds to the land, too many valleys to choose from.

It was Duguay who found an answer, though it wasn't one that made any of them feel easier. The road they had followed was relatively flat and unmarred. The other fork was marked with deep ruts, as was the way ahead, clear sign that heavily laden wagons had passed by recently.

"Y'see here," he indicated, motioning for Elora to hunker down beside him as he waved his hand over what was to her an indecipherable mess. "We have footprints between the wheel ruts."

"Ah," she said sagely, ignoring a derisive snort from within the folds of her cloak on her shoulder where Rool was snugly ensconced.

"A lot of folks walking," Duguay said. "And off to the

side, shod horses, right along the border of the road as well as overlaying some of these signs."

"Which means?"

"Outriders," Rool replied, for her ears alone. "Fore- and after-guard."

"Outriders," Duguay told her thoughtfully, munching absently on a long stalk of grass. "Together with a fore- and after-guard."

"Told you," said Rool.

"You're a hunter, Rool," she told him in mindspeech. "I expect such insights from the likes of you."

"A freight train would have an escort," she said aloud.

"But not all these folks on foot. We ever reach the vil- lages along here, it's my bet we'll find them empty."

"Awfully specialized knowledge for a troubadour, Duguay."

"I like wandering, Elora. I like surviving more. On the frontier, a body's pretty much on his or her own. You'd be amazed at what you can learn, and how it can save you."

"Hush," said Rool suddenly, rising to his full height on Elora's shoulder, "the lot of you."

"What's the matter, Rool?" she asked.

"I mean it, Elora. Listen!"

"For what?" Duguay wondered. "It's a quiet day but I don't hear anything out of the ordinary. Plenty of birds and the like."

"Be *quiet,* will you?" Rool snapped, exasperated. "I'm talking to Elora." Then, to her: "*Listen!*"

"To what? Nothing's here but what Duguay said."

"Precisely. I was going to ask the local dryads for in- formation on this convoy. They're social creatures, they love to gossip. Yon great, thumping, lumpen Daikini there, he might scare 'em off, but I figured word would get about that we meant no harm. Eventually I expected someone to brave our campfire and pay us a visit."

"Probably fled my singing."

"They fled something, Elora. Use your InSight, tell me if there's a dryad within view."

She did as she was asked and her voice and manner grew very still.

"There's nothing, Rool," she said at last. "As far as Lesser Faery is concerned, this stretch of forest is barren. But why? Where did they go? What are they afraid of?"

"What's behind us, I 'spect," said the brownie. "And what's ahead."

Elora's brow furrowed.

"When a war starts," Duguay agreed, with a nod, "you don't want to be caught between the two sides."

"The Maizan are here," Elora asked.

"No," Rool said sadly. "This is new, this is different, a conflict between Greater Faery and the Daikini Realm as a whole."

"It was just a raid," she protested, but her heart had already accepted the essential truth of what she heard.

Rool indicated the rutted track, and then the forest about them.

"They think different."

From that crossroads, they picked up the pace. The mood had changed and none among them could find desire or determination to win it back, either during their daily hike or around the evening campfire.

Each morning, Elora sent Bastian forth with a specific purpose, to sweep the way behind for any sign of threat and forge ahead to find a sign of Daikini habitation.

On the third day, beyond the crossroads, Bastian flashed her a view of a town, a hub community sited mainly to serve as the anchor for all the far-flung settlements beyond, in a locale where there was nothing much else of value. Good timber, true, but the river was too rough to use it to float the logs downstream to any market. Fair terrain for farming, more to serve as subsistence for the town than for export, and with the apparent abandonment of the forest by its caretakers and inhabitants among the Veil Folk, the country would be wide open for a boom in the fur trade.

What Elora saw through the eagle's eyes, courtesy of

her InSight, was a fair-sized natural meadow that had been expanded fivefold by an aggressive and thorough clearance campaign that left a huge stretch of open ground on every side of the bustling stronghold. The timbers had been put to good use, to form a stockade better than twenty feet tall atop an earth-and-stone-reinforced redoubt that itself rose ten feet above the ground. Within the walls was an open square twice the size of a jousting yard, dominated at one end by a massive, multistoried structure that was hostelry and fortress combined. Ringing the yard were lesser structures, barns whose residents were split between horses and livestock, coupled with an equally extensive smithy. A slaughterhouse and smokehouse were attached to the kitchen, itself an adjunct to a large communal lodge. The storehouses would most likely be underground, since the clearing ran right to the shore of the river, which also probably meant a buried channel bringing freshwater in from the stream to supplement any wells.

"Now there," Duguay muttered as she described what lay ahead, "is a castle worth the taking."

"I'm certainly impressed."

Scattered out from the fort were individual homesteads, structures as stoutly designed and constructed as the stronghold itself, hard by fields of cleared land that were thick with late-summer crops, almost ready for harvesting. Close by the walls stood a circle of wagons, a train of settlers out to make a new life for themselves. Duguay shook his head at the news, commenting that they'd waited far too late in the year to travel, they'd be buried in snow long before they reached any decent land.

In the meanwhile Elora made her way to the comparative seclusion of a convenient stand of brush and raided her traveling pouch for a change of attire. Buckskin leggings to cover her from hip to ankle, tied to loops that hung from inside the waist of her tunic. Gauntlets for her hands, a wimple to mask every part of her head but her face. At the last a long scarf of patterned muslin, which she wound and draped over and around her skull in desert style until only her eyes were visible. It wasn't a terribly comfortable arrangement, especially since she'd grown so used to the more casual and open style she'd adopted these past weeks, but altogether preferable to someone catching sight of a crop of silver hair or gleaming argent skin.

To the outward eye, she now appeared as a High-lander, one of that breed of iconoclasts and loners who roamed the most remote and inaccessible reaches of the globe. In temperament and reputation, they were considered close kin to the Cascani, though they were held in regard more as warriors than merchants. They preferred the solitude of their own kind, and any who crossed their path with malice were as likely as not to lose some major body parts, if not their very lives.

Elora wasn't cheating by wearing their colors. During their flight eastward from Angwyn, she and Thorn had spent a turn of seasons among one of their clans. Thorn tended their sick and from them Elora received her tartan-wool greatcloak.

"Something the matter?" Rool inquired as she stretched and wriggled each leg in turn, then tugged ineffectually at her leggings.

"They're tight, Rool. And they've shrunk!" The lower hem was meant to rest on the top of her foot, but that left a gap of exposed skin at the top of her thigh. When she pulled the leather to her hip, where it was supposed to be, the bottom rode up past her ankle. Elora muttered something foul.

"I thought your clothes didn't do that."

"They're not supposed to. Oh, *bother*," she cried, deciding that since she was wearing high boots she'd tie the leggings as snugly to her belt as they'd go. "And the damn boots aren't that comfortable anymore, either!"

"Perhaps it isn't them, ever consider that?"

"I beg your pardon?"

"You heard. You're the Royal Highness, you figure it out."

She plumped onto her backside and covered her face with her hands.

"Bollocks," she said miserably.

"Well, you wanted to be bigger. Me, I think you're quite large enough already, but since when did my opinion ever matter?"

"Why now, for heaven's sake?"

"Perhaps because you're finally running about in a world where you've room to grow."

"Ugh!"

"What is your problem, Elora Danan? I'm the one, standing beside a walking mountain, have to shred my throat raw just to say hello. I ride your shoulder still, I'll most likely suffocate, bouncing up so high there's no more air for me to breathe."

"Don't talk like such a silly. If I can breathe, so can you."

"Someone big as you, figure you'll use it all up."

"Is there any way," Duguay interjected carefully, from a respectful distance, "I might be of assistance?"

"I'm growing," Elora lamented.

"Oh."

"Out of her clothes." Rool chuckled.

"Ah. It's certainly a different look," Duguay commented as she stepped around the bush and into full view.

"It's necessary."

"No need to explain, Elora. You're the right size and apparent age for an apprentice. Any problem with a Highlander hiring on to an outsider to learn a trade?"

She shook her head. "Highland bards are as renowned as their fighters. I may draw looks but no real questions. Best of all, given the reputation of the clans, no one's likely to give me any trouble."

"Splendid. I'm tired of this load anyway."

She'd carried his pack before, it weighed the proverbial ton. As befit her adopted station, she let him take the lead as they made their way to the road. They were spotted the moment they emerged from the treeline. Bastian's eyes gave Elora a spectacular overhead view of a sentry pointing from one of the blockhouse watchtowers set at each corner of the five-sided stronghold. Its longest wall was the one facing the river, where it would be hardest for any invader to mass his forces for an attack. Someone up there had a spyglass. Sunlight flashed off its lens as it was brought to bear. Duguay paid the distant hubbub no heed as he made his way forward with a jaunty and effervescent step while Elora trudged behind him in the best tradition of a slavey.

He waved a merry hello to the settlers as he passed their encampment, spinning his cloak out and around with the flourish of a born courtier as he offered so elegant a bow to a clutch of girls playing by the roadside that they scampered away, giggling, to tell their parents someone wonderful had come to town. The menfolk looked on him as major trouble and the smile he offered in return to their warning glares did nothing to reassure them. While Duguay worked the crowd Elora assessed the nearby horseflesh. The traders at the bazaar favored mountain ponies, sturdy short-legged creatures one step removed from mountain goats, built to survive in extremes of weather and terrain. These, on the other hand, were massive, hulking draft animals, half again her height at the shoulder and averaging better than a ton in weight. The herd was all of the same stock, a mixture of duns and chestnuts with close-cropped coats, long manes, and a feathering of similar hair about their fetlocks.

While the horses were similar, what they pulled here was not. Barely three or four qualified as shipping wagons, the kind used by merchants at the Cascani bazaar to transport their goods. The rest were a mismatched hodgepodge of carts, drays, buckboards, light transports, and other carriages. Some were in good condition, others looked like they'd just come from the junkyard, where they'd been up on blocks for years.

The same dichotomy applied to the travelers as well. Well dressed, comfortably and practically clothed, these were people of some substance, yet there was a palpable air of apprehension to them, bordering on outright fear.

They were folk on the run, from something too terrible to contemplate, much less confront. They were here because they had no choice and they had no faith in these stout walls to protect them.

"Rool," she muttered.

"Not outward bound at all, you had that assessment backward."

"The ruts we saw in the road. These could be the wagons, they could be from that other settlement."

"Prob'ly heard what happened to the village we found, hit the road that selfsame night."

"Look at all their faces—the grown-ups, I mean."

"Walking dead, the lot, that's how they see themselves. Figure they can run where they like, it won't save 'em. An' who're we to say they're wrong?"

The sheer excitement of the place, even more than its size, took her aback as they made their way to the main gate. Even though the approaches to the fort were clear, to allow defenders an unobstructed field of fire, a stretch of about a hundred yards or so on each shoulder leading to the main gates was a veritable thicket of tents and stalls, a bazaar in miniature, with wandering entrepreneurs offering all manner of trinkets and gewgaws, souvenirs, talismans, snacks, fortunes, whatever, in such variety and profusion that Elora had to marvel. The scene was thick with customers, which made her assume that this must be a market day. A vendor wafted a length of translucent cloth before a trio of appreciative young women, letting the light play across the shimmering metallic threads woven at random through the fabric, though it quickly became clear they weren't entranced enough to buy. Seeing Elora's interest in the fabric, Duguay stepped into that breach, charming both the ladies and the merchant with one of his trademark smiles as he bargained the man down to a fraction of the price that had been quoted before.

Elora couldn't help a grin of admiration to watch the troubadour at work, sidling this way and that through the crowd, leaving not a whit of ill feeling in his wake.

She didn't try to follow, there wasn't space to fit both her and the pack she carried, and frankly it was more fun to watch him from a distance.

"He's very good."

"He's paying," groused Rool. "Doesn't count at all."

"What, you want us thrown out of here before we've even properly arrived?"

"If he was *very* good, Highness," the brownie mocked, "it shouldn't come to that. A *good* thief—"

"Such as yourself, I assume, Master Magpie?"

"I name no names, but a good thief could strip this lot bare and leave them none the wiser."

"You don't like him much."

"He flashes too many teeth when he smiles, and he smiles far too much."

"A man of good cheer, Rool, where's the fault in that?"

"No. He's a man who's in on the greatest joke ever told, and he's the only one who knows it. There's a difference and it makes me nervous."

"Well, I do like him."

"You're young, you don't know any better."

"Thank you, Conscience."

"You think this is a joy for me, Elora? Cast as chaperon to a willful, growing, stuck-up—"

"Am *not*!"

"—know-it-all—!"

"R-o-o-ol!"

"Nice noise."

She made a worse one, the kind of whine that came easily to her in Angwyn, but that now made the both of them laugh.

Then, as suddenly as if a door had slammed, her laughter stopped.

"On the notice board, Rool, that proclamation."

There was a large, framed rectangle of wood posted between the encampment and the gate, one half listing the general rules and codes of conduct of the stronghold, while the other was for announcements of general interest. It was dominated by a single sheet of parchment, relatively clean still and without weathering, which meant it hadn't been up for very long.

IN THE NAME OF

MOHDRI

CASTELLAN OF THE MAIZAN

A REWARD OF

1000 GOLD SOVEREIGNS

IS OFFERED FOR THE

RESCUE AND RETURN

ALIVE AND UNHARMED

OF

OUR BELOVED PRINCESS

ELORA DANAN

A description followed, fairly sparse in details because no one knew how tall she'd grown or how her features had matured (*hardly at all,* she muttered to herself, *in either case*). Its key point was that the fugitive could most easily be identified by the fact that she was silver in color, from head to toe. Silver skin and silver hair, like a forging come to life.

" 'Alive and unharmed,' " Rool noted. "How considerate."

"I like 'our beloved princess.' Nice touch."

"As is 'rescue and return.' Makes a body think he's doing something noble."

"Do the Maizan a favor, get on their good side. It's beautifully worded. Provides every incentive for playing along and giving them what they want." She made a face. "Well, no one ever said the Deceiver wasn't cunning."

"Not so impressive a price. He's trying to get you cheap."

"Hardly."

"A thousand sovereigns?"

"*Gold* sovereigns," she corrected.

"Is that significant? I mean, I'm sure it's a lot to these rustics. . . ."

"Rool, if he's using Cascani standards, there are a thousand crowns to a single gold sovereign. Outside of Angwyn City itself, and I assume Sandeni, a thousand crowns will support a major household prosperously for a year."

"A tempting sum, is it?"

"Suddenly I feel like there's a bull's-eye on my back."

"Move on, then?"

"Soon as we can."

"You realize, I hope, that this is why Drumheller wanted you to stay with Torquil."

"Thank you, I'm not wholly dim."

"Now there's a relief."

She glared at the brownie. He didn't appear the slightest bit bothered.

"I simply don't want to depend any longer on the kindness of others," she said slowly. "If that's all right with you."

"Hola, Elora!" she heard from a short ways to the rear as Duguay rejoined them.

"What about him?" was Rool's final question before lapsing into silence.

She had no answer. Duguay spared the board hardly a passing glance but she knew that meant nothing. His sight often proved more keen than hers and he had the infernal knack of seeing things while appearing not to.

"I don't know about you, apprentice, but I am tired of the road," he announced as he promenaded to the main gate of the fort in full view of the sentries and their officer of the watch, who had the power to admit them or turn them both away. "A few days' rest and relaxation, to replenish the body and the purse, should set us both to rights."

He shot Elora a sudden, sideways glance that was so quick, that caught her so by surprise, that for the merest split instant her eyes met his. In that flash she felt as though she'd just stared into the heart of the sun. She couldn't remember any details, the inrush of sensation was too intense. The moment passed so quickly, in a space of time so small, she didn't have a word for it, she was left only with its residual aftertaste. She felt a vague mix of exhilaration and danger, a desire so pure she ached to possess it even though that would mean oblivion.

The only outward sign of this was a faint gasp from her, nothing from Duguay, which immediately made her wonder if it was all her own imagination. His words, however, told her he'd seen the sign and made all the right connections. They were meant to reassure. They didn't.

"Trust me," was what he said. And strode right up to the gatekeepers.

"Don't," was Rool's warning.

Duguay met the guards' challenge with a smile and a wave and in short order, to the accompaniment of glib words, irresistible charm, and finally the clink of coins changing hands, and they were admitted.

Of a sudden there was a riot of sound from within the stockade, beginning with a single shout in the distance that doubled and redoubled, crashing toward the gate like an aural wave as voices mingled with the crash of steel and the falling of heavy objects. Heads turned out along the road, none of the patrons of the bazaar quite sure what was happening, their interest manifesting itself more as curiosity than alarm. The gatekeepers knew better, they'd been galvanized into action right from the start. Elora saw pikes tossed to waiting hands while others leaped with trained precision to close the gates.

Elora barely had time to register the sound of hoofbeats before a cavalry charger bulled its way past her through the crowd from the opposite end of the bazaar, its bulk and the harsh cries of its rider acting in concert to clear a path. As it reached the gate a figure launched itself from the interior shadows. The rider bellowed, the horse screamed in startlement, rearing up onto its hind legs. Too much happened too fast as the rider tried to maintain control of his mount and defend himself. The poor man simply didn't have enough arms. At the same time the horse had lost all memory of its training, reverting to a natural state of panic. It overbalanced, lost its balance, tumbled to earth with a palpable crash. As it fell the rider's assailant launched itself from the saddle with a fearsome roar.

Unfortunately Elora was right in its way.

She felt like she'd been thumped by a thunderstone. It really didn't matter much that Duguay's pack caught the full brunt of the impact as the pair of them hit the ground, the collision still hurt.

She struck out reflexively, not a conscious thought behind any of her blows beyond a primal desire to protect herself. Each one, though, brought her an increasing sense of recognition. This was no stranger atop her, and no enemy.

At least so she assumed until Ryn Taksemanyin bared fangs and uttered a snarl that set babies immediately to shrieking and sent onlookers scrambling desperately for cover or weapons. Elora couldn't help flinching as wicked claws flashed across her body, the look on his features was so fierce she was sure he'd cut her. Then he scooped her out of the severed pack straps and heaved her from his path.

Again reflexes superseded intellect. She twisted in midair, managing to salvage a decent landing. Ryn cast about for an escape route through the crowd, but a burly armsman took him down with a chest-high tackle. An elbow to the solar plexus took the Daikini out of the fight, but two of his mates slammed into Ryn as the Wyr scrambled to regain his feet.

A cudgel rose and fell, and Elora hissed as the blow drew blood. For each opponent Ryn cast aside, easily two or three more piled on to take their place, and the Wyr was quickly buried beneath a mass of pile-driving punches and savage kicks. There was no elegance or finesse to this encounter. It was a brawl, and these men were masters at the art.

The crowd kept a respectful distance. The authorities appeared to have the situation under control but no one wanted to find out the hard way that they were wrong. A couple of horsemen were waved back by one of the troopers on the ground. This was a foe better handled on foot. Shackles were quickly and roughly fastened into place about ankles, wrists, and throat. A thick hobble chain prevented Ryn from walking with anything better than quick little stagger steps and his arms were wrenched painfully high on his back in a pair of hammerlocks, to be hooked onto the back of his collar, making it a struggle for him even to breathe. A restraint gag had been applied as well to keep his fangs at bay. Elora's hand itched toward her traveling pouch, and the weapons within, as she heard a chorus of loud comments that the prisoner, this *beast,* would be better off hamstrung.

Duguay's hand covered hers and Elora felt a madcap flash of agitation at how easily he'd caught her unawares. She knew that this was no time for a rescue, but it was agony to stand by and do nothing while her friend was dragged away.

Manacled as he was, Ryn still stood taller than many of his captors, tall even for his own ocean-dwelling race. He was broad in the shoulders, long and lean along the body, built better for swimming and scampering than for walking upright. His fur had suffered from the scuffle, and whatever imprisonment had come before. Usually immaculate, with a glossy sheen that made it look polished, it was now scored with dirt and mud, matted in places, and stained with what Elora hoped was water but suspected was blood. His face was usually expressive as any Daikini's, though while their fangs were vestigial, his were not. Ryn's intelligence should have been a match for the best among the jeering crowd of onlookers and his sense of honor put more than most to shame. But now, snarling through his gag, foam flecking his muzzle, a mad glare in his eye, Ryn appeared more beast than human.

The Wyrrn spanned the gap between land and sea. While they made their settlements along remote and wild shorelines, they were equally at home far out upon the Deep Blue, as they called the Mother Ocean. They breathed air but could swim underwater for periods that would leave the hardiest Daikini drowned and dead, as well as plumb depths that surface dwellers could only reach in their imagination. They were as ubiquitous and far-ranging at sea as Daikini were on land, and in the main a far more collegial species. Their partnership with the Cascani was legend, so much so that stories labeled them as related offshoots of the same parents. When challenged on that point, the response of either race was generally a broad and knowing grin, and the offer of another glass of something good to drink to make the encounter pass more enjoyably. The main difference between them, aside from the physically obvious, was that Cascani lived for the deal and had their fun on the side. Wyrrn apparently were born laughing, the better the game, the happier they were.

Damn, she thought as she watched Ryn dragged away, and then gave the feelings voice, "damn damn *damn!*"

"You were hanging back before," Duguay noted, the sound of his voice yanking her from her reverie. "Of two minds about staying?"

"Nope."

"Nasty business, that."

"Yup."

He got the message and mentioned no more of it as he led her beneath the portal of the main gate. Passing within on his heels, Elora was impressed to note that the redoubt was twice her height in thickness and that the tree trunks which formed the wall above were themselves doubled.

"These folks take their security seriously," she said quietly, as much to Rool on her shoulder as to Duguay by her side. The troubadour had taken charge of his pack, keeping hold of it with one hand and her with the other.

"Then we've every expectation of a sound, safe sleep this night," Duguay responded.

The promise of a performance gained them a cubby for the night, and supper. The closet had a feather bed that might comfortably fit a Nelwyn, provided he was modestly sized and didn't move much in his sleep, and there were peg hooks on the wall to hold their gear, plus a single shelf. No candles, and when Elora inquired about them she was greeted with an explosion of derisive mirth from the serving lass who had showed them the way. No door, either, only a curtain to afford them a marginally threadbare modicum of privacy. Common washroom and privy out back. Light, such as it was, came from a line of sconces in the hallway. There were quality rooms of course, for the quality folk with means to pay for them. Still, the mattress was clean, as was the floor and the staff, and the room had a minimal sense of bugs. Duguay commented that he'd seen worse.

He sat Elora in the corner farthest from their "door," plucking off her greatcloak to hang on the frame and shroud the pair of them in near-absolute darkness. Mage-Sight allowed Elora to see perfectly and she wondered if the same held true for him until he folded back one corner of the cloak to spill a wedge of light over his pack. From there he drew a small metal container, pulled off the tight-fitting top to expose the wick. He handed her the lamp, struck flint to steel, and within seconds the room had illumination. At his direction she set the lamp on the shelf, while he refastened the cloak to enclose them completely once more.

"This could get us into trouble," she told him.

"Only if they notice, which they won't, and only if we set the place on fire, which *we* won't."

"You're sure on both counts?"

"Trust me."

"You keep saying that."

"I haven't betrayed you, Elora, and I won't."

She said nothing but cocked an eyebrow.

"Please," he said, "don't dissemble. I saw that warrant out front same as you and I have to ask, how many silver-skinned people are there in the world?"

"I haven't met the whole world, have you?"

"Suit yourself, but you can't wander about this fort dressed like that."

"Highlanders do."

"And when you eat or drink, what then?"

"I can stay here."

"Won't be doing your friend much good in that case, am I right?"

He was, and she sighed to show she knew it.

"How could you tell?"

"I watch people. I observe the way they react to things. From yours, that Wyr was known to you and on a more than casual basis."

"He's my friend, Duguay. I have to help him."

"Best then you begin by helping yourself. There are two ways to hide when you're on the run." It sounded like firsthand knowledge. "Play the titmouse and stay so deep within yourself you're never noticed. Or grab center stage so flagrantly no one'll dare think of you as a fugitive."

"Speaking from experience?"

"Not every engagement ends happily. Some audiences carry a grudge."

"And your preference?"

"People don't like surprises, Elora. It's always better to play to their preconceptions and prejudices, to be precisely what they expect. You're apprentice to a bard. When was the last time one of that breed was ever shy and unassuming? Besides, if you make sure to direct everybody's attention one way, all manner of schemes can be hatched behind their collective backs."

"I should warn you, Duguay, if you mean to cast any sort of glamour, magic doesn't hold on me."

"A glamour, this isn't. That sort'a nonsense doesn't hold much for me, either." His mouth quirked, an expression too wry and rueful to be a proper smile. "Besides, you've seen and touched parts of me no one else has. A good heart, I'll own to, albeit reluctantly, since I prefer the role of a rogue and roué. But magic"—and Elora heard a definite sense of sorrow to his tone—"not at all."

He turned his gaze toward her, and try as she might she still couldn't meet it. "I owe you my life, Elora with the silver skin. This is small and scant repayment." He took a big and deliberate breath to break the mood and returned to his original discourse. "Anyroad, magic is too easy, first thing any truly suspicious mind looks for. In a stronghold this big, probably three or four household spooks on retainer, just to sniff out the slightest whiff of any renegade spell casting. Me, I'm an old-fashioned player. I work with my hands, with whatever comes to hand, and with my wits, and so should you."

"What about the reward?"

"Am I a liar or a fool to tell you no way? I've the wanderlust in my soul, Elora, same as you. That's more money than a man like me will ever see in his whole life, but what'll I do with it? Carry it on my back, I'm branding myself a target for every robber worth the name. Even if it was possible to spend so much, I'm not sure I'd want to try. That much money has a way of twisting a body's spirit, spin its thoughts around a practical, sensible turn. Some are born to be men of property, but I've yet to see one of those I truly liked, and I've certainly no desire to see one staring back at me each morning from my mirror. So, in the balance, I *am* tempted. I'm only human. But not so much as to act on it."

"Fair enough."

"You're not convinced."

"It's a good speech, Duguay, but these are times that cast shadows across the best men's souls. Maybe you're right, and that means it's better to throw in with scoundrels born. In my case, I sure hope so. But under the circumstances, it isn't as if I have a whole lot of choice. So . . . ?"

He had her strip to the borderside of decency, shorts and a singlet that didn't quite cover her midriff, and at the sight of her even he had to sit back on his heels and simply stare. She dropped her eyes and hunched her shoulders forward, struck by an unaccustomed fit of modesty she'd never felt around the brownies. She locked her fingers together in her lap, to keep from little helpless gestures meant to cover her body, apologize for her shorn head.

"That poster doesn't do you justice."

She didn't trust herself to speak. She wanted to shriek at him, *This isn't me, this isn't who I really am!* Yet at the same time she wanted to face him with pride. She'd never felt this way, so wholly and fundamentally unsure of herself. Everyone loved her when she was a baby because everyone loves babies. Growing up in Angwyn, the Vizards who were her guards and constant companions were no more real to her as people than she was to them. Her own opinion of herself was so flawed that theirs didn't matter. Afterward, when she was reunited with Thorn and came to have an appreciation of her own worth and potential, she deliberately refused to think of herself in terms of physical beauty. That wasn't the standard she wanted to be judged by. She set out to learn skills and shape her body to accommodate them. She always knew the day would come when she would want to be seen as a woman, but she never had anyone to prepare her for the moment.

"May I touch you?" Duguay asked, and was answered by the shallowest dip of her head. The mere thought of it gave her another attack of goose bumps and she pursed her lips in agitation as she tried to understand how she could feel as though streams of ice-cold and near-boiling liquid were intertwining themselves throughout her body.

It's not as though he's doing *anything,* she thought in frantic confusion. *Rool wouldn't allow it if he tried.* She blessed Rool for his presence and hated him, all in the same moment.

"Your skin's warm," he said, marveling, as he took her forearm in hand. Then, as if realizing how absurd he sounded, he broke out in a low chuckle.

"Forgive me, Elora," he apologized, gathering himself to his knees and dropping head and shoulders slightly forward in a proper bow. "I must appear one great and thumping lummox."

"It's all right."

"You really do appear a statue come to life."

"The one spell I've encountered that hasn't washed off. Unless, of course, this is how I was supposed to look all along. The question is"—and here she hardened her voice, holding fast to the original subject of their conversation as though it was a lifeline—"how do I hide it? As you said, in plain sight."

"Clothes are one way, that you know. But for our purposes . . ."

Duguay rummaged in his pack, came up with a smaller box that opened to reveal a cornucopia of jars and pots, ointments and pastes.

"The trick," he considered thoughtfully, picking and choosing among its contents, "is not to cover the silver, but make it appear as though the silver is covering something else."

"Suppose I sweat, and what about when I bathe, won't your paint wash off?"

"Some will, others not, that's the key. Apply the makeup in layers, you see. . . ."

He left her hair spiky, but washed it with an unguent that turned it a black so dark she could have been dipped in an inkwell. He used a pencil to shape her brows so that they rose up and away from her eyes in a dramatic sweep, and then took a razor to her scalp to deepen and extend the arc formed by her natural widow's peak.

Paint came next, swashes of vibrant color, primaries all, highlighting and accentuating the shapes and planes of her face in ways that both added years to her appearance and, paradoxically, made it increasingly difficult to tell precisely what she looked like. The overall design was wonderful, Elora never imagined she could ever look so beautiful, yet even she found she couldn't fix any coherent image of herself in memory.

Over the rest of her, every part that would be visible, went a subtle base coat that didn't so much submerge her argent skin tone as cast it in a wholly different light. With paint, Duguay somehow replicated the same effect that occurred whenever Elora blushed, giving her body a faint but discernible roseate accent, the end result being a woman with exceedingly pale but otherwise normal skin.

The final effect was striking. Elora looked utterly wild, with more than a deliberate hint of Faery to her features.

"The main idea for now, though," he told her in what was meant to be reassurance, "is to make sure they look more at your face than anywhere else."

"For now?"

"Face facts, you don't have that distracting a body."

She hit him for that. He got his revenge by producing the costume he wanted her to wear. She held the gauze scarf before her face and looked at him right through it.

"I don't think so," she said warningly.

As it turned out, her apprehensions were pretty much unfounded. There were light sandals for her feet and thin silk trousers that hugged legs and bottom like a second skin. They didn't reach her waist, however, like proper pants, but sat right atop the line of her hips, as did the flounce skirt that tied over them, itself made of a gauzy fabric similar to her scarf, ankle length and laced through with spangles and beads designed to reflect and refract the light with every movement. Despite its seeming lack of substance, the skirt was weighted to allow it to flow with her movements, billowing outward when she turned with a sleek and sensuous grace that by rights should be doing justice to a woman who knew how to use it. A set of golden chains encircled her waist, with dangles of metal and crystal hanging from where it clasped together over her navel.

The bodice was an equally theatrical mix of the fantastic and the practical. A shirt of fine cotton that had the feel and presentation of silk, fitting snugly to her shoulders and billowing outward where its bell sleeves fastened around her wrists. A high collar swept around to a neckline that plunged to the blouse's hem, right below her breasts, cut in a way that masked her lack of prominence there. The sleeves were slashed from top to bottom, exposing the full length of her arms, which were decorated with bangles and bracelets galore, as well as with a set of stylized tattoos which Duguay painted on in ink as black as her new hair. The designs represented nothing Elora was familiar with, they were abstract shapes that she best described to herself as interlocking spear points.

More jewelry for her face, a clip-on ring for the septum of her nose, with a double line of light chain attached to rings at the tip and lobe of her left ear. A broad choker necklace, more gold, around her throat, rings for every finger and one of her big toes.

"Might this not be considered," she wondered as the session progressed, "a tad gaudy?"

Duguay grinned so infectiously she had to respond in kind. "You haven't seen me yet."

The thought of that set her to laughing outright.

"You're painted in hot colors," he told her, "clothed in warm ones, accented in gold, rubies, amethysts. Every element is intended to take the watcher as far as possible from a vision of you as you truly are."

"Will it work?"

"Ask me tomorrow."

"I find that *so* comforting. What about Ryn?"

"Your furry friend?"

"His name is Ryn Taksemanyin."

"We establish our own rightful place here first, then we can begin to maneuver about. The one thing we cannot do is rush."

"All this preparation doesn't matter a damn if we lose him!"

"Then you'll have to trust that the Fates aren't in a malicious mood."

She stuck out her tongue at him, and then settled back to watch as he began to ready himself for the evening's performance.

Chapter
7

Duguay was very good, there was no denying that.

He charmed the crowd as individuals and as a whole, and possessed that rare gift of making a song sound as if it had just been written right then and there, a personal creation for every person in the room. The dining hall was an imposing space, broad more than deep, with room for two impressive hearths along one of the long walls. Its twelve-foot ceiling was broken at intervals by the massive beams necessary to support the upper floors of the building. Rough wood all around, creating a dominant impression of rustic strength and solidity rather than elegance. This was a functional building, with few pretensions, like the people it served.

Light was courtesy mainly of the hearth

fires, plus a multitude of thick-bodied candles on standards and lamps arrayed throughout the room. Meals were served on a line of trestle tables and benches, with the high table on a dais along the wall between the two hearths and beneath a magnificent rack of antlers, so broad and thick with points that many visitors assumed it couldn't be real.

All around Elora, the hall shook with the raucous assemblage of permanent residents and transients, all of whom were in a mood to enjoy the troubadour's ribald and occasionally acerbic wit. In return, Duguay entertained them with songs and stories that made men bellow with laughter and their lady companions blush and giggle. A beat later he would come back to those same tables with a selection that provoked entirely the opposite response, howls and scandalized shrieks of delight from the womenfolk and grumbles of bluff discomfiture from their mates.

At the same time the room was a frenetic bustle of activity as a veritable army of serving men and maids rushed to and fro, laden with trays of food and drink from the kitchen, equally weighed down by dirty dishes on their return. For the most part table manners were atrocious, as the several courses of the dinner were attacked with a ferocity that would have put many so-called animals to shame. Elora was a bit taken aback by all this manic hubbub. Growing up, she always sat at the high table at meals, and was the one waited on. Since those were invariably state dinners, the most formal and dignified of occasions, she found them deadly dull. She had little experience working the other side of the table, especially in a crowd like this.

As a consequence, after Duguay made his entrance she kept close by the wall, trying her best to follow his injunction that at the very least she look decorative and suspecting she was making a royal botch of it. She felt stiff and frighteningly ill at ease, certain her disguise was a joke, that any moment she'd be denounced and seized. Or, far worse to her way of thinking, the crowd would fix on her every imperfection and laugh at her pretensions to prettiness. Because she'd never done this before and didn't know any better, she cared too much what the audience thought of her, and that very nearly proved her downfall as she took advantage of Duguay's opening ballad to slink toward the nearest hidey-hole.

She never made it, the troubadour didn't let her. His hand caught her by the scruff of the neck, and without missing a lyric or a beat of his song, he paraded her before the mob. She thought she would die, and then determined not to go without killing him first.

Thankfully, at least Rool wasn't here to see this humiliation. (Though, chances were, he'd make a great show of enjoying every moment and would never, *ever*, let her forget it.) She'd cut him loose before following Duguay inside, to find where Ryn was incarcerated and see how he was. Later, when the show was done, she'd follow and together they'd work out a plan to set him free. She couldn't help wondering how the wily Wyr had been captured in the first place and what sort of mission had brought him so far from Thorn. She tried not to think about the moment of their collision. In the midst of their struggle she'd called out to him with voice and mind-speech, but there's been no reply. No acknowledgment of his name, and worse, not the faintest awareness of her. She might as well have been yelling at a brick.

Gradually it dawned on her that hardly anyone in the audience was paying her the slightest bit of attention. They had far more important things on their minds, she was simply part of the background, to be admired momentarily and then soundly ignored just like the antlers on the wall.

This revelation, of course, left her so miffed that she had to laugh out loud.

It was a liberating realization and with it she cast aside much of her stiffness and reserve. The smile that had till now looked pasted on her face, and badly, came more spontaneously and began to draw equally genuine responses. She watched the serving staff as they slipped and sidled their way along the narrow passages between the tables and let her own body adopt their rhythms and manners. It wasn't as easy as it looked, she quickly discovered as she found herself drafted into service.

There was a challenge to keeping track of orders and delivering them promptly, and as well to handling trays of food that were nearly as broad across as she was tall. The tables allowed precious little clearance between them and anything that spilled was likely to land on a paying customer, which meant that was to be avoided at all costs. The problem was dealing with louts and yobbos who took her mere presence as an invitation to be rude.

Quality folk were tabled right below the dais and its high table and were accorded the privilege of choosing their dinner from a menu. They were presented with a selection of wines as well, for which they were handsomely charged. Everyone else, who actually had better seats, since their tables fronted both hearths, enjoyed whatever repast the cook had in mind. Tonight, that meant a hearty game stew—mostly bison, with leftover boar and venison from the night before, mixed in a rich, spiced broth with potatoes, leeks, carrots, onions, and other assorted vegetables—served in cast-iron pots that went straight from kitchen fire to table, each kettle serving a dozen customers. No wine for the cheap seats, either, only beer or plain water. Unfortunately there were thirsts to match a fair number of equally considerable appetites, which kept the staff busy with refills from the first plating of the night to the last. The only saving grace was that the crowd forced the Commandant to banish the fort's resident pack of wolf- and elkhounds to their kennels for the evening, thereby removing one formidable hurdle from the tavern's nightly obstacle course.

Through it all, Elora obeyed Duguay's injunction to watch and listen. She worked as hard as she ever had in her life *(as hard,* she concluded with a groan when she realized that the evening was barely half over, *as in the whole rest of my life put together),* and she learned more.

"What's a lovely lass like you doing in a dump like

this?" she was asked by a strapping young man too altogether certain of his ability to set ladies' hearts to fluttering.

"Why," she replied in the tone of a breathless ingenue, as she'd seen the other girls do, and stealing one of their lines as well, "hoping beyond hope to meet a wonder such as yourself!"

She fluttered her lashes becomingly (at least, that was the idea) and made a moue with her lips. Then Elora's eyes met a fellow serving maid's, who made the exact same expression back at her, and the false mood of the moment was thoroughly shattered by a mutual attack of the giggles. The lad didn't get the joke, and rose up to take righteous umbrage, but the other maid flicked a foot lightly between both of his and the next the young man knew he'd dropped hard back down onto his bench without the slightest clue as to how he'd just lost his balance. The maid immediately topped off his mug with beer, gave him her brightest smile and a kiss on the cheek; by the time he realized he'd been abandoned, he was altogether smitten, and she and Elora an entire table length away.

"Weren't our fault, what happened!" she heard from a middle-aged man, among a clutch of people determined to resist the general merriment. She recognized some faces from earlier in the day and knew without another word that these were from the wagon train encamped outside the gates. Immediately, Elora sidled closer to hear what they had to say.

"Weren't right, Maug, what they did," countered another, half again as old, as deep in his cups, as haunted in his eyes.

"You sayin' those poor devils deserved what happened to 'em?" Maug cried. "By the Realms, Hobi, there was *children* slaughtered in Ganthem's Crossing!"

So, Elora thought, *the village had a name.*

"There was *babies,* man. An' you know how ogres love the taste o' meat that fresh!"

"Shut'cher damn hole, Maug," snapped another.

"There's women here with babies, an' folks with kids, who want no more'n for folks to mind their business an' their manners so's we can all eat a decent meal in peace!"

"We earned that land of ours fair an' proper, Asa," Maug said. "We shoulda stayed."

"Go back, then," came a challenge. "See how long you last before it's your head decoratin' a Faery pikestaff!"

A mug was hammered down on the tabletop, spilling much of its contents. Maug was pulled back down by his fellows before he could respond in kind or worse and cause an incident. The fort was peace-bonded, no weapons allowed to any save its own detachment of soldiers, and there were always proctors close at hand to quell any disturbance. This was only a flashfire altercation, yet Elora spotted two of those deputies looking their way. They'd already marked these refugees as potential trouble.

"Behave, Maug," snapped one of the others, "else we'll have the law toss you in with that damnable beastie for the night, see who walks out come the morn."

"Meant no harm, not words nor deed," Maug said, but from the way he cringed in his seat, Elora knew he took the threat seriously.

"Those raiders from Elfland, they meant plenty harm."

"We lived in peace, our kind an' theirs, for as long as always."

"What can I say, Maug, or any of us? Times have changed. Looks like there be new powers beyond the Veil don't care for peace. Don't care for Daikinis. They want us gone from their land, or they want us dead."

"Give it a rest, Hobi," someone demanded. "You're as bad as Maug."

"Whole world's gone to hell," lamented Maug over a fresh beer.

"Teach you to believe in that damn 'Sacred Princess' nonsense, ya dumb duffer."

"She was hope."

"For who?" "Sure, not for us." "B'sides, you seen that poster, she's gone missing." "Ahhh, but if we could find her . . ." "Dream *on*." A clutch of voices, overlapping as one.

"More money there than all of us put together could dream of spending," Hobi proposed enticingly, "if we had all our lifetimes to try. We could start again."

"If wishes were pigs . . ." scoffed Asa.

"Where can we live," said Maug, "that the lords of Greater Faery won't claim for their own?"

"Among the Maizan, maybe," Hobi offered.

"Aye," agreed another at the table. "It's said none of the Veil hold any sway in Maizan land."

"How long'll *that* last?"

"It's better'n we got now."

"Girly!" With a start, and after a second and third call for her attention, Elora realized that call was for her. "More ale!"

"It's hope, damn it!" said Hobi, but Maug shook his grizzled head.

"We got no hope," he said. "We got no hope."

Elora topped off their mugs, cleared what plates were ready, allowed herself to drift around the periphery of the room. She didn't need any special abilities to see now how forced and almost desperate the general good humor was. That it existed at all was because too many of those present refused to consider anything more than the immediate here and now. The analogy that came most readily to her mind was of the calm surface of the water, hiding the vicious riptides that lurked a body length below to doom any unwary swimmer. Ryn had told her a long time ago that one of the first things that young Wyrrn learned was how to recognize those treacherous strips of water because even the strongest swimmer could find himself in deadly trouble if he let himself be caught.

The image turned her thoughts to Ryn but there was still too much to do in the dining hall, she had no opportunity to slip away. What bothered her was hearing no news from Rool.

A stocky figure of average height paused a moment in the doorway, returning the wave of an officer at a front table and quickly threading his way through the crowd toward him. He caught Elora's elbow as he went and gave her a rushed order for food and water. He wore mail, his surcoat emblazoned with the sigil of the Sandeni cavalry corps and the piping of a captain. There was dust all over him, worked deep into the creases of his mouth, and he smelled of both human sweat and horse. He was armed with long sword, short sword, and daggers but he'd left his helmet at the door. His stiff gait and the way his legs bowed told her he'd just come from a long ride, as did the way he eased himself onto the proffered bench.

He drained a full glass of water the moment she set it before him, so she brought a large carafe with his meal, returning in time to catch him in mid-conversation.

"No word from the Paradise River patrol?" he was asking his fellow officer who'd cried the greeting.

"No reason to expect any, Sam, they're not due for a week yet."

"This is black business, Ran, an' that's no error. Bara-clough's Station, up by Tooley Crest . . ."

"I know the place."

"Gone. As bad as Ganthem's, so my scryscouts said."

"You didn't press on to see for yourself?"

"No, I did not. I'll tell you what I just told the Colonel, I'll not be throwing away good men we'll likely be needing before winter."

"Your scouts couldn't establish contact with the Paradise patrol?"

The Captain shook his head. "That's what's got me scared. The raiders, I think they let us see Baraclough's same as they did Ganthem's, so's we'd spread the word across the whole of these highlands. I'm also thinkin', any settlement that isn't down here by week's end, they won't be comin' at all." He blinked, surprised to find a bowl of steaming stew beneath his nose, plus a plate with extra bread. His hunger matched his thirst and he ate wolfishly, shoveling the food into his mouth without regard for its taste. He could have been eating swill for all he appeared to notice.

"Colonel says no crops go downstream this harvest," the other officer told him. "Everything consumable is to be brought within the walls and stored for siege. We're to make a residence plan as well." He took a hefty swallow of his ale. "You've seen the crowd outside, Sam. If more come, can we accommodate them all?"

"For their sakes, we'll have to."

"First the Maizan, now this. What the hell is happening to the world?"

"Looks like war, lad."

Elora blinked rapidly, shaken not so much by the news but by the resignation underlying it. Events to these men were out of their control, they could do no more than try to cope with the consequences. That same air of despondency flickered through the emotional atmosphere of the hall like a heat haze, carrying with it an unpleasant aftertaste of acid and grease that reminded her of the time she'd been caught downwind of one of the Nelwyn smelters. The effect could be endured, even though it made the lungs burn, but it was no place to linger because a lengthy exposure would kill.

She looked for Duguay, hoping to find him as the sole shining point of light amidst the gloom. Instead she found the lad who'd made a clumsy pass at her earlier.

"Uh," he said, in the manner of boys, to break her reverie, and then as her eyes focused in on him, "hi."

He was as stumble-tongued as the other maid had made him stumble-footed when she tripped him, bravado packed away now that he was out of eyeshot of his fellows. He had size on her in every dimension, and years, too, by the look of him, yet Elora had a strange intuition that he regarded her as the older and wiser of the pair.

"Hello," she returned with polite reserve. She was leaning back against one of the pillars that supported the ceiling, both arms wrapped lightly around a large pitcher of beer she was holding close to her belly.

"I'm, uh, Luc-Jon."

"Elora."

He bobbed his head and flashed a lopsided grin. "I know. I asked. He's pretty good," and indicated Duguay with a jut of the chin. She said nothing, which made him react as if the ice beneath his emotional feet was beginning to crack. "You, too, I'll bet."

"Thank you. You're very kind."

Something wet and cool poked her in the side and the sad eyes of one of the household wolfhounds gazed beseechingly up at her. The dog stood as tall at the shoulder as her waist and easily doubled her weight. Big head, big body, with a keen intelligence that marked it much more as companion than pet. These were hunting animals, bred and trained originally to battle the terrible dire wolves of legend, who held such sway in these mountain forests that they were once revered as gods themselves and in turn gave rise to the earliest known tales of heroes. Those stories told of how the wolves had exchanged the true and vaguely human form they wore in their own accursed home for this most fearsome of predator shapes, and came to this world to hunt Daikini for sport.

Daikini being Daikini, so those age-old tales went, which is to say stubborn beyond all belief and even more cunning, they fought back. They adapted, by learning new ways to fight and finding allies to help them, forming a bond with these hounds that had lasted unbroken through the ages. Every other time, every other place, the depredations of the dire wolves lasted until they grew bored and departed of their own accord, satisfied that they had marked both land and people with blood and horror enough to scar them to the end of time. Against the Daikini, for the first time in their own history, they found themselves actively repulsed, leaving behind only tales and a name that was never spoken lightly, if at all, to this very day, because it still had the capacity to inspire dread in any who heard it.

This most ancient and feared race called themselves the Malevoiy.

Elora laid her hand on the wolfhound's head, and the

beast gave her palm a single lick with its broad, warm, altogether slobbery tongue.

"You've made a friend," the young man said.

"You like puppies?"

The lad chuckled. "This'un ain't been a puppy for years now, got pups an' gran'pups of his own."

"No fooling? I wouldn't have guessed, to look at him. He seems as young as you."

"You're funnin' me."

"No, really."

Elora set down her jug and folded herself at the hips and knees until she was sitting on her heels, still braced against the pillar, her head on the same level as the hound's, who proceeded to give her a thorough sniffing. For a moment she felt a surge of panic at the thought the hound might move from sniffs to licks and thereby make a mess of her disguise, but a good look into the dog's eyes instantly calmed those fears. He and his kind meant her no harm. Quite the opposite, in fact.

He knows who I am, she thought in amazement.

"Given his bloodline, Elora Danan, hardly a surprise." Rool's voice, mindspeaking inside her head, and Elora flushed hot to realize how carelessly she'd broadcast her thoughts to give him so strong an awareness of what she was seeing. "These wolfhounds," the brownie continued, "have been bred to sense the difference between good and evil, light and shadow."

"Rool, in his heart—!" She struggled a moment to put words to the absolute and unwavering faith she found there. "He'll defend me to the death!"

"As would Drumheller," the brownie replied, "as would Ryn, as would I."

"Rool," she said, unaware that she was speaking aloud, "I can hear it in your voice. What's wrong?"

Sensing her sudden surge of distress, the hound whined and gave her a nudge with his muzzle.

"Anything the matter?" the lad asked, hunkering down himself and not convinced in the slightest by the emphatic shake of her head. "Thought I heard'ja say

197

somethin'. Too blessed loud in here for anybody to make sense with less than a shout. Come on," he told Elora in a take-charge tone he hoped would brook no back talk, "you've the look of someone needin' fresh air."

She acquiesced until she'd risen once more to her feet, then made her apologies.

"You're right on both counts," she told him, "the noise and the need for a break."

"So stuff 'em," she was told conspiratorially. "Stuff *him,* too, while yer at it. Everyone deserves a moment to play hooky, this'n's yours."

"Right now I can't. I'm really sorry." That was where she meant to end it but her body acted of its own accord, the line popping free before she even realized she was speaking. "Some other time, maybe?" She swallowed hard, not sure which of the possible answers was making her the more nervous.

"I'd like that," he said. "Soon, yah?"

The grin she answered with popped every bubble in his head about her being older, for it was as youthful and conspiratorial as his own.

It stayed with her out onto the porch and beyond to the broad expanse of the parade ground. She cast about for some sign of the brownie, was about to call with mindspeech, when Bastian reached out to her instead. The eagle stood atop the apex of one of the blockhouse watchtowers, which gave him a commanding view of the entire yard. InSight did the same for Elora through his eyes, and since he already knew where to look, that single glance was all she needed to guide her to her friends.

Ryn had been locked inside a corner of the horse barn reserved for wild mounts who hadn't yet been broken to the saddle. The timbers were as stout as any in the fort and Elora doubted even an ogre's punch could easily break them. Moreover, massive ringbolts had been mounted on the walls and floor, the prisoner shackled so comprehensively he couldn't do more than stir. The weight of the metal alone that bound him was probably greater than his own. There was no provision for hygiene either, beyond rushes strewn haphazardly over the floor, and Elora's nose wrinkled in acknowledgment of the smell.

All this she saw through Rool's eyes. There was a pair of guards at the entrance to the stable and all the windows had been latched shut.

"Ryn," she called softly with mindspeech.

There was no reply as a small form dropped lithely from a chink in one of the wall seams.

"It's no use, Elora," Rool said with a disconcerting edge of bleakness to his utterly professional tone and manner. "A wasted effort."

"What are you talking about?" she demanded in a whisper. "He hasn't answered me," she realized. "Surely he heard—!"

"No doubt."

She fingered his long canvas duster, a fresh double line of parallel slashes that opened one whole side of it along Rool's flank.

"I got too close," he said in answer to her unspoken query. "I approached him like a friend. My mistake."

"He attacked you?" She didn't bother trying to hide her incredulity.

"He was hungry, I was meat. He was bound, I was free. Who knows? So used to seeing him play slybones all the while, you forget how fast Wyrrn can really move when there's need. Happily"—a ghost of a smile that lacked the smallest scrap of humor—"brownies can move even faster."

"I don't believe this."

He nodded. He'd expected this response.

"Ride with me back inside, then," he said, meaning that she should use her InSight to bond her thoughts and spirit temporarily with his, a more complete merger than she normally utilized when she just wanted a peek through another's senses. "But what you find won't be pretty. Bastian," he continued in the same matter-of-fact tone, trusting the eagle to hear him, "watch over her body while she's spirit-strolling."

"Always," was the reply. "And I won't be alone in that regard."

Both girl and brownie looked over their shoulder as the wolfhound dropped heavily to his belly. His dark coat was ideal camouflage for the heavily shadowed alley, only the glint of his eyes gave him away.

"I must be getting old," Rool muttered disgustedly, "to be so lackwit as not to notice something big as that sneaking up on me."

"Maybe it's because he meant us no harm?"

"Fine. What's Faralorn's excuse?"

"Duguay?"

"Back at that tower, Elora, I had spirit-scents from the goblin, the two elves, the ogres. I marked the carrion smell of all the leavings piled in the ground floor. Nothing more. Nothing since, where Duguay's concerned."

"You telling me he's not real, Rool? I helped the man heal himself. Trust me, he's as real as any of us."

"Oh aye, girl, I can see him, hear him, touch him. On every tangible level, he exists. But go a step beyond and there's nothing but fog. The only spirit-scent I read off him is a residue of yours, from that healing."

"Are you saying he has some magic?"

"I don't know what he's got, or even what he *is*! I've never seen the like of him before."

"Why haven't you said any of this before now?"

"There's a saying: Keep your friends close, your enemies closer. You weren't about to abandon him, I wanted to learn what he had in mind."

"He's done nothing but help, Rool."

"To serve whose purposes, Elora Danan?"

"I don't care right now. And I don't want to talk about it anymore. It's Ryn who needs us."

She was really angry, which wasn't the ideal state of being in which to use her InSight in this manner. It made for a rough ride, and unfortunately the person she bonded with was the one who bore the brunt of the grief. In Rool's case, the net result was a moderate to awful head-ache.

She pressed on regardless, reaching out to Ryn with her thoughts the moment the Wyr came into view. Her heart leaped to see him and the sight only made her rage all the more. He was manacled in a sitting position, on the floor, arms and legs outstretched, shackled seemingly at every major joint: wrists and ankles, elbows and knees, plus waist and throat. A spiked skullcage enclosed his entire head, locking his jaw closed tight on a thick gag.

"They haven't seen to his wounds, Rool," she said with mindspeech. "One's close to festering."

"I can smell the rot, Elora. Can you work from here? I'll go no closer."

"What happened before? How'd you get into trouble?"

The brownie sounded chagrined. The fault was his. "They didn't bind his fingers."

"His claws . . ." she began.

"Are very sharp," he finished.

"I'll fix the damage."

"You can sew?"

"Heavens forfend, no! I'll simply sing the appropriate song of shaping and remind the threads of how they used to lie together. The little darlings will do all the work for me."

It was a splendid deadpan delivery and he fell for it like a brick.

"You can't do that!" he accused after due consideration.

"Of course I'll sew it," she chortled, delighted to get a bit of her own back against the brownies. "I learned a lot of useful skills in Torquil's household."

"Proper marvel you are, that's obvious."

"Hey, what can I tell ya, being the Sacred Princess isn't what it used to be."

This was a tiny interlude of repartee but absolutely necessary for Elora. There was no way she should attempt a healing with her spirit wrapped tight in skeins of violent, negative energy. To reach out in anger might well make the wounds worse and, by example, flashfire the infection she had sensed into full-blown gangrene.

As with Duguay, the first requirement was to assume a measure of control over the active life processes, most notably pulse and respiration. The difficulty here was that she was manipulating two physical bodies while her spirit was apart from both of them. If something went wrong, the first set of reserves she'd have to draw on would not be her own but Rool's, since she was sharing his body. Worse, since the energies she wielded were those of primal fire, any kind of uncontrolled surge would consume him utterly.

He knew that full well but didn't raise the point. His trust was absolute, as was her determination never to betray it.

There was no resistance from Ryn to her incursion but she pulled back from him regardless, as if that merest touch was poison.

"What?" Rool asked her, sensing shock and distress and a horrified grief.

"It's not Ryn," she said, aghast.

"A changeling. Some double, you mean?"

"No, no, nothing like that. It *is* Ryn, yet it's not. Rool, it's a spell. He's been cursed."

"Ah. A very good one, it must be, for me not to notice."

"I spotted it just as I began to merge with him, like a spiderweb beneath the skin. I'll have to be really careful here, Rool, I can't finish the healing all at once."

"Should you try at all? You might be trapped yourself."

"It doesn't feel powerful enough to hold me, but damaging the pattern might have an effect on Ryn. There's a total absence of spirit, or *self*. What's held here is the shell of him, able only to function in its most bestial state. It has nothing to do with being a Wyr, I don't believe even the most crazed of them would act so. His humanity's been stolen, and replaced by this brute."

"Very sly."

"You talk like you admire what's been done!"

"Abomination this may be, Elora, but an exercise in supreme cunning nonetheless. You have the essence of the man all for your own and at the same time prevent him from resisting you in any meaningful way. He can't turn to friends for help, or explain what's happened, and he's so dangerous he has to be locked away lest he slaughter those who wish to save him. Should the body somehow escape, as Ryn obviously has, he won't be that hard to find."

"Rool"—her voice was rough with dismay as she fought back tears—"I don't know from spells. I can, I can help his body heal itself, but that spiderweb inside him, that was grafted on by someone else. It isn't natural. I'd have a better shot manipulating the iron of those chains."

"Help him as you can, Highness. Then let's get out of here."

She worked on only one wound, and that only to erase the infection. It was a long way from healed but it was all she wanted to try until she had a better idea of the limitations imposed on her by the spell that held Ryn.

The yard was silent as she slipped free of Rool's body and returned to her own. Torches burned along the parapet and at intervals throughout the yard, but almost none of the windows visible were illuminated. The scene possessed the eldritch stillness of deep night.

"How late is it, I wonder?" she asked rhetorically as she took a wary look about.

"Late enough for all good souls to be in bed. We shouldn't tarry."

"You're not going to." The forcefulness in her tone made the brownie look sharply up at her.

"I'm of no use to Ryn," she said, "neither are you. There's only one person who can help him."

"Out of the question."

"Don't be obstinate, Rool, you know I'm right."

"Observation and conclusion, top-notch. Where this is leading, madness."

"Someone has to tell Thorn."

"Bastian can go, I'll stay with you."

"That won't work. Because we were merged, you saw what I saw, Rool. Firsthand observations are critical, especially since you can explain it a whole lot better than Bastian can. You're both of the Circle of the Flesh, that's true, but Bastian's wholly of the world; he's bound to the Realm of the Daikini. Rool, you're of the Veil, you have a comprehension of magic, an insight and understanding, that he doesn't. No offense, Bastian," she added hurriedly with a mindcall to the eagle, fearing she might have hurt his feelings with her blunt assessment.

"None taken. And she's right."

"I won't leave you alone," the brownie insisted stubbornly.

She smiled. "I have my wits. And as we've discovered tonight, I have my puppy."

Obligingly, the wolfhound *whoulfed* at them from where he lay.

"Perhaps that's why he made himself known to me," she went on, "because he sensed a moment like this was at hand."

"It's too dangerous, Elora. There's that Maizan price on your head, and who knows what repercussions from what happened at that village." He left the line unfinished but Elora had no doubts as to the conclusion of his thoughts: *and no matter how much you try to take his part I'll not trust that dandy troubadour!*

"I'll be careful, Rool," she told him, "I'll be fine," and then administered the coup de grâce. "Unless you have a better idea."

He paced, he fumed, he worried a thumb knuckle, he would have ranted, but none of them wanted to draw the attention of the nightwatch sentries.

"Please don't be foolish," he implored at last, as his concession of her victory.

"Sooner you're gone, the sooner you're back. We'll be waiting."

With a rare formality, he took one of her fingers in his hand and bent at the waist in a proper court bow to kiss it. She took him in her palm and with the same regal gravity lifted him to her lips to bestow a kiss on his head where he'd been wounded weeks ago. She rose to her feet, placing Rool on her left shoulder, lifting the arm in invitation to the eagle.

Silent as any wraith, Bastian swooped out of the night, wings and body curving to embrace the air even as his claws did the same to Elora's outheld arm. Any sane falconer would be wrapped thick in protective garb from shoulder to gauntleted wrist, yet Bastian's touch was so considerate, his balance so exquisite, that the dagger points of his talons made hardly an indentation in the fine cloth of her blouse. He partially extended his nearside wing to form a ramp for Rool, who obligingly scampered to his perch straddling the eagle's shoulders. Elora gave Bastian a gentle stroke along the feathers of his broad breast.

"Fly fast," she told him. "Stay safe."

"No less," he replied, "than you."

A powerful thrust of the legs propelled him from her shoulder. The moment he was clear, his wings pumped the air to gain him altitude by brute muscle power alone.

As the eagle swept across the yard Rool let out a banshee screech that turned heads and set dogs to barking throughout the stronghold, leaving Elora understandably impressed that such a wee bit of a creature could utter so caterwauling a noise.

And then she was alone. Until a weight pressed against her hip and her hand quite naturally cupped the hound's massive head.

Duguay made no comment as she slipped gingerly over the threshold and hunkered down into the space he'd left her on their pallet. She'd stripped herself to pants and shirt in the washroom, divesting herself of everything that might make noise enough to wake him. She could see by her reflection in what passed there for a mirror that the body paint had survived the night remarkably intact, but even so, the twenty-odd strides to their room were the longest and most harrowing she could recall. She wedged herself into a corner and tucked her greatcloak snug about her until she was completely covered save for her head. She slept where she sat, as in a chair.

Paid for it, too, come the morning, with a grimace or a groan for every attempt to shift position. She knew he'd been awake when she returned and was grateful for his pretense, her estimation of him rising another notch when he said nothing about the absence of either Rool or Bastian. She was used, sadly, to being feared, for that was but a short step removed from the veneration accorded her in Angwyn as the Sacred Princess. It was a far different feeling to find herself, even now, respected. She still wasn't sure she deserved it but found herself thankful just the same.

The troubadour had news, revealed after a hearty breakfast as Elora found herself led to a different floor of the hostelry and a much nicer room. Evidently Duguay's performance had so impressed the innkeeper that, in return for a guarantee of a week's run, minimum, she had upgraded them to a chamber with a door, together with space to move around in, a window overlooking the parade ground, and an actual bed.

By night, the pair of them worked from first seating to last, Duguay entertaining, Elora serving meals. She didn't explain where she went for an hour or so afterward, nor did he pry, except to offer a sympathetic eye at the hollows on her features and the tension strung through her body when she returned. It wasn't a huge bed, though a comfortable enough fit for two. The problem for Elora was that she'd never really shared one before. She of course had no siblings, and because of her status had never even shared one with a maid. She didn't know what to expect of him or of herself and the first night she resolved the problem by curling up on the floor.

That day, Duguay took some of their earnings and presented her with a nightgown. Soft flannel, because the weather was showing far more signs of fall than summer, long-sleeved and floor length with an arrangement of delicate floral embroidery about the bodice. His generosity had limits, however. He would share the bed but not give it up.

The solution, since she didn't much like the floor either, was to divide the bedding and the mattress equally, each of them rolling in a set of separate blankets as though they were separate sleeping bags. They might well touch as they moved about during the night, but only through a major thickness of cloth. This was a source of considerable amusement to Duguay, and of perplexed self-consciousness to Elora. She enjoyed his company when they were awake, and his proximity when they weren't. She felt safe and secure to have him in reach, all Rool's concerns notwithstanding. She acknowledged them but did not share them and as time passed saw less and less reason to give them any weight.

Her days quickly proved far from free, for Duguay took her role as his apprentice quite seriously. They didn't work anywhere within the fort, she was far too shy for that, but each morning he would lead her along the river to find a stand of rocks or a clearing within a grove of standing trees. He started her with scales to warm up her voice, and exercises to unlimber her body, and then push both to their limits.

For all her initial protestations, Elora discovered that she had a voice, and a surprisingly good one. It lacked the purity of classic sopranos, she was no match for the soloists among the stronghold choir and probably not for any of the chorus, either. Those weren't the kind of songs she sang, anyway. Hers was a bar voice, meant for smoky rooms where the competition was wine and conversation and the occasional thump of knuckles on nose, and the counterpoint to a good line of verse was the crash of pewter dinnerware, or worse, china, hitting the floor. She had a fairly broad range for someone without training, and she hit her notes the way a master swordsman crosses blades, sharp and clear and with an edge that cuts. Better yet, she had the endurance to sustain those notes and the diaphragm strength to make them heard.

It was her passion, though, that had the power to make her memorable. Duguay found within her the talent to present a love song with the innocence of someone who'd never even been kissed, for whom the whole of life was nothing but possibilities and dreams. Or lament a loss so piercing she'd surely wrest tears from hardened campaigners. By lesson, and example in the evenings when he took the stage, Duguay taught her to gauge the mood of her audience and pitch her performance accordingly, sedate one moment, roguish the next, drawing heat from them or striking out at them with her own, as if it was a weapon.

At the same time he made improvements to the design of her makeup, offered suggestions for her costuming, switching conversational subjects from one line to the next, as though they all ran along parallel tracks, allowing him to jump randomly from one to another and back again.

"Do you really believe this works?" she asked him.

"I didn't hear any shouts of discovery last night, or the night before, or during either day."

"That's because everyone was looking at you."

"I rest my case. As my apprentice, you have a place and an identity. Your function is to draw attention to yourself, because that draws attention to me, and *that* is how we bards earn our living. But when people look at you, they see what they expect to see, a troubadour in training, not that far removed—in the eyes of so-called quality folk—from the village tart. They can't be bothered to look past the prejudice to see the fugitive beneath, especially if that fugitive is supposed to be some kind of royalty. They resolve the conundrum according to their bias: royalty dresses a certain way, acts a certain way, you neither dress nor act like royalty, therefore you cannot be royalty. Therefore, ultimately, you cannot be the personage everyone's looking for. By contrast, a girl traveling alone, folks might wonder why. Wondering why, they'll wonder who you are, where you hail from, what you're doing here. Wondering who and where and what, they'll pick at any disguise until they know."

"You're as twisted a trickster as a brownie."

"I trust that's a compliment. A touch more kohl for the eyes, I daresay, to seat them deeper in the sockets, hmnh yes, and enhance your general air of exotica and mystery."

"Will this ever come off?" she wondered with a dollop of concern.

"Undoubtedly, and at the most inconvenient moment."

"Oh joy."

"First law of the universe, everybody knows that— Whatever can go wrong, will. Or is it, I'm making this up as I go along? Hoy, Elora, stop giggling there, you wretched creature, these lines have to run straight." Then, a while later: "How's your friend?"

She knew whom he meant. "Better," she said. "Looks worse than ever but I've done what I could for his wounds."

"Obviously, from your tone and expression, there's more to it."

"Someone did this to him, Duguay."

"That's the way of sorcery, 'lora. There always has to be a victim."

"Every spell has its counter!"

"That's the hope. But does every poison have an antidote, every sickness a cure?"

"You sound like all the people in the fort."

"All? In what way?"

"They're giving up. A lot of them have *given* up. It's like they're dead, only none of them knows it yet."

"So do something about it!"

"I'd love to! If I only had the power and the knowledge I could cage the Maizan before they could conquer another city, and make the Great Realms behave. There was a Demon Queen once named Bavmorda. . . ."

"I've heard songs about her."

"I'll just bet. She was as evil as could be but there are times I'd love nothing more than to wave my arms like her and cry the proper arrangement of syllables, and presto, turn a whole invading army into pigs."

"And that would make things right, you figure?"

"It's a place to start, isn't it? At least it'd bring some order and peace to people's lives."

"Is that what they want?"

"Why wouldn't they? Why wouldn't anyone?"

"Blessed if I know, Elora. Why not find out for yourself? That's what a bard does mostly—listen, to the ebb and flow of conversation, who's doing what to whom and why, where folk come from, what they dream of, what they fear. Stir it all together, offer it back to them in songs to make them laugh or cry or think, but always to feel. I mean, it's all very well to be a legend"—she shot him a sharp and piercing glance from under lowered lids—"but who do you think spreads the word?"

His face moved close to hers, his breath warm across her cheek. Somehow, though, the touch of it on her skin made her shiver as a chill breeze never did.

"Tonight, I think," he mused, "we'll go a bit bloody."

He was talking about lip paint and nail polish and quickly mixed a color that was both darker and more red than burgundy wine. The application made her mouth stand out dramatically, even against the backdrop of her painted face, and he used a variation on the shade to accent her eyes.

"I can do this," she told him as he expertly drew a brush across her nails.

"It's my pleasure," was his offhand reply.

Mine, too. The thought popped unbidden into her head.

Her hand lay on his thigh, just above the knee, the two of them sharing a seat on a flat-topped slab of a boulder overlooking the river. There weren't many trees along this stretch of bank, the ground cover was a mixture of grass and wildflowers. He finished her last finger—*making a better job of it,* she conceded easily to herself, *than I possibly could*—but otherwise made no move. Toward her or away. His gaze had to be intense, though every other aspect of his body was casual and relaxed, but Elora couldn't bring herself to lift her eyes to his for confirmation.

He extended a pair of fingers and lightly stroked the tendons of her hand as if they were guitar strings.

She started to say "please," but couldn't decide what was to come next: "stop" or "more." That was when the dog coughed.

The wolfhound sat at a discreet remove, tongue lolling as direct sunlight warmed his sable coat. He was the picture of innocence and as effective a mood breaker as any chaperon.

"How does anything that big"—Duguay marveled—"approach so silently?"

He patted her hand, a more companionable gesture, and proceeded to pack away his pots and potions. "I must say, Elora," he told her, "you make the most damnably infernal friends."

"Being one, Master Faralorn"—she laughed—"you should know."

Where the hound roamed, Luc-Jon wasn't far behind. Or perhaps it was that he knew the hound would invariably lead him to Elora. Either way, she didn't mind as the young man rambled over to where she sat, Duguay having returned to the fort to prepare for this evening's performance.

The sky was supernally clear, with a crispness to the air that held more than a promise of winter, though by the calendar it wasn't yet autumn. Luc-Jon pulled his collar tight and made to gather Elora close, to share some of that warmth. He was tactful enough not to press the point when she didn't take his hint.

"Cold?" he inquired.

"Is it?" she queried back. "I hadn't noticed."

"Dressed like that, I figured you'd be the first."

She dropped her eyes and felt her cheeks grow warm. He left her in peace again and occupied himself by tossing a stick for the hound to fetch. The dog hardly seemed to make an effort, yet not a single time in a half-score tries did that stick touch the ground once it had been thrown. The hound would mark its line of flight and be there to catch it, eating up the distance between with a stride that would put a horse to shame.

"Bears move like that'cha know," said Luc-Jon.

"How do you mean?"

"Ya sees 'em," Luc-Jon explained, "they look like these big, plush, stuffy toys, all fat an' lazy like. They see something they want, summat that angers 'em like, they get really rollin', boy you better watch out. They'll be on you quick as lightning."

He tried to fake a toss, but the hound merely gave him a look of such patience and contempt that Luc-Jon didn't even try the bluff he'd prepared but heaved the piece of wood as far as he could.

"Do you work with dogs?" Elora asked him.

"Na, jus' like 'em is all. I'm an apprentice."

"Me, too."

"So, you'll sing an' play someday, like hisself in there?"

She shrugged and shifted the subject back to him. "What about you?"

"Scribe, that's me."

"You're not!"

"What, I look that much a thickwit?"

"I'm sorry, I didn't mean to be rude." She flushed, she stammered, she lost all pretense of mystery and found herself once more acting her age. "It's just, I thought, I mean, I am, I am *so* sorry."

"Not to worry," he told her, enjoying her discomfiture even as he tried his best to ease it. "Ain't the first to react that way, given the way I talk. I know the woods—can't grow up here'bouts without learnin' that—know animals. I can ride fair an' I'm decent with bow and blade; I can stand my place with the militia. But the best at what I do is letters. A sure an' elegant hand, my master says."

"I'm impressed."

"First one in my whole house, I am, can read an' write. First one as far back as any can remember in my family. Problem is, the knack I got with words on paper, it don't carry over as easy to speech."

"What do you write?"

They were strolling with apparent aimlessness toward the compound, the wolfhound pacing behind them. Luc-Jon took her hand in his for a bit, she didn't mind, but he let her loose in short order because he used his hands when he spoke, weaving his pictures like a born storyteller with gestures as well as words.

"Letters, o' course. I read 'em also, them what arrive in the post. Contracts an' the like, though the master's seal has to go on all formal documents, to make 'em all proper an' legal. An' it's fun sometimes, t' take the stories I hear an' put 'em down in ink."

He paused, but clearly there was more to tell, so Elora prompted him with her expression. He looked endearingly shy.

"I change 'em when I do. A little."

"In what way?"

"T' add some spice, maybe make the characters a little more like local folk might recognize but also mix in some of what I've heard an' read 'bout folks from other lands. Sort of what the world might be if it was all mine to make over. I mean"—another pause as he searched around him for inspiration—"this is home an' all, an' it's a place of wonder for those with wit to truly look, but it's still wood an' hill an' meadow an' stream, as it's been my whole life. The same old, same old. My dreams, they're full of all these places I've never seen. If I can make 'em real in my words, it's as good as goin'."

"Why not go for real? You've a craft that'll serve you as well downriver as here."

"Once I'm certified, aye, then I'll have my craft."

"But . . . ? I hear a *but*."

"This is home. An' I'd hate ta find out my dreams was better. I got time yet, though. Maybe I'll stay. Maybe

213

I won't." Then, abruptly: "Y'know, Elora, my master, he owns *books*!"

"Oh."

"*Lots* of books."

"Ah."

In her tower in Angwyn, there'd been a room of no mean size shelved floor to very high ceiling with books, the knowledge of the ages she was often told, donated for the education of the Sacred Princess. But while she'd been taught to read, the library was denied her. Like Elora herself, in the eyes of the Angwyn King, it was solely for show.

Which turned out to be a mistake, because she was stubborn as well as willful and she refused to be locked out of anywhere. The more she was forbidden something, the more she rose to the challenge of achieving it, especially when she had to outwit Vizards and servants galore in the process. It was an arduous task she set herself, and not always successful. More than once, she was ready to chuck the whole project, deciding the reward in no way compensated for the aggravation. What ultimately decided her was the anticipation of knowing things her minders did not, though she had no notion at that point of how she'd turn that learning to her advantage.

She'd barely scratched the surface of the library before she had to flee Angwyn. She hadn't pushed herself before then, she thought she'd have a whole lifetime to explore.

Luc-Jon's master was working in his scriptorium, at a partner's desk he shared with his apprentice, so large that it nearly filled the entire room. The two sat facing each other across a tabletop angled to form a comfortable work surface. The entire ceiling was a skylight, as was the wall that faced the scribe's garden, to take full advantage of the day. The walls behind each man were broken floor to ceiling into cubbyholes of various dimensions, some squares, others rectangles that were wider than they were high, filled with raw materials, tools of their craft, works in progress, pending commissions, and anything else that might prove useful. There was a hearth in a corner, tightly grated to prevent the escape of any sparks.

So as not to disturb him, Elora and Luc-Jon slipped barefoot past him into the library, a room of similar size and design set right next door. The shelves here were rough-hewn, in keeping with the basic nature of the fort itself, the collection eclectic, again what you'd expect from someone who made his acquisitions while traveling. There were parchment rolls tied into tubes, flat sheets of the same pressed between tablets, more modern bound books inscribed by hand, plus some of the latest titles to come upriver from Sandeni that had been printed by machine.

A glance over the study told Elora that the master's focus was more on decorative illuminations. He left the actual calligraphy to Luc-Jon. None of the titles meant anything to her. They were in a half-dozen languages, some of which she could barely understand when spoken and had no hope of reading. Sadly, in that regard, Luc-Jon wasn't much help, for many of these languages were a mystery to him, too. Some were so ancient, from lands so distant, he had no idea of the cultures they represented.

"This is Hansha," she cried delightedly as she flipped open a volume that was almost as big as she was.

"Wha'chy'say?"

"The language. I know this! It's a variant of the Chengwei main tongue, from the islands off their coast."

"You can understand this?"

"I wish. I have a smattering of speech, and I can puzzle out some of the meanings of their written words, but no one'll ever mistake me for a native."

"So what's this, then?"

"An abstract of some kind. Census, maybe, tallying populace, possessions, moneys earned, moneys spent."

"Not very exciting."

"Life rarely is, if you're lucky."

"I thought bards lived for adventure."

She laughed outright. "It's the lively bits get told

around hearth fires, my sweetling. Nobody's much interested in the days and days and *days* it takes the heroes to get wherever they're going."

Elora slipped her left hand along the edges of the shelves, occasionally touching the spine of a book, the bindings of a manuscript. One she looked at was emblazoned with the figure of a dragon, though it looked nothing like the one she'd actually seen, but the text was a mass of indecipherable glyphs.

"Would your master mind me looking at more of these?" she asked Luc-Jon.

"Can't figure any reason he'd say no," the lad told her, leaning knuckles on the arms of her chair so that he loomed over her. He was looking very intently into her eyes, with hardly anything remaining of his earlier shyness. Apparently, he'd passed that aspect of character right over to her, as Elora's breaths turned quick and shallow and her lips went infernally dry.

He's going to kiss me, she thought with a dispassion she in no way felt.

And then, he did. Very lightly, his lips hardly brushing hers, in a touch that was mostly tease and promise and left her suddenly hungry for more.

She was about to kiss him back when the wolfhound began to growl.

It was a fearsome sound, that instantly stiffened the hackles on her neck and set goose bumps racing across every square inch of Elora's skin. Luc-Jon heard the challenge as well and, from the way his face changed, experienced much the same response.

Without another word, both youngsters fled the room. In the foyer, halfway down the short hallway from the house's double doors, Luc-Jon grabbed a broadsword from the household weapons rack. Two-handed haft, the straight, double-edged blade almost as long as Elora was tall, it was intended for use by footmen against cavalry.

The wolfhound stood on guard, waiting for them on the porch, his own hackles stiff as rumbles continued to rise up from the bottom of his chest. He wasn't alone.

The rest of the stronghold's resident pack were all in view, their eyes fixed on the main gate.

Beneath its arch, and under the watchful eyes of the sentries, rode a troop of horsemen, a light squad of seven warriors. One of the hounds started barking as soldiers of the garrison moved out along the parapet, splitting their attention between the riders inside the walls and the view beyond. Bows were already in hand, every one with an arrow nocked, ready to be drawn and fired.

"Not ours, I'm thinkin'," Luc-Jon said in hardly more than a whisper. "None of our patrols're due back an' nothin's scheduled from downriver neither."

"No," agreed Elora. "They're Maizan."

Chapter
8

THEY SAT ASTRIDE THEIR CHARGERS WITH THE EASY arrogance of a race who believed they were destined to rule the world. Given recent history, fewer and fewer were inclined to argue the point. Big men on big horses, sable on ebony, made all the more imposing by dark armor and horned helms that intentionally hid their features.

There was a stiffness to the squad's leader as he swung his lanky form to the ground that bespoke long, hard days in the saddle, if not weeks. For a race that was fond of boasting they were born on horseback and more at home there than in any hut or palace, it was nice to see their nomadic ways taking their toll.

Elora didn't hear what was said as the Commandant met the squad leader on the porch of the stronghold's central keep, but the stance of their bodies marked it as a formal exchange.

"What d'you think?" she wondered aloud.

"Mos' likely, askin' permission to kip here for the night," Luc-Jon replied, a tad unsure now what to do with his bare blade. " 'Pears they've spent a fair piece on hard an' open ground, prob'ly wouldn't mind a change to soft bedding an' decent grub."

"They can sleep on rocks, for all I care. The more jagged, the better."

"Don't like 'em?"

"There isn't much *to* like."

"First Maizan I've ever seen."

"The way they're spreading across the continent, it's doubtful they'll be the last."

"Hmmph." He paused a little, then tried a joke. "I were expectin' someone taller."

It was an honest effort, so Elora had grace enough to reply in kind.

"That's what they all say."

"You laughed."

"I have a kind and overly generous nature, inclined to take pity on those less fortunate."

"You laughed," he said again, with perfect deadpan.

"You're impossible." This time the laughter was in no way forced.

Across the compound, all the Maizan dismounted, two of their number leading the horses under escort toward the stable while the rest gathered their gear. The Provost Marshal, the garrison's military lawman, and some of his proctors had materialized to gather their weapons. They'd be locked securely away in the armory until the visitors' departure. To all outward show, there was nothing exceptional or untoward about the scene, merely the arrival of some new travelers to the fort.

Elora marked, though, how the wolfhound hadn't relaxed his vigilance in the slightest, and how the rest of the pack took their cue from him. None of the hounds approached the Maizan, they maintained a respectful distance. However, so long as any one of those warriors was in the open, he had a hound for a shadow.

"Well"—Luc-Jon sighed—"that appears to be that, then, blessed be. No more need for this," and he brandished his sword a last time. "I'll just nip back inside and tuck it away. If you'll wait, Elora, I'll walk you home."

"All right." She was glad for the company.

By sunset, the entire community was abuzz with news of the Maizan's arrival.

"Think it through, Elora," Duguay cautioned as he sat on the long porch of the tavern, "what you intend." His guitar rested on his belly and he lazily played with chords as he pushed his leg against one of the roof's support pillars to tilt his chair backward.

"Pardon?"

"They're on horseback, those Maizan. And from all accounts, very good at their craft, am I right? You start trouble, light out of here on foot, or even on a horse of your own, how far d'you think you'll get with them in pursuit? And after, of course, everyone'll know this disguise. One less weapon for your arsenal."

"I'm not that dim, Duguay. I've no intention of raising a ruckus with them. It's Ryn I'm worried about. Suppose he's recognized? Suppose it's him they've come for? What then?"

"I don't know yet. And neither do you. Got to figure, though, doubtful it's coincidence. For a Wyr, he's far from home. See 'em maybe around Sandeni, working the riverboats or having a bit of fun running the cataracts, but the streams here'bouts, they're too shallow. More for naiads than the likes of them."

"So it's like what you said about me traveling alone—simply seeing him is enough to raise a question."

"An' one question almost always leads to another, that's the nature of things. And from there, just as certainly to trouble."

She watched a pair of Maizan stride back from the stables. Everyone in eyeshot stopped to stare, they

220

couldn't seem to help themselves. As well, anyone in their way gave them the widest possible berth.

"They always walk in pairs," she noted.

"Safety in numbers. Always guarantees someone to watch your back. And to talk to." He punctuated the final comment with a decorative riff.

"Why do you think they're here, Duguay?"

"You tell me, apprentice. Consider it today's lesson."

Luc-Jon was booked solid through most of the evening, as the Commandant drafted him to work with his own secretary on a new batch of communiqués to go downriver with the next dispatch rider. Couriers had been sent out within the hour of the Maizan's arrival to alert those Sandeni patrols still in the field. The stronghold itself was advanced to a heightened state of readiness. The leader of the refugee wagon train wasted no time adding to the Commandant's burdens by demanding an immediate escort to the lowlands. He was rejected out of hand. There was no state of war in Sandeni nor any imminent expectation of one, and the level of brigandage, even this far out along the frontier, in no way justified such a diversion of resources. Granting the level of protection they requested would subject the stronghold itself to an unacceptable level of risk. The wagon master asked permission to bring his train within the wall, and that, too, was denied. People and livestock, yes, but not their movables. There simply wasn't room. Voices were quickly raised and words heatedly exchanged but the Commandant's decision remained unchanged.

All this, Elora learned from Sandeni troopers gossiping at the horse trough, from customers in the sutler's store, from strollers in the bazaar outside the gates, from menfolk bellying up to the bar at both the fort's own tavern and a refreshment booth set up outside among the itinerant merchants. In addition to refining her face paint, Duguay had also expanded her wardrobe, providing a loose-fitting gown that brushed her toes when she walked and decorously covered her to the wrists and collarbone. It was slit to the waist along both side seams, exposing the full length of her legs, and was likewise slashed across her shoulders and down her arms as well, held in place solely by clasps at the wrist, elbow, and shoulder. She caught more than her share of scandalized stares as she made her rounds, until the onlookers saw that she wore her silk trousers beneath the gown and realized she'd merely tweaked the nose of propriety, not flouted it. Some appreciated the joke, some condemned her all the more.

As she roamed the grounds she had to concede Duguay's point: she was drawing eyes every which way and hardly a one among them spared her a second glance except perhaps to reinforce what they already saw. She was still nowhere near as relaxed as the other girls she worked with in the dining hall but she'd come a fair piece from the ill-at-ease creature who'd followed Duguay inside that first night, expecting nothing but disaster.

So, when she saw the doors open to the barn where Ryn was imprisoned, it seemed only natural for her to saunter over to see what was up. As she joined the small-ish gathering close by his cage, she decorously draped her gossamer shawl across her forehead and one of its long edges across the bridge of her nose to shroud her features.

A warder had come over from the guardhouse to sluice down both cell and prisoner, that was the occasion for the show. While an assistant enthusiastically applied himself to the levers of a pump, the warder directed a powerful stream of ice-cold river water from the hose in his hands onto the floor and then the prisoner. Ryn writhed in his bonds, making futile attempts to evade the tormenting spray. Unable to give voice to his misery because of the skullcage and its gag, he hammered the iron frame as best he could over and over again into the wall behind him.

Elora didn't know what to do. Part of her wanted to scream, to horsewhip the onlookers back from the stall, to set her friend free. Yet his every response to this situation was a painful reminder that he wasn't the friend she remembered.

Someone pitched a partially munched carrot through the bars, that bounced off Ryn's skullcage. His aim was applauded but the crowd had clearly hoped for more of a reaction.

"Can't'cha poke him wi' your pike there, laddie?" came a call to one of the guards, who hastily demurred, protesting it was worth his stripes and maybe even his posting to manhandle a prisoner so. The rules evidently applied to beasts as much as men.

How civilized, Elora thought, and then, *Bastards!*

A sotto voce chorus of catcalls ensued, offering rude commentary on the guardsmen's antecedents, gender preferences, sexual prowess (or rather, the total lack of same), and anything else duly insulting that came to mind. Elora's time with the brownies had spoiled her for such invective. This wasn't even minor-league material, but it made their targets bristle.

"You mind'jer manners there, lout," one guard told the crowd, brandishing his own pike for good measure, "else *you'll* be the one gettin' poked."

"Sure you know which end's the one to use!"

"Be off wi' ya, the whole lot o' yas!"

They couldn't care less about the guard's threat, but there appeared to be precious little fun to be had in this venue. The crowd began to drift on in search of some other amusement. As they cleared away, Elora stepped close.

"Oi, girl, what'cher?" called the guard who'd warned off the others, now intent on doing the same for her. "Leave the poor creature be now. He's done ya no harm, how's about offerin' the same kindness in return?"

"Precious little kindness in evidence about here that *I* can see," she flared before a thought could stay the words.

"You mind'jer mouth, missy. We'll have no sass nor back talk on *my* watch!"

"What did you do to him?"

"Nothin' we wouldn't do to any other placed in our custody. What's it to you?"

"He looks like he's in pain."

"Well, I ain't about to step in there to see if he's hurtin', an' neither's the sawbones. Be better for him to die anyway, if the claim o' them Maizan holds true."

"What claim?"

"Some paper or other marks that critter as their property."

"The Commandant would honor a Maizan warrant?"

The soldier sighed in a big huff. "Not for me ta say, missy. Ain't for me to make those decisions nor pass judgment on 'em, an' blessings galore for that. Still, they're guests an' the rules o' hospitality apply. Orders are to make nice. An' where's the harm? It's only a beastie, is all, an' we sure as hell ain't doin' wonders for his life."

"He's not a beast," Elora snapped intemperately, "he's a Wyr!"

"Aye," the guardsman agreed, "an' some o' them can't be touched by madness, same as Daikini? Best for all t' keep him penned so, cruel as it may seem. Them sodbusters in that wagon train out beyond the gate, they're already in an uproar about 'im, sure an' certain he's one o' those t' blame for their troubles."

"But he's not!"

"No matter, when a body's out for vengeance. Trust our colonel, missy. He'll deal square an' fair with the Wyr, an' that's no error."

Throughout, Elora had gradually closed the gap between herself and the cage until she was right up against its bars. There was no sense of recognition of her, of her scent or her mindspeech, and she didn't need InSight to show that the spell still held him fast.

"Oh, Ryn," she keened so quietly she hardly expelled breath enough to stir the words past her lips.

Ryn Taksemanyin, she called in mindspeech, casting the summons forth with all her strength as a fisherman would his net, only to see it sink beneath the surface without a trace. Reaching for his thoughts, for any aspect of his spirit, was like making a free dive into the Great Deeps he spoke of so fondly, plunging down and down and down into an icy darkness that never seemed to end.

Her body saved her, reacting before her mind became aware she'd moved, hurling Elora back from the bars even as ravening strands of energy erupted from Ryn's body to where she stood. The guards saw nothing of these, they reacted solely to Elora as she fell, legs scrambling for purchase on the dusty hardpan as she struggled to kick herself out of the reach of the onrushing tendrils. She hit her rump and kept going, heard the delicate fabric of her scarf tear as she flipped through a sideways roll that yanked her legs back under her and put her back on her feet in a combat crouch that left her perfectly balanced for attack or evasion. Most of the runners discorporated the instant they touched the iron bars of the cell. The three that survived to press on after her were speedily dispatched by slashes of the blade she plucked from her traveling pouch. Then, remembering her role and realizing the threat was past, Elora collapsed to her knees, back bowed with hands to her mouth while she let her dagger fall from nerveless fingers and uttered a wail of utter misery. She didn't have to feign a sense of shock, or stark terror, she felt both in full measure. The tendrils had been a deadly surprise.

Her own fault, she knew. A sorcerer formidable enough to capture a soul as cantankerously independent as Ryn's would have set layers of trip wires to protect his handiwork. She'd been right to take care with her healing, but the thought now struck her that she might have inadvertently triggered some other defense.

Could I have set off some kind of beacon, she thought, *that gave away his hiding place to the Maizan?*

Everything happened so quickly that the guardsmen had no chance to react before the danger was past.

"What the hell," the older man cried as he sprang to the fallen girl's side. "What the *hell?*"

"I'm sorry," she gabbled. "It's all right, I'm all right, really I am, no harm done, it was my own silly fault you see for going too close, I'm sorry, I'm so sorry!"

225

"Damn me, Marn," the younger one said to his companion, his pike held at the ready in both nervous hands. "I dint know better, I ain't seen with my own eyes, I'da sworn you was attacked, girl!"

"Well, she weren't, Roke, so give your imagination a rest. But you called it right, lass, for goin' too close. Your fault for bein' so lackwit, ours for givin' you leave. It's a blessing you ain't hurt none."

"Tell that to my backside," she told him with a pout.

Out of nowhere, a pair of hands closed about her shoulders to lift Elora to her feet with breathtaking ease. She knew without a glance, from the feel of his gloves and the texture of his spirit, that it was one of the Maizan.

"You've lost your scarf, lass." His Sandeni was fluent but strangely shaped by his native plains accent. "If you like, it'll be my pleasure to retrieve it."

Somehow, in the confusion, it had ended up inside Ryn's stall.

Looking up at the Maizani, Elora had a flash of insight as to how the Daikini world in general must look to Nelwyns. This warrior was a living, breathing, walking, talking embodiment of *big*, and she felt sympathy for the poor horse that had to carry him. He was smiling, too, but his expression lacked any of the gentleness she'd seen in Marn. He'd seen her, he desired her, he would possess her.

"No," she said flatly, keeping her replies simple so there'd be no misunderstanding. "Thank you."

"Wouldn't allow it anyroad," Marn said, and Elora noted the quiet shift in his own stance as each warrior took the other's measure.

The Maizani raised an eyebrow, as though to say, *And you'll be the one to stop me, old man?*

Roke bristled at the unspoken insult, but Marn didn't react in the slightest, which immediately marked him as the more formidable of the two.

"Take it here," the Maizani said, referring to Ryn, "or on the road, it's of no matter."

"What do you mean?" Elora demanded.

"Ours by claim, ours by right."

"Not if our Commandant says different," snapped Roke.

"We are Maizan," the warrior replied. "Better to be our friends."

He still had his hands around Elora's arms, tight enough to hold her fast though not enough to hurt. He was daring her to struggle to escape or beg for her release. Either would be a victory.

Instead she cocked her hips as she'd seen other young women do when ever so slightly peeved, and assumed an air of such boredom that Marn couldn't repress a snort of raw amusement.

The Maizani knew instantly his ploy had turned against him and that he'd become the butt of someone else's joke. Neither suited him, and like all Maizan he reacted with lightning speed by shifting once more to the attack.

So quickly she had no chance to slip from his grasp, Elora was spun 'round to face the man and then lifted off her feet. His lips closed on hers. There was no comparison between her kiss with Luc-Jon and this. That was invitation and entreaty on both their parts, where this was outright invasion.

She didn't resist, she didn't respond, and when the Maizani held her away from his face, the self-satisfied smirk on his features was greeted by an expression even more bored than before.

"You mock me, girl?"

She shrugged her shoulders. "Why bother, when you do such a superb job of it yourself?"

"Diseased dog whore," he snapped at her in Maizan, unaware she knew perfectly well what was being said. The two Sandeni troopers didn't understand the words but the tone was plain. It was Marn who stepped forward, while Roke stood watchfully to the side, bringing his pike down to guard position.

"I think enough has been said and done this day," Marn said companionably. "Set the lady down, if you please, an' be on about your business."

"And if my business is with this piece of excrement?"

"Not within these walls, not the way you mean. You're guests of the Republic of Sandeni. Don't abuse our hospitality." With each phrase, there was less "companion" to Marn's speech and much more steel. The Maizani's eyes flicked arrogantly from him to Roke, balancing present pleasure against future pain, gauging the amount of damage he could inflict on the two troopers versus the punishment meted out to him afterward. Then Elora heard the faint creak of gut and yew that marked a longbow being drawn to full extension. The Maizani's eyes moved upward to the hayloft and the archers who'd quietly taken their positions. Though he'd yielded his weapons to the garrison Provost Marshal, the Maizani wore heavy mail beneath his leather tunic. No matter, the bowmen's shafts were tipped with points designed to punch right through, and they had skill enough to place them wherever they pleased.

The Maizani set her down.

"No harm done," he said, thick with mockery, daring them to fire.

By sundown, it was the talk of the fort. Eyes shifted Elora's direction, and whispers followed, everywhere she went—and no longer because of the way she looked. With each retelling, even over the course of a single day, the confrontation grew more extreme and her response more devastating. It was as though the entire complement of the fort, military and civilian, soldiers and dependents, had been waiting for the merest excuse to put the Maizan in their place. Elora was the catalyst to ignite all that pent-up animosity.

There were no demonstrations of hostility, collective or singular, no one was that stupid. Or suicidal.

There was simply . . .

. . . laughter.

This patrol represented the nation who'd conquered half the continent, whose proclaimed goal was to bring the whole of the world beneath their feet, yet they couldn't quell the spirit of a single, solitary slip of a girl. The aura of invincibility they used to armor themselves had taken a nice dent, and each chuckle from then on marred it that much more.

They sat alone at dinner, with an entire table to themselves.

Elora worked the far end of the room that night, keeping close by the Commandant's table, partly to steer well clear of the Maizan and thereby avoid the possibility of another incident, but mainly because she wanted more than gossip from the evening. She guessed rightly that the garrison's officers would be focusing on their guests and that the conversational "shop talk" would involve not simply the tactical aspects of fighting those legendary warriors but the strategic ramifications of the Maizan's eastward expansion running up against Sandeni's borders.

"Stairs of Heaven to the south," a captain said, referring to the monster mountain range that split the continent just above the equator, one spur forming the secondary range where the Rock Nelwyns made their home, "Ice Lands to the north, an ocean behind 'em, our Wall in front. They're boxed, same as that creature outside they've such a hankering for. They might as well get used to it."

The Commandant wasn't convinced, Elora saw it in his eyes, sensed those doubts skibbling across the surface of his thoughts. He kept them to himself, however, he was here to listen to others' counsel.

"You think?" queried another troop commander, likewise a captain. She recognized him from her first night here, returning from his patrol. His name was Sam.

"Fact of nature, Sam my dear friend, the way the land lies. They're reaching the natural limits of their ambition. I mean, they already rule near half the continent, how much more do they want?"

"Forgive me, Captain," came an interjection from the Commandant's left, "I'm just a plain, old, country doctor. . . ."

The self-deprecating introduction was greeted with snorts and chuckles and pro forma protests. The physician may have gotten his age right but he was in no way plain and the respect accorded him by the others was very real, as glasses of wine were raised to him here and there in salute.

". . . but it's my experience that some ambitions have no limit. Neither does human ingenuity. Why are you so sure of our security?"

"The Wall, of course."

"Yes?"

"Doctor, half the continent's two thousand feet higher than the other, demarked by a sheer cliff that runs from these mountains north to the sea."

"Actually, Captain, it slopes. Travel far enough, there isn't any sort of cliff at all to bar your way."

"No, Doctor," the other man countered with a laugh, "merely some of the most raw and unwholesome terrain ever created, land that must have been cursed the day it was formed. I did my first tour of duty in those Ice Land territories. Believe me, if the mud and flies don't finish you in what passes there for summer, the ice and cold of those endless winter nights will for certes."

"Smugglers manage."

"A band of outlaws is hardly an army. I mean, if this Castellan were to cut a deal with some of the Veil Folk or other, then we'd have a different story. But to all accounts he's death to them. And magic besides."

Here, the discussion turned along lines she'd heard before, as some spoke for the ways things had always been and others about what might be coming. Again, there was a sense of loss, for magic added an element of spice and wonder to the world, a spectrum of colors and possibilities that enriched both the eye and the imagination. At the same time she heard an undercurrent of eagerness, a hankering for an age when the Daikini could reign supreme and gather the future of the globe wholly into their own arms.

"You see," the Commandant spoke at last, with a

smile that was mainly sadness, "there is no limit to ambition. You dream of a day when Daikini might reign supreme over the world, the Maizan of one where they reign over the Daikini. Different perspective, same goal. Yet what of the cost, to our spirits as much as anything, if all the Gates between ourselves and the Veil Folk are sealed shut forever? Do any of you wonder *why* this is happening? We accept the *what,* that the Maizan are doing *something,* without a clue as to their reasons?"

"It suits our interests," the Doctor noted idly. "As a species, as one of the Great Realms, we chafe under the restrictions imposed on our lives by the Veil Folk. Of all the absurd things, asking permission of dryads before logging a single tree, much less a forest, or of naiads before building a dam. It's a wonder *anything's* gotten done these past eons."

A lieutenant spoke up. "Forgive me, sir, but would you go into a neighbor's house and take their possessions without permission—cook a meal in their kitchen, serve it on their china? It's not our world alone; others were here before us. We owe the courtesy, the *respect,* of sharing that we'd expect for ourselves."

"Bravo, Lieutenant. From out of the mouths of babes. We are not alone, gentlemen. We of the Twelve Great Realms have lived in various measures of comfort and relative harmony for the whole of recorded history. Being creatures wholly of the world, we do not understand the Veil, much less those races and Realms that lie beyond it. There are some who presume we fear what we do not understand and there's something to be said for that. Worse, though, to my eyes, is that we have no regard for it. We log that tree I spoke of without a thought for the dryad who perishes with it. We plow the land with no concern for the fairy nests or brownie burrows we ravage in the process. We create reservoirs that doom naiads who must live in the active, running water of streams and rivers.

"And moreover—to borrow your analogy, young Lieutenant—because that neighbor's house is so much

grander than ours, because the covenants on the land—
that have existed for far longer than we—prevent us from
building ours to equal or surpass it, we content ourselves
to turn a blind eye to an assault on its foundation. If it is
diminished, we profit. If it is destroyed outright, we
profit. Secure in the certainty that whatever happens to
our neighbor, *we* remain unassailable."

"Which is," the Commandant continued for him, "utter rot. Of course"—and he fixed his gaze on the visiting
patrol across the hall before returning it to the captain
who'd spoken first—"Sandeni can be taken. It's a fixed
position. *Any* fixed position can be taken, given sufficient
resources."

"As you proved, Mikal," the Doctor told him, but the
Commandant waved off his proffered hand, choosing instead to refill his glass to the brim.

"And I might point out, gentlemen," the Commandant finished, "that whatever happens to our capital, *we*
have no wall to stand as our bulwark, save those we've
built ourselves."

"Perhaps, sir," hazarded another lieutenant, in hopes
of lightening the mood, "the Sacred Princess Elora Danan
will save the day for us all?"

That jape occasioned its apportioned share of laughter, but again Elora sensed the rising heat haze of despair,
a foul coloration to the mood that made every attempt at
humor sound forced to her ears. All their lives, these men
and women had lived in a world where magic was an integral, intricate part of its primal fabric: gods could be
conversed with, enchantments cast, blessings requested,
and curses overthrown. At some time or other, through
the whole of a Daikini lifetime, it was inevitable that
there'd be at least one point of contact with one of the
Veil Folk. Many dealt with them on a daily basis. Whole
economies were based on that ongoing interaction.

Now, before the eyes of the world and wholly beyond its control, that relationship was being deconstructed. Old loyalties no longer had weight, covenants
that folk on both sides of the Veil lived by were crumbling

to dust, to the point where lasting friendships were giving way to active hostility.

If that verity of being no longer held, why should any other? If magic could be stolen from the world by the Deceiver, could impregnable Sandeni likewise fall? How could it possibly survive?

That was the moment when Elora Danan took center stage.

She'd been working on this with Duguay but hadn't considered herself anywhere near ready. Tonight changed that. She could no more stand aside in the face of this growing miasma of the spirit than she could deny a soul who needed healing.

She stood in a pool of candlelight, cast in shades of gold that accented the stark black red of her lipstick and nails. She glistened, but except for the barest, accenting highlights, there wasn't a hint of silver to her coloration. Instead she seemed to flash fire, little chips of glitter scattered across fabric and flesh, adding to the illusion by making it appear as though she was striking sparks simply through contact with the air.

She stood stock-still and swept the room with her eyes, waiting for the background noise to ease past the point where she could be heard.

The audience was a bit confused. They were expecting Duguay, used to seeing her waiting on their tables. And this was something altogether new and unexpected for Elora. Though she'd played the apprentice and dutifully begun to learn the trade, she never once seriously considered assuming the stage. From the instant she stepped forward, she knew she was making the right decision.

It was a story from Angwyn's past, long before the nation had become respectable, that she'd found in her library. It wasn't the first she read but it quickly became her favorite. The words she spoke, the melody she used to shape them, slipped free of their own accord, as naturally as breath, coming from a part of her more akin to soul than mind.

It was olden days, because all the best stories were set in olden days, when a good and noble people suffered beneath the cruel yoke of a tyrant. A monarch of consummate cruelty, whose lust for power no amount of conquest seemed able to satisfy. He held sway in great cities and trading towns and tiny, outland villages, and no affront was so slight as to go ignored or unpunished. The people endured because, despite their proud history, they knew no other way to survive. Resistance guaranteed only a retribution so terrible that death, when it came, was considered a mercy.

In this time of shadow, against all odds, a simple man strode forth to plant his feet and set his sword and tell this dread liege, "No more."

When the monarch sent a troop to arrest him, he was nowhere to be found. Assassins were dispatched to murder him, and were never seen again. Royal tax collectors were routed, their moneys disbursed to those who needed it most. Royal warehouses were raided, their contents used to feed the hungry. Royal edicts were mocked, and throughout the length and breadth of this land of sorrow, for the first time in a generation, whispers of defiance were heard.

An army was sent, to discover that they no longer dealt with a man alone. Others had flocked to his side, and the monarch's soldiers were sent back to him on foot, stripped to their tunics, with a warning that he and his were no longer welcome in this land. The monarch had those hapless souls impaled for their failure, his warning plain for those who would soon follow: return in victory or return not at all, the only alternative is death.

And so began a war. And soon the realm entire was drenched in blood. A line was drawn across the soul of the nation and eventually all its citizenry—noble and common, secular and religious—came to the moment when they had to choose their sides. On the one hand was a puissance almost beyond all comprehension. Against it, a desperate yearning for liberty, for the triumph of right over might. This man, this rebel, spoke of equality, of a future where every man and every woman would be judged by character and deeds, rather than the accident of birth. He spoke of honor, he spoke of justice, and found himself loved for it.

And hated.

Who knows how the battles would have ended? Some were won, others lost. Like tides upon a shore, the campaigns flowed back and forth across the countryside, ultimately resolving nothing. War has its own implacable dynamic: the best of the breed are often the first to die. Those who remained began to whisper among themselves, that no matter how many battles were won there was always another to be fought tomorrow. Victories against this monarch brought no peace, in a conflict where defeat meant sure disaster.

In the beginning the rebels had everything to gain, and that gave them courage. After long years of struggle they found themselves with too much to lose, and that made them afraid.

So, at the last, telling themselves this was for the best, they betrayed their chieftain.

In chains, he was dragged to judgment and thence to the place of execution, before a massed crowd of those with cause to hate him most, the nobles whose estates he had burned, the abbots whose treasuries he had looted, the common folk dispossessed of property, or worse, of the lives of loved ones who had gone to their deaths in battle against him. They cheered to see him helpless and could not wait to see him bleed.

Before their eyes, the chieftain was subjected to unspeakable tortures, a death that was guaranteed to be as slow as it was agonizing. It was so terrible a sight that some in the crowd cried out in sympathetic pain and horror.

Yet the chieftain uttered not a sound.

The flesh was peeled from his bones, long past the point when any lesser soul would have fled its casement, yet he breathed. And said nothing.

Where there had been cheers and catcalls, there was only silence now, broken by sobs from those who could not endure the awfulness before them.

"Kill him," someone cried, but there was no hatred in this voice. It was a plea for mercy.

The Lord High Executioner—a wizened stick of a creature, from whom had been sucked every scrap of kindness or decency—leaned close by the chieftain's ear and whispered: "Beg for mercy, and it shall be yours."

When he heard no reply, he tried again.

"Be sensible. We have barely begun. You can see this sun set and tomorrow's rise, in such agony as the mind cannot conceive. Or we can end it. Quickly. Cleanly. Plead for mercy, and you shall be at peace."

The crowd was growing restive. The chieftain still lived, he was still awake to hear every word and suffer every torment, and not one among those who watched could find the temerity within themselves to mock such absolute courage. He would not speak and he would not die and that was more defiance to their monarch than any one of them had thought possible. And the whisper began among them, in the most secret hidey-holes of their being, that perhaps their ruler was not so all-powerful after all. Perhaps there might be hope.

The Executioner spoke again, with an edge of desperation to his voice because he, too, sensed the shift in the crowd's mood. He could not let the chieftain die, not without publicly breaking his spirit, yet no longer could he afford to let the rebel live, since each breath was like an arrow through the foul heart of his monarch's majesty. He bent to his task a final time, his voice as soft and caressing as a lover's, for the bond that had grown between him and his victim was as intimate, to win through deceit what could not be forced.

"This has gone on long enough. You have done enough, and more. Your task is done. Ask for mercy, and you shall be free."

At last the chieftain spoke, in a voice that filled every corner of the war yard, that made strong men weep and women gather their companions to their breast.

A great shadow fell across the square and every eye looked up, to behold on every parapet, atop the crown of every tower, at the summit of every mountain that could be seen about this haunted, hated spot . . .

. . . dragons.

A score, a multitude, more than any present could remember seeing, more than anyone could conceive of ever being, gazing down on this place of execution with ancient eyes to witness the chieftain's final act of supreme and lasting defiance. One took for its perch the peak of the monarch's own battlements, directly across the yard from where the chieftain hung, of such a size that none could understand why its weight didn't crush the stone to rubble beneath it, with wings so broad they could envelop the entire castle. Its eyes, that had witnessed the birthing of the world, gazed into those of this Daikini—and when the chieftain smiled, the dragon wept.

As the echoes of the chieftain's cry began to fade, that dragon lifted his own face to the heavens and roared defiance of his own. First one, then the others on the walls, and those in the distance, took up that self-same cry and cast it forth in pride and joy with force enough to shatter the casement of heaven itself.

A single word . . .

. . . against which evil ultimately has no power, nor can tyranny long endure.

"Freedom!"

Elora spoke in the barest of whispers, the selfsame voice that the chieftain had used to speak it into the Executioner's ear. Yet so still was the room, so skillful her projection, that every ear took note.

She was crouched low, shoulders bowed, head bent, a posture of grief and loss. Suddenly, in a movement as smooth and fluid as quicksilver, she rose to her feet, the upward thrust of her body giving her utterance added force. This outcry was full-voiced and she prayed it would be heard in Angwyn by all the innocent souls imprisoned there.

"*Freedom!*"

The acoustics were wretched and the echoes of her shout faded quickly, as though the room itself had gobbled them up. In the vacuum that stillness caused there was a sudden creaking and groaning of the wood, as if some incredible weight had settled on the roof. A wind skirled past doors and windows and the flames flashed brighter in both hearths, and more than a few listening clutched charms or loved ones or both and whispered of dragons, some in fright and some, delight. For Elora herself, it was a reminder of her rescue of the firedrakes, when her blood burned white-hot, every pump of her heart sending another surge of glory through her system. It was a passion so intense she was surprised to find herself still whole and thankful she wasn't actually glowing; a wonder so all-encompassing, all-consuming that she was reduced to ash and resurrected in the same fantastic blip of time.

By the Great Gods, she thought, *words* do *have power!*

Another moment followed and with it a distancing from the storyteller's magic Elora had spun with her tale. There was no holocaust in her heart, only honest blood. One set of hands came together from the audience before her, then another and another, and faster than a line of falling dominoes the whole room exploded in applause and cheers, leavened with hearty sighs of relief that it was only a story and jovial chuckles at how they'd all been spooked at the end by that gust of wind.

Elora herself was drenched, top to toe, as if she'd just plunged into a pool. She was trembling, too, when voices began to chant her name, more exhausted than she'd ever been after a hard day at Torquil's forge. The beginnings of a smile tickled the side of her mouth as Duguay gathered her into his arms from behind, offering his strength to sustain her—in the nick of time, too, because her knees were on the verge of total collapse.

"Elora," they chanted. " 'lor-ah! *'lor-ah!*"

In the face of such adulation, she basked and couldn't understand for the life of her why she was sobbing.

"What did I do?" she cried to Duguay.

"What came naturally, that's obvious," he replied into her ear. "There's a born bard in you, Elora, an' that's no error, am I right?"

"Sure wouldn't have thought it to look at my past. Do they understand? What I was trying to say?"

"Some more than others, but that's always the case. Yon Maizan, they got your message, sure. Left before you finished, all in a clump."

"What?"

She searched the room, with all the Sights at her disposal, and saw that Duguay was right. The Maizan were nowhere to be seen.

In a flash of intuition, she knew where they had gone and what they were about. She was on the move herself that selfsame moment, realizing she hadn't a prayer of making her way through the crowd and out the main doors. The audience was already pressing forward, clapping, cheering, wanting to touch her, congratulate her, to try through that little bit of contact to reclaim some of the wonder of her performance. If she let them catch her, she'd never get out. She wasn't sure she'd even survive.

She dropped loose of Duguay's embrace, kicking herself sideways in a crab scuttle that took her to the dais. Then, proprieties be damned, she flung herself over the high table and dashed for the kitchen entrance beyond the far hearth. Through the door, returning the applause of the serving staff who'd been watching with smiles and nods and waves, trying her best to be gone before anyone was sure she was actually there. Out the back to where the trash was dumped, trying not to gag on the stench or wonder how the cooks could stand it, leaping for the near balcony and going up the wall much like a monkey, thankful both Ryn and the Rock Nelwyns had taught her how to climb.

It took neither time nor effort to reach the roof, but as she clambered to its peak she almost came to disaster as one foot found open air where it expected shingles and she thumped down hard on her front, the pitch so steep that she was propelled headlong toward the gutter and a four-story fall to the ground below. Fortunately, a flailing hand found the same hole that had tripped her up. That broke her slide and provided a solid enough anchor for the moments she allowed herself to regain a semblance of breath. Even so, when she opened her eyes, she saw more spots than not before her vision and each breath hurt as though she'd been soundly punched.

"There's a hole in the roof," she told herself stupidly, and to her surprise found three more on the other side. Looking along the building, MageSight revealed an identical pattern, almost all the way to the other end. They looked like claw marks, and if called to testify, she'd have to say they most resembled the footprints of some giant creature coming briefly, and lightly, to rest. . . .

Here, she stopped herself, not at all comfortable with where this line of thought was going.

What! she scoffed in silence. *Are you going to presume that a* dragon *dropped in to hear your story! How come no one saw!*

But then, memory reminded Elora of the story Thorn Drumheller told, *no one saw Calan Dineer, the dragon that had brought him and my bear to Tir Asleen the night before the Cataclysm destroyed it.*

At that point all her speculations were banished by the clash of steel from the direction of Ryn's cell. Instinct prompted her to look that way, conscious thought overrode the impulse and turned her eyes toward the main gate instead, to find one door wide open.

She almost cried, *Alarm,* but another sweeping glance in a circle all about her confirmed her worst fears. The battlements were clear, without a sign of the normal scattering of sentries. She heard horses in the distance, more sounds of a struggle, the faint thump of chains against a padded target that she suspected was covered in fur. The stable was closer, but she suspected she'd have a better chance catching them at the gate.

She used the length of the building as a runway, then launched herself in a wild leap for the parapet beyond. She tried too hard, she made it with room to spare and so much excess momentum that she crashed full tilt into the palisade beyond, leaving her sore and a little winded and glumly anticipating a sensationally dramatic bruise come the morrow as decoration for playing such a daredevil. She ignored the aches and protests of her flesh as she made her way along the walkway, accelerating with every step until she was flat-out running.

There was one corner tower between her and the gate. She guessed that if she was going to find trouble, it would be there. Without breaking stride, she twisted the clasp that held her skirt in place and rolled the waistline once about her hand. Not much as weapons went, but all she had, and with that thought, she promised herself to find a way to integrate at least one of her bottomless traveling pouches into any future costume.

Through the doorway, a Maizani was waiting, the warrior who'd confronted her at Ryn's cage. The instant he realized it was she, a huge and unpleasant grin split his face. He was between her and the exit, and set himself to make sure she went no farther.

She caromed off the wall ahead without slackening speed, then used the opposite wall as a springboard, kicking herself up into the air as though off a pair of tightly coiled springs. In mid-flight she tucked arms and legs together into a somersaulting ball, rolling as she went so that she'd bounce off the next wall on her feet. As she passed the Maizani, who wasn't sure what to make of her acrobatics, her movements so quick and dramatic that he was a fatal half second behind them in his reactions, she snapped the skirt into his eyes, flicking it the same way boys do towels at one another's backside when they're feeling particularly obnoxious. Didn't do him any lasting harm but she made him flinch. That was all the opening she needed as she came at him from above and behind, giving voice to a great war cry as she hammered clenched fists down close on either side of his spine, at the base of the neck. She struck the nerve clusters perfectly, right above the protective collar of his leather tunic. He made an odd little noise, his eyes glazed, his limbs lost all ability to hold him erect, and down he went with a formidable clump.

He'd be unconscious quite a while, and more sore than she for a bit longer after that.

He had no sword but Elora relieved him of the long knife she found sheathed to the outside of one boot. Double-edged, well-balanced, it'd suit her fine.

So much for peace bonding, she thought, *not to mention the rules of hospitality.* Then she was off again.

Someone had sounded the alarm. She heard a chorus of basso barks as the wolfhounds responded to the threat, saw people boiling out of the dining hall like ants from an unearthed nest. Too late, though, for the remaining Maizan were already racing for the gate on horseback, leaving the stables afire in their wake to forestall any pursuit. Much as the Commandant and his men might like to stop these raiders, the critical priority was to save the livestock, as well as prevent the fire from spreading to the body of the fort.

The lighting was uneven, moonlight mixed with torches, but MageSight easily made up the difference, showing Elora that Ryn was tied belly down across his animal's back, the reins of his horse in the hands of the Maizani galloping ahead. Two mounts were saddled but empty. One was presumably for the warrior Elora had already dealt with, the other for whoever had opened the gate.

She didn't take time to think. If she did she knew she'd be too scared stiff to act. She reached the gate a few steps ahead of the Maizan and without a heartbeat's pause hurled herself for the warrior leading Ryn's animal. She let his body bear the brunt of the impact, and before the Maizani knew what was happening, he was un-horsed, pitched into the face of his comrade, who'd emerged from the shadows by the gate to mount up himself. In those few, frantic moves, she managed to throw a well-planned and executed escape into utter disarray. The challenge now was to get herself and Ryn out of the mess intact and unharmed.

Elora yanked on the reins, digging her heels into her horse's ribs to make the beast rear up on its hind legs, forehooves lashing out instinctively to make anyone in front keep a respectful distance. At the same time she pulled its head to the side, trying to turn her mount back into the fort.

She thought she knew the location of every Maizani. She thought she had a clear lane open to safety for herself and Ryn. She was just kicking the horse into gear when the Maizan Captain loomed up out of nowhere, so close at hand and coming so fast that Elora barely had time to recognize her danger before she was struck down, to crash in a clumsy heap through a roadside pile of compost.

By the time Elora struggled free, clothes and body now adorned by a wild variety of filth, the Maizan were past the tree line. In their wake they cast torches among the tents that lined the approaches to the main gate, and set fire to some of the wagon train as well, breaking the refugees' livestock loose from their paddock. Of the two who'd fallen, one had managed to make his escape. His companion, though, had been tackled by a pair of wolfhounds, a fearsome shock since their size was a match for his and their combined weight greater. He knew neither mail nor any weapon would be fair protection against jaws powerful enough to tear limbs from their sockets, and so he yielded. A quartet of Sandeni troopers managed to evade the roadblocks the Maizan had set and thundered past Elora in hot pursuit. If the Commandant knew his business, and her reading of him was that he did, their orders would be to follow but not engage, to mark their trail for a larger, more heavily armed force. With all the confusion, the need to bring both fires and loose animals back under control, those re-inforcements wouldn't be leaving soon.

She sensed the presence of the wolfhound who'd adopted her before she actually saw him. He whined his concern, then lifted himself on his hind legs, making her grunt with the strain as he placed forepaws on her shoulders and looked down into her eyes. He was a dog, yet standing in this position he had height on her by better than a couple of heads. She didn't reprimand him, she knew he just wanted to make sure she was all right. She even endured a slobbery lick of his tongue because it was to make her feel better. Once, though, was enough, and with a heave she returned him to all fours.

What she wanted now more than anything wasn't comfort, she wanted to give chase herself. Her failure to rescue Ryn, when she had him right in *hand,* left a bitter, angry taste in her mouth. The fact that she'd outmatched the Maizan warrior in the watchtower only made her feel worse. Winning every battle, she raged to herself, didn't count for much if ultimately you lost the war.

She said as much to Duguay, when he found her helping fight the fires outside the stronghold walls, turning the upper-body strength she'd built at Torquil's forge to good advantage by working the rocker bars of a water pump. It also proved a splendid outlet for her frustrations, maintaining a steady flow of water to the fire hose.

He appeared as elegantly turned out as ever, and she hated him for it, painfully aware of how wretchedly bedraggled she looked.

"Depends on the war," he noted. "On how you define the terms of the conflict and the victory to be won. You should pay more attention to your own songs."

"I should have been paying more attention to that mess at the gate. I was totally blindsided."

"The Captain's a warrior. That sort of thing's his stock-in-trade. You've the beginnings of a decent bard."

"I'm not supposed to be either, Duguay! *Hey,*" she bellowed suddenly as the bellows clunked on air instead of water, "get off the damn hose, you great thumping pillocks! Can't'cha see we're working here!" Retorts came in a blend of apology and insult as the offending wagon was shoved clear of the line that linked pump to the river. For the next couple of minutes Elora said nothing, save for some random grunts, as she worked the rocker arm all the harder to rebuild pressure in the hose. Now of course, there were cries of dismay and protest from the other direction as the spray faded fast to a trickle and then to nothing.

"Conversation's a duet, Elora my sweeting," Duguay prompted gently when the silence began to drag. "You have to know the right moment to come in with your part, else you'll cock up the tune worse than any traffic accident."

"I'm a little busy right now, Duguay," was her pointed reply. "You could always pitch in and help, you know."

"I like to think I am, in my own way. Talk with me, Elora, it'll make the work go easier. I can guess partly what this is all about, the bare bones seem pretty obvious."

"Oh?"

"A prophecy," he said with a small smile that, despite her fatigue, she couldn't help returning. She liked the shape of his mouth, the firm set of his jaw, the way this one infernal forelock refused to yield to any amount of styling pomade but always slipped free to curl across his brow. She had a solid sense of every aspect of his features, except his eyes. Without them, the picture was incomplete. Worse, she feared it was meaningless.

"A Princess," he went on, thankfully oblivious to the path her thoughts were taking. "Everybody wants the prize. I've the distinct impression hardly anyone really knows why. Except perhaps this Mohdri fella. He's offering a pretty penny, think he has the answers?"

"If he does, we're all damned."

"An old familiar face, then?"

"We've crossed swords."

"Prophecy and Princess. Noble heroes, a grand and

glorious villain. Must be a fable, then. An epic confrontation between Good and Evil!"

She gave him her best basilisk glare for that remark, which only made him laugh.

"What exactly does that mean, good and evil?" she wondered afterward, in all seriousness.

"Substance versus style?"

"Is everything to you nothing but source material for a joke?"

"No more or less than it should be for you, lass. We're troubadours, we tell stories, our purpose is to entertain, am I right?"

"I bet," she said, bypassing his question because a part of her agreed with him, "if you took a poll of our audience, a decent number would say the Maizan conquest isn't such an awful thing. That the Daikini Realm is a better place with the doors to the Great Realms of Faery closed and sealed. Probably find as many among the Veil Folk of the same opinion."

"House gets too crowded, Elora, somebody generally has to move out."

"Suppose you have a pattern of glorious beauty and complexity, a weave whose whole is far stronger than the sum of its parts? When you split it into its component threads, is it then as lovely, as rich? As lasting?"

"Lovely for cloth, perhaps, but I've never heard of one thread having any sort of opinion about another."

"Listen harder."

"Oil and water don't mix, Elora, why should every race and culture?"

"Isn't that one of the responsibilities of sentience, Duguay, to rise above even natural prejudices?"

"Especially with a Sacred Princess to show the way?"

"Who's to say? The job didn't come with instructions."

"Now who's making light?"

"It's true. The only person with any real clue is the Deceiver. . . ." Her voice trailed off, as if the words themselves constituted a sudden and unexpected revelation.

"What?" came a prompt from Duguay, after she'd been silent awhile.

"Something Thorn Drumheller said . . ."

"That name I've heard before."

"My guardian, you might say."

"You mean I've a rival for that role? Heaven forfend!"

"Keep this up, Master Faralorn, I'll have them hose *you* down."

"Hmm, I'd best behave. You're always most formidable when you call me 'Master Faralorn.' "

"And you're worse to deal with sometimes than any brownie!"

"So what did this Drumheller fella tell you?"

"That the Deceiver seemed to know everyone better than they did themselves. Cherlindrea, all the other monarchs, Thorn himself." *And especially,* she thought, feeling apprehension descend her spine like a trickle of ice, *me. He knows me, and his spells can do me harm. But why? How can he alone have such power? Where does it come from, where does* he *come from?*

"As the sages are fond of saying, Elora, knowledge *is* power."

"And I have next to none. I don't even know who I am."

"Could have fooled me."

"My mother was murdered the day I was born, Duguay. I have no fit memory of her, I know *nothing* about my father. If anyone else did"—a pause, as a vision all in scarlet and black, with haunted features and hating eyes swam across the panorama of Elora's memory, the Demon Queen Bavmorda, who'd tried so hard to end Elora's life before it had even begun—"they never told me. What are you smiling at?" she demanded suddenly of Duguay, tempted to clout him for his rudeness.

"Just listening, is all. I can't speak for the whole of your destiny but at this time, in this part, it's clear you were meant to be a bard."

"Stop."

"It's the way you frame words, almost as well as I do music—and that's saying quite a piece."

"Thank you," she told him, but her tone made plain that she didn't believe. He didn't appear to mind, which infuriated her all the more.

"So," he said. "That elf, back at Ganthem's, when he lay dying he named you 'Deceiver.' "

"That's not the same!"

"The accusation struck a chord, that much is plain. Do you fear some connection with your enemy?"

"It would explain a lot."

He considered. "Think to when we were deep within the forest. Suppose you ask me what the shape of the world is and I tell you straight it's made of naught but trees. Can you prove me different?"

"Easily."

"How? Look about you, Elora, what do you see?"

"Trees. But—!"

"What do you see?" he asked her again.

"*Trees!*" she repeated with some asperity. "And if we travel a ways," she went on, daring him with a glare to interrupt again, "we'll see meadows." She waved an arm to illustrate the point. "And plains. And mountains. And an ocean."

"Absolutely right. The more you know," he announced triumphantly, as though presenting a fundamental law of the universe, "the more you know! And you"—for emphasis, he gave her a sharp poke on the breastbone—"know damn all. Am I wrong, or am I right?"

She let out her breath in a deliberate and obvious sigh and pursed her lips. "You're right," she said, with a shallow nod.

"Absolutely." He surveyed the scene, pursed his lips, came to a decision. "Come with me," he told her. "Time you did some good."

"And this is . . . ?" she said, wearily indicating the pump.

"Something any stalwart soul can do. What I have in mind is for you and me alone."

He produced a jug of mint-accented water, deliciously cool, so she could slake her thirst. She splashed a double handful across her face and head, won a nod of self-appreciation from Duguay at how well his paint withstood the night's onslaught, and asked for something to eat. All he had to offer were road biscuits, which tasted like sawdust but took the edge off her pangs.

Then his rich baritone voice rang out in a roundelay familiar to the locals, used during harvesttime in the wheat fields, to make the cutting and threshing go more quickly. Elora came in on cue a half phrase behind him, taking the harmony to his melody.

No one paid much attention at first. The most response they got was a volley of sharp complaints from those who had to replace Elora at her pump, and by the hoseman who felt the replacements didn't do as good a job. Elora took the challenge personally and without missing breath or beat moved back to her old position and took hold of the rocker arms. She matched the cadence of the pump to that of the song and turned it into a duel with Duguay to see who could complete each verse with more energy and panache.

The hoseman couldn't help a laugh at the discomfiture shown by the four Elora had supplanted, who themselves were trying to figure out how this girl could outperform them. Duguay moved over to him, gestured him to pick up the next verse, only to roll his eyes in overplayed scorn at the hesitant attempt that emerged. The four pumpers took that as an opportunity to get some of their own back and took up the roundelay themselves, engaging in a four-part harmony as they accepted the handoff of the pump from Elora. Which in turn inspired the hoseman to better efforts.

And so the troubadour and his apprentice spread music through the night, easing the pain of those who'd suffered loss, energizing the spirits of those who fought to help them. Their repertoire were simple tunes that everyone knew or that could easily be learned.

As battles went, this was quickly won, and the cost was surprisingly cheap. Aside from some aching heads—

drugged wine flasks—and a couple of abstemious sentries who'd been thumped, there were no casualties. While the risk of disaster had been significant, the actual losses turned out to be far less so. Scorched timbers and a roof in need of repair about the stable, a number of tents that would have to be replaced, one wagon that was a total write-off.

True, the Maizan had stolen Ryn away, but two of their number had been left behind, the one from the gate and his companion, whom Elora had clocked in the watchtower.

Elora wanted to confront them herself. To her astonishment, she found herself summoned to the Provost Marshal's office for an interrogation of her own.

She wasn't under arrest, or even under suspicion, she was assured, despite the fact that a couple of armed proctors had been sent to collect her. This was only a formality.

Luc-Jon sat at his scribe's table in the corner of the Marshal's austere office, to record all that was said. He tried to look reassuring as Elora was marched inside but couldn't hide the worry in his eyes.

She told the truth. Just not all of it. About the confrontation at the stable and the Maizan's determination to win back what they considered their property at any cost. Her flight from the dining hall after her performance, she ascribed to panic over the audience's response. She'd never done this before, she didn't know how to cope with their reaction. She wanted some time to herself, to regain her composure, and heard the commotion at the stable. She didn't sound an alarm because she didn't know what was happening. By the time she did, there was no more time. Her reason was simplicity itself: she believed the Maizan intended harm to that poor creature and she wasn't about to let them have their way with him.

It was a well-told story. The Marshal made no attempt to discount it, but also made none to disguise the fact that he knew this was a bard's stock-in-trade. It was plausible, which was why he chose to accept it. He also believed there was more.

She asked if the Maizan prisoners had said anything, received no more than a thin-lipped smile in return that told her it was none of her business. She was thanked for her cooperation and dismissed, and just as she stepped over the threshold she was informed that until this matter was fully resolved she and her companion were restricted to the fort.

As morning edged away night, after all the others had gone to bed, she sat by herself in the dining hall staring into the hearth until the last of its embers finally guttered out. Every now and again she would reach a finger, or all of them together, through the flame of the candle that stood before her on the table. Sometimes its fire was like the lick of a serpent's tongue, at others like a caress of heat. Once, she closed her palm around it, to see if she could steal it away, but the flame slipped from her grasp and held its place firmly on the wick. Such a puny thing, yet it could ignite a blaze capable of consuming the entire fort, if not a goodly portion of forest. At the same time, it remained so fragile that she could extinguish it with a fingertip, or the smallest puff of air.

She thought of dragons, and asked how they could possibly hold a fire as hot as the world's heart within their bellies and not be devoured themselves? How could firedrakes exist, composed of nothing *but* molten essence, of such incredible intensity that their mere presence could vaporize steel and stone? How could she swim with them, be one with them, yet not be annihilated?

Thinking of swimming reminded her of Ryn, and that the word which came most naturally to mind when she pictured him was *joyous*. Life was a delight and his sense of wonder was so infectious that all who encountered him couldn't help but be swept along with it. His features weren't even human, when she was younger she took him for a living embodiment of her guardian bear, whereas Duguay was a heartbreaker. Without a thought as to why she measured these two against each other, she realized that she could look Ryn in the eye, and what she found there was a soul as winning and noble as could be wished for.

She ached with the loss of him and raged at her inability to find a way to go to his rescue.

The rational side of Elora told her to go to bed, that no good purpose was served by such ruminations, but she wasn't in the mood. Her spirit wasn't weary and her body was beset by too many angry sensations, as though all of her joints and bones had decided they were done with living in harmony. She snorted then, remembering her analogy with the cloth and wondering if all the parts of her had decided they were better off wandering their separate ways.

She puffed out the candleflame and stepped past the wolfhound onto the porch. In the early-morning silence, with the stronghold mostly asleep, natural sounds once more held sway. She could hear the wild progress of the river as well as the rustle of wind through the aspen groves that intruded upon the more numerous spruce and highland pine. The breeze brought with it a myriad of scents that weren't so noticeable by daylight. There was no moon, but neither were there clouds to obscure the magnificent panoply of starlight overhead. Black sky she beheld when she looked up, against the blacker silhouette of the forest. Peace at last settled around her like a shawl, and she thought to go to bed.

"Elora Danan," she heard from behind, "you're dead."

Chapter 9

"THANK YOU *SO MUCH*," ELORA SAID TO THE WOLF-hound, who merely opened his mouth wide in a luxurious yawn and then let his teeth close with a resounding *chop*.

"You should know better," said the warrior, in a familiar voice.

Elora considered a rude reply, but decided on a more temperate one and made a face instead which she knew the other could not see.

"Hoy!" she heard Luc-Jon cry from the Commandant's porch, where he'd been working through the night. "What'cher there! Put up them swords!"

"It's all right," Elora called as the young man's alarm brought an instant response from guards, whose nerves were already on hair triggers. "No harm meant, no harm done!"

She stepped clear of the blades' embrace and heard them sing through the air as the warriors returned them to their scabbards. Boots thundered on floorboards all around them. In surprisingly short order near a dozen armed men had taken position before her, to face Elora and her supposed assailant with a formidable array of bows, pikes, axes, and blades.

"Who goes?" demanded the Sergeant of the Watch.

"Khory Bannefin," said the warrior, stepping into the torchlight where she could be properly seen. "In the service of Thorn Drumheller, himself adjunct to the office of the Chancellor of the Republic of Sandeni."

She hadn't changed much since the last time Elora had seen her two years earlier, any more than since the first. Broad shoulders, long arms and legs, hair as naturally black as the false color Elora wore, cropped as close to her skull as a day's growth on a man with a heavy beard. She wasn't pretty, she wasn't ugly, Khory existed in that realm where features were defined more by character than design. High cheekbones framed a strong, square jaw beneath a broken nose and wide-spaced eyes, their oval shape and upturned setting marking her as a native of the Spice Lands, though her features were too angular, her skin too rich a gold, to be mainland Chengwei. Thorn's guess was that her heritage was Hansha, off the coastal archipelago, but had no notion how one of her race had come to Angwyn, to meet her doom ages ago in the dungeons beneath the old royal palace.

Tribal tattoos marked biceps and thighs, and especially her face behind and above her left eye, covering her eyelid and filling the whole of the brow ridge before flaring up and out along the flank of her skull until it met her hairline. The image was as brilliantly colorful as Elora's makeup, and most closely resembled the facial feathering of some exotic raptor, as if transposed directly from the head of that great hunting bird. The odd thing was, in all their travels together, none of their party had ever been able to identify *which* bird. Thorn didn't know, neither did the brownies, nor the two golden eagles Bastian and Anele, nor did anyone they met along the way.

In her previous life Khory had been a warrior. That had been plain at the start from the tone of her body's musculature and the calluses on her hands, as well as the few scars that marked her flesh. While death claimed her soul in those catacombs, the reaper found it had a challenger for her body: a demon imprisoned since time immemorial in the very stones used to construct the ancient stronghold that served as the original seat of power for Angwyn's rulers. The demon saved Thorn's life, and offered to help save Elora's, provided the Nelwyn sorcerer gave life to its own unborn offspring. The demon was a prisoner from time's beginning to its end. It would not allow its child to share that fate. The child was soul without body, Khory was body without soul. Thorn would be the catalyst that brought the two together and made them one.

He had never spoken of that ceremony. Neither had Elora, and she never would. Necromancy was considered a Black Art, province of such evil wizards as Bavmorda. Trafficking with demons was worse. Revealing Khory's true nature would be an instant sentence of death, for her and Thorn both.

Then again, Elora considered as she accompanied the other woman to the Commandant's, *what is her true nature? Demons have always been considered spawn of the ultimate evil, yet Khory's been nothing but a true friend, a woman of courage and honor.*

"I sent for Thorn," Elora said.

"And he sent me, little Princess." Plain as spoken words between them was her silent rebuke: *He has duties, Elora Danan, and there's more at stake here than the life of any friend, no matter how dear.*

"You should have been here sooner." She was unable to keep a hint of accusation from her tone.

"So I gather."

"Or at least sent Bastian and Rool ahead to let me know you were coming! With their help none of this might have happened."

"I don't care *who* she claims to be," they heard the Commandant roar. His anger was as palpable as an expanding field of burning gas, making those outside extremely reluctant to make their presence known. "What I want to know, gentlemen, is how the hell she entered this stronghold unnoticed?"

"Sir—" one of his officers began, but that was as far as he was allowed to go.

"I don't want excuses," the Commandant snapped. "I also don't want this to happen again. Find out what happened and make it right."

The officers hurried out, radiating their own little puffballs of humiliation and fury, promising an equivalently hard time for their own subordinates. The troopers who composed Elora and Khory's escort exchanged rueful glances at the sight. This promised to be a bear of a day.

The Commandant didn't ask how she accomplished her incursion as she presented both credentials and a packet of dispatches. A brief but thorough sweep of the eyes across her body, taking the measure of her stance and weapons, told him all he needed to know about her abilities.

He looked rumpled, he looked worn, with none of the cultivated veneer of the visage he normally presented to the world. He was a figure as rough-hewn in his way as the garrison he commanded, who'd grounded his life in as firm a foundation and built it solidly piece by piece. He would never be flashy, he was rather the kind who would endure. Right now, to Elora, he was very much the bear who'd been rudely wakened from his winter's hibernation. Not happy at the disturbance and less so to be presenting himself at so much less than his best, with grizzled, unshaven cheeks and red-streaked eyes sunk too deep in their sockets. He'd obviously grabbed whatever lay closest at hand to wear, belting his sword on over a nightshirt.

He ran his fingers through hair that badly needed a wash, scrabbled about the desktop and drawers in a vain search for something to tie it back from his face.

"You seem to be the focus of quite a lot of interest, young woman," he noted to Elora.

"A misfortune of fate, sir?" she hazarded lightly in response.

He gave that line no more credit than the story she'd told him earlier but chose to accept it anyway. For the moment.

"Are you familiar with these assessments?" he asked Khory, indicating the thick bundle of dispatches she'd delivered. The warrior nodded. "Is there hope for a negotiated truce?"

"Defensive mind-set," she said simply, voicing her own opinion. "Defensive strategy. Automatically cedes the initiative to the enemy. Peace will last until the enemy decides to break it."

"At which point," the Commandant mused thoughtfully, in agreement, "the question becomes, can that attack be repulsed? I'm to hold fast here, then."

"As best you can, and for as long, yes. Those are the orders."

"With no more resources than what I have?"

"In light of Testeverde, the decision has been made to concentrate Republican forces at Sandeni itself. If the Maizan mean to scale the Wall, that's the nut they have to crack to do so. The hope is that the Castellan and his warlord will conclude it is a shell that can't be broken."

"There's more at play here than just Maizan, does your master, Drumheller, understand that? Does the council? The Maizan are no longer the only enemy with territorial ambitions. We've had skirmishes all along the frontier."

"Those were no more than raiding parties, weren't they?" Elora interrupted. "I'm sorry," she hurried on as both Khory and the Commandant turned their gaze on her, "I guess I'm wrong but what threat could they pose to a place like this?"

"That the High Elves of Greater Faery raid at all is cause enough for concern," the Commandant told her. "But they've enlisted allies to their cause. Every which way you look, there's someone new who feels they've been pushed hard into a corner. Daikini who believe the Veil-Folk mean their extermination, to whom the Maizan appear their sole salvation. Veil Folk who see how magic is being expunged from Maizan holdings and assume the same in return. And those nations of the Daikini caught in the middle, unwilling to bow before either camp. We're none of us being left with any option save total commitment, because the perceived alternative is annihilation."

"What will happen here?" Elora asked Khory as they returned along the porch to the inn.

The taller woman shrugged. "Maybe nothing."

Her gaze was always roving, sweeping the space immediately surrounding her and flicking from point to point across whatever lay within eyeshot to check for any possible threat.

"You don't believe that. The Commandant doesn't."

"The government in Sandeni has decided. They have to make a stand."

"What's that mean?"

"The best I can do, little Princess, is tell you what Drumheller told me before I left. The Republic has to hold what is theirs, not only against the Maizan but against these marauding forces of Greater Faery. The Maizan must be made to bleed for what they wish to conquer, not only to maintain Sandeni's independence but to demonstrate to the Veil Folk that there are Daikini who will stand in their defense. There is no longer any middle ground, as the Commandant said. Testeverde was proof of that. To save the lives of its populace, the decision was made to surrender the city, even though that meant the eldritch power of its World Gate would be stolen away by the Deceiver. Instead, some force beyond the Veil shattered Testeverde's Gate with a spell so foul that the land there is death for any Daikini who even comes close."

"Like Angwyn."

Khory shook her head violently. "No. What happened at Testeverde was an abomination. For all the enmity we may bear him, the Deceiver has committed no such atrocity. Angwyn is ensorcelled, as Thorn's stories say your Tir Asleen once was. Consider the Deceiver more like a drain, drawing to himself the magical essence of the world. That upsets the balance of things. Because the Realms are interlinked, what affects one affects all. The less energy a thing possesses, the colder it becomes."

"So if the Deceiver wins, we all freeze?"

Khory exhaled sharply and both of them watched the thick cloud formed by her breath as it chilled.

There was a bite to the air strong enough to make others clutch their jacket collars about their throats and exchange knowing nods about how quickly summer was giving way to fall, but neither woman appeared to mind.

"Everyone's desperate," Elora noted, using the term to encompass far more than just the Daikini within the stronghold's walls, "everyone's scared. That's why they're lashing out so fiercely, they figure there's nothing left to lose. That's the Deceiver's doing," she told Khory, "that's the responsibility he must bear. He's the one who's pushed us all into these corners." She looked around the whole of the parade ground yet again and exclaimed, "There has to be a way to help!"

"The decision has been made."

"That this fort is to be sacrificed? I refuse to accept that!"

"You have no choice, Elora."

"Do you ever wonder," Elora asked her, "about where you come from?"

"Formlessness into form. I was not and then I was."

"Trust a demon to speak in enigmas."

"I am not a demon, Elora. Any more than I am this woman whose flesh is foster home to my spirit. I am myself entire. Beyond that, all is discovery."

"You sound like Ryn."

"Not so poor a way to embrace existence."

"Do you deny your heritage?"

"I assume, like most, my whole is greater than the

sum of my parts. Do you deny yours?" she asked Elora suddenly.

The question caught Elora off guard and the answer burst out before thought could temper it. "I don't have one."

"No?"

"I've a Destiny. That's apparently all that matters."

"You haven't the experience to be clever, girl. Save it for better days."

"I'm serious. I think. I mean, who *am* I? Princess by name, but what's my *blood*? Hellsteeth, Khory, you know more than that about yourself and you're not even wholly *human*!"

"Piss and vinegar will only take you so far."

"That's for damn sure."

"Bed, girl. Now."

"I'm not sleepy."

"You've a hard ride ahead come morning."

"We're going after Ryn! Why wait till sunup, I'm ready now!"

"Ryn is my responsibility, girl. I'll bring him home safe."

"I'm coming with you!"

"You'll do as you're told. Don't look so downcast, Elora, you're getting your wish. You're going to Sandeni to join Thorn."

Khory was gone within the hour.

Elora would have followed, but the warrior had left her in the charge of a brace of proctors, with orders to keep her under close confinement until morning when she'd be sent downriver under escort. Even if she gave her minders the slip the gates were closed and bolted, with a full wartime complement of sentries on the walls. For her, the fort was a closed box.

There was no sign of Duguay in their room, which provoked a mixture of emotions in Elora. She was thankful for the solitude, upset at his absence. She wasn't in a mood to sleep, though she knew she'd pay for that later when the excitement of the evening finally faded, and so busied herself packing away her costume finery into a traveling pouch, replacing it with her buckskins.

The mare Khory provided for her wasn't much to look at, mahogany coat accented with russet in the mane and tail, dark socks on all her legs, in the same autumnal red, white blaze down her forehead like someone had laid down the basic outline of a broadsword. Across shoulders and flanks was a network of pale lines, some long, some short, some wide, some narrow that first glance registered to Elora as scars, long-healed. A moment's reflection rejected that presumption on the grounds that no creature living could survive such an onslaught, and most certainly not in the prime of health and condition that this animal radiated.

There was pride in her stance and a *knowingness* in her gaze that Elora had rarely seen in her breed. Though she wore saddle and bridle, this horse had never been broken, nor did she acknowledge any rider as her "master." With that exchange of looks, Elora understood that here stood one who faced her as an equal, whose friendship and loyalty and, above all, respect had to be earned.

The distinctive *clip-clop* of another set of hooves alerted her to the approach of another animal and a few moments later Duguay Faralorn led a mount of his own around the corner of the paddock.

Elora greeted him with a tense flattening of the lips and continued her examination of her tack, tugging on the saddle girth to make sure it was securely strapped in place. She offered the mare a fresh carrot and smiled at the *whuffle* of the horse's warm breath as she took her scent as well as the proffered snack.

"What's all this, then?" she asked the troubadour as she slipped the bridle into place and fed her mare another carrot, stroking her soft muzzle as she ate.

"You don't get rid of me that easily, lass."

"Bound at the hip, are we, Master Faralorn?"

"We make good music together, Elora," he said in all

seriousness. "I don't want that to end. I don't think you do, either."

"I have other obligations."

"They're mutually exclusive⸮"

"Ryn's my friend. I won't abandon him."

"Don't you think that your warrior friend might be better qualified to go to his rescue⸮"

"So I just stand idly by and wait, while others do the work and take the risks⸮"

"It happens. It isn't even so bad a thing."

"You live with that attitude. I refuse to."

"How will you find him⸮"

"The same way Khory will, with Bastian and Rool's help. I caught a whisper of their presence a little after sunup. She brought them back upriver with her, but she's got them ranging way wide of the fort, I assume to mark the Maizan trail from the air."

"And they'll help you⸮" She shot him so fierce a basilisk glare that he held up his hands in a placating gesture. "All right, all right, no offense, we'll set that one aside for a moment, there's no need to cry."

"I'm not crying," she snuffled, physical evidence to the contrary.

"Of course not. Take my handkerchief anyway."

She blew her nose but didn't give it back right away, letting her forehead rest against the seat of the saddle. She heard the mare whicker in concern for her.

"I felt so *good* the other night," she told them both, her voice thick and huskier than usual.

"And deservedly so."

"I felt I had made a kind of contribution! Taken all the despair that was in the room and galvanized it into something brighter and stronger and more positive. I felt *hope* from them, Duguay. And then Ryn was taken and I couldn't stop it and now I'm being told to run away to where it's safe while all these people here, they're doomed, and I don't want to be told there's nothing to be done, I'm *sick* of being told there's nothing to be done!"

"So what will you do⸮"

She huffed. "I can't fight, like Khory. I can't wield magic, like Thorn. I'm a fair blacksmith, but Torquil's better. All I know, that I'm *good* at, are singing and healing. Those I can do. That's where I'll have to start."

"I've heard of some building more with less."

"Thank you."

Elora circled the mare's hindquarters, keeping one hand lightly on the horse's rump so she wouldn't make the animal nervous while she moved through the blind spot in her vision. Circuit complete, Elora once more stood before the mare, noting that the horse stood higher at the shoulder by better than a head than Elora herself was tall. Blue eyes met brown, in an exchange of looks and an equivalence of mien that was as utterly formal as any court introduction.

"I am Elora," she told the mare. Almost immediately she became aware of the name offered in response. It wasn't that the mare answered—this was a creature whose sentience was defined by the act of *being* rather than by literal intellect, a mentality structured along wholly different paths than the human mind—but that Elora intuited a simple and obvious truth about her.

"And you are Windfleet," she continued, gaining a whicker of acknowledgment and a bob of the head in response.

She knew the story from both brownies, Rool and Franjean, though she'd never met the horse. Before coming to Angwyn, they and Thorn Drumheller encountered a young Angwyn pathfinder. Together, the four of them and the Pathfinder's mount faced down a hunting pack of Death Dogs that had been set on Thorn's trail. In the course of that terrible fight, the mare was mortally wounded. Thorn brought her back from the brink of death, and that struggle far more than the one with the hounds was what inspired him to come at last to Elora's side.

For the better part of a decade Thorn had roamed the world, taking stock of all its crippled and broken places, those sites of power which had been destroyed by the same Cataclysm that had claimed Tir Asleen, unwilling—afraid—to accept that he himself numbered among them. Windfleet's healing was the first active, *positive,* step he'd taken in that time, the long-overdue reassertion of his proper role in the shape of things.

"I am honored," Elora said, bobbing her own head.

She grasped the pommel and the reins and hoisted her left foot to the stirrup, swinging herself into the saddle with an ease that belied the fact that she hadn't been on horseback in years. There were some moments of adjustment, as Windfleet settled the new weight on her back and Elora tried to get used to straddling the powerful chest.

Now, she thought, *I know how a wishbone feels.*

She'd been taught to hold the reins in both hands, back in Angwyn for a brief, lost time when the Emperor had seen her as a surrogate for his own lost children: his son, who'd disappeared the night Elora had appeared, and the boy's twin sister, the Princess Anakerie, who'd run away from home rather than serve as the first of Elora's Vizards, the guardians of the Sacred Princess.

The Emperor was a warrior born. It was his wife who actually ran the kingdom while he served ably and well commanding the armies that defended it. Tragically, she had died the night of the Cataclysm and he had been forced to relinquish the duties of warlord in favor of those of Angwyn's monarch. He tried his best, and wasn't so bad in the job, but it was painfully much like fitting a cavalry charger between the poles of a dray. The animal may well pull the load but it isn't the best use of its skills and talents.

To compensate for those awful losses, he began to lavish care and attention on Elora. With a fondness that surprised her, considering how she came to hate her time in Angwyn, she found herself now remembering how he'd sit her before him on his saddle when she was barely able to walk and trot about the castle's war yard. She hadn't been afraid, snug in that seat with him, even when he took the huge animal over some small jumps, and couldn't wait for the day when he promised to take her riding on a pony of her own.

That day never came, of course, for the Emperor's advisers prevailed in their objections, proclaiming endlessly their concern over the consequences to Angwyn should the Sacred Princess be injured during one of these excursions. Or worse, be abducted by some other power among the Great Realms. Or worst of all, escape. She was Angwyn's prize and Angwyn's talisman, a gift from the Almighty, cast halfway around the face of the globe itself into the monarch's very courtyard. She was a treasure beyond price and must be secured accordingly.

So, a tower was built, adjacent to the palace, and from the day of its completion Elora was never allowed beyond its gates.

On the ground once more, she led her mare across the sprawling yard to the hitching post in front of the inn. Her leggings were more uncomfortable than ever, which gave her a wry appreciation of the old saw about "sprouting like a weed," but they were an absolute necessity on horseback, especially in rough country. She'd once more wrapped her head and shoulders in her tartan scarf, and lashed the much heavier greatcloak to her saddlebags and bedroll. True to Duguay's word, her face and body paint hadn't faded in the slightest and the dramatic patterning drew more stares now than when she strolled about in costume.

"Got to go, I hear," said Luc-Jon from the porch.

"What can I say? My first solo performance, and next I know, I'm being run out of town."

"Aye, truly there's no justice in world."

" 'In *the* world,' " she corrected. "Scribes should know their grammar, if no one else."

"Pfaugh!"

"Nice noise!"

"You should talk, some o' the ones you've made."

"Nice manners."

"Even more so, back at you!"

"Children!" remonstrated Duguay, at which point

both Luc-Jon and Elora burst into a rampaging fit of giggles.

"Better take care, Elora, else you'll make y'r master old afore 'is time."

"If I do, it's no less than he deserves."

A volley of hooves on hardpan heralded the approach of their escort, a light patrol of a dozen troopers with a fresh-faced lieutenant to command and a grizzled sergeant to actually run things. The Sergeant was Marn and he greeted Elora with affection. The Lieutenant was in a rush, and obviously considered this "baby-sitting" detail beneath him, so farewells had to be quick.

"Just my luck . . ." Luc-Jon began.

"Damn straight," Elora told him, stopping him with a finger to his lips before he could say another word. "It's a young world, Luc-Jon, and we're a pair of young lives. Anything's possible."

"You believe that?"

"I know it." *This time,* she thought, *I'm going to kiss him!* And she did. It was as gentle as the first, though it lasted a bit longer.

He has nice eyes, she thought. *He makes my heart race.* Her hands rested lightly on his neck and through her fingertips she could feel the pulse of the big vein just beneath the skin and the tips of her mouth twitched in delight at its tempo.

"I brung you something," Luc-Jon stammered.

"You a magician then, to whistle something out of nothing? The only thing I see in your hands is me."

"In y'r bag a'ready. From my master's archives. With permission," he added hurriedly as she reacted to the thought he might have stolen it.

Finally they heard a cough from the Lieutenant, apparently the latest in a series.

"Where's the puppy?" she asked, more to tweak the Lieutenant than to prolong the moment.

Luc-Jon shrugged. "Ain't seen him nor any t'others in his pack all the mornin'. Maybe they're huntin' Maizan."

"Say good-bye for me, will you?" Elora asked as, with

far more outward confidence than she actually felt, she climbed back onto Windfleet's saddle.

"You take care," Luc-Jon called after her as she turned to join the patrol.

"You, too!" she called back to him with a wave.

The Lieutenant offered a salute to the Commandant, to the colors, to the Officer of the Guard at the gate. They hadn't even left the fort and already Elora was bored enough to die.

She'd thought of kicking her mount into a full gallop the moment they were outside, but common sense scotched that notion right away. That's why there were miles of cleared ground on every side of the fort, so the defenders could see everyone coming or going. In the best of circumstances, she'd only have seconds for a head start and she doubted she could maintain that lead for long. The only way such a bolter would work was with a monstrous huge distraction.

The wolfhounds gave it to her.

The patrol was hardly out the gate when the dogs came at them from every side, raising a terrific hullabaloo of barks and snarls, baring fangs with fearsome growls, lunging forward in a stiff-legged attack posture as though they meant to grab the horses by their fetlocks and pitch them over. The horses immediately assumed the worst and their riders, taken by surprise by the attack itself as well as by its ferocity, had no argument for them. The animals panicked, and the men, who should have been trying to calm them, were suddenly left desperately trying to hold their seats.

They didn't have a chance. In lightning succession, the entire patrol was unhorsed, the terrified animals charging across the parade ground for the sanctuary of their stables to the jeers and catcalls of watching troopers. Duguay's horse skibbled in anxiety. It would have joined the others given the chance, but the troubadour proved himself as expert a horseman as he was a balladeer and kept the beast under control. Elora of course was lost, lacking both training and experience, but with her it was Windfleet who saved the day. The mare wasn't bothered in the slightest by the hounds' display. She had fought Death Dogs and lived. She knew there was no threat.

"Bravo, puppy!" Elora called, and without the slightest urging on her part Windfleet shot into a gallop.

The wolfhound looked indecently pleased with himself as he loped to a small rise past the wagon train's encampment to watch them go. Behind him there was a wild succession of shouts and curses, yelps of the purely human variety, and then a monstrous huge crash as one of the other dogs, very keen on initiative, streaked from the gatehouse as the portcullis thundered into place.

Feeling very pleased with himself, the hound lifted his head high and howled, as his ancestors had to tell the Dire Wolves their reign of blood and terror was done, and that now they were faced by foes worthy of the name.

"Did you *see* that?" Elora crowed, in between heartfelt prayers that the base of her spine not be pounded to powder. "Did you see what my puppy *did?*"

"Very impressive," Duguay agreed as his mount held pace with hers. "A prince among canines, truly."

"He did it for me, bless his heart." A frantic look over the shoulder. "There's nobody following!"

"Not really expecting anyone."

"What was that big crash, d'you think?"

"Portcullis. Not so hard, really. They're designed to come down in a hurry. All you have to do is release the brake."

"Absolutely brilliant."

"They're working dogs, wolfhounds are. Bred for brains as well as brawn."

"A whole lot of things in the world are smarter than they appear, Master Faralorn. You simply have to find the way to communicate and comprehend. Is the portcullis broken, d'you think? Is that why they're not after us yet?"

"Takes time to raise the gate, though not a lot. Takes

time as well to round up another patrol, though not a lot. By then, we'll be near the trees, if not outright in 'em."

"They have trackers, though, and scryscouts."

"If they want us badly enough, Elora, they'll find us. And run us down. We've only these animals here, they'll come with remounts so they can maintain a constant pace and faster. But I don't think they'll come."

"Why not?"

"There's been no word from that patrol went haring after the Maizan. If the rumors are correct about the Commandant being told to make a stand, he'll need every man and every blade."

"They are true, Duguay."

"I figured as much in the stable. By his lights, if we're this hell-bent set on suicide, he hasn't the resources to spare to save us from ourselves."

They slowed somewhat once they reached the shelter of the tree line. Open ground gave way to a succession of forest trails, but Duguay didn't call a halt for the better part of another hour, when they reached the crest of a rise that allowed a surprisingly panoramic view of the fields and the fortress at their hub.

"Well?" he challenged Elora.

She looked at him uncomprehendingly.

"From here we still have a decent sight of the fort," he explained. "It's not so hard to pretend we got lost if we decide to call this quits. We press on, girl, we cast away that luxury. But if we do press on, we need to know which way to go."

"Right."

He caught one of her reins, close by the bit.

"I know what this means to you, I know Ryn's your friend, but those others you're counting on, if they shut you out, we're done here. We go no farther, are we agreed?"

" 'We'?"

"If I have to hog-tie you, girl, I will. Think now what *you* mean to those we've left behind! That boy, that damnable *hound*! You talk about being worthy. Well, worth is grounded in honor, and honor in truth, to yourself first of all! And there's neither worth nor honor nor truth in being dumb. Now, are we agreed?"

She sat very still and very proud, because it was rare that she was ever spoken to in such a tone and rarer still when she acknowledged the moment was deserved.

She answered with a small and shallow nod of the head and didn't realize how truly regal she suddenly looked.

"Rool!" she called in mindspeech, firing her thoughts skyward like a beacon. "Bastian!

"I know what Khory probably told you," she explained. "I know what she told me. I'll understand if you don't reply. I hope and pray you will. Please. I beg you. Let me help."

She took a shuddery breath and chewed a moment on her lower lip. Duguay's horse was still a bit nervous, expecting another dog attack any moment, and kept shifting its feet. Windfleet remained totally calm.

"How long should we wait?" Elora asked.

Then her eyes went wide and she sagged back in her saddle as if a great and invisible hand had suddenly pushed against her chest. The air went right out of her and Duguay was halfway to the ground to catch her, certain she was about to fall, when she regained both breath and balance.

"Oh my," she said, and took a long moment to enjoy the view.

Bastian soared to the north and west, in the general direction that Elora was meant to travel. Below him was a hedgehog range: old-growth mountains whose majestic summits had been worn away by the passage of the eons and cast in gentler forms, so named because of their general resemblance of those animals. Rool was riding with him, and with his first word, Elora knew she'd made the right decision.

"Come," he said, with the finality to his voice of a warrior facing battle.

"Where, Rool? What's happening?"

"Stay merged with Bastian, he'll show the way. There's a fast trail, I'll explain as you go. Be quick, Elora Danan. Be here by moonrise. Be ready to fight."

Rool was good as his word and Bastian a superb guide. Once they gained the track he spoke of, Elora merely gave Windfleet her head and trusted the mare not to make any missteps. It proved to be a wild, wonderful ride, even if the young woman spent much of it with her eyes closed.

Abruptly, shocking the girl's eyes wide open, Windfleet jerked to a stiff-legged stop. Tension raced with fatigue straight through the mare's body, and from there through Elora's, with such force and intensity that both sets of nerves were nearly crackling. Duguay felt it, too. He'd pulled his own mount beside her, his free hand clasped tight around the haft of a drawn sword.

Ahead and above rose a mound. Nothing near as impressive to look at as many peaks she'd seen, that was true of all these ancient mountains. Worn away by the elements of nature as a body is by time, they had all been reduced to the merest ghosts of their original selves. Yet this one in particular possessed a *gravitas,* a primal weight of spirit, that put the whole rest of this range to shame, and a fair portion of the Stairs to Heaven as well.

The night of the Cataclysm, not only Tir Asleen was destroyed. As Thorn discovered during a decade and more of roaming the face of the globe, that selfsame malefic force annihilated a score of similar sites, on every continent and on both sides of the Veil, savaging those special places that were the main repositories of arcane energy.

Once upon a time, this hill would have been among that number, a nexus of the ley lines which sustain all magic through the uncountable eons. But just as with every other physical property of the world, the intersection points that once existed here had moved on, leaving only the residue of that eldritch force, the palest echo of the glory that once had been.

Windfleet danced sharply on her hooves and laid her ears back flat atop her skull. This was not so much a posture of fear but of readying herself for battle. Flight was certainly a considered option. Brave she was, not stupid. There was a stillness to the air, akin to the gathering of forces before a thunderstorm. It felt supercharged with an infinite number of tiny, invisible lightning bolts that burst over every inch of Elora's skin, whether clothed or not. Even her hair, short as it was, stood on end. Sounds faded the way they do in terrible cold, when the air becomes too dry to carry noise very far. Yet, paradoxically, Elora felt the beginnings of a wind, not so much the movement of air . . .

. . . but of forces *through* the air, winding their corkscrew way up from the base of the steep-sided mound.

"What is this place?" she asked, in a voice as hushed as the moment.

"A high tor," she heard Rool say aloud, and Bastian swung out of a tight circle to claim a perch on a nearby outcrop of stone. A nudge with her knee sidestepped Windfleet close beside it and she raised her arm to make the transfer easier. She noted a harness tucked beneath the eagle's shoulder feathers. Rool used it to swing to her hand and from there he made his swift and surefooted way to his usual perch on her shoulder.

"A place of gathering," he finished. He wasn't happy to see Duguay alongside but chose not to press the issue.

"Something special about tonight?" asked the troubadour. "You made it sound urgent."

"We're at the midpoint between solstice and equinox. It's a window of opportunity for the casting of major spells, if you've the knowledge and the heart."

"Let me guess," Elora noted. "Someone up there has both."

"I see horses tethered in that hollow," Duguay noted. "No riders visible."

"None alive, leastways," was the brownie's grim comment.

"Maizan?"

"The ones who stole Ryn had comrades waiting in the forest. And more here."

"Those poor bastards." At Duguay's exclamation, Elora looked at him in startlement until he explained. "The patrol, those four men sent out to mark the Maizan's trail."

"They were alive when they were brought here. And when they were dragged up the slope."

"What about Khory?" Elora demanded.

"She dealt with all the Maizan she could find. Then she followed. We've seen an' heard nothing since."

"The summit's obscured," Bastian explained with mindspeech. "And something about the mist that shrouds it made me keep clear."

"Made us both," echoed Rool, who'd heard him.

Without a word, Elora swung herself to the ground, leaving Rool behind on the saddle.

"Elora Danan," he snapped in protest, but his mouth clacked shut as she tossed the reins to him.

"Keep her calm," she said, meaning her mare.

"And mine as well, small master, if you please," said Duguay, slinging his own reins over Elora's saddle horn.

"And his as well," she agreed, since he clearly wasn't about to be denied in this.

"Suppose there's trouble!" Rool cried.

She ghosted a grin. "If there is, I'm counting on you and Windfleet"—she gave the mare a comforting stroke to the muzzle—"to bring help. Watch over him, Bastian," she called.

"Always, Royal Highness."

With that, she was gone, Duguay by her side.

Dressed though she was for the road, Elora was glad whatever forces shaped her physical being had gifted her with a marked resilience to extremes of weather. The temperature was closer to cold than chill, and a skirling breeze put sharp teeth into its bite. Thickly layered as he was, in wool and leather and fur, she could feel Duguay shiver.

At this altitude, the air was thin enough to permit a spectacular view of the firmament, a sight Elora had beheld often before but one of which she never tired. It was a cloudless night, and with the moon wholly occluded there was no competing radiance to detract from the overarching glory of the heavens. Even when she told herself there was nothing new to see, she found herself casting forth the net of her imagination and picturing a different kind of Elora on some distant peak looking back at her across that inconceivable gulf. Usually those dreams made her laugh, because it was hard enough to conceive of the myriad and conflicting aspects of life on her own world, much less crowd an entirely new and different order of creation in beside them.

There was more. As Thorn said resignedly, there was *always* more. If each of those dots was a sun much like the one that sustained this world, and if each of those suns had planetary children, and each globe inhabitants, then the universe, already so vast and unfathomable, grew utterly beyond all hope of comprehension.

That's usually when she stopped thinking about it, for the concepts made her head hurt, as when she spun herself around and around like a dervish until she found herself no longer able to stand. A dizziness of the spirit to complement the vertigo of the flesh.

She saw a flash, high above and toward the horizon, brilliantly scoring the darkness for the merest moment before it was gone.

"Shooting star," she and Duguay said together, and both made light of their impromptu congruence.

A mist rose in the time it took them to make their way to the base of the tor, across a jumbled scree that reminded her of a child's messy playroom, with building blocks all tossed carelessly about. Save that these blocks were stone instead of wood and weighed tons, not ounces, and could only be held in a giant's hand.

The smell of blood drew her to the first sacrifice. He'd been stripped, but Elora assumed he was one of the four Sandeni troopers. He'd been staked head down toward the base of the tor, with his feet directed at the summit. His aspect was due north. Elora assumed that if they circled the tor they'd find the other three men at the remaining cardinal points of the compass. There were a pair of Maizan close at hand, as dead as he, with their torturer's tools smashed and scattered about them on the ground. One was twisted back on himself in a way that indicated both his spine and neck had been broken. The other was minus his head altogether.

"It's called the blood eagle," Duguay said in a voice totally devoid of emotion, as though flat reportage was the only way this scene of horror could be endured. He was on one knee beside the sacrifice and with a hand indicated the ruin that had been made of his chest. "The object of this atrocity is to keep the victim alive until the ceremony's complete."

"Look at his face. That's a man at peace, not in agony."

"Your friend Khory's doing," Duguay reported in that same matter-of-fact tone. "She took care of the Maizan, then gave this poor devil the mercy of a quick, clean death, to put an end to his torment. Should we try to find her?" he wondered.

"She'll be after Ryn." Elora's gaze rose up the slope before them. "That's where to look."

"Let's go, then."

She shook her head.

"Not you, Duguay. Not any farther."

"I'm not having this discussion another time, Elora."

"No, we're not. There's sorcery afoot here, so foul I don't have words to describe it. But at least I have some immunity."

"Suppose there are other Maizan. You're not that good in a rough-and-tumble scrap that you can't use someone to watch your back."

"If Khory's gone ahead, there are no other Maizan. Stay by the horses and heed Rool. If he says, you bolt."

"You need me by your side, Elora!" he called.

She didn't look back. He didn't follow.

She heard the first scream when she lay foot upon the actual slope of the tor. There were no evident paths, to Mage- or InSight, and while the grade wasn't anywhere near vertical, it was steep enough to be a trial. This first stretch was the most difficult, mainly because the footing was so treacherous, the surface littered with stones that threatened to skibble out from underfoot with every step, and handholds equally ready to betray her.

It was a man's voice, the kind of bellow that mostly comes from a physical shock, cut off with a finality that left her no illusions as to his fate.

Elora felt something grab at her, twisted instinctively to break its hold, lost her balance in the process, the sharp tip of a rock making her cry out as it poked her, and began a madcap toboggan back the way she came, managing to stop herself by frantically splaying every limb to full extension and scrabbling for purchase with fingers and toes together.

She was on her back, and therefore had an uncontested view into the heart of the mist. She didn't consider that a blessing, as a twisted, glowing shape leaped from those skirling clouds to swipe at the laces of her tunic. The attack was so quick, the creature was out of reach before Elora could even register her danger, much less attempt any defense. It wasn't alone, either, as a glance up and down the course of the mist revealed almost as many glowing shapes within as there were stars above, all of them racing pell-mell for the tor's summit.

A second creature began its charge and this time Elora took a swat at it, only to see it loop around her hand with an ease that beggared birds and insects both and zoom back to safety with her sleeve slashed open to the elbow.

This time, though, she'd caught a decent look at her attacker. It was a fairy.

All her life she'd thought them the most inoffensive of beings, little more than adornments on the form of Creation in the same way that decorations adorned the Yule trees. They were always said to be the kindest of souls, who never tormented a stranger in their midst out of malice, but tried their best to entrance with play.

The emotion she saw now was anything but gentle, and the blow that struck her was likewise rich in hatred.

A third and fourth broke from the cloud to come at her, but this time the surprise was theirs as she spun to her feet and sprinted uphill, accepting the risk of an occasional slip as she blazed a crablike switchback trail—racing to her left, to her right, to her left—that gained her distance with every reversal of direction. She didn't evade these new attacks, she refused to pay them any mind, keeping her concentration focused instead on the need to reach the summit.

Rock soon gave way to grass, a rich, thick, loamy sod that had no business being on these slopes at all, much less at such an altitude. Here and there Elora could see patches where peat had been worn away to bare rock, and the image came to her of waves pounding ceaselessly on a shore, each crash of surf inexorably peeling away another layer of sand. Same here, in its way. Magic sustained the life represented by this grass. But with the passage of the ley lines, the magic was no longer renewed. Eventually that residue would be exhausted, the grass would wither, the soil fly away on each gust of wind as dust. Snow and stone would claim this peak, as they had all the rest.

Another scream, a gargling ululation so piercing Elora had to cover her ears and blink away a wicked cascade of tears before they overflowed her eyes. The first death, however brutal, had been quick and in that way merciful. Not so the second, in either respect: not quick, not merciful. She couldn't recognize the voice, and prayed it wasn't Ryn's.

Elora had come better than halfway, and forced herself pause not so much for breath but for the opportunity to take stock of herself and the situation. The strands of mist had been thin when they started rising around the tor, their course following the whirlwind form of a tornado. In the time Elora had been climbing they'd thickened and widened, to the point where they'd closed the gaps between them totally below her into a solid mass of cloud. She could see more lights as well, sparkling brilliantly within that gray mass. Each one, a fairy. Each fairy with a blade.

She couldn't retreat now if she wanted to.

Her clothes were a shambles, hanging off her body in great droops of cloth, with every seam slashed through. She salvaged what she could and cast the rest aside. She'd grown so used to the style and manner of the fairy attacks she gave them little mind any longer. It was a nuisance having her clothes literally cut from her body but hardly worth the effort needed to defend herself.

This one came sharply around the curve of the hillside, in a blindingly fast, diving attack that Elora didn't catch until it was nearly too late. Even then it was only a reflexive snap of the head away from the *pop* of fiery radiance that was the fairy that saved her eye. She felt a blow strong enough to stagger her, heard a howl of triumph that was a poor imitation of a wolfsong as the tiny creature swept back into the misty skystream, and then felt something wet across the curve of her cheek.

The gash was barely two fingers long, only a surface cut, although it bled freely and stung worse than any wasp or hornet. More than the attack itself, what disturbed Elora was the crazed grin the fairy wore, as it took a feral delight in an act that its kind would have once considered obscenity.

At least now Elora understood why they'd been tearing at her clothes, and realized as well that even the shallowest of wounds, in sufficient number, can cripple if not outright kill.

As the fairies came for her she attacked the hill, scrambling the intervening distance to the summit with a frantic, four-limbed gait that was an unconscious but disconcertingly effective echo of Ryn when he was in a rush. Her assailants redoubled their own efforts, no longer striking singly but descending in a swarm to scourge and harry her, determined to claim sole credit for this one life in the face of the score run up by whatever ruled the summit.

Rounding a last pile of boulders, she crashed headlong into a Maizani hell-bent on flight. The collision pitched them both to the ground, though Elora caught the worst of it, since the warrior had the advantage in bulk, not to mention the remnants of his armor. He struck out from the moment of contact, fists and feet flailing with such fury that to protect herself Elora had no choice but to curl into a tight ball, knees to chin, her own hands closed into fists, forearms crossed before her face, taking the blows on bones, gambling that none would strike so hard to break them.

The Maizani wasn't interested in doing her harm, merely in driving her away. Once she was out of reach he lumbered on. Elora's instinct was to follow and bring him down, for in his state and on this sharp a grade, his course would lead him only to disaster, but she uttered not a word, made no more than that sole halting gesture. She'd seen the man's eyes in the moment of contact and there was no intellect left in them for commands or comfort to reach. He had been reduced to little better than a beast, obedient only to the most basic of inborn natural directives.

The fairies appeared to view his attempted flight as more important, possibly more sport, than her ascent. None attempted to defy the current that spun them all ultimately to the summit, but those below who'd been gathering against Elora now turned their full attention to the Maizani. She saw him in bursts as he emerged from each line of mist, with every appearance more and more dotted with flashes of radiance until he might well be mistaken for a creature of light himself. In far less time they stripped him to the skin, and then they stripped him of his skin, only to discover a prey too dumb to know it was doomed.

The fairies could make him fall, they couldn't keep him down. Elora found herself thankful that the arid air, so sharp and dry each breath scored her lungs, kept his outcries from her ears. This was hard enough to watch, unbearable to hear as well. Sworn enemy though he was, being a Maizani, she had to acknowledge him a marvel of a man, brimming with strength and life. She wished he had less of both—so he could die.

It was a spear that claimed him, cast from the summit as swift and sure as any arrow. Elora's heart leaped to see it, for she knew only one person with so deadly an aim and the strength to make it good.

"Khory," she whispered. "Alive!"

But for how much longer, she thought as a last glance down the slope saw the Maizani collapse to his knees, the spear standing up from his body like standard, while the fairies burst away from him like a nest of glittering hornets.

Elora began to run, and prayed there wasn't far to go.

The summit was roughly the size of the fort's parade ground, dipping down and away from where she stood to form a shallow bowl before rising to a crest two thirds of the way to the other end. It should have been barren save for the natural adornments of grass and flowers. Any sarcen stones and plinths to mark the cardinal points of the physical as well as arcane compass should have worn away ages past, for once the lines of power moved on there was no reason to use this tor any longer. It wouldn't even be effective as the setting for a World Gate to and from the Veil Realms.

Yet stones stood before her. The perimeter ring marked the rim of the peak. It was composed of the smallest pieces, wedge-shaped and no taller than her knee. Narrower at the top than base, they reminded Elora of the battlements of long-lost Tir Asleen.

A slightly larger set, each stone approximately Elora's height and breadth, demarcated the bowl itself, with the primary stones arrayed in a circle about the altar. Those last dwarfed all the rest, and for the life of her Elora couldn't imagine how anyone had set them in place.

The perimeter was rough-hewn, giving Elora the impression that a load of boulders of approximately appropriate size had been gathered and then chiseled into shape on site. By contrast, the primary sarcen stones were an obsidian so dark and gleaming they might have been touched with oil and polish just the hour before, surfaces so smooth, corners so sharp, they must have been quarried and then finished by master artisans. She'd rarely seen steel come from Torquil's foundry in so excellent and flawless a state.

Khory was waiting.

Perhaps there'd been fewer fairies to oppose her, or they didn't much care even in madness to pit themselves against a warrior with a demon's soul; whichever, she'd reached the summit in a far better state than Elora. There was blood on her, and some of it was her own, a testament to the prowess of her foes.

"Are you all right?" they said as one and each spared the other a fleeting smile of reassurance to discover they were.

"What's happening?" Elora asked.

"I think I'm happier not knowing," was the taller woman's laconic reply. "The Maizan knew I was coming, there were ambushes set for miles back. This had already begun when I arrived."

"Makes sense. Begin at moonrise, climax at zenith." Elora skated a glance across the heavens but the mist lay too thickly overhead. "There can't be much time."

"I thought, if I finished those men below before their time . . ."

"It was a kindness, if nothing else." She turned toward the heart of the stone circles. "I have to go in there."

Khory nodded. "Saw you coming. Figured I'd wait."

The altar was where all the elements of the battle crashed together. As they approached, Elora could make out a glow at ground level, a defensive sphere of energy whose blood-hued shades rippled like fine satin in a breeze. Directly above it the rising column of fairies came together as clouds do to form the anvil forms of thunderheads, so innocent and beguiling in the one incarnation, puffballs finer than blossoms of unspun cotton floating through space. In the other, they form the embodiment of violence and destruction, giving birth to thunder and lightning, torrential rains, and winds of such fury even stone houses could not stand against them.

She remembered something a Highlander she knew

had told her when she was cooing over the dogs that jogged happily at his heels: "A pup alone is a wondrous thing," he said of his mixed-blood herders, "but put two together, they'll sure an' find a sheep to kill." Because then they were a pack and became subject to hereditary imperatives that overruled the character of the individual.

Alone, a fairy was the quintessence of loveliness. In this mass, they roiled together with such intensity the construct they formed couldn't hold a wholly stable shape. It was meant to be vaguely human, with correct extremities in pretty much the proper arrangement—allowing of course for the horns and wings and tail—but the details couldn't remain constant from one moment to the next. Each new arrival altered the blend, which in turn had a cascading effect on the final result. The changes never ended, so many occurring in so short a span of time that Elora couldn't bear to look at it. There was nothing tangible on which to anchor her perceptions, it was like trying to keep her balance on a floor composed of nothing but marbles and ice. Merely trying made her eyes burn and her head ache.

Like swimming with firedrakes, she thought.

The figure cried out and the sound it made was worse than the sight of it. There was no single voice, but a chorus of every creature that composed its being. It had no coherent form of its own, but was an amorphous compilation of this horde of fairies, crushing themselves so tightly together that their individual luster blended to cast the illusion of something greater and more terrible.

As with any great enterprise, there was a commensurate cost. The fairy that blazed most brightly does so for the briefest time, and these were burning with an intensity that seared the eye. That made the melody of their blended voices as unendurable as their glow, for within the mass, individual songs suddenly vanished, as did the light that signaled that fairy's life force. They were dying, one and all, killing themselves willfully— *gleefully*—in defense of this most holy ground. Any creature not of their own kind who trespassed on this hill tonight was an enemy, and therefore to be destroyed without hesitation or mercy. Within the globe of energy, a sorcerer's last and most desperate line of defense when all the other spells of protection had failed, was the person responsible for this sacrilege, the object now of the fairies' greatest hatred.

When Elora started forward, belatedly aware that she was next to naked, clad in her belt with its traveling pouches, from which hung the tattered remnants of her shorts, the fairy conglomerate swept out an arm toward her, casting a blistering lash of raw energy across the curve of its foe's globe. Rainbow fire exploded on the surface of the globe, tendrils striking back at the assaulting arm, Elora crying out in sympathetic horror as they left avenues of shadow in their wake. Tiny bodies rained down to carpet the stone like ash. She recognized the nature of those defenses, they were the same that had attacked her in the fort when she'd called out to Ryn. Yet she took no pleasure in the discovery that she'd run her prey to ground, and that the fairies' enemy was also the sorcerer who'd enslaved her friend.

Above her, those countless scores had no sooner perished than their place was taken by hundreds more, and the bolt of fire which struck toward Elora was tenfold more powerful than the one unleashed against the globe.

With a desperate cry, she shoved Khory to cover beyond the circle, but there was no time for her to follow. She staggered as the blast washed over her, but that was mainly from the shock of contact. She thought there'd be pain, sufficient to dash her shrieking to her knees for the brief moments allowed her before she was utterly consumed.

Not a thing.

On either side, rock blistered, slagged, exploded under the terrible onslaught. Elora remained untouched, unharmed.

In amazement, she stared down at herself while the conglomerate howled frustration and redoubled its efforts against the figure within the globe. She believed she'd been cut more times than she cared to recall, yet there wasn't a sign of it on her skin. Dried blood on the loincloth, yes, but not even the ghost of a scar elsewhere.

She sensed movement, caught a glimpse of Khory slinking from cover to cover, called out to her to stay clear. This was a moment for Elora alone.

An avenue led from the perimeter to a circle of station stones, and from there to the heart of the ancient shrine. Elora took a breath to compose herself and then set off with a formal and measured cadence, approaching the altar with all due respect and solemnity.

At the station stones, she paused, ignoring (though it was blessed hard) the monstrous creature that loomed so high above the tor, it now dwarfed these sarcen stones that in their turn dwarfed her, and the now visibly shrunken (though no less colorfully bright) globe of fire huddled at the base of the one that stood at the head of the altar.

Lifting her arms to either side, stretching her hands, she found she had just enough height to brush her fingertips over the lower surface of the gateway plinth.

"Revered heart of grace," she said, and wished for something more majestic than her husky and broken voice. "I come in peace. I mean none harm, I do none harm. I ask your welcome."

She didn't know what to expect by way of reply, didn't really expect one at all, and so wasn't surprised when none was forthcoming.

Elora drew about herself the same dignity she'd have projected in any royal palace, with herself gowned and coifed to the eyebrows, and took the twenty steps that brought her at last to the basalt center court. It was easier to ignore the battle now that she realized none of the weapons could do her harm.

She stood before the altar and repeated her invocation.

There was no sense of foulness when she placed palms flat on the worn and pitted slab. Alone of all the aspects of the shrine in view, it showed full evidence of its tremendous age. Whatever was intended here by the person in the globe, it had not come to pass.

Then and there, Elora took a slow, steadying deep breath. She shook her hands in a vain attempt to stop their trembling, frightfully aware that if she was in any way wrong about her invulnerability she'd only find out the hard way. A last and final lesson in humility.

She put her back to the creature, aware of a tickle of sensation along her spine as she stepped forward into the path of its bolts. She strode right to the edge of the glowing sphere, spared a moment to kneel and lay her hand in sorrow and apology on the scored and savaged rock that had borne the brunt of the damage.

Then as easily as strolling through an open doorway, she breached the sorcerer's wards and passed through the globe.

Within crouched a woman twice Elora's age, garbed for war, in a pose that suggested cornered predator more than human being. Soft leather garbed her snugly, a costume designed as much to distract the eye as for comfort and ease of movement. It was dyed the color of rich red wine, more black than scarlet. Spike-studded gauntlets reached to her elbows, boots to the top of her knees. She wore a tunic laced as tight as any corset, slashed in battle to reveal a layer of fine chain mail sandwiched between those of leather. Elora had no doubt the woman was armed to the proverbial teeth, but knew as well she hadn't strength or concentration to spare to draw a single one. All her efforts and resources were devoted to the maintenance of her wards. The slightest relaxation and she'd join her comrades. Elora understood, as did this Maizan sorceress, that their agonies would pale to insignificance compared with hers.

It was a beautiful face, she saw, though now to Elora it seemed haunted. There were great dark circles beneath her eyes, which themselves appeared sunken within their sockets, eloquent testimony to the toll this struggle was taking. The battle was literally eating her alive. She lacked the nigh-inexhaustible numerical reserves of her foes.

Fairies could be easily replaced on this slaughtering ground, not so the substance of the woman's own flesh. Her cheeks were deeply hollowed as well, and there was a loginess to her movements, as though every particle of her was pulling against the resistance of a great and growing weight. Full lips, pressed thin and bloodless from strain, elegant hands made more for holding a dancing partner at court than a sword.

Beside her on the ground lay Ryn. Alive, and to Elora's eye unharmed.

"You've lost, Maizani," Elora told the woman.

"Never."

"Take my hand."

"Rather have your heart." Defiance had its moments, this wasn't one of them.

"Are you surprised at their resistance? This is their home. Whatever you had planned, the fairies want none of it."

"There's a new order in the world. They have to move aside."

The woman grabbed for her blade. Elora tapped her on the breastbone with its point.

"How—!" the sorceress gobbled.

"Magic." It was nothing of the sort, really. The sorceress was too fixated on the need to maintain her wards. By the time she noticed what was going on around her, Elora had stolen her sword.

"You're not magic, you're not even human."

"There's been enough bloodshed, and too much damage done already."

The woman's expression changed, twisted by a burst of comprehension. "I *know* you," she hissed.

"Yield."

"This is your companion, that's why we took him. We hope to lure Drumheller to his doom, but you'll do just as well."

"I'm not the one here who faces doom."

"I have his spirit, I have his"—and the way she spoke the word made it a curse—*"soul."*

"And I have you," Elora said, with a calmness she didn't feel. "Fates willing, if you've wit to realize it, I can be your salvation."

"His life for mine, is that it?"

"I'm not the only one you have to deal with, remember."

"You don't speak for them, you're nothing like them."

"Consider those my advantages. You haven't much time to decide, you're weakening with every breath."

"This World Gate must be *closed*!"

"Why? There hasn't been the power to sustain a Gate here in longer than the Daikini race has even been alive."

"No matter. It was a place of power once, can be so again. That must never be! Limit the access of the Veil Folk to our world, limit their power over it. Over *us*!"

"Is that what Mohdri told you? Is that what you believe he wants? The spells you cast don't simply seal World Gates, they strip the land of its magic and deliver it to him. He's betrayed you—so you can betray the world."

"Liar!" she screamed. "We're *saving* the world for our people, for our children!"

"What about the Veil Folk? Isn't this their world, too?"

"They have proper domains of their own, we Daikini this one alone, what right have they to pieces of ours?"

"That may be true for Greater Faery and those who dwell in the Circle of the Spirit. But this is sacred ground for Lesser Faery. They're partly of the Veil, but mainly of the world. They've as much right as we to live here."

"Then why haven't *they* ever offered to share?" There wasn't hatred in the woman's voice, although she well and truly snarled her words. To Elora she seemed more like a child who'd spent too long staring through a set of gates at something wondrous and untouchable, heartsick and crying out in sorrow because no matter how hard she begged, she'd never be allowed through.

"We're not arguing over toys," Elora told her with a gentle but matter-of-fact tone. "Not possessions of any kind. We are *all* of the world, on both sides of the Veil. Diminish a part, we diminish the whole."

"Words." Another snarl, thick with rough contempt.

"Your companions are dead. Is that what you want, to join them?"

"I'm willing to die for what I believe in."

"Then you die for nothing."

"Kill me, then, you silver bitch, and have done with it, if you've the courage!"

Elora shook her head. "There's been enough killing. You want to show me courage, try living! Try building something, *creating* something."

"Stop it. I don't want to hear any more. Leave me be!"

"There are beings out there who love their lives as much as you do yours. They're immolating themselves, like moths on a furnace flame, to get to you. I walk away, they die, you die. I refuse to accept either."

"You're a fool, then."

"Then I'm a fool."

The bubble around them creaked, as though from the pressure of some great wind, and a moment later the Maizani groaned in sympathetic pain as the force deployed against her shields made itself felt within her body. She was breathing in deliberate pulses, almost akin to an automaton, each breath proclaiming her will's domination of her flesh. Yet in stark defiance of that state of being, her sunken eyes were awash, tears of sorrow streaming across her proud, ravaged cheeks. She knew her life was done, and she was afraid.

"There's a time for every death," Elora told her. "And somewhiles even a purpose. This isn't yours."

"You're trying to trick me!"

Elora snorted.

"You're a sorceress," she said, trusting her instincts to guide her words the way they did her songs. "If you're any good at all, that means you've touched the glory. I can't work magic. I'll never know, but I've heard sorcerers speak of it." Thorn spoke of it only in the most simple terms. The words weren't important, Elora understood that now more than ever. What mattered was the light that gleamed deep in his eyes, like a lighthouse beacon against the darkest nightfall, and the joy that gathered around him as snug as his most favorite quilt. To touch the glory, he told her, was to know wonder, and from there find your way to the heart of the dream.

"Remember the joy of that moment," Elora cried out, "the sense of hope, the surety that all things are possible. Where's that wonder"—and she waved her arm to encompass not simply the interior of the sphere but the battlefield hidden beyond—"here?"

Elora reached out to the woman, but held short of actually touching her.

"Your heart knows the truth," she said. "Your soul knows. This is wrong. You are wrong. And you should stop."

She saw a tremble ripple across the other's chin that she took to mean assent, for in every other aspect the woman appeared to be carved from stone, as immovable and eternal as the rocks of the tor itself.

With that, Elora simply stood up to her full height, bringing the crown of her skull up against the substance of the energy field.

With a *pop* much like a soap bubble, the globe burst, its substance fast-fading in a shower of firefly particles, leaving a scene dominated by the ghastly greens and blues generated by the fairy creature towering above.

The globe had comprised a circle with a diameter of roughly twice Elora's height. The boundary itself was marked by a wall of ash, the remains of fairies who'd sacrificed themselves in onslaught after futile onslaught, creatures the size of dust motes piled as high as Elora's hips and considerably farther back.

Without the globe to restrain them, the entire bulwark collapsed inward, with a soft *shooshing* that sounded louder than any church carillon in the sudden hollow silence. The spillage flowed like mercury across the earth, almost to their feet, and Elora blinked back tears of her own at the sight.

So many hopes—the thought came to her, not one she had herself but overheard from another—*so many dreams. Lost.*

The creature stretched its great arms to the heavens and roared in triumph. The Maizani took no notice as she stroked trembling fingers across the fairy remains, barely touching them, the wake left by her hand moving through the air enough to stir them into a dance that was a pallid and poignant reminder of what they'd been capable of when alive.

Did fairies come to dance for you, Elora thought, *the night of your Ascension, when you touched the glory and claimed the fullness of your natural power? Is that what you're remembering?*

"What have I done?" the woman breathed. "What have I *done*?"

"WE WILL HAVE VENGEANCE," thundered the great mass overhead.

Elora took a step sideways to place herself between it and the sorceress, and shook her head, painfully aware of how hard her heart was suddenly pounding and wishing as suddenly for a whole host of things, all of which would place her as far as imaginable from this place and this moment.

Then, in the face of the creature's fury, she smiled.

"This is a place of passion," she told the fairies, and felt the faintest tingling in her toes as the stones below remembered what that meant over countless eons, "but most of all, of peace."

"IT IS NOT WE WHO HAVE COME TO DESECRATE THIS HOLY PLACE. WE ARE ITS DEFENDERS, ITS CHAMPIONS!"

"And you have done that work well. But the danger is past."

"Suppose We say different."

A single voice, single face, emerged from the verdant radiance to take a stand before the altar. He viewed the scene with a proprietary air that marked his rank, his true place in the scheme of things, far more eloquently than any crown. He stood shorter than Elora, though not by much, and not so broad as a Nelwyn, though she could see strong similarities in the shape of his body and the structure of his face. His robes seemed to be formed of leaves, and since it was late in the growing year he was a riot of autumnal color, russets and scarlets and golds. Long hair the color of mahogany was woven into multiple braids, though his beard, by contrast, hung loose. Elora spied the tiny heads and bright eyes of fledgling birds poking out from its thicket.

"Such is your prerogative," she replied, "but that doesn't make it right."

"And what's been done here, be that 'right'?"

"If it were, I wouldn't have stopped it."

He said nothing but his manner made his anger plain.

"I am—" she began, but was rudely cut off by a peremptory wave of the hand.

"Your name is known, and your claim. Whether We acknowledge either remains to be determined."

"As Your Majesty pleases," and she bowed her head in affirmation of the King's rank.

"Death has been brought to this sacred place, and foul desecration attempted. Those scales must be balanced."

Too late Elora realized that the King wasn't engaging in a dialogue but was passing sentence. A blast of energy ripped forth from him. She'd been expecting any attack to come from the mass above, yet even as the King struck at her she saw the monstrous creature burst apart into all its component parts, the sky around her suddenly filling with fairies, thick as snowflakes in a blizzard and infinitely more lovely.

She had a heartbeat to realize the purpose of this distraction before the King's bolts struck both her and the warrior. Coherent thought shattered like breaking glass, all the numberless pieces of her self cast forth on bits of crystal, each to be snatched up by a fairy and hidden away in some secret spot known only to them, nevermore to be found. In this way would the old persona be irreversibly annihilated, leaving the way clear for something new and altogether different to be born.

She would have cried out, but the pain was so blindingly intense that her breath caught in her throat. Her mouth opened wide, the sole means left her to express those feelings of suffering, but then to her horror her jaws separated even wider, as though her flesh had become pliable and elastic. The shape of bones shifted beneath her skin like soft clay, squarish jaw becoming sharply pointed, skull elongating and narrowing to match, eyeteeth stretching into fangs, ears curving up and out to triple their former size, a fan shape ending in sharp points top and bottom. Her vision splintered, reformed, developed multiple facets, as though the lens of her eyes had been replaced by cut diamonds. She felt her shoulders compress, then her hips, accompanied by an elongation of the spine. She registered a dull, distant thump as her belt dropped from a waist grown too thin to support it. Legs came to resemble stilts, uncommonly long and thin as twigs, nothing but bone and whipcord muscle beneath their tautly wrapped envelope of skin. Her arms grew much the same, to end in fingers dominated by wickedly sharp, retractable claws. She didn't need a look at her toes to know they were the same, accompanied by a spur that extended from her heel to make it easier to grasp hold of a landing perch.

The last was the worst, as flesh and bone and muscle and sinew were reshaped a final time to bring forth her wings.

She found herself wrapped in a cocoon of her own making, pliant wings folded protectively across her body. She unfolded herself gracefully, because there was no other way for one of the fairy folk to move, to find the King standing before her, hand outheld to help her to her feet.

Elora turned her head to the side, and beheld the sorceress, curled up in much the same pose, having undergone an identical transformation. She was larger by far than most of the fairies, though little more than a small child by Daikini standards. She awoke slowly, haltingly, confused at first by the strangeness of all that lay about her, but speedily entranced by the wonder of it all. Every experience was a discovery, and each of those, a delight.

Her wings unfolded with a snap, and the moment they did so her feet left the ground. It took no effort on her part, and there was only the barest of breezes across the crest of the tor. Neither mattered. Her place was the sky, and as she rose a triple column of flashfire creatures spiraled about her until she was as radiant a being as the massive creature that had tried so hard to claim her life.

Elora felt a terrible yearning in her own heart, an itching down the length of her spine as her wings stirred of their own accord.

She closed hands into fists, felt the pressure of blunt fingernails against her palm, held them out for inspection, and realized with that sight that she viewed them through a single smooth lens rather than the prism of a fairy's eyes.

"Elora Danan," the King breathed while she tried to master the pain of reversion, and she found herself thankful to be already on her knees as she rebuilt herself from the inside out.

"It *is* you."

She was folded totally in on herself, on her knees with her forehead resting on the rough surface of a paving stone. She wanted nothing more than to sleep away the season, if not the year, if not the rest of her life, but instead pressed herself up until her spine was straight and sat on her heels in the Chengwei manner. She and the King were eye to eye. She met his gaze and did not bow.

"I am Tyrrel." His public name, of course, for the revelation of his True Name would give sorcerers power over him, as would knowledge of his rank to his more temporal foes.

"Majesty," she replied.

"My spell did not hold."

"None do, on me."

"You don't sound so pleased."

She flicked her eyes skyward, to where the woman who had once been a Maizani had joined hands with other fairies in a joyous dance of rebirth and welcome.

"It would have been nice to fly just once. What have you done here, Tyrrel?"

"As I said, balancing the scales. A bloodgelt. A life in payment for the slain."

"Your fairies took their toll of her companions, why spare her?"

"They fought, they were slain in battle. She yielded. That brought her before Our justice. Rampant slaughter is a Daikini trait, Elora Danan."

"What will become of her?"

"She will serve as Our consort. Her children will take the place of those who were slain defending this most sacred place. And mayhap her power as a sorceress will help defend Us against any others who would do Us harm. On either side of the Veil."

"She won't be enough."

"Shall We then depend on you, Sacred Princess?"

Elora made a wry face and rose to her feet, grimacing at every pop of every joint as they were reminded how to properly work. She felt sore and pummeled, worse than she ever had after a day's work at Torquil's forge. She scooped up her belt and pouches as she stood, and cast about for something to wear.

"I was thinking we might help each other. You know of the Sandeni stronghold on the river, to the south and east?"

Tyrrel nodded.

"One way or another, war will come to them before long. Either the Maizan, or Faery. Those Daikini are taking a stand to defend your homes as much as theirs."

"Tell that to those dispossessed when they clear-cut the forest for their buildings and their farms."

"Will you argue till we're all ghosts and these Realms we cherish no more than a memory? I say to you what I did to her, there's room to share. Or do you choose to be just as deaf? They're prepared to *die,* for you as much as for their own. But if you of Lesser Faery join with them, that doesn't have to be."

"Fairies," Tyrrel said slowly, "are but one of the races of the Realm of Lesser Faery, even as Maizan and Sandeni, Angwyn and even Tir Asleen are but nations of the Daikini Realm. They cannot speak for all."

"I'm not asking them, Majesty. I'm asking you."

"And who am I?"

"When my adversary, the Deceiver, who wears the shape and seeming of the Maizan Castellan, ensorcelled the monarchs of the Twelve Realms who'd assembled for my Ascension, his goal was to seize dominion over them all. He failed. I escaped. Instead the governance of those Realms has been thrown into disarray. Out of that chaos comes opportunity."

"Not only for him."

"You plead my case for me, Tyrrel. Together we have a better chance than alone. And who knows where such an alliance might lead?"

"You could command Us, Elora Danan. As you could have commanded Us earlier to forbear. Such is your right."

"I didn't think you'd listen," she confessed. "And I haven't earned that right."

He nodded.

"You are learning, child. All life grows according to a *natural* order. A quicker way might be found, that growth could be forced. But *should* it?"

"Puzzles?" she groaned in dismay. "Why does it always have to be puzzles?"

To her surprise, Tyrrel actually chuckled.

"You want it to be easy?"

"Yes?" she hazarded.

"Then you'd be your own adversary."

"What's that supposed to mean?"

From beneath his cloak, that spread out from him like a fall of forest leaves, Tyrrel drew his staff of office. It stood as tall as Elora herself and was composed of strips of all the woods of the world, wound lengthwise together. She didn't think much of it, beyond an appreciation of the wood-carver's craft to combine examples of so many different trees, until a closer look revealed that no piece of the staff had been cut or carved. The staff itself was as much a living thing as any of the trees it symbolized, its component elements blended because it was the natural and proper thing for them to do.

In one hand, he raised it shoulder-high and held it parallel to the ground so that he stood on one side of the altar and Elora on the other. Without urging, trusting yet again to instinct and inspiration, she reached out with both her hands and placed them on either side of his.

"We speak as Prince Regent of the Realm known in the Daikini tongue as Lesser Faery," Tyrrel said, and with those words came the barest hint of sunrise behind him to the east. "For all who swear Us true allegiance, We pledge to the Sacred Princess Elora Danan Our lives, Our souls, Our most sacred honor. When needed, We shall come. Her battle is Ours. As are her foes."

"I speak as Elora Danan," she said in response. "And to you and yours, my lord, I pledge my life, my soul, my most sacred honor. When needed, I shall come. Your battles are mine. As are your foes."

"So mote it be," cried the green man, and together they slammed the staff down upon the altar.

Silence. Not so hollow and lifeless as before, just the ordinary quiet of a mountain dawn, highlighted by the ever-so-slight *shush* of a breeze around the rocks and stones jumbled across the hillside, stirring air in much the same burbling manner as a current might water over a riverbed. The towering plinths were gone, all the sarcen stones, the perimeter blocks. Even the altar was once more a wind-worn lump of obsidian. The last stars of morning blazed defiantly in the heavens, grass tickled the folds that marked the knuckles of her toes, and each slow breath tasted sweet.

She buckled her belt across her hips because she had nowhere else to put it, thankful beyond words to once more *have* hips, and began to root in a traveling pouch for something to wear.

"To the victor," Khory noted, joining Elora from where she'd been watching behind one of the middle rank of stones. She held forth some of what the Maizan sorceress had worn.

"I don't think so." Elora wrinkled her nose in distaste.

"You're of a size."

"I don't *think* so," she repeated, comparing her own image with that of the sorceress.

"Consider the alternative."

"I'll find something."

"That fits⸮" She didn't mind Elora's basilisk glare in the slightest. "Considering the company⸮"

"Ryn," Elora cried, "what about Ryn⸮" She dashed to where the young Wyr lay. "He's still unconscious—no!" She corrected herself excitedly, "He's *asleep*!"

Her smile was a wonder to behold as she lay her hands gently on the young Wyr's temples. "Khory, the bindings are gone. His soul is his own again."

"A good night for us all around then. About time."

"What should we do⸮"

"Sleep's the best thing for him now. Rool has some herbs to help in that regard. While he takes his ease we'll transport him to Thorn. He's the Magus, mind you, he'll be able to make sure of the lad's recovery." She turned her head downslope in the direction of their companions below. "We've certainly horses enough for the journey, between our own and what the Maizan rode. And Bastian can find us a gentle track. Ryn should come through fine."

"From your mouth to the Almighty's ear⸮"

"I know things. He'll be fine."

Who knows, Elora thought with an irreverence that made her laugh out loud, *maybe we all will.*

Chapter
10

From horseback as on foot, views are always limited. The horizon is a flat line off in the distance, that distance determined by the height of the vantage point. It can be the mountains that define the shape of the land along the southern frontier of the Republic of Sandeni, or the trees arrayed ahead or on either side. You see what there is to see—until something gets in the way.

Bastian had no such impediment. For the eagle, perspectives were boundless, the nature of the world was laid out before him. That was the practical reason Elora loved looking at it so often through his eyes, to provide herself both a sense of true direction and of progress. She could actually see where she was going, and determine from that sight how long until she got there. It allowed her to view things as a whole, rather than in isolated bits and pieces. There was a context from on high that wasn't always clear at ground level, in much the same way that the surface of the ocean provides only the most general clues of the shape and texture of what might lie thousands of feet below.

The Stairs to Heaven formed the spine of the continent, as well as its literal, and mythical, summit. They were the highest point on the globe, whose paramount peaks soared to realms where such as Elora could find no air to breathe nor those like Bastian sufficient air to support even their mighty wings. Snow was a constant on those rugged and towering slopes, right through the hottest days of summer. These were young mountains, their silhouettes only lightly touched by wind and weather, with edges so sharp they might have been etched in acid against the cerulean backdrop of the sky.

The range stretched east and west like a belt across the belly of the continent, forming a natural barrier between the upper and lower hemispheres. Because the crown of the chain lay closer to the Chengwei coast than Angwyn's Sunset Ocean, there was no gradual fall off to the east. The phalanx formed by these peaks charged right to the water's edge, ending in a line of breathtaking cliffs and the most forbidding coastline ever charted, while out to sea for another two hundred miles was scattered an archipelago of sea mounts, the tops of peaks whose bases stood hundreds of feet if not miles beneath the water's surface. It was almost as if they were pathfinders for the army that followed, marking the way for the rest to ultimately form some impossible land bridge to the opposing shore.

Thanks to generations of mapmakers, the general shape of the Stairs to Heaven was seen as resembling a vase, fattest like a bulb where the peaks rose highest, slimming and lowering as it stretched westward in a gradual descent to sea level. As it progressed, offshoot secondary chains sprayed to the north and south in a way that was reminiscent of the spray off a fountain or the curve of flowers in that vase, blending ultimately with lesser, independent ranges thrown up along the north–south orientation of the coast.

The most dramatic feature of the continental land-mass occurred roughly two thirds of the distance from Angwyn eastward to Chengwei. It was as though count-less eons past some titanic force had simply *lifted* the en-tire surface of the world to create a plateau of incredible dimensions. Its western boundary was a chain of cliffs for the most part better than a thousand feet high that stretched from a subsidiary branch of the Stairs to Heaven almost all the way to the top of the world, where it merged indistinguishably with the equally mag-nificent Ice Land glaciers.

To the Daikini, it was known with simple eloquence as the Wall.

From the earliest chapters of recorded Daikini his-tory, the Wall appeared to be an insurmountable obstacle to travel between east and west. True, there were trails and passes through the southern mountains, but they were traversible only in summer and they passed through so many different domains of the Veil Folk that anything more than the most minimal traffic and trade proved uneconomical. Too many tolls to start with, since each domain had to be negotiated with in turn. It was difficult enough to get the locals to acknowledge any Daikini right to use the land at all, much less arrive at some mutually agreeable formula for compensation. This left almost no hope of laying down the roadwork necessary to sustain regular traffic. Dryads might be per-suaded to accept the felling of a stretch of trees in the for-est, but would the naiads who resided in the lakes accept the use of their water by stock and travelers? Ultimately for both sides, there was too much grief and aggravation for far too little reward.

This was the classic story of relations between the Great Realms. Everyone had ambitions, but could find neither clue nor desire in regard to achieving a compro-mise. In a world where no one accepted that they had anything in common with their neighbor, how then to determine a common good?

But where the Veil Folk possessed actual, direct power over the physical world—the ability, through magic or innate talent, to individually manipulate their environment—the Daikini were blessed with a formidable intellectual capacity, married to a gift for engineering even brownies knew to respect. For every problem there was a technological solution. That was the Daikini way. Every obstacle was merely a new challenge to be overcome. If they found a wall they couldn't go around, they'd find a way to go over it.

In this instance, while the Wall was high and altogether forbidding, it proved in no way unscalable. Water, as always, tended to flow downhill. Streams that began in the highland reaches of the Stairs to Heaven became rushing torrents by the time they reached the foothills both above and below the cliffs. Some rolled east toward Chengwei. Others cast themselves from the precipice in a series of breathtaking waterfalls and cataracts, cascading thunderously off outcrops of primordial rock to crash into the great basin below, there to combine with another stream of far less visual drama but considerably more strength flowing out from the mountains to form the official headwaters of the Cascadel, greatest of the westward flowing rivers.

From the Wall it was a relatively smooth run to the sea and the river's terminus at the southern end of the Bay of Angwyn, along a course so wide in some points that one shore could not be seen from the other, while at others a good stone's throw would reach the far side, so deep that for near a thousand miles it could take the largest oceangoing vessel.

Water formed the key to prosperity both for the ranches and farming homesteads that dotted the Cascadel's shores and for the merchants who plied their trade from one end to the other. Naiads ruled the lesser streams, but their influence waned in direct proportion to the size and strength of the water. The great rivers were the province of the freshwater Wyrrn, as the oceans were of their blue-water brethren. These Wyrrn also acknowledged the special relationship their blue-water cousins shared with the Cascani. Out of that grew a similarly beneficial relationship. Once the requisite treaties had been negotiated, the Cascadel became a highway that opened the way to the heart of the continent. After that, surmounting the cliffs was a minor hurdle.

Approaching from the south and west, as Elora and her companions did, afforded one of the truly spectacular views in the natural world. Heavily forested highlands yielded near the end to a barrier wall of peaks called the Shados because of the shadows they cast. This mandated a climb past meadows of grass onto barren slopes of scrub rock. Around the flank of one mountain, through the shadow of its neighbor, along a turnpike that would have been impossible for wheeled traffic had not a veritable army of workers hammered a path through any and all barriers—and there you were.

There was nothing gentle about the transition, none of the usual sequence of foothills leading to the lower range to the high reaches. There were plains, there were peaks, punching up into the air as dramatically as the plateau itself. That contrast was just as spectacular, only not quite so extreme, a vertical descent measured in thousands of feet. To the west Elora found herself gazing down upon an apparently endless prairie that disappeared over the far distant horizon. The sole defining feature of the landscape was the Cascadel, winding outward from the magnificent lake formed at the base of its waterfall, the foot of Lake Morar forming the first of a succession of cataracts.

To the east stood the Wall.

From her vantage point on the pass that cut through the last rank of Shados, Elora was actually above the level of the plateau, which provided her a view of the upper boroughs of the city of Sandeni. Here at a massive and recently reinforced barbican that straddled this end of the pass as its twin did the other, the road branched. Travelers could either descend to the prairie below along a sequence of wild switchbacks or make their way over a series of equally daunting viaducts to the upland city.

Like the prairie, the plateau stretched off to the distance, well beyond the limits of her vision. To Elora's dismay, not to mention a modest measure of disbelief, she discovered it reached far beyond Bastian's as well. It was one thing to hear the stories and read the accounts of this natural marvel, quite another to confront it face-to-face.

The Wall wasn't entirely straight, she observed, but was marred by promontories and depressions. In some places, a promontory had collapsed, leaving a butte to stand alone like some giant column amidst an otherwise denuded landscape. The plateau's general construction reminded Elora so much of a coastline that she couldn't help but wonder if, at some unimaginably ancient moment in the past, these plains had been underwater.

Though the falls were miles away, the shape of the Wall combined with the serried ranks of the Shados themselves to form an effective amplifier that allowed Elora to hear the rolling thunder of the falls the moment they came into view. The Cascadel flowed directly to the plains but she could see at least six other rivers of varying sizes come together on the plateau, where they plunged over the edge in three distinct streams. The largest dropped straight to the lake, the others bounced and showered off jutting outcrops of granite and basalt, creating a perpetual mist that kept the base of the cliff shrouded in romance and mystery.

The lowland boroughs of Sandeni weren't tucked up close beneath the cliffs. Quite the opposite in fact, the land appeared substantially undeveloped until hard by the cataracts, where she made out what appeared to be quite a substantial community. There was an extensive waterfront of piers and warehouses, far more lake traffic to and from the falls than along the roads that ringed the lakeshore. She saw granaries as well and a clear network of trails ranging off to the north and west across the well-nigh-endless prairie. She saw no bridges across the first cataract, but given the width of that gorge and the force of the water below, could understand why none had been attempted. A single span wouldn't reach and there was no practical way to anchor pylons in that tremendous flood.

Though the sun was quartering toward the westward horizon, it didn't take much imagination to comprehend the other reason why there was very little building close by the Wall. On a clear day, the view from the plateau was said to be better than fifty miles. The drawback for those below was that the extraordinary shadow cast by the Wall lasted until close to midday. It must be a strange sensation, she thought, to stand on a balcony atop the Wall in brilliant morning sunlight, and then look the other way to behold land that would remain wrapped in the semblance of evening for hours yet to come. Stranger still, perhaps, to live below, knowing that the day would never reach you with its full force until it was half over.

About ten miles along the Wall and as many out into the prairie, which placed them almost directly ahead of her, stood three lean pillars of stone. They'd been christened the Three Maidens, because they seemed to have no geologic connection with the plateau. Their substance was a variant of sandstone, a dun-colored base coat shot through with reefs of umber and scarlet.

To the distant west, she recalled from her reading, beyond the final cataract, the shore along the Cascadel was a dark, rich bottomland that provided some of the best farming between Sandeni and the sea. The prairie itself was mainly grassland, home to migrating herds of buffalo and deer, but also to sprawling cattle stations. The country surrounding Sandeni was pretty much as it had always been. Few Daikini made a mark on those plains, and it didn't last. Those changes were reserved for the city and its environs.

And what a city!

Elora had never seen anything like it. Even from this remove, Sandeni dwarfed the only municipality she had to compare it with, that of Angwyn, and she couldn't begin to imagine the number of people who resided within its confines. Of all the cities of the world, what made this unique was that in Sandeni there was hardly any magic. It was located at one of those rare points where the influence of the eldritch ley lines was at an absolute minimum. It was the balance to those places where magic came as second nature, and words had to be chosen wisely lest an untimely, ill-thought-out curse might actually come to pass. In Sandeni, since there was no convenient reservoir of energy to draw from, the easiest spells took more effort to cast than they were worth, while their greater counterparts took more than any sorcerer could afford.

On the face of it, Sandeni seemed an odd location for Thorn to go to ground, considering that many of his abilities as a mage would be crippled. Then again, since their foe was likewise a sorcerer, perhaps this was the ideal place to make a stand.

They'd ridden hard since leaving the tor, to get Ryn as quickly as possible to where Thorn could help him. The hours of daylight passed either on horseback or leading their mounts on foot as they made their way through the mountains to the carriage route. From there, at least for Ryn, once he was loaded onto a coach, the journey was easier. Khory's assumption was that Elora would accompany them to a reunion with her guardian and protector.

That had been ten days ago, better than two hundred miles up the line, when they broke their journey at one of the taverns that lined the turnpike at intervals from Sandeni to the distant frontier. It hadn't begun as a pleasant conversation.

"I'm going my own way," Elora said.

"The hell you are," was the taller woman's response. She spoke matter-of-factly as they put their animals to bed, Khory more concerned with them at the moment than she was with Elora.

"It's not safe, child," she said a moment later, looking across the back of her own mount to where Elora was busy tending to Windfleet.

"I'm not a child, Khory." Elora turned to face her. "True, in Sandeni, I'm below the age of legal majority, but among the Nelwyns I'd be an apprentice."

"Barely."

"In Chengwei, married and probably with child!"

"And that's your ambition?"

"I know my own mind, enough to try to chart my own destiny."

"It's not safe."

"The world hasn't been safe for me since I was born!"

"This is an argument better left for Drumheller. I'll have none of it."

"By then it'll be too late."

Khory made a face, dismissing that contention out of hand.

"*Listen* to me, will you," Elora cried, confronting her across the back of Khory's horse, who wasn't at all pleased to be caught in the middle and made that opinion plain by shifting its feet nervously.

"I'm not a baby anymore," she went on in a great rush. "I can, I need to, I *must* take part in my own defense."

"Fine. What's wrong with doing so from a place where *you* can be defended?"

"Thorn's achieved a position of some responsibility among the Sandeni, yes?"

A nod from Khory.

"If I were the Deceiver, I'd have spies watching Sandeni and especially watching him."

No reaction at all from the demon warrior, but she was listening intently.

"Because the Deceiver wants me, seemingly more than anything. And Thorn's my guardian. Sooner or later the Deceiver's got to figure I'll go to him or he to me. Wait long enough, watch hard enough, he'll have me. My best hope is to stay away."

Again, no reaction. Elora took that for a positive sign and pressed ahead.

"Think about it. He knows my name, but I share it now with *how* many girls? A lot, judging from Angwyn and the places we've visited since. And a lot who are now about my age. He knows my face, but he hasn't seen it since Angwyn. I'm not the girl I was then."

"With one slight exception," Khory interjected mildly, and Elora realized this wasn't an objection so much as a test to see if she'd considered this element as well. Khory was taking this discussion very seriously.

"True enough, the Sacred Princess has skin of silver, and hair to match. How about Elora the apprentice bard?"

"You think that paint will hide you, girl?"

"I'm not *trying* to hide, don't you see? *Hiding*, the way you mean it, will draw the Deceiver's agents right to me! When they look my way, I want them to see exactly what they expect."

"That's no small gamble."

"I'm not just being willful. Look at the people, Khory. Did you see them inside the tavern when we arrived? It was the same back at the fort. They're terrified. Their world's coming apart at the seams, leaving them with nothing to hold on to, no anchors against the storms to come. They're losing hope."

"And you'll give it back to them?"

"I can remind them of the time in their lives when they had faith, and what that faith was, and why it's important to take tight hold of it." She made a gesture with her hands, of acceptance as much as frustration. "Right now, that's what I'm good for."

"I saw you on the tor, remember? Don't sell yourself short."

"Khory, you're a warrior. Tell me the truth, can Thorn defeat the Deceiver? Can I?" She was answered with silence, as she knew she would be.

"If my contribution to the struggle is to behave exactly as everyone expects, how will that ever change?"

"This is war."

"I know."

There were ghosts in Khory's soul as she said, "You don't."

"And who's kept me from learning?"

"This isn't a thing you hurry to embrace, or wish on anyone else."

Khory reached out to Elora, lightly stroking the young woman's jawline in a gesture of surprising tenderness. "You are so young," she said softly, and the pain in her voice slashed like a razor.

"It won't stop, Khory, until we yield or we win. You know that. You know I have a role to play."

"Better I should lock you in your room."

"I'll pick the locks."

"Brownie locks."

"I'll do them faster!"

Khory gave her the shallowest of nods. "He won't be happy," she said, meaning Thorn. "But that's his lookout. Bastian I'll keep with me. Eagles are rare enough to be noticeable, and golden ones, especially. Rool stays by you."

"He's pretty recognizable himself."

"If he's seen, which I don't expect to happen. *Ever,*" she finished pointedly, with a glance up and over her shoulder that was followed by a discreet cough from the shadows of the barn's hayloft.

"Damn," the brownie muttered as he lowered a rope and rappelled down to Elora's shoulder. "And I thought I was doing so well, eh?"

"Consider that your one mistake," Khory told him, with a curious flatness to her tone that served as plain warning of the consequences of any future oversights.

"Spying on us, you wretched little bug boy?" Elora chastised the brownie in a shocked tone as she returned to the care and feeding of Windfleet.

"Haven't called me that in an age," Rool grumped.

He rose to his feet, hands on hips as he glared up and back at Elora.

"Haven't deserved it. But you can make it up to me."

"Is that a threat?"

"A challenge, O font of all the world's wisdom."

"I do *not* like the sound of that."

"I want to know about myself, Rool."

"Look in a mirror, there's the place to start your education."

"Been there, done that, don't get snarky. I'm serious, Rool," she told the brownie.

"As am I, Elora. You are what you are, anointed before my eyes by Cherlindrea herself."

"Why me?"

"Born at the moment foretold by prophecy, bearing the equally foretold birthmark."

"*Why* me, Rool," she repeated. "Why *me*?"

"Blessed if I know."

"You're a brownie, you claim to know the way the world works. Aren't I part of the world?"

She expected at the very least a smart remark.

"I don't know," he said at long last, in distress.

"What?" Her confusion was genuine.

"Whether or not you're part of the world. I don't know. You speak to *demons,* child. You're a part of the tapestry of legend of every race I know, whether Daikini or Veil Folk, on levels I'm not sure even *they* understand."

"What do your legends say?"

"A child shall come, apparently of Daikini stock, but bound to *all* the Great Realms. Her birth shall presage a time of great change. Of boundless possibilities both for good and ill."

"That's all?"

"The essentials."

"What, you weren't paying attention during catechism class?"

"We glean our knowledge the way we do our prizes"—he sniffed dismissively—"from around the edges of events."

"Find out more."

"Those doors are closed to us, Elora, I told you."

"Guess what, Rool? I don't care. You're so great a thief, lemme see some proof. If it's written, find me the book, or at least directions to the library where it's housed. If part of an oral tradition, I'll take the song or the storyteller. Whatever their origins, Rool, I want them all."

"As you command, my princess."

She started to smile, and protest that she was "asking" not telling, but realized in the same thought that that wasn't true. She'd given an order, expecting as a matter of right to be obeyed, and Rool had responded accordingly.

"I ask but one boon in return," he told her. "Leave Faralorn. Ride on alone."

"I can't."

"What's this, then?" Khory wondered.

"The bard," snapped Rool, making the title an obscenity.

"Why don't you like Duguay, Rool?" When he didn't answer right away, Elora asked, "Are you jealous?"

"As good a reason as any"—he huffed back at her—"for those too damn dim to know better."

"Liar."

"Why do you like him?"

She shrugged. "He makes me laugh. He's shown me parts of myself I never knew were there. I like to hear him sing."

"But you can't meet his eyes."

She blinked rapidly and looked from place to place to place, as though Duguay himself had suddenly materialized before her. She thought of a thousand quips to dance free of Rool's challenge but in the end confined her reply to a single word.

"No," she said softly, flatly.

"Why is that?"

"I don't know. Others seem to."

"And they love him for it."

"You think he has magic?"

"I don't know. And I should, at a glance. I've said before, we brownies know the way the world works. We know who possesses the talent of a sorcerer and who does not. I look at Duguay and everything tells me he is precisely what he seems, yet for all that certitude, I don't believe it. And no, I won't meet his eyes either."

She and Khory parted company the following morning, when the demon warrior rode out with the stage. Elora and Duguay remained that night at the depot, singing for their supper, then set off themselves on horseback. Their reputation preceded them down the road, and each time they broke their journey they found growing audiences and publicans more willing to make them welcome. By the time they reached the Shados, they had earned a decent sum, even by Sandeni's inflated standards.

From the barbican, they took the turnoff toward the upper city. This last leg was the easiest, as they passed along another magnificent example of Daikini ingenuity. The road had been carved out of the body of the mountainside, wide enough for two freight wagons to travel side by side with room to spare. A stone wall, hip height on Elora, ran along the outside of the entire route as a barrier to the precipice beyond.

After a fortnight on Windfleet's back across all manner of country, ranging from mountain trails barely wide enough to accommodate the mare's hooves to the broad, well-maintained expanses of the Republican highway, Elora had become used to the mare's incredibly smooth gait. She'd also learned that the horse could be trusted to keep to the road without active supervision. Through the thickness of the saddle Elora could feel the interplay of Windfleet's powerful muscles, the easy ride rocking her ever so gently back and forth. The young woman let her awareness drift, until each of the mare's breaths struck a resonance in her own lungs, each beat of that indomitable equine heart striking fire through human arteries and veins. Elora felt a security that reminded her of the comfort she used to derive solely from her bruised and battered old stuffed bear (now tucked away securely in her traveling pouch), an assurance that here was a friend whose faith, and likewise trust, was wholehearted and unconditional. Windfleet would stand by Elora as she would her own foals, and fight as fiercely to protect her.

She let her eyes close, her shoulders slump, the way she might in a favorite chair when she wasn't quite ready for sleep but found herself unable to stay wholly awake. She found herself in the grip of a yearning she could not deny. The immediacy and passion of the mare's life was plain before her, neat and uncluttered, obligations strictly defined without the slightest confusion or doubt, all bound together by a contentment that had no physical equivalent in her own. Elora wanted to throw herself forward, to stretch herself full-length along Windfleet's back with her arms wrapped around the horse's neck until flesh dissolved and these two lives flowed into one. The temptation was so strong that Elora felt actual pain, enough to sting her eyes with tears . . .

. . . but instead of fighting, instead of yielding, she spread wide her wings and leaped for the stars.

Not really, of course. Although that single beat of her shoulders thrust Elora so high that the figures she left behind of herself and Duguay were reduced to little more than dots, she knew that her body still rode astride the mare. Physically, she had gone nowhere. Only in spirit did she soar.

It was the most magnificent of sensations.

Elora couldn't believe the way she looked, this grandly terrifying form she'd conjured in what she told herself had to be some fantastic and wondrous kind of waking dream. The strangest aspect was that, to her own mind, she remained unchanged.

She couldn't help a giggle, and as soon as she started, it grew into full-throated, belly-busting laughter. Three rings to encompass all the signal aspects of Creation, and here she beheld three distinct aspects of herself. A purely

312

physical being, that she was leaving far behind. Another of spirit, that mixed what was with what she dreamed of being. And a third that she had no label for whatsoever, save that it appeared to have some manner of literal being and seemed to be taking her to the farthest reaches of her imagination.

She turned her neck right the way around, as limber as any swan, to behold this new self, and found a sight to take her breath away.

Tremendous wings stretched from her shoulders, from a body that matched them in grace and timeless power. If she landed in the center of a parade ground, an easy stretch would allow her to touch opposite parapets with her tips. From nose to tail she doubted she was much shorter. Her skin gleamed with a shimmering iridescence that reminded her of Angwyn Bay at night, when she would look out from her tower to watch the moonlight play across the water. The sparkles she saw then were silver; these comprised more hues than she had names for, that changed continuously in a fantastic interplay of color and intensity with every ripple of her skin. There was a gleaming sheen to the flesh as well, that gave it a familiar metallic cast; in it, she saw the reflection of a head that was shaped like a blacksmith's wedge, whose mobile features allowed for an unexpected range of expression. She bared fangs longer than most Daikini were tall and knew she'd assumed the form of a creature that knew how to hunt and fight and kill. A pair of horns curled up and back from her temples, in a manner more aesthetic than functional. From their base grew a double line of secondary ridges that made their way along the length of her spine, peaking in size at her shoulder blades, then fading away as they descended her tail.

I've never done this *before,* she marveled, giddy with the joy of flying as well as the myriad sensations that came to her from this new and wondrous body. She remembered her wistful comment to Tyrrel atop his tor, about flying, and thought with delight, *Now I know.*

This is like the story Thorn told, she thought further, *when the dragon brought him to Tir Asleen. Except in his dream he only got to ride a dragon,* and she felt a set of subsonic rumbles that passed in her for chuckles, *where I—!*

"Yes, you are," she heard from above and behind. "At long last."

First thought: *There's someone on my back.* But the quality and timbre of the voice was all wrong. Too deep for someone small enough to climb aboard, and too far removed. A turn of the head should give her a sight of this new companion, but she decided on something more dramatic. Impulse combined with physical instincts and linkages well beyond the reach of her still primarily human consciousness to make desire reality as she closed her wings, twisting eel-like the whole length of her body as she'd seen Ryn do in water, dancing wickedly across all three dimensions of flight in a snap roll meant to loop her around her mysterious companion and essentially reverse their positions so that she'd be on *his* tail.

It was a totally outrageous maneuver, especially for one whose active flight time could be counted in minutes. It might have worked, too, had not the other dragon rolled the other way in that selfsame instant, the pair of them racing around each other in wild circles until Elora belatedly realized that every attempt to shake free of him had failed.

Elora heard laughter and redoubled her efforts, the pair of them darting from the top of the sky to near its bottom, slashing their way through the mountains with the reckless abandon of children playing tag, brushing treetops with their bellies, mountainsides with wing tips. There wasn't the slightest hesitation in Elora, any more than in her rival, the thought of disaster was utterly inconceivable to them both. It was the invulnerability of ignorance and it cloaked her as surely as any armor.

She couldn't remember when she'd had such fun, in dreams or awake, though her fiercest efforts didn't bring her close to catching him, nor did they provide any opportunity for escape when she found him on her tail.

In the full dark of night she couldn't get a kinetic sense of him even with her MageSight. Try as she might, she could grab only the most fleeting of glimpses as his body briefly occluded the stars beyond. He had the ability to bar her InSight as well, she couldn't merge her consciousness with his.

The sight of the tor brought her up short, the one great sweep of her wings it took her to come to a full stop striking the air with such a shock that the sound of whipcrack thunder echoed through the mountain passes.

She wasn't sure if it was the perspective granted by flight, or some enhancement of her vision that came from her change of form, but the shape and structure of the hill below appeared more clear to her now. A pattern was visible where before she'd seen only stands of stone.

The altar stood dead center atop the tor, in a space formed by the intersection of three circles, each of those demarcated by a border of sarcen stones. The stones themselves began as paving blocks, hardly bigger than Elora's human foot, set flush with the ground at the point of the circle farthest from the altar. She counted twelve in all, set in tandem at equidistant points around the circumference of each circle. Each pair doubled the height of the one before until they reached the last, directly opposite the first and a tall Daikini's body length removed from the altar. Those three cardinal stones formed an equilateral triangle with the altar at its heart. At the same time Elora beheld another pattern overlaying them, the sense of a fourth circle, running through those cardinal stones and enclosing the altar.

A sudden swoosh of air up and across her back heralded the madcap arrival of her pursuer, but as she frantically twisted around to catch at least a partial sight of him, the only figure to greet her eyes was a boy, standing by himself in the third circle, leaning nonchalantly against the cardinal stone as though he'd been lounging there all along.

In the moonlight he appeared as silver as she, though to be honest, a second, stronger look forced her to call his gender into question. He seemed of an age and body form where either pronoun—he or she—might be applied with equal justification. His clothes were no help, either. He wore a snug-fitting suit of fabric that splintered every element of radiance that struck it into glittering pieces of light and color. A dazzling enough display at midnight, well nigh unendurable, she suspected, at sunrise. His hair was as black as Duguay's dyes had made hers; another aspect he and Elora shared in common was their barber, who'd done neither of them any favors.

"I know you," she hazarded, delicately balancing herself on her hind legs atop the other two cardinal stones, as though claiming the Circles they represented—of the World and the Flesh—for her own. He stood at the heart of the Circle of the Spirit.

The faintest nod was the only reply. The manner of that gesture, the crinkle about the eyes, the mix of familiar and strange within them, clinched his identity for her. She wished it hadn't. The sudden insight was like a spear through her soul.

"You're dead," she breathed.

"Join me," Kieron Dineer said, and held out his hands as though to invite her to join him in a dance. He had a lopsided smile that was just off-kilter enough to be endearing.

She never had a chance to know him. He alone among the whole assemblage at Angwyn had stood to her defense. His sacrifice had bought Thorn Drumheller the precious opportunity he needed to rescue Elora.

Then she remembered the other portion of Thorn's story, that all he'd assumed was dream that fateful night was in fact reality. Somehow a dragon had plucked his spirit from his bed and made it flesh, and brought him across the leagues and miles to Tir Asleen so that he might see his dearest friends a final time and unwittingly carry away the brownies Rool and Franjean to safety.

And most important of all, to deliver his birthday gift to Elora Danan: a stuffed bear he'd made with his own hands, and imbued with a portion of his own magical strength, together with the injunction that it keep her safe till his return.

Reflexively, her hand went to her traveling pouch, where she kept the bear—but in this incarnation, this aspect of reality, neither was there. Her heart was starting to pound faster and faster, like a drummer sounding the tocsin call to arms, as she raked her gaze across the horizon to see how clearly every feature of the landscape was etched in place. It was as though a moment had been plucked from time and then gone over by some celestial artist whose task was to integrate all its component elements into a perfect harmony. The peaks to the east were touched with the faintest roseate glow that hinted at a dawn she knew would never come, blades of grass and the edges of leaves glistened from a decorative application of dew. Nocturnal animals had just tucked themselves into dens and burrows and nests, while those who stirred by day had yet to rise. There was a preternatural stillness to things that should have been a wonder, but in this instance left Elora terrified.

"What have you done?" she demanded of the boy. Unspoken, the twin injunctions, *to the world, Kieron,* and then, *to me?* "What is this place? Where am I?"

"Where you must journey, Elora Danan, for your own circle to be complete."

"Don't speak in riddles, that isn't fair!"

"This isn't about fair, and it isn't meant to be easy. Some prizes must be won, little Princess, and others earned."

"What do you want from me?" she cried.

"Your life," was his reply, and he *burned.*

They weren't the flames of honest combustion but dragonfire, the most extreme manifestation of sorcerous might. Kieron blazed from top to toe, with such intensity that he should have been consumed in an instant. This was energy in its most raw and primal state, that might have been scooped from the foundry of Creation itself, an essence of nature so profound that *nothing* mortal could endure its touch, much less stand against it.

On Tyrrell's tor, in the Hour of the Wolf, when the night is darkest and the boundaries between the Realms are at their thinnest, in that terrible moment where the NightGaunts hunt their prey across the Field and Forest of Dreams, it seemed to Elora Danan that Kieron Dineer had come to repay her in kind for his life, and in full measure.

She tried to fly, blind instinct prompting wings to lunge for the sky, but even as she clawed desperately for altitude an awful paralysis gripped her and she tumbled to earth with a crash that shook the hills like the fall of some colossal thunderstone. Her frantic struggles had thrown her wholly beyond the circles, the size differential between herself and Kieron so extreme that even flat to the ground as she was, she still looked down on him across the crest of the tor.

He didn't look pleased. Matters were not going as desired. She wasn't in her proper place in his scheme of things, the pristine perfection of the setting had been marred, she hoped irreparably. She was glad.

She struggled to move, denying the lethargy that wormed its way through bone and sinew and gave her flesh the immobile consistency of metal to match its appearance. She was growing cold inside, as still in her own way as the ground she lay upon, and saw that the only source of warmth available to her was Kieron's burning, outstretched hand.

"Why are you doing this?" she cried, angry with herself because she wanted only a warrior's strength and defiance in her voice and what she heard sounded too much the girl.

"Because I must. You must. *We* must."

"I deny this!" She heard her name called. "I deny *you* the power to do me harm!"

Again she heard her name, and from Kieron's reaction so did he, and from his scowl came the realization that this, too, wasn't part of his program.

A third time, her name. With the last of her will, for her strength was nearly gone, Elora screamed her reply:

"Duguay!"

The hearty aroma of spiced chicken soup told her she was safe, and the toasty comfort of a down quilt. To begin, she simply lay where she was, luxuriating snuga-bug in her cocoon of bedclothes and using those sensations as bulwarks against the aches she knew lurked just offstage.

She was in no place she recognized, taking stock of a fire in the hearth beyond the foot of the bed. She arbitrarily labeled it as "cheery" because that's how it made her feel, as did the warming pan tucked a bit beyond her toes.

It was a huge bed, her kinesthetic judgment confirmed that when she creased her eyelids open for a proper look. Best she'd seen since Torquil's. She'd stayed in rooms smaller. She could stretch full length from its center, arms and legs both as long as she could reach, and not touch the edge of the mattress in any direction. *Lots* of pillows. The design of the bedframe was as simple as it was elegant, composed of smooth and gracious curves, and the bed in keeping with the rest of the room. Furniture was functional but well crafted, the harder edges smoothed by accents of cushions or throw rugs. There was personality to the room, as well as considerable taste, but it was of a general nature that told Elora she was in a hostelry rather than someone's home.

At the moment the only light came from the fireplace, which consisted more of glowing coals than outright flames. Elora gathered a pillow to her that was so big she could easily wrap both arms and legs around it. She folded her legs up within her nightgown until her knees were almost to her shoulders, making herself as small as possible within this cozy little nest. She was trembling, a physical reaction that had nothing to do with being cold. Her eyes were wide and haunted, as liquid as a trapped fawn, though she felt no urge for tears. She didn't want to touch any of the memories of what had happened, but found they were like a scab that itched abominably until she just *had* to pick at it, no matter if doing so made the wound bleed afresh.

So like a dream, she *wanted* it to be a dream yet knew it was not. The shape of her body didn't fit her quite as it was supposed to; she was too small and every twitch of her shoulder blades only served as a reminder of wings that were no longer there. She could recall every moment that had passed atop the tor, with a clarity that transcended what she beheld now with open eyes. It was nothing like what she'd experienced with the ghosts at Ganthem's Crossing. There'd been hardly any sentience to them, they were shades of spirit as much as of flesh, the leftover resonances of what once had been, defined mainly by their rage and their pain at the manner of their death. Kieron was something altogether different, as alive during this encounter as in Angwyn. Yet she knew he was dead, and with that acknowledgment, she wept for his passing and for the role she had played, however unwitting, however unwilling, in it.

"Mama," she whispered, the barest outrush of sound, hardly discernible at all, much less as a word. In her thoughts, that word burst forth as a cry from the farthest depths of her being, with all the passion and grief she was capable of. A cry of loss, at being alone, and one of rage, at being so abandoned.

"Papa," as quiet in one form, as loud in the other.

It came to her then, in a flash of realization that once might have been dismissed by all and sundry as childish pique, that she hated her life and title as the Sacred Princess. Not for what it was, but for what it represented. She'd been too long the Princess in her bejeweled cage, a bauble fit only for display. She hadn't accepted until now how wonderful it was to be a part of a family, of a community, as she'd been with Torquil and Manya, among the Rock Nelwyn.

She buried her face in the pillow, using its case as an impromptu cloth to wipe her eyes dry, then called out to the figure whose presence she sensed lounging in the sumptuous armchair close beside the bed.

"Duguay?"

She heard a hesitation in breathing patterns that told her she'd been heard, and realized with the texture of his next breath how terribly wrong she'd been.

"No," Rool said softly, without any inflection to his tone to give her a clue to his reaction. "Shall I summon him, Elora Danan?"

The brownie was up and gone before she could muster any reply. She gathered the comforter about her shoulders like a cloak, feeling very small amidst this vast expanse of bedding and wondering if the bed could be persuaded to eat her.

"Are we in Sandeni?" she asked the troubadour from her down-and-cotton redoubt upon his entrance.

"Safe and sound," Duguay noted cheerily. "And rest assured, we're at a fair remove from your mentor Drumheller's residence. Lads may come from far and wide seeking Elora the songstress, but not a Princess of any kind, sacred or otherwise." He perched himself on the edge of the bed and lifted the lid from the bowl of soup that was set on the bedside table. "I'll confess, though, that last stretch through the Shados gave us something of a turn, me and your brownie both."

"What happened?"

"We were riding along, normal as could be. Thought you might be dozing. Then, of a sudden, you screamed. That horse of yours, she's one damn smart animal, sidestepped right away straight to the Wall so you wouldn't tumble far. If she'd had hands, I daresay she'd have caught you in the bargain."

"Windfleet, is she—?"

"Nicely stabled." His eyes roamed the room appreciatively. "As are we."

"A tavern?"

321

"Food and drink and lodging, and no objection to an evening's entertainment."

"That's good."

She pulled the quilt over her head to shut out the world, but it quickly grew too warm beneath the covers and she was forced to poke her head, then most of her body, back into the open. Duguay leaned forward, a quizzical expression on his face, to press splayed fingers on the mattress.

"What?" Elora demanded, seeing this.

"Just curious, is all. Wanted to see who in here would spend the night on a cat's-claw bed." Then, mockery gone from his voice, he asked, "Care to talk?"

"How'd I get here?" she wondered.

"Dissembler."

"No such thing!"

"Answer my question with one of your own, what else d'you call it?" In a single, smooth motion he pirouetted to his feet from where he sat on the edge of her bed, the utter, raw grace of the movement taking Elora's breath away as he held out a hand. "You've played the slug too long, Elora my pet. Up with you before you're mistaken for a piece of furniture."

"That's mean."

"Aren't we all, given spur and circumstance?" She flushed with anger as she struggled free of the covers and he spread hands wide in a placating gesture. "I'm not the one whose spirit went wandering, Elora," he said, temporizing. "You ever stop to consider that answers sometimes can't be found because there are none *to* be found."

"Bollocks."

"Think a bug looks at the world the same as you?" he asked her, scuffing the toe of his elegant boot across the floor, stirring dust in the darkness that floated more like ash from the body of something long since dead and decayed. "Or I? And where stand we"—now he waved his arms to encompass not only the room, but everything that lay beyond—"in the face of all that is? Everything has its place and proper purpose; if nothing else in Creation holds true, it's that. Bass baritone might have one hellacious voice, but don't expect him to hit a soprano's notes."

"No transcendence, Duguay? No dreams? Then why are the circles interwoven?"

Surprisingly, he needed no explanation of what she meant, though she'd been ready to present one.

"Are they truly, Elora? Or just because that's how you want to see them?" He faced her again, a glorious figure of a man, and oh, how he knew it. By movement and manner he dared her to join him.

"Myself," he continued, "I'd rather form circles of my own." Eyes flashed at her from beneath hooded brows, a come-hither glance that gave her chills and goose bumps that were nothing like how she'd felt when Luc-Jon kissed her. The sensations were electric and tantalizing but they left her vaguely unsettled, as though she'd been sent signals she had no desire yet to comprehend.

Almost in defiance, Elora swung one leg across the other and as smoothly as though she were on ice pirouetted up from where she sat in a match for Duguay's turn.

His eyes were waiting, and his hands. Avoiding the one, she almost took the other.

Right before they touched, her eyes fell toward the table where her belt and traveling pouches lay, and the small figure that stood there, holding them out to her. Duguay responded with the savoir faire of a cat, as though he'd known all along this was how the moment would end. His fingers never closer than an inch to hers, he pivoted as she ducked beneath his arm and past him, paralleling her movements so that it seemed he was the one casting her loose, rather than Elora departing of her own volition.

"Am I interrupting?" Rool inquired, making it obvious that he was, and intentionally so.

Duguay's response was another of his trademark smiles, though he held an outstretched forefinger toward the brownie and mimed the action of pulling the trigger on a crossbow. On the surface it could be taken as an exchange of physical banter with no harm meant. Rool clearly considered it something altogether different. He watched the troubadour as if Duguay was the incarnation of a Death Dog.

"The room's paid for," Duguay told Elora. "But if we want to stay here, we'll have to work for it. I promised tonight at least."

"I'll be down directly," she replied, "as soon as I've bathed and dressed."

"Fair enough. See you then." And he was gone.

There wasn't a shred of apology in the brownie, not for his manner toward Duguay nor his refusal to leave Elora in private. She retaliated by ignoring him, as if he wasn't there.

The establishment was called Black-Eyed Susan's, so named for the proprietor, a handsome woman of middle years whose calm and generous nature made her the ideal host. When Elora found out its address was the Street of Lost Dragons she directed a very sharp glance Duguay's way, assuming some deliberate confluence with her dream. All he did in return was shrug and proclaim all innocence with such a lack of guile that she threw up her hands in despair. There was no way to tell when he wasn't dissembling, he was too good an actor.

Tavern and street were located on a small island called Madaket, one of the modest parcels of earth and rock scattered across the floodplain formed by the upland rivers as they rushed toward the falls. They were connected by a network of bridges that linked them to the main body of the city, but even that small separation allowed each to develop its own separate charm and character. Madaket, being most convenient to both the university quarter and a whole host of government ministries, attracted an eclectic mix of students and professionals. On any given evening a tour of its taverns and coffeehouses could provide a fair example of the young passionately declaiming to their seniors about how badly they'd screwed up the world and getting just as impassioned a response that they couldn't possibly know anything until they worked a real job.

Construction here was predominantly brick, which held true across the whole of the city, since good clay was more economically feasible on the plateau than forests. Also, it was far more effective at withstanding the onslaught of damp from the rivers. Civic design was more regular on the mainland, buildings tended to be set in rows, sharing common walls along the length of an entire street. On Madaket, by contrast, and many of the other islands, houses were snugged together on stand-alone plots which allowed for some quite spectacular gardens.

Elora had hardly any opportunity for sightseeing this first day. The afternoon was spent in introductions to the staff and preparation for the evening meal. It was a communal enterprise, everyone pitching in as and where needed, so Elora found herself dragooned into accompanying Susan and the chef to market and then to work peeling and slicing the vegetables she brought home. Then, after a visit to the washhouse, she and Duguay closeted themselves in her room to make whatever repairs were necessary to her paint. No work was needed to her costumes, because it had already been done, with the invisibly fine stitching that was the hallmark of a brownie's hand. Thanks to Rool, the clothes looked better than they had when they were new and Elora felt churlish for her anger toward him.

She wanted to apologize, but he was nowhere to be found.

Early arrivals, once the tavern opened for business, were regulars, with favorite seats and favorite dishes, who greeted Susan companionably and were more than a little intrigued by the new guests. There was no requirement for Elora to help with serving meals but she found that she enjoyed the work. She had had so few opportunities to mingle with people before now, especially those of her own kind, that she wanted to take full advantage of them. The more she watched and listened, the more she learned, not only about the news of the day but how people reacted to it, hopes and fears, ambitions and frustrations. Each moment, each life, was a thread that she wove into the tapestry of every performance, the means she used to make it a personal and lasting experience for her audience.

From one clutch of ministerial scribes she heard of Thorn's status within the Sandeni government. The Nelwyn had done well for himself as an adviser without portfolio, his status as high within the councils of power as his title was intentionally nebulous. The net result was that he had access to the Chancellor whenever required and that his advice might actually be heeded.

Her own reputation was somewhat less stellar.

"The Sacred Princess has a reputation?" she asked a student in all innocence.

"No more than any self-respecting lightning rod." One of his companions laughed as he polished off the last of a pitcher of beer and took the replacement Elora held out to him.

"Not so bad a strategy, that," commented an older man at a neighboring table. He wore the robes of a lecturer and the students deferred to him. "If you spread the tale that everywhere Elora Danan takes refuge falls before some terrible onslaught, how long before none will dare to take her in? And with every door closed to her, how then to raise an effective resistance against the Maizan?"

"Your pardon, Professor," said a student, "but suppose the tales are truth? It's said Angwyn is sheathed in the hoarfrost of a bleak and perpetual midwinter."

"No traffic on the Cascadel anymore worth a damn," a trader noted in passing. "Short-haul, that's all that's left, town to town on this side of the High Desert of the Saranye. Nothin' goes beyond the Ramparts"—which were the range of coastal mountains that fronted the Sunset Ocean. "Whole of Angwyn Bay's s'posed to be frozen, an' a piece of the ocean beyond. Surroundin' country's glaciating worse than any of the Ice Lands. The Ramparts are as good as their name for now, holdin' back the worst of this false winter. But mark my words, young masters, there'll come a time, and soon, when they won't be enough. Summer'll be a memory from the Wall to sunset."

From a far distance Elora heard the staccato drumbeat of fingers on a "doumbek," establishing a rhythm that fit her body as naturally as her own skin.

Her feet began to move in time to the drum, hips and shoulders articulating ever so slightly to match its infectious beat. They were small movements, flowing so effortlessly one into the next that once started, there seemed no natural way to stop. Elora was the active partner in the dance, Duguay assuming the passive role with his drum, the hub around which she revolved.

She flung her arms up to full extension as she sidled clear of the tables into the open floor before the hearth that Susan had cleared for their stage. Then she brought them back to her body with an almost languid grace, sometimes in total harmony with the music, others intentionally at odds. The drum became her pulse, each hammer of her heart adding fiery spice to the flow of her blood as it went coursing throughout her body. She spun on the ball of a foot, threw back leg and shoulders and head until her body was bent double, then followed through on the motion to kick herself up and over in a sensuously acrobatic flip. She drew on the performances of gymnasts she had seen, and warriors, to craft a dance that was part purest movement, part combat, all suffused with an elemental passion that entranced the gathering crowd almost as completely as she was herself.

Always, Duguay was there to complement her, keeping fair distance to make clear to the audience that this was Elora's solo, but likewise never relinquishing the equally unequivocal sense that he was the principal half of their partnership. Whenever he extended an arm, hers curved toward it in response, as a plant seeks out the life-giving radiance of the sun. Any move he initiated, she echoed in gentler resonance. The merest touch would instantly bring her back to him.

Duguay took Elora's left hand in his right, pulled it up and across her body in a gesture so natural that she couldn't help but follow and complete the circle. He spun her once, twice, a third time, then followed those triple pirouettes by bringing her close into his arms, gripping her snug about the waist as he led her through a fourth and final circle that somehow encompassed the first three, making what had been a solo into a duet. She not only let him do so, she welcomed it.

At the end, as the pounding rhythms built to their final, almost violent crescendo, the bodies of the two dancers appeared to flow together, as though both beings were composed of nothing but wiry sinew without a decent skeleton between them. How else, those watching wondered, to appear so elegantly, inhumanly limber?

He meant for Elora to finish facing him but at the last she twisted in his grasp so that they came together back to front. Duguay didn't seem to mind, taking hold of her around the waist and by the right hand with such remarkable ease they must be following long-practiced choreography.

Elora spun gracefully to her knees before him, settling on her heels in the Chengwei manner while her back arched along its entire length like a drawn bow. Duguay stood above her, apparently ready to receive any arrow she cared to hurl forth. Presumably of love, but from the undertone of their performance in the raucous opinion of many onlookers, more likely of sin.

There was a moment of absolute stillness, the only sound that of Elora's breath pumping in and out through a mouth that was curved into a smile of exultation. Otherwise, the whole of the tavern seemed to be holding its collective breath.

Then came applause, and cheers, caps materializing in the hands of both performers as they slipped among their audience to gather every coin to come their way.

Elora was exhausted, yet at the same time she was flush with the most intense and incredible energy. She'd stopped dancing, not for tiredness, but because she'd come to the end of that song. Given that music, and players whose vigor matched her own, she had the giddy certainty she could go on forever. Even now she couldn't stay still. She was too receptive to every wayward rush of sensation without and within her own body, each providing the impulse to a new movement, and each of those the inspiration for a new dance.

People stared. Those who hadn't given her a second glance when she served their meal found themselves fascinated. Elora didn't care. She thrilled to the adoration, but more important to what she had achieved.

The talk had been of winter and despair. She'd grabbed tight to their spirits and lit a fire there she hoped would warm them, sustain them, for a good long time to come.

They would need it.

Chapter
11

Alone in her room, Elora Danan opened the present Luc-Jon had given her.

It was a small book, quite a contrast to the massive tomes piled in the cubbies and on the shelves of his master's library. The bindings were a leather whose condition made no concession to its evident age, and it was fastened by a single strap. Few details survived on the cover but the leather had been lovingly polished and oiled by the hands that held it to the point where its mahogany color was so rich it created the illusion of depth. Elora had the thought that if she placed her hand on its surface it would pass right through, as though she'd reached into a pool of water. She had never touched anything that felt as smooth or lustrous.

The pages were no less special, sheets of a parchment finer than vellum but far more durable. It was a book of illuminations. On every recto sheet, the right-hand page, Elora found the representation of some fantastic creature. Opposite, on the verso pages, were what she assumed were the arcane symbols for each image. The brushwork was of a piece with the construction of the book, the pictures so lifelike Elora half expected them to move. She had no trouble recognizing the ones she knew but those proved only a small proportion of the contents. The colors were breathtaking, blazing forth with such vibrant intensity that they might have been applied only yesterday.

Luc-Jon had included a letter. The book was from his master's collection, freely given over to Elora because despite its antiquity, this master had no great regard for it and little hope of ever deciphering its contents. Luc-Jon wasn't altogether sure why he himself had chosen it, save that one of its images was recognizably a dragon and the book had struck a resonant chord with the song she'd sung the night before her departure. Strange as it might sound, he wrote, this was a book that *felt* like it should be hers. He also included a note of recommendation from his master to a colleague at the university in Sandeni; if she wanted anyone knowledgeable about the history of the Great Realms to talk with, it was he.

She smiled, curling up on her bed with the letter in her arms, the book left for now off to the side. She could see Luc-Jon in the scriptorium, hunched over his half of the partner's desk, wearing fingerless gloves to keep the fingers of his writing hand warm and limber while he worked. He used a variety of crow-quill pens and as needed would pause to sharpen the nib or shift to a different edge. There was an elegance to his handwriting that bore little relationship to the rough-hewn facade of the young man himself, which provided as effective a disguise to his true nature as Elora's makeup did to her own. Yet, though she was sure she'd given him no clue, he'd divined her identity. She didn't have to read too closely between the lines to see that. He was trying his best to be of help.

"Rool," she called, "this is serious. I need you."

"Milady," he replied from a perch on the bedside table, as if he'd been there all along.

"Don't start, all right? Come here, would you, and tell me what you can make of this."

He forbore the temptation to belabor the obvious and pursed his lips as she turned the pages.

"That's a firedrake," he said, pointing.

"So would this be its sigil?" she asked, indicating the symbol opposite.

"I don't know, I'm sorry."

"A bestiary, perhaps?"

"If so, it applies to creatures that either no longer exist or those who reside far beyond the Veil for the likes of any of us. There's nothing like this in the worlds I know, either among the Daikini Realm or those I'm familiar with beyond the Veil. Unless"—he brightened—"it's fiction, the product of some poor soul's dementia."

"Good imagination. The dragon and the firedrake are perfect representations."

"I can give it to Thorn," Rool suggested.

Elora shook her head. "I want to speak to Luc-Jon's professor first. He went to the trouble of securing me an introduction, it'd be a shame to waste it."

"Look here toward the back, Elora. These pages are blank."

"Only the images. The sigils go right to the end."

"You know some of them, don't you? I can hear it in your voice."

"Not 'some,' Rool. One. The symbol Carig forced me to form."

"A name but no face."

"Precisely."

"Shall we try to find one?"

She discovered while dressing that Rool had been busy again with needle and thread. The Maizan woman's leathers now fit like they'd been made for her, and there was enough play left in the material and stitching to allow for further growth. It was a sinfully comfortable suit but the mirror's reflection once she was dressed confirmed her initial impression, that it swung a tad too far onto the side of daring for her taste. Then, of course, she caught what she decided was a scowl of disapproval from Rool, which immediately stiffened her spine and put some sass in her stride as she proclaimed the style wholly and forever her own.

"Not so used to this high collar," she noted in mock complaint. Flat in front, it swept up on a steep flare to shield the entire back of her neck to the base of her skull.

"Style's all the rage around town."

"Oh joy."

"Color suits you."

"Wine on silver?"

"You're forgetting Duguay's face paint, Elora. Combine that with the way yon outfit's cut, I guarantee nobody will look first at your face."

"What a relief. I feel more reassured already."

The brownie was proved right yet again at the foot of the stairs as Elora descended for some breakfast. She took a seat at the counter, trying to ignore the gawks from a couple of students and concentrated instead on the heady aroma from the mug of steaming tea Susan set before her.

"Bless you," she said as she took a hesitant sip, and meant it.

She wolfed down a bowl of fresh porridge and an omelette flavored with herbs and mushrooms and melted cheese. One of the other women who worked there took a seat beside her and picked off a mouthful of egg, trading a chunk of fresh sourdough in return.

"You eat and eat, girl, more than is decent," Pilar groused in good humor. "Why doesn't it ever show?"

"The way we work each night," Elora retorted, "you have to ask such a thing?"

"I'll concede your performances. Those are hard."

"And I'm a growing girl."

Pilar offered the most jaundiced of looks that raked Elora from top to toe. The younger woman had the grace to blush.

"This is ridiculous," Elora fumed. "Everyone's looking at me like I've just grown a second head! I'm fully clothed here, Pilar. I don't get this much attention in costume and that shows off just about everything!"

"On occasion, sweetie, it's the assets you hide that become more enticing than what's on active display. Don't mind them, though." She indicated the students. "Scholars have no lives."

"Actually, I need one."

Pilar raised her eyebrows, looking from Elora to the students and back again with disapproval.

"Not that way, not socially," Elora protested, "and not them. Excuse me," she called to them, sidling off her chair and over to their table, "I'm looking for this professor." She handed them the envelope on which Luc-Jon's master had scribbled his name.

"He's in Keeys College, yes?" asked one, to nods all around.

"But you'll not get in to see him till, oh, mid-afternoon at the earliest. Classes today, you see."

"Partial to high tea, though. Scones and cakes, the way to win his heart."

"We're easier conquests, Elora. You've won our hearts already!"

"Aha." She nodded, and then asked for directions.

Dominating the city was a massive edifice called the Citadel, of which Thorn's tower was a part. This was the seat of government, so vast it bridged two of the rivers that plunged over the Wall and added better than a hundred feet to the height of the cliff. That prominence wasn't so evident at first glance, mainly because of the sheer bulk of the stronghold. In shape, from an eagle's-eye view overhead, it described a rough half circle, which presented a curved defensive palisade to the east (since it was assumed that no attacking force could possibly scale the Wall itself) that in its turn enclosed a massive complex of interconnected buildings and fortifications that extended for the better part of a mile along the escarpment. It was near half that in depth, with far more available space than was ever actually used, since it was also intended to serve as a refuge of last resort in case of attack.

Those had been dangerous days, when the feuding warlords of Chengwei had been in an expansionist frame of mind, each determined to seize control of the trading routes to the west—the fabled "Silk River"—as a means of consolidating power to the point where they could proclaim themselves "Emperor." Some proved little better than brigands and were dealt with accordingly, as were their descendants to this day. Others represented more formidable threats and came across the sprawling tableland in massed formations on horse or on foot, assaulting Sandeni with forces temporal and, on rare and terrifying occasions, magical.

From the beginning the greatest danger came from the sunrise, and the east was where the city concentrated the bulk of its attention and defenses. Paradoxically, it was also where Sandeni enjoyed its most impressive growth as the city expanded inland from the cliff face as well as along its edge. Fanning outward from this hub were streets and buildings too numberless to count, representing a mass of humanity that easily eclipsed all Elora had known in the past. Tir Asleen and Nockmaar, the preeminent castles of their respective realms, would both be lost within this Citadel. Even mighty Angwyn couldn't compare.

Being the confluence of a half-dozen rivers and lesser streams, the land above the falls formed an extensive floodplain interspersed with a fair number of islands, of which Madaket was one. Some were rock, others were composed of silt that thickened over the decades into solid earth. During the initial expansion from the stockade that would quickly become the Citadel, bridges had to be built, traversing not only the free-flowing waterways but the bog and marshland surrounding them, thereby allowing troops to reach the solid land beyond. The swamps were more than a strategic nuisance, though. Summer brought not only a stench that was often indescribable, but hordes of insects who made the citizenry's life a misery from equinox to equinox. To deal with both problems, a massive public-works project was instituted to drain the marshes and replace the natural landscape with a metropolis worthy of Sandeni's substantial, and increasing, wealth and power.

The end result, at least in the eyes of the civic fathers, more than justified the cost.

Sandeni was laid out much like a wheel, with the Citadel its hub. After generations, if not centuries, of rampant development, the shape of that wheel had been thrown significantly off center. There was much more of the city to the north, where the ground was more substantial, than in the opposite direction. Broad avenues stretched straightaway from the huge plaza that fronted the Citadel. There'd also been two moats, channels connecting the rivers that ran beneath, designed to serve the plaza's original intent as a clear killing ground. Under constant fire from the walls, it was believed impossible for any attacker to make a successful assault across such a broad expanse. But there'd been no war for two generations, nor had the city itself been under direct siege for centuries before that. The original purpose didn't seem so essential any longer, and since the plaza was so much more useful for peaceful activities, the moats had long ago been filled in.

Major intersections on the avenues followed the same basic curve established by the Citadel's walls. The difference was that the cross streets derived their inspiration from the plaza moats, and alternated solid thoroughfares with aquatic canals. Those canals in their turn were linked so that it was actually possible to travel from the Citadel's water gate to well beyond the official boundary of the city without once setting foot on dry land. An arrangement of dikes and bulwarks diverted the force of the rivers themselves, preventing the canals from being too affected by their swiftly flowing currents, and likewise keeping any boaters from being inadvertently swept over the falls.

Every so often some bravo or other, convinced either of his genius or invulnerability, made the plunge, in a contraption "guaranteed" to survive the attempt. Thus far, the falls remained unconquered.

In concept, the city was simplicity itself, laid out according to a grid with streets essentially at right angles to one another. Six boulevards, named for the six rivers whose waters fed the falls, stretched outward from the Citadel as the "spokes" of the great half wheel, while a mix of numbered avenues and named streets formed the rings that intersected with them. On those boulevards could be found the most impressive and renowned demonstration of the city's inventive genius, its tram system.

From the founding of the city, the inhabitants respected the power of the falls. Being Daikini, and finding themselves in a portion of the world where the Veil Folk appeared to have little interest or influence, they dreamed of ways that power might be harnessed. The principle of using a water wheel to power a mill's grinding stone had been long established. Roughly a century earlier an engineer had the inspiration of applying that same notion to public transport. A whole series of wheels were constructed, connected by an ingenious network of gears to what was essentially a giant pulley system buried under the street. Water spun the wheels, which turned the gears, which pulled the perpetual cable, which dragged along anything clamped to it. Tracks were laid on the street bed to keep the vehicles properly in line, and the Sandeni Municipal Railway was born. Day and night without pause its trolley cars trundled back and forth along the avenues, creating a safe and efficient means for those who lived on the outskirts of the city to visit its center, and vice versa.

Plans existed, had for some time, to expand the system to the major cross streets, but there remained too much opposition from the Watermen's Guild, who rightly saw the trolleys as a significant threat to their own livelihoods. As a consequence passengers rode the trolley to the required intersection and transferred to a water bus or taxi, or on a noncanal street, a horse-drawn coach. Otherwise, folk made do with mounts of their own, or rickshaws, or their own feet.

The streets also served as convenient boundaries for the political subdivisions of the city. The area between the boulevards, roughly the shape of a giant pie slice, was designated a council borough. Districts were delineated by the avenues, which then were broken down into precincts. Unfortunately the expansion of the city, and the equally expanding arc of each borough's "pie slice," meant that outlying districts comprised a far greater population than those closer in. They wanted power in council commensurate with their greater number of precincts. By the same token, the older, more established districts were equally reluctant to yield their own influence or status. It was a debate as long-standing as the city itself that had in recent years grown increasingly fractious, with positions hardening on every side, as Elora had heard herself while serving dinner.

The points of the "pie slices" that abutted the plaza comprised the city's business center. Here could be found the home offices of Sandeni's major banks, mercantile houses, cathedrals, each proclaiming to the world their own absolute preeminence in their respective fields. There were also the official residences of the ambassadors of all the major continental Daikini powers, even one whose gate was still adorned with the crest of royal Angwyn.

Off to one side of the plaza Elora spied an island, sensing instinctively that it was one of the original plots of solid ground on which the rest of the city had been constructed, and positioned in such a way as to provide a deliberate flaw in the otherwise superbly symmetrical design of the esplanade. It intruded no small distance into the body of the plaza itself and took a divot out of the terminus points of the two adjoining boroughs. Here the moat had not been filled in, nor had the race of water been checked in the slightest. Both sound and sight testified eloquently to the ferocity of the current and to its purpose as a deterrent. It was too great a width to jump and far too dangerous to attempt a crossing either by boat or by swimming.

There were structures visible on the island, but only as disconnected elements, being mostly hidden behind so majestic an assortment of trees and shrubbery that the island might well be mistaken for an arboretum. A promenade ringed its shore, with paths fading into the shadows cast by the full branches, giving it a marvelous air of mystery and enchantment even at the height of the day. For a stretch of the isle's circumference Elora beheld a magnificent stand of wild roses, still in bloom despite the lateness of the season. She felt a pang of sympathy for whoever was responsible for pruning that nasty tangle, as well as for anyone fool enough to try to slip through it.

Rounding the whole of the moat, she found only one way across, a stone bridge too narrow for any vehicle, with barely space for two Daikini to walk side by side. Thinking at first this must be some public garden, she made her way from one shore to the other only to discover a thin length of silver chain, so fine it would hardly qualify as a woman's necklace, strung between a pair of stone pillars to block the way. It was apparently a permanent obstruction, a quick examination provided no sign of any lock and the links themselves appeared to disappear into the fabric of the lacquered stone. There were no seams visible in the rock, or tool marks of any kind, which gave Elora the distinct impression that these two obelisks were two perfect crystals, either grown in place or brought untouched from the quarry. And while the surface gleamed as though from the ministrations of a daily and thorough polish, there was absolutely no reflection to be seen.

She considered stepping over the chain, or crouching underneath, but after a glance at the carved gargoyles crouched watchfully atop the obelisks, thought better of it.

The isle and its dwellings might be empty, even abandoned, but that didn't mean caretakers hadn't been left behind to look after things.

She slumped down onto her heels and chewed on her lower lip while she stared at the island in frustrated fascination, ignoring the faint burr of warning sent her way from above.

At that point both brownies together decided this was the moment for discretion to prove the better part of valor.

"Walk away from here," Rool hissed in one ear.

"Now!" echoed Franjean in the other, in a remarkable imitation of a cat's *raowl*.

So strong and urgent were their injunctions that Elora didn't stop to question or argue but let her feet take her quickly off the bridge, back the way she came. She didn't pause or even look back until she was once more well into the broad, sunlit expanse of the plaza.

"Have you lost *all* sense, girl?"

"Pleased to see you, too, again, Franjean."

"If you could see yourself through my eyes—! Elora *Danan,* what cut your hair, you go all dozy too close to a herd of sheep?"

Common sense put a brake on the retort that sprang to her lips. Franjean was already in rare form and could cut with epigrams more deeply than Khory with a sword. Moreover, experience told her that his acerbity in this instance came from a genuine fright.

"Where did you come from?" she asked instead.

"Thorn lives there," the brownie replied, with a turn of the head to indicate the Citadel that created a wall of its own along the far border of the plaza. "Thorn works there. I live and work with Thorn. You don't want contact with him, that's your lookout."

"I have good reason, Franjean," she tried to explain, but he would hear none of it.

"Not passing judgment, wouldn't think of it, your decision after all, but don't see a need to be bound by it either, especially when your foolishness looks to put my friend Rool in jeopardy."

"I would never—!" she protested.

"Turn about," Rool told her. "Slowly."

"What's this all about?" she asked instead.

"Take in the sights."

"What do you see, then?"

"Buildings." A pause. "People." A longer pause. "Lots of people." There was the merest thread of unease running through her ostensibly casual tone. "I've never seen so many, not up this close. Not in Angwyn, nor at the bazaar in the Valley of the Mountain Kings. Where do they all come from? How can they live so chockablock, all one upon the other?"

"Daikini and ants," groused Franjean. "Go figure."

"I'm serious, Franjean."

"And I am not? Don't imagine there's a species born that isn't social, one way or t'other, Elora. It's just you Daikini tend to carry that impulse to extremes. Brownies now, we like communities where all the names are known. Big enough for spice and variety but not so much that there are strangers among us. Hive like this, everyone's a stranger. Don't see the sense. But then again, in the eyes of most folks hereabouts, I'd wager the likes of us are considered too small to matter in their scheme of things."

"The way you talk, Sandeni's already pretty much in the Deceiver's camp, with no time or truck for any people but themselves."

"You misunderstand, Elora," Rool offered laconically. "They have both time and truck, just not a whole lot of gratuitous respect. Big folk beyond the Veil, elves especially, aren't used to that. Don't much care for it."

"Right now, I don't much care for *you*," snapped Franjean to his friend. "If I hadn't seen with my own eyes, I'd never have credited it. You let her stroll across that bridge, pretty as you please, *knowing* what was waiting!"

"What was waiting?" Elora asked, resisting the urge to steal a glance over her shoulder.

"That's of no mind right now. D'you see the strollers on this promenade, where they wander?"

A nod. In actuality, she'd noted the difference even before the question was asked.

"None of them near the bridge. None even close to the moat. Wards?" she asked, after brief consideration.

Franjean was taken slightly aback. He'd assumed he'd have to take her through this step by laborious step. Instead she was leapfrogging ahead.

"Passive mainly," he explained, "innate to the land and structures themselves, radiating a pervasive background suggestion that you'd be better off somewhere else. Reinforced by the gargoyles, of course. They woke up when you looked like you were about to stay awhile."

"So I felt."

"Anyone else would have leaped from there faster than from a red-hot skillet. You hardly noticed and walked through the rest as though they didn't exist. If not for us, you'd be there still."

"Would they have attacked?"

"Doubtful, given who you are," said Rool. "She was in no danger, Franjean."

"Run up a flag, why don't you?" Franjean's tone was acid mockery. "Build a platform in the center of the plaza and reveal her true nature. Save us all a lot of fuss and bother."

"What *is* the matter, Franjean?" Elora demanded.

"Got time, and patience, to hear the list? That island doesn't even wholly exist in this plane of being! It dates from long before the founding of the city, that's why no attempt was ever made to move it or alter its shape. Supposedly, in its heart is an ancient World Gate. No one's ever found it, wouldn't matter if they did since there's no energy left here'bouts to power it."

"Like the tor," Elora mused.

"I heard about that," said Franjean, "from the demon child," which was his term for Khory. Of them all, he still refused to refer to her by name. "Bad business."

"Happy ending," Rool commented. "And you should

342

be more polite, Franjean, since we're sworn allies now, Lesser Faery and Elora."

Franjean retorted with such a face coupled with the most disrespectful of noises that Elora nearly burst out laughing.

"The physical aspect of the world changes with age," she said, returning to her thought. "And why not, since the world's a living being? The patterns of force it generates change with it. What's true for one age may not prove so for the next."

"Is that helpful?" Rool wondered.

"Not really," she confessed. "Not yet."

"Regardless," Franjean announced, reclaiming the conversation, "that island serves as home for all the local embassies of the Veil Folk! No one visits uninvited, same as no one finds a brownie burrow unless we're of a mind to allow it. Walking on that bridge is trouble enough. *Not* being attacked brands you for certain."

"I understand, Franjean. I'll be more careful."

"You're in the world, Elora, as you so proudly proclaim. Ignorance—rather, *stupidity*—is a luxury you can't afford."

"You rather I hide?"

Franjean, always the more voluble of the pair, made a noise of extreme exasperation.

"Faint hope of that, the mind you're in," he told her. "But mark me, girl, in the scheme of things you've only now come into your milk teeth. You're a fledgling with more down to your wings than proper feathers."

"I'm not helpless, Franjean."

"Not *that* helpless, perhaps," he scoffed.

"I've held my own pretty well so far."

"And our charge is to ensure that doesn't become your epitaph."

"You *are* in a choice mood."

"Clothes are adequate," he said dismissively, abruptly changing the subject with the most minor and grudging of compliments, which was as quickly undercut. "For traipsing through bogs and fens and the like."

343

Elora rolled her eyes and tried to exchange expressions with Rool, but the other brownie was nowhere to be seen on her shoulder. Nor, when she turned her head the other way, was Franjean, although his voice made his presence as plain as his opinions.

"I suppose you hate my body paint as well," she dared him.

"Actually, that has possibilities."

"I'm so glad."

"Truth," he conceded grudgingly, "if I hadn't known from the demon child and Bastian what to look for, and hadn't spotted Rool in the bargain, I'd most likely have passed you by. You've gone through more than a skin change, Elora, and walked a far piece from the girl you were, in both body and spirit."

She said nothing, where ordinarily she'd have been floored by Franjean's unexpected and gracious compliment. Indeed, she seemed to have hardly heard him.

"Elora," asked Rool suddenly, "what's the matter?"

"What I said before. All these people. All this noise . . ." Her voice trailed off.

The plaza was the center of urban life for upper Sandeni. From it ranged a whole network of walkways and esplanades that took strollers to the edge of various falls, or right to the cliff itself. Portions had been cleared of stone, over the strenuous objections of the military, and planted with stands of trees, so long ago that those saplings had grown taller than the surrounding buildings. Both groves and flower beds were interspersed with plots of grass and benches where citizens could enjoy some quiet contemplation, or a meal in the open air. Strolling buskers entertained, speakers harangued, children played, cutpurses cruised for marks while avoiding the watchful, wary eyes of the patrol constables. Elora heard the sound of shoes on flagstones, the background susurrus of thousands of voices, skeins of music, all battling to be heard over the constant rush of water over the falls. Nothing before her stayed still, all was constant motion in a never-ending panoply, a feast for her eyes that she found both entrancing and terrifying.

Of a sudden, in a way she'd never experienced before and didn't understand, she felt tiny, like a fairy among giants. And most awfully alone.

"There are so many!" she wailed softly, to herself. "And this is just one piece of one city of one domain among the whole Daikini Realm. And that Realm is one among twelve."

"Thirteen," reminded Rool.

"The Realm of Elora," she snorted.

"If you're afraid," Franjean said with uncharacteristic kindness, "knock on the Citadel door."

"Is Thorn watching, Franjean?" Her eyes scoured the battlements but they were too high and too far away. She could find no details she was sure of.

"No. More fool him. The demon child pled your case, he accepted. Won't watch for fear of someone watching him."

"It was easier at Ganthem's Crossing, or on Tyrrel's tor," she said. "The goals were tangible, they were right in front of me. Someone needed saving, I did it, hooray for me. The consequences were immediate and personal." She took in a deep breath, released it in a rush. "I look around here and see all these *people*—!"

"There's no harm in accepting your limitations," said Franjean.

She reached into her pouch, to find Luc-Jon's gift at hand. She stroked her thumb on its cover, thinking her skin would never feel so sleek, and to her mind came the vision of the sigil that stood alone.

Another breath, this one of acquiescence, and for an instant both brownies feared she had given up.

"I gave my word, Franjean," she said simply, before casting about for the trolley stop. "Just like Thorn did to Cherlindrea, when she asked him to take me to Tir Asleen. Knowing your limitations is a good and necessary thing, my friends. Knowing your honor," she finished, "is more."

345

The university was larger than many towns she'd known, a community unto itself chockablock with subordinate colleges that dealt with each other much like rival states. She enjoyed the stroll through the school's environs, painfully certain from the way she marveled at every sight how much the country bumpkin she must appear despite her leather costume, and soon got used to the brusque manner the students applied to anyone not of their college. The brownies were less charitable. Within short order they were gleefully plotting between themselves the nature of their spectacularly malicious revenge against all and sundry.

As predicted, the professor was in class, but Elora had timed her arrival so that she didn't have long to wait. Also as predicted, he had an abiding fondness for sweets.

"Ah, Luc-Jon," he mused, picking crumbs off his faded black robe and popping them in his mouth with a diligence Elora had never seen. "I told Parry"—Luc-Jon's master—"that if he'd send the lad downriver I'd sponsor him myself."

"He'll be honored to know you think so highly of him, sir."

She offered the plate of cakes. He made a show of reluctance, then shook his head, scratched his beard, and plucked the richest of the lot.

"You'll pardon me for saying, miss," he said to her between mouthfuls, "but you're not the sort we're used to seeing about these precincts."

"Sort of what?"

"Person, for one. Your appearance is rather more . . . theatrical than most."

"As is my profession."

"Yet you come to me for some assistance."

"A need born of a regrettable lack of education."

"I would scarcely credit such a statement."

"Appearances are deceiving, Professor." Elora laughed. "To be well-spoken is not necessarily to be well-read. To be well-read doesn't always provide one with the knowledge one requires."

"What do you require?"

She almost answered him but caught herself over the way he'd phrased his question.

"I ask," she said, offering an entreaty where he'd been expecting a command, "your help."

"Regarding?"

"The prophecies of Elora," she told him.

He made a tremendous *whoulf* sound that turned heads at some of the neighboring tables.

"And the nature and truth about dragons," she told him.

He made the same sound, louder than before, and tossed his hands up in the bargain. A waiter hurried to his side, concerned that the professor might be having some sort of seizure.

"And this," she said at the last, when the waiter had departed. She set the book Luc-Jon had given her down before him.

He steepled his fingers before his face, stared at the book, then at her, and was silent for long enough to make her nervous. If not for the brightness of his eyes and the vibrancy of his spirit, she might have made the waiter's mistake and assumed the worst as well.

"Do you know what you have here?" he asked in a tone meant for her ears alone.

"I've heard it described as a kind of bestiary."

"Fascinating. I've never heard it described at all."

"But you know what it is."

"I suspect," he said with gentle emphasis, and a succession of qualifiers, "I may know what it is supposed to be, that is possible, yes."

"Why are you so afraid, Professor?"

"Truly, you don't know?" She shook her head. "I am a man of letters, the closest I've come to weapons are the knives I use to cut my meat. That's as it should be, for I've no skill whatsoever with the bloody things. But as I am a man of letters, I've read accounts of weapons and battles by those who know both well. I know, for example, there are blades of so fine an edge that any fool struck by one

347

will see the offending limb fall, completely severed, before the body has had time to realize what's happened."

He reached out a finger as though to tap the book by its cover, but never made contact.

"This is much the same. Do you know why Parry gave it up to you?" he asked her.

"Luc-Jon didn't say, beyond that it had no value and he despaired of ever deciphering its contents."

"Hard to decipher what you can't blessed see," chortled the professor. "I'll wager any sum you like that the one time, and one time *only,* Parry opened this book he saw naught but blank pages. Tossed it on a shelf after and never gave it a second thought, not even to use for himself."

"The pages aren't blank."

"You've been told," he inquired sharply, "or you've seen it for yourself?"

"I've seen."

"Then, my dear, you are singularly blessed. Or cursed. It is an encyclopedia, a census if you will, of those who are said to inhabit the Third Circle."

"Have you seen it?"

His mouth quirked a little ruefully, at opportunities set aside. "I have been told about it. I am a scholar, not a sorcerer. Only they can perceive its true nature, and thereby its contents. Only a magus"—and his eyes met hers a moment before dropping away—"can actually use the summoning sigils."

"Setting the book aside, Professor," she said, and did so, sweeping it casually back into her pouch, "what about the rest?"

He slid a key across the table to her.

"You are welcome to my library at any hour. Whatever is in my power is yours for the asking."

If Keeys College were the castle it pretended to be, the professor's lodgings would be one of the subordinate keeps, three stories of stout stone whose interior was as solid and conservative in design as the building's facade. His actual residence was little more than a closet, and as she passed it by Elora felt a surge of sympathy for who-ever was responsible for keeping it tidy. While those rooms were a veritable chaos, the work spaces were any-thing but. Cases of volumes climbed every wall to the ceiling, while others, not quite so tall, stood alone in ranks across the floor. A space was set aside for desks and there was a whole collection of ladders to reach the topmost shelves. At the far end of the room she could see a circu-lar stairway of wrought iron, leading, she assumed, to the floors above.

"Iron steps," the professor said idly, "iron mullions between the windowpanes, iron facings on the doors. Simple precautions"—a flare of a smile, as quick as the blink of an eye—"but effective."

"Against what?"

"Knowledge is power. And ambition is not solely a Daikini trait."

"I have to go, Professor. Do you know the Street of Lost Dragons, on Madaket?" He nodded. "Come by Black-Eyed Susan's some night. I'd like you to hear me sing." She took him by the hand. "I'll be back," she said.

"The books will be here. I will be waiting."

A long embankment formed the southernmost boundary of the university along the shore of the Paschal, smallest of the six rivers that flowed through Sandeni. It was also the only one that stayed wholly independent all the way to the edge, forming a cataract all its own from the heights of the cliff to Lake Morar below. As she strolled along Elora could see the sparkling trail made by the Paschal as it plunged off the heights of the Shados in a series of wild cataracts that brought it to the level of the plateau. The mountains met the tableland like the point of a wedge, in an arrowhead formation of jagged and im-posing peaks, as though they meant to crack the land asunder, the way an ax might split a log.

"Think they've ever been found?" Elora asked no one in particular, basking in the warmth of a lowering sun, the air cast in comforting autumnal hues, her thoughts full of the possibilities she'd seen in the professor's library. She assumed the brownies would reply.

"Who's that?" Duguay asked in return, and Elora stumbled in startlement. She struck the parapet, hissing with annoyance more than pain as she barked her hip, and the troubadour's hands closed over her to keep her from falling farther.

"The dragons." Whatever her innermost feelings, her smile of welcome was genuine and a decent complement to the daystar beaming overhead. Duguay looked like he was about to kiss her but chose instead to stroke his thumbs lightly along the column of her throat. The sensations were delicious, they made her tremble like a cat. She'd have purred as well if she'd known how.

"They're a vexatious breed," he said. "Comes of heeding no law but your own."

"Know 'em that well, do you?"

His smile turned lazy and possessive in a way that made her want to melt inside. "I've heard the stories and sung the songs, like any troubadour worth the name."

"Street of the Lost Dragons," she mused. "I wonder, does 'lost' mean missing, or doomed?"

"Or nothing at all? Does it matter? It's only a street sign."

"Just a thought, is all. What are you doing here, Duguay?"

"Thought we'd go a-wandering tonight, pet. Dance for our pleasure . . . ?"

"Don't we always?"

"Gauge the competition, so to speak?"

"Answer my question."

"Asked at Susan's where you were. Got pointed toward the university. Came looking. Not so big a place to search, nor are you so hard to miss. Now you answer mine?"

"It sounds like fun. Though I warn you, Duguay, if the performances of the last few nights are any indication, once we're done at Susan's, it's bed."

"I'll take my chances."

He took a hand in his, sliding fingers between hers to intertwine their grasp. She let him for a few more steps, then slipped free before his hand could close. She had no thought of direction when they started their stroll, the only requirement being that they return to Madaket in time for dinner. They passed along lanes barely a few handspans wider than their shoulders and from there into proper streets, crossing bridges when they came to them. Given the layout of the city, that proved fairly often. Few words passed between them as they walked, but to those who passed they seemed the most familiar of couples. Not quite lovers but more than simple friends, bound by an intimacy that went beyond the simply physical.

It was her inspiration to ride the cable car. She saw it at the end of the street and took off like a stone from a catapult, crying at the top of her lungs for the car to stay just a bit longer until she could leap aboard. There were hardly any passengers, which was fortunate because she'd built up so much momentum she very nearly hurled herself straight through the open-sided carriage. At the last instant she caught hold of one of the brightly polished poles that supported the roof, swinging one leg out and around in a huge circle, embracing the pole with both arms wrapped about it and a great, goofy grin on her face as she beheld Duguay huffing after her.

Her entrance earned her a stern reprimand from the conductor and she took it with such courtesy and good grace that he hadn't the heart to pitch her off. She snugged herself down on the wooden bench beside the brakeman, legs folded tight beneath her, one arm wrapped around her ankles to hold them in place, the other draped along the back of the bench while her gaze swept the buildings on either side of the magnificent boulevard. A greenway promenade bisected the roadway for its entire length, providing a lovely mix of grass and flower beds and trees.

Somewhere or other Duguay had managed to come up with lunch, and he presented Elora with a sandwich from a roving vendor. Bread hot and fresh from the oven, spiced meat, grilled mushrooms and onions and peppers, plus melted cheese. It smelled delicious and tasted even better. The aromas were too enticing to hide and it seemed discourteous to hog such bounty to herself, so Elora broke off a pair of decent-sized pieces and offered them to the trolley's crew.

"I'm Elora," she said cheerily. She didn't hold out her hand in greeting because both of the brakeman's were covered in heavy, grimy gloves, but he returned her smile with one of her own, a bit more shy. The offer of food was appreciated but they weren't allowed to eat while on a run, so the gifts were stored away for later. In return, the conductor offered one of their own dinner flasks of hot spiced cider, and as the car trundled on its route they chatted amiably about the city, about politics, about sports, about their lives.

"Damn daft, is what they are," grumbled the brakeman, referring to politicians in general. He was a young barrel of a man, whose compact form belied an exceptional and formidable strength of body in a way that made Elora wonder if there was Nelwyn blood in his ancestry. Such occurrences were exceeding rare, and actively discouraged by all the races on both sides of the Veil, but they happened nonetheless. Duguay had a song about two such lovers, doomed of course. No matter how true their love, the world was against them, the tragic end preordained and inescapable. Far sadder than the ballad itself was the occasional comment from some lout or other in the audience that it served the lovers right, they merely got the fate they deserved.

The brakeman's name was Tam.

"I mean," he said between small grunts as he hauled on the great, polished lever handle mounted on the floor to tighten the clamp on the cable buried beneath the street or release it. As the car slowed he took hold of the brake to bring it to a halt. Lastly he sounded the bell by tugging the lanyard by his head. All these actions occurred in sequence, in a matter of seconds, so practiced a series of moves that the trolley slowed and accelerated with hardly a jerk. "It's a big world, innit?"

"What's your point, Tam?" wondered the conductor, whose name was Rico, sneaking a sip of cider from the mug he'd given Elora.

"Well! How many weeks to Angwyn, d'y' think, by boat or horseback? How many to Chengwei, t'other direction? An' d'y' know of *anyone* been south o' the Stairs to Heaven, I mean regular like? It's no small business, is what I'm sayin', travelin' from place t' place. Hardly none of it's what'cha call a regular service, like what we provide. Caravan leaves when it's good an' ready, ain't no set schedule. How's one guv'ment, *any* kinda guv'ment, s'posed t' bind it all t'gether, is what I'm askin'?"

"We don't do so bad, Tam, movin' folks from the Citadel to Wivlesfield."

"What, you suggestin' we stretch a cable from here t' the ocean?" The brakeman found that concept so amusing he nearly choked on his mouthful of cider, splurts of laughter interspersed with bouts of coughing. He never once lost his rhythm on the levers, and the car likewise lost no headway.

"What I'm saying, *dolt*—"

"Wa'cher yap, there's a lady present!" Tam tossed Elora a wink and a lopsided grin and got a fair smile from her in return.

"I am saying," the conductor repeated patiently, conveying the sense that this was not the first of such discussions between the two men and that the heat it generated was actually a form of play, "that we started our journeys afoot. Learn to stand, learn to walk. We graduated to horseback, and let them do the bulk of the work. After domesticating the animal, we harnessed them to carts. When we came to rivers, we discovered how to make boats. We built these trolleys. We Daikini— we learn, we grow, we *invent*. That's our nature. You may not see how a single state might effectively rule a continent, or even a world, but does that mean it can't be done? Or shouldn't be attempted?"

"Where's the benefit?" Elora asked.

"Be nice never again to have to worry about marauding warlords out of Chengwei. Or possibly establish a regular shipping service across the continent, from top to bottom as well as sunrise to sunset."

"Accordin' t' me ma, had fairies present to bless me at my birth," Tam said quietly. "Cost me da a pretty penny in obligation, but tha' was work he was glad to shoulder, an' I in my turn after he passed on. If I have young of me own, I'm hopin' they'll come again. And for me grandkids in their turn. A world that denies us tha' beauty, whatever else kind of peace or prosperity it offers, comes at too high a price."

"But I've heard said that the Veil Folk oppress us," Duguay said, playing devil's advocate. "They deny us the nature your partner speaks of."

"They do oppress," Rico said slowly, placing words and thoughts together with due deliberation. "They *do* deny our nature. But I'm like Tam, I'll miss them if they go. I'd like to find another way."

"At least in Sandeni," Tam interjected with no little civic pride, "we each of us have our proper say in the making of things."

"However small that may be," noted the conductor.

"We've our franchise, Rico, we got our vote. Them what rule do so by the consent of the governed. The decisions they make, they're answerable to us."

"The Highlander clans are much the same," Elora said. "And brownie burrows, so I've heard tell. In fact, there's a story that Nelwyns passed the idea to the Cascani, who mixed it in with a holdful of beliefs gotten from the Wyrrn, and the founders of Sandeni stole from them all!"

"Most excellent thievery"—Duguay chuckled—"if this is the result. No wonder, though, the Royal Realms are so nervous about them. It's always been hard to mesh the right of monarchs with those of the individual."

"Heard talk out of Angwyn, before the Frost," which was how folks had come to refer to the overthrow of that city, " 'bout some yob came up with a way to harness steam as a means of propulsion. Imagine, Tam, cars like this moving along a set of tracks, with an engine to pull them instead of our cable."

"That'll be the day. Remember the stories? All the grief the city fathers went through with the Veil Folk just to get these trolley lines laid? An' this be land where most beyond the Veil don't lay no claim. You stretch iron from here to the sea, in *any* direction, Rico, *then* you'll see a war, an' tha's no error!"

"You two at it again," said a new arrival, by way of an introduction of his own. He was a Daikini of middling height and apparently slighter than average build, though Elora noted that could have been as much a result of stance and style of dress as the actual shape of his body. Chestnut hair, neatly combed, otherwise the man was utterly unassuming. The same true for his clothes and diffident manner. At a glance he could be marked as a member of any number of professions, nothing physical like a foundry worker but by the same token nothing higher than mid-list on the economic food chain. One of the multitude of unexceptional functionaries essential to the well-being of the state.

Only his eyes gave him away, and only then because Elora had learned from Khory and the brownies what to look for. They missed nothing about him and did so without drawing the slightest attention to their scrutiny. His interest wasn't confined to the trolley, either. He regularly swept his gaze over the frontages they passed.

She offered her hand and her name. The conductor supplied the response.

"This is Renny Garedo," he said.

"Constable?" Elora hazarded mischievously, to be rewarded with a pleasantly surprised chuckle from him, and a nod of acknowledgment.

"You two been corrupting minors again," the constable said, tossing a gentle gauntlet down before the two transit workers. His manner was relaxed, his tone unthreatening, as he sat on the opposite side of the car from Elora.

"Shaa," scoffed Tam. "We never!"

"More likely the other way 'round, Constable," said Elora cheerily. "As you'll see if you come to our show tonight."

"Last stop," Rico sang out from his own perch in the back. "Citadel terminus. All passengers off, please!"

For the crew, this also represented the end of their shift, as Elora and Duguay and Renny joined them and their replacements in hauling the car around on its turntable, thereby reversing its direction and positioning it to catch the outbound cable.

It seemed like a wonderful idea at the time.

From the start, though, the mood was jangly, with an undercurrent that made Elora nervous. Patrons were brusque and uncommonly hard to please, and there were occasions in the evening that made her glad the constable had decided to accept her invitation, and that the professor had chosen not to.

Then Duguay sang the doomed lovers' song. Elora started toward the stage intending to follow with another tune entirely, but the japes and catcalls from some of the audience were harsher than usual and the casual cruelty of that intolerance sent a tidal wave of anger coursing through her. She took a seat before the fire and didn't move, gathering a stillness about herself that made Duguay look up sharply, reminded of the prelude to her performance at the fort weeks ago. Renny looked as well, and as intently, for different reasons. Unbidden, a tune and lyrics flashed from lips and fingers as Elora strummed a sequence of basic but increasingly passionate chords on her guitar, accenting them by striking a dynamic percussive beat with her hand on the face of the instrument. There was no ambiguity about her position, nor any mercy. It was an anthem and a slap in the face to every person here who'd offered a rude remark about Duguay's song. Strangely, though, it was as strong a refutation of the song itself. His lovers were doomed, hers defiant. His were victims, hers seized hold of their fate. There was a neat ending to his. Hers was a call to the barricades, with nothing settled and nothing guaranteed. Hers had rage, and it had hope.

There was a large table of students, not from Keeys College, she was glad to see, who were responsible for most of the rude commentary. They caught the brunt of her fury when she sang, and knew full well, as did everyone else in the room, that her words were meant for them. They weren't happy about it, either, and harsh glares followed her back to the table she shared with the transit workers.

Tam was on his feet, hands held overhead as he pounded palms together, counterpointing his applause with piercing whistles.

"Damn fine," he cheered over and over, "damn fine!"

"You liked?" Elora asked.

"I'm not altogether certain 'like' is a word I'd apply to that song," said Renny, "but a powerful performance nonetheless."

"I'm afraid," Elora said, flexing sore fingers, "I'm still learning the guitar."

"Better at it than I ever was," Tam told her.

"With fingers like yours, that's no revelation."

Four heads turned as one to fix themselves on the student who'd commented just a bit too loudly.

Renny started to his feet, but Susan was there before him, sidling easily through the press of customers and tables to place herself between the constable and the students.

"With respect, gentlemen," she said, "you've finished your meal and these tables are needed for other customers. If you don't mind, perhaps it's better that you take your leave."

One started a protest but another gave him a thump to the shoulder and used his own body to shunt him from his seat. None of them looked happy but they all did as they were told. As they departed Susan and the staff all exchanged glances and nods, silently confirming amongst

357

themselves that it would be a long time before any of those faces were welcomed back.

That flashfire confrontation, brief and seemingly inconsequential as it was, defined the evening from then on. Duguay took Elora's response to his song personally and for the first time harsh words were exchanged between them.

"I wasn't aware I had to ask your permission what to sing," she told him during a break after he'd hustled her into an alcove.

"Nor was I that I should be so actively and publicly insulted by my apprentice."

"I meant no insult."

"Spare me, girl. What else would you call it?"

"It wasn't you, Duguay," she tried to explain, but her thoughts kept stumbling over the irrefutable truth that he was right. "The song made me angry. . . ."

"And you couldn't find another outlet? Another way to express yourself? You saw no alternative but to turn this into open conflict between us?" He hadn't raised his voice once but even a casual onlooker couldn't help but realize from the pose of his body that this was a private conversation. "You have so little regard for me?"

She blinked, quickly, as though she'd been actively struck. She said nothing, could find no words to close the sudden breach between them. Worse, she wasn't sure she wanted to. His song had acted on her like a gauntlet and she found she could not, would not, apologize for taking up that challenge.

Throughout the evening, right to the very end, the constable's eyes never left Elora for long. It was a very underhanded scrutiny, she'd catch him out of the corner of her eye watching her from the corners of his. She'd flick a surprise glance his way, to discover his gaze conspicuously elsewhere, which paradoxically left her all the more convinced he'd been watching. He sat with his back to the wall, his chair angled toward the other two men, but in such a way that his field of vision easily included Elora, so that even when he wasn't looking at her directly his awareness of her was total.

"Tell me, Constable," she asked at last as the tavern gradually emptied, "what is it you're looking at?"

"You have good bones, Elora, why hide them beneath all that paint?"

"I like to be seen. I want to be remembered."

"But the paint is artifice, the memory a lie."

"I'm a performer, Constable."

"Nothing to hide, then?"

"Everything. Nothing." She batted her eyes. "Mystery is my stock-in-trade, Renny, as keen eyes are in yours."

"Point an' game t' 'lora, Renny, tha's my way o' thinkin'!" chortled Tam. "Pay him na' mind, lass," he continued to Elora, "man's a sponge o' questions."

"Another useful talent in my profession, Tam," Renny said.

"Too damnably suspicious by half, Renny, an' y'ask me!"

"Right," Rico announced, rising wearily to his feet and stretching his back to ease the kinks. "Your pardon, gentles, but it's been a long workday and I've bairns a' home I'd like to see afore they're off to class in the morning."

"It's not that late, Rico," protested Elora.

"Puttin' y'r garden abed on the morrow, are y', Rico?"

"Aye, that's my thought, Tam. Might leave some veg till the first hard frost but better this year to be safe than sorry. Will we see you then?"

"Said I'd help. But prob'ly not till after midday."

"Not a problem."

"No obligations?" Elora asked Tam, after the taller man had departed.

"Single man, single life."

He smiled. She smiled back. They both turned their eyes on Renny, who was tactful enough not to mention the hint as he smilingly took his own leave.

There was no sign of Duguay at closing, not downstairs nor up in the rooms they shared when Elora changed from costume to what had become her favorite everyday leathers. An inquiry to Susan revealed that he'd gone his own way soon after their performance was done, to find a companion for the evening who wasn't quite so judgmental. That proved the final seal on Elora's decision to walk with Tam partway home—if he was interested, which he was.

As they passed the Citadel there were still lights to be seen at various windows across the otherwise dark and featureless expanse of stone, testifying to those still at work on state business despite the midnight hour. To Tam, what was the value of work that took you forever away from home and family, and what then the point of having either if you allowed your work to so dominate your life, and finally, what kind of person allows himself to be caught in such a tangle? Is that someone they really want deciding the fate of the nation?

"What do you say then," she demanded, with a fair portion of the passion she'd put into her song, because she was thinking of those she knew and loved, no less than herself, "of those who've *lost* home and family but struggle on regardless?"

"Would those things ha' been lost, my girl, had they paid proper mind?"

"The world isn't always so easily ordered, Tam. And I'm not *your* anything." She said it deadpan, but the twinkle in her eyes gave the game away.

"So," Tam began, hesitated, almost began again, hesitated again, in the manner of a deliberate man working himself up to something spontaneous. *Very much a Nelwyn trait,* Elora thought, reacting to him with a mixture of exasperation and amusement. "You an' the bard." Another pause, before he backed away from the question he wanted to ask. "Y' sing well t'gether."

"We have our moments," she conceded, "good and bad."

"Y' like him."

"There's a lot to like."

"An' a lot, I'll wager, makes y' want to slap him upside his noggin with the flat of a cast-iron pan."

She chuckled, then said, in answer to the question he hadn't asked: "He's my teacher. We travel together."

"Companions, then."

"Not the way some mean that word, no," she said hurriedly, for she knew in many contexts it described a relationship one small step shy of marriage. "Why do you ask?"

"Man likes to know where he stands in the scheme of things."

"I never realized the scheme of things could get so complicated."

"Couldn't tell that from the way you sing."

"Duguay's the master in that regard, Tam."

"You should give y'rself more credit, 'lora. He's got the voice, tha's certes, can't remember myself hearin' one better. But there's no heart. No truth. I don't *listen* to him. Wi' you, it's near impossible *not* to.

"Hightown's not so bad for a visit," he then said, responding to her comment about the city. "Got the view for certain, and some sights to match. It is quite the proper venue"—without missing a beat, Tam presented an acid, dead-on mockery of the accents practiced by many of the university students, with lots of smoothly rounded vowels—"for proper people." Just as smoothly, he reverted to his normal way of speaking. "But the prairie's the place t' live."

"I thought they called it Lowtown."

"They would."

At the terminus of each cable-car line, a broad set of stairs descended to a level beneath the plaza, where Elora found a huge arcade connecting them all together. There were stalls aplenty, all shuttered and locked, offering goods and services of every conceivable description.

Their footsteps set up cascading echoes in the silence, adding to the quietly sinister mood cast by the lanterns. Staccato spots of sound that complemented these spots of light amidst the otherwise all-encompassing shadow. It was a lonely place, the kind where it seemed natural to expect ghoulies or some other, worse monsters to leap from the darkness to wreak unholy mayhem on all in their path, and more than the evening chill made Elora shiver.

Would Tam think the less of me, she wondered to herself, *if I unlimbered my cloak from where I tossed it over my shoulder and wrapped myself up snug inside?* And then, a counterpoint question: *Would that make the slightest difference? Is it this gallery that makes me cold, or my own imagination?*

The unnerving quiet wasn't as absolute as first she'd thought, either. There was a faint vibration, set up through the soles of her boots, of a piece with a roar so muted and distant that it was likewise felt more than actually heard.

"Is that sound," she asked, "the falls?"

"Tha' 'tis," replied Tam. "Can't get away from it in any part o' Sandeni, plateau *or* prairie. Shouldna' sound so ungrateful, tho', since it's wha' helped make us what we are."

"They sound so far away. But they aren't really?"

"Had to do somethin' t' mute their thunder, else the din would make this depot unusable. Tha's why there's a quarry's worth o' stone 'tween us an' free water."

"I keep forgetting the city here's mainly built on platforms."

"Y're na' alone in tha' regard, 'lora lass," Tam told her, "an' we live here. Least you have the excuse of ignorance."

"Thank you. I think."

"Meant no slight, take no offense. The ignorance of an outlander, is what I'm sayin'. There's a whole rat's-nest maze o' tunnels down here, natural an' man-built, some the province o' them what was here b'fore us Daikini, so many I don't think they ever been properly charted in the altogether."

"Wow," was what Elora said.

And then "Wow" again, when they came upon the funicular.

As with the trolley cars, there were six lines, only

these were set right beside one another and dropped almost straight down through the floor of the platform. There were three stages—or levels—to the cars, allowing them to carry a total of better than a hundred passengers each per trip. The same principle operated them as the trolleys: a series of cables, running vertically along perpetual loops about huge wheels that were partially visible overhead where they extended from their housings in the roof. In this instance, each vehicle rode a double cable. Tightening the clamp on one line initiated a controlled descent to the plains below, while the other brought the car back up again.

The journey was in a tunnel all the way. Tam explained that there was an external funicular consisting of two sets of cables and much smaller cars but that was mainly for tourists and sightseers. These were to move people, and freight, between plateau and prairie with all the speed and ingenuity Daikini wits could muster.

At bottom was another tunnel, another network of cable cars to take riders from the cliff to the first cataract. There'd been plans for years to use the same technology to establish funiculars and trolleys the whole of the distance to the sixth cataract, but the farther out from the cliffs the city expanded, the more opposition its planners and engineers had encountered from the Veil Folk.

He was close behind her, on an observation platform cut through the face of the cliff that offered the most spectacular view of the prairie beyond. In the background the clank of gears announced the departure of the next descending funicular. They'd held hands on and off along their stroll, initiated by one or the other, briefly maintaining contact until some impulse pulled them apart, and had gradually learned that each was more shy than the other had expected. Tam had set himself on a step that allowed him the slightest height advantage, which was a bad thing for Elora to think about because the fact that she was taller, if only by a bit, almost made her giggle. Then he placed his hands on her sides, where she curved out from her waist and over her hips.

"Could they be afraid of what they don't understand?" Elora asked.

"Fates forfend!" Tam sounded legitimately shocked. "Why, would'na' tha' make them," he paused for effect, "just like us?"

"Troll-boy," said a voice from out of eyeshot to raise the hackles instantly on Elora's neck, "you are *nothing* like us."

Tam spun about like he'd just been stroked by a bull-whip and his face was ugly with rage as he reflexively shoved Elora behind him.

"Who?" she stammered as a handful of shapes moved in the gloom between them and the funicular. There was less light than before, a number of wall sconces had been extinguished, but she'd been so wrapped up in the moment, in her enjoyment of it, that she hadn't noticed.

"Tha' lot from y'r place, looks like t' me," Tam said. Then, louder: "We want no trouble here. This is a public place!"

"All the more reason to enforce a modicum of civilized behavior, don't you agree? If you and your slut desire to do the nasty, Tammy Troll-boy, find one of your burrows or whatever."

"You take tha' back!" Tam took a step forward. Elora locked both her hands on one arm but he broke her grip as though her fingers were made of straw.

"Which part, pray?"

"All of it, damn your eyes!" She grabbed for him again, he broke her grip again.

"Tam, don't do this! You're giving them what they want!"

"More's the pity for them!"

As he lunged forward Elora felt a wild twist in her own perceptions. In that moment, but fortunately only *for* that moment, her awareness was yanked wholly from her body, as InSight splintered into a half-dozen component elements to merge her perceptions with those of her attackers.

In a flash, spirit and flesh restored, she dropped to a

crouch on one bended knee, bracing most of her weight on her hands as she used them as she used arms and foot together for a pivot point and swung her remaining leg around like a scythe, catching Tam right behind the knee and dumping him to his back a heartbeat before a pair of crossbow bolts whizzed past.

After that, a whole host of events seemed to happen all at once, even though memory after the fact strung them all together in a linear sequence. Tam, delightfully quick on the uptake, rolled one way, and Elora the other. No time to grab for a weapon from her traveling pouch, she had to make do with whatever came to hand. She heard a scream from along the vaulting passageway, that redoubled with every echo until she had to hold her ears against its fury. Then there was a gust of wind as a golden eagle—not Bastian, Elora recognized, but his mate, Anele—swept through the opening in the cliff to strike at one of the bowmen with beak and wings and, most especially, her murderously deadly claws. The would-be assassin worked his mouth like a puppet, ruined eyes above, gaping throat below, flailing with both arms in a futile attempt to protect himself before collapsing to his seat, dead before he'd realized the eagle had stripped him of sight, of voice, of life itself.

Another bowman—Elora tagged three so equipped, from a total of eight—yelped and leaped like someone who'd just had his socks turned all to brambles. He slapped at his cheeks, at his breast, at his butt, making noises like a dog in agony until Elora put her shoulder into his belly so hard he folded right over with all his breath slammed right out of him. There was a sliver of thorn on his face, proof positive that these attackers weren't the only ones armed with bows. Brownie arrows may be small as splinters, but the poisons they were coated with made hornet and wasp stings seem mild. Worse, both Franjean and Rool were such formidable archers that neither clothes nor mail, nor on occasion even steel-plate armor, was any protection against them.

Elora swung back to the main body of the fight, having yanked the fallen man's dagger from his belt, in time to see Tam take down three at once, two with his hands and a head butt for the last. Bastian had harried another into headlong flight. She did an instant head count, came up four short.

That was the cue for disaster. A bolt caught Tam in the back of the thigh and he toppled to the polished floor. At the same time Elora was tackled herself. She grappled with her attacker like a leech as they tumbled, landing with her on the bottom. The impact put stars in her vision but she ignored them, using the fact that she was angled downward on an incline to give her leverage enough to pitch the man off. He didn't go far, she didn't want him to, as she kicked herself up and over and delivered a knee as hard as she could to the junction of his legs.

A fist connected right beneath her breastbone, did her assailant more harm than her as the force of the blow, and maybe some knuckles on the bargain, were broken on the sandwich armor of her tunic. Unfortunately, the advantage was as minimal as it proved short-lived as the man unloaded a tremendous backhand to the side of her head that immediately connected all the stars she'd been seeing with bolts of lightning.

He pitched her on her face and straddled her, putting his greater bulk right across the base of her spine and using his good hand to haul her head up and back from beneath the jaw. If dancing hadn't made her limber, the move would have snapped her spine. As it was, the sudden shock of being bent backward like a bow, and torqued a little sideways in the process, made her grunt in pain. He knew his business, he had her too well pinned. Try as she might, even with two arms free and one of his out of commission, Elora couldn't get a grip on him to free herself.

There was no sign or sense of Bastian or the brownies. Wouldn't be, in a mess like this. It would take no effort at all to snap her neck. Even the deadliest brownie poisons wouldn't act fast enough to stop him.

On the other hand, the instant he relaxed his hold, or his vigilance, even the slightest . . .

That moment wasn't in the cards. A shape approached, loomed, his voice marking him as the student who'd challenged Tam.

"Bitch!" he raged at her, and raised his hand to strike.

"Do that," growled the man holding Elora, "we're dead."

The bravo didn't understand. He blinked and raised his hand higher.

"You hit her, I lose my hold, we're dead," the man repeated. "Look about, an' you doubt my word. She had an eagle come when she's needful, an' other friends besides. We breathe 'cause we hold somethin' they value. She's our talisman, the only hope we have to walk away clean."

From the bottom of Elora's belly came a cry of rage and defiance, and she flashed fangs of her own as she made a final, ultimate effort to dislodge her captor. The student sneered, his teeth startlingly bright amidst a countenance of shadows.

That sneer was his last expression as his head suddenly, startlingly, departed from his neck.

Elora and her captor cried out at once, and then she felt a spray of hot liquid across the back of her head, followed by a cessation of the pressure on her head and spine. The weight fell one way, she pushed herself the other, and never once looked back. She knew what had just happened, but her eyes were only for Tam.

He lay sprawled facedown where he fell, the crossbow bolt sticking upright from the meat at the top of his thigh. The whole lower part of Tam's leg was sodden as she rolled him over, but loss of blood wasn't the real threat. Elora sensed it from the blue-black tinge to his lips, the rictus of pain that drew them away from his teeth. Placing hands gently on his leg, bracketing the wound, confirmed those fears. The bolt had been poisoned. Whatever their intentions, these attackers had intended to leave no witnesses.

She bent forward for a sniff, wrinkled her nose, and made a face at the strong odor of corruption, as though Tam had been struck by an instant case of gangrene.

"Franjean!" she called, "Rool! I need an antidote here!"

"There is none," was Rool's reply. The brownie stood across Tam's body from her, splashed head to toe with blotches she suspected were blood. Franjean had been equally in the thick of the battle, yet had emerged wholly unscathed, without even a torn thread. Beyond them, Khory Bannefin emerged into view, sword in hand. To her left strode Renny Garedo.

"I don't want to hear that, Tam's dying!"

"His killers have paid the price," the constable said. "Our friend will not leave this world unavenged."

"He won't leave at all, not yet he won't, if I've any say in the matter."

"Even a healer can't stop poison this deep in him."

There was no time to explain, here was an instance where seconds were crucial. She laid her hands around the wound, enclosing it in a rude circle formed by the crook between thumb and forefinger. She began to croon a song of Making, casting her InSight down through the layers of reality, first separating his clothes into their component threads to allow her passage, then beyond to the outer layers of his skin. It seemed so solid from one level of perception, yet another placed her beside pores that seemed as large as Lake Morar, where the hairs stood higher than the sentry spires of rock that heralded the presence of the Wall itself.

Smaller still, she slipped her awareness through these flakes of flesh into a veritable soup of interwoven tissues that was the body beneath. There wasn't even a pretense of health here. Blood moved sluggishly, if at all, and she sensed a chalky quality to the cells that made her think Tam was being transformed to dust from within. There was worse than an air of death about his body, there was despair, as though even the tiniest components of his being had given up the fight, believing there was no hope.

No problem, Tam, she thought with wild defiance, *I'll hope for us both till you can manage once more on your own.*

There were five edges to the crossbow bolt, all nicked

and scored in such a way as to do far more damage going out than on the way in. The arrowhead was forged steel, capable of punching through plate armor, too dense and formidable a material for her to manipulate in the time allowed. She turned instead to Tam's flesh, teasing apart the bonds that anchored cell to cell and gave him cohesive form, to the point where what was solid became a kind of viscous fluid most akin to soft putty. At the same time she reached up a physical hand to grasp the bolt's shaft. She didn't realize she was sweating, she didn't realize she was glowing, as the fire she sent surging through her own blood cast its glow outward through her argent skin.

This was a tricky procedure. She had to draw the head free and reverse the effects of her own chant in virtually the same movement, or she'd end up doing the arrow's work for it.

She let out her breath in a long, slow slide and in the moment where body and spirit grew absolutely still, as smoothly as drawing sword from scabbard, she pulled the arrow free.

Someone plucked the deadly shaft from her fingers. She didn't look to see who, didn't really care. This had been the easy part. Now there was the poison to deal with.

Once more, she used InSight to cast herself altogether from her own bodily casement into Tam's. No fun right from the start, like immersing herself in a lake of noisome sludge, waste pond for the filth of a world, but she pressed on regardless. When "riding" the eagles, she was essentially a passenger and therefore ever-mindful of her responsibilities as a good and hopefully welcome guest. Yet InSight was more than a passive tool of observation, because through access came the opportunity for control. If her will was stronger, she could take control of the host's physical being. The drawback was that this linkage represented a two-way street. As she could apply human direction to the actions of a lesser being, so, too, could that creature's more elemental and passionate nature have an equally powerful effect on her. Duguay had a song about such an experience, of a sorcerer who'd merged his soul with a kindred beast and found the experience so much to his liking that he never went "home" again. The sorcerer gained a lasting and ultimate contentment, but at the cost of everything that made him human. By the same token, there were tales of those who'd attempted such possessions, only to become possessed in turn. Supposedly, that was how the race of Shapeshifters came to be.

Elora had little fear of either happening to her in this instance. Tam had so little life in him to begin with, the remaining force of his own will was sadly negligible. She didn't expect to find any resistance to her assumption of primacy. The danger was his dying. By so merging with him, binding themselves tighter than identical twins, almost to the point where they became a single entity, Elora made herself vulnerable to whatever ailed him. She'd already tasted the poison, she had no doubts about her ability to counter its deadly effects. But if the damage done to Tam was too great, if he was already too far gone, she might well find herself unable to pull free when he died.

She knew enough to be afraid. She refused to let it deter her as she pulled a rill of fire from the torrent coursing through her own arteries and veins and set it loose in his, to consume the poison that was killing him.

She started from the wound, because that was the source of the infection, and let the natural current of his body sweep her from the lesser tributaries into the femoral vein and from there to the great central vessel that led up the trunk of the torso straight to the heart.

She'd seen her share of bodies, and helped Thorn with wounded over the years. She knew what the heart looked like, inside and out.

So it came as no little surprise when she burst from the darkness of the inferior vena cava onto the starlit expanse of the fairies' tor.

Shock froze her where she stood. She refused to believe her eyes and feared in those initial moments that she had gone mad, or simply died herself. This had never happened to her, she'd never imagined it was even possible, to be seized in the middle of a trance and transported somewhere else.

"No," she said to herself in reflexive denial, repeating it over and over again as though the words alone would craft the spell that would return her to where she rightly belonged, "no no no no no no no!"

It didn't work.

All was as it had been before, with one exception. The last time she'd come to the tor as a dragon; now she stood amidst the stones in human form, with a dragon waiting for her, perched delicately atop the principal stones of the Third Circle. Elora herself was across the altar from him, flanked by the equivalent stones of the Circles of the World and the Flesh.

The dragon was the personification of every noble word she knew. He was power and grace and a beauty that made her eyes burn and teeth ache, because he represented an order of being so far removed from her humanity that not even imagination could bridge that gulf.

She had seen him killed.

As though that thought was a cue, Kieron Dineer's great, wedge-shaped head snapped forward, baring teeth that were longer than Elora stood tall. They came together with the crash of the greatest steel trap ever conceived, but they closed on empty air.

She rolled to the base of one of the primary stones, not even considering a break from the circle she'd found herself in. Size, in this instance, was Kieron's liability and her only advantage. The stones were on a scale to match him and set too close together for him to fit his body between them. The only way he could reach her here was by stretching his neck or a hand to full extension.

Like the man who held me during the attack, she thought wildly, ducking a wayward grab of the dragon's forehand with a crab scuttle that skibbled her sideways past the altar to the stone directly beneath him. Kieron looked almost comical as his head curved upside down to follow, but to reach her properly he had to take flight and try to catch her from the air. As he moved, so did she, denying every possibility to catch her. *He couldn't let me go for fear of what the brownies or the eagles would do. I can't leave these stones for the same reason. But I don't even know what I'm doing here, I'm trying to save Tam's life!*

She told Kieron so, he wasn't interested. She was the prey and he the predator. His only goal was winning.

Unless she killed him first.

"I saw you slain once, dragon," she cried aloud, denying the thought that followed, *even though it wasn't my fault,* because she still believed she should have found a way to defend him and all the others against the Deceiver's power. *"Never again!"*

"Consider the alternative," Kieron said for the first time, in a voice that was all the more heartbreakingly magnificent (as all dragons' voices are magnificent) for its youth, and a promise unseasonably cut short. It made Elora weep. "Consider the consequences."

"Why are you doing this? Do you want to die again?" She screamed the last, leaping from her latest hidey-hole to the altar, to take her stand full in the dragon's face.

"Is that what you *want?*"

He looked pleased.

But the voice that answered was Duguay Faralorn's. "No!"

With the utterance of that single word, Kieron's mouth opened like the maw of a blast furnace that enclosed the heart of the world, and Elora's defiance turned to terror and pain for the flashfire instant left her before oblivion as she found herself engulfed in raw flame.

There was a roof gleaming overhead when she found courage enough to open her eyes. Next came an absurd tidal wash of relief that her experience on the tor—whether dream or something else—had had no lasting physical effect, and with that, her body was shaken by a series of profound sobs that racked her as hard as any beating.

Somehow, during the healing trance she and Tam had turned themselves around. The last she recalled was crouching over his thigh while he lay mostly on his belly. Now he was on his back, with his head cradled in her lap. There was color to his features and he breathed with the ease of sleep. The touch of fingertips to flesh told her that all taint of infection had been removed, the young man as well as he'd ever been.

More than could be said for her, she decided, conscious of a bitter chill that centered so deeply in her bones she had to fight to keep from shivering, though she found no way to check the trembling in her hands.

"It's cold," she announced, and was rewarded by her cloak being draped across her shoulders, gathered snug about her and Tam both.

"Brought some soup," Renny said, crouching before her with a steaming bowl. More like stew than soup from the smell and look of it, and utterly enticing. Too bad she didn't have strength enough to even lift her arms.

Apparently Renny recognized the lack and proceeded to feed her, not so easy a task considering that the moment she opened her mouth her teeth began to chatter.

The brownies were happily at work, stripping the slain of anything that might prove of value, while Khory remained close by Elora's side, unsheathed blade resting in the crook of an elbow, another couple laid out close at hand in case they were needed.

Spices in the stew made Elora's eyes tear, and a great sniffle made her realize her nose was badly running. So with what she labeled a "supreme" effort, Elora drew a handkerchief from her pocket and indulged in a spectacular sneeze.

"Bless you," said the constable.

"How long?" she asked.

"An hour," Khory replied, "if that."

"Since I started working on Tam?"

"Since the attack."

"Well," said Rool, "you were the one who wanted to see the world."

"Still do."

"Milk teeth won't save you, Elora." The brownie's

tone was light, his meaning deadly serious. "And we may not always be at hand."

"I'll manage, Rool."

She touched Tam's cheek in a gesture as affectionate as it was tender. "Ah, Tam, you sure know how to show a girl a good old time."

"You're lucky you can laugh."

"Hardly luck, Constable, considering the army I had at my back." Elora fixed a gimlet eye on Khory, who didn't seem to mind in the least. "How did you know?"

"You've me to thank for that," said a voice she knew better than her own. "I like to think there's little that occurs in Sandeni I don't know about. That holds even more so for the catacombs beneath my tower." He looked about the carnage and sighed. "This should not have happened.

"It's not the way I wanted to welcome you, Elora Danan," Thorn Drumheller told her as he opened his arms and gathered her into a hug so strong she was sure she heard her bones creak. There were tears on his cheeks, too long held back, but she didn't mind, since they were a match for her own. "But I'm glad you're here."

"No less than I, old duffer."

Chapter
12

SHE'D GROWN SINCE LAST THEY MET, THAT WAS IN-
stantly obvious to her, standing more than five
feet tall to his barely four. Like many of his kind
Thorn's limbs were proportioned to a different
aesthetic than Daikini, long arms and stunted
legs on a barrel torso. Hard for getting around
yet powerful nonetheless, and his long fingers
were capable of far more delicate work than
many twice his size. His was a good face,
though stricken with more lines than Elora recalled, and what shone most clearly still from
his features was his innate generosity of spirit.
He loved to laugh, so infectiously that for all
the grumbling and grousing forced on him by
circumstance, those around him couldn't help
but take on a portion of that good cheer as well.
There was intelligence in his wide-set hazel

eyes, but more, there was empathy. He was a wonder at seeing the essential passion of things, which in large measure formed the core of his ability to work magic.

Clean-shaven as he was, he looked surprisingly young. Elora knew better. In years and experience there were few among the Daikini who could match him. If he lived a normal Nelwyn span, none of his companions save perhaps the brownies would see him die. His hair was neatly combed, the color of pale oak, swept straight back from his brow and held at the nape of the neck by a silver clasp. As for the rest, Elora was suitably impressed.

She was used to him in homespun, wools and cotton and shearling, depending on season and terrain. This incarnation of Thorn Drumheller wore a velvet robe that probably weighed a goodly portion of what he did. It buttoned up the front to a high collar, fitting snug at the torso, flaring below the waist into a wider skirt to allow for a long and easy stride. Over that went a brocade surcoat, sleeveless and floor-length. This hung open, as did the overcloak that covered it. She suspected trousers rather than tights because Thorn preferred them, and she knew he would only yield so far to the dictates of fashion. His own shoes as well, because Nelwyn feet weren't constructed for anything approaching Daikini footwear, even at their most practical. Around his neck and hanging off his shoulders was a chain of office, its links composed of representations of the crossed spears and bound sheaves of wheat which symbolized the Sandeni Republic.

Renny took charge of the scene, seeing to the disposition of the bodies. The fight had been brief, but also brutal. The only two survivors had fled without raising a weapon to anyone and they were quickly taken into custody. Elora's presence was duly noted in the crime report, but only as a potential victim who'd actively defended herself against this heinous and unforgivable attack. Renny's friendship with Tam and the fact that they'd all been seen together earlier explained his appearance. As for Khory, although the funicular station was a public thoroughfare, it was located beneath the Citadel. She was in Thorn Drumheller's service and known to be a warrior of some considerable renown, who was said to have an "instinct" for such things. No one reading the report would think twice about her intervention. The brownies simply were not present, nor were the eagles.

Tam's survival, concluded the report, was Thorn's doing.

"You want to see how the world works, Princess," Franjean noted from where he lay sprawled on his belly across her right shoulder, watching what transpired with his chin resting on crossed arms. She had never seen bureaucracy in action before, though she'd been enmeshed in one all her childhood.

"It all makes such sense." She marveled. "The elements are mostly true. They're *all* plausible. Yet the end result is a total fabrication."

"You'd prefer to reveal the truth?" Rool asked her.

"That'll be the day, her and Drumheller both." Franjean cackled.

"You two are in rare form," she said.

"It's been a rare night," Rool commented.

"A rare day preceding it," agreed Franjean.

"As I recall, Rool," Elora told them, slipping the smallest width of steel into her voice, "I gave you a task not so long ago. I've heard nothing since."

"There is a domain among the lords of Greater Faery called the Tadjeek." The savage twist of emphasis he gave the name of that Realm wasn't very nice, and Rool spat the words like darts. "Alone among the Veil Folk, they hold to life as a flat state of being, with but two aspects: you are, you are not. To them, life is nothing but a test, each of its moments presenting a choice of how you interact with the world and with others. There is no going back, there are no second chances, what's done cannot be undone save perhaps by some action yet to be. The only forgiveness, the only atonement, is what we find or make for ourselves while we yet live. Once dead, while the book may continue, our chapter is closed."

"Being of the Veil, aren't they immortal?"

"That's a cheap word, Highness."

"Immortal?"

"Compare a mayfly to a Daikini, does the one consider the other immortal because his life spans numberless generations? To some among the Veil Folk, Daikini are mayflies. To others, so are those Veil Folk. Legend says only the Malevoiy can speak firsthand of the dawning of the world, but no one's knocked on their door to ask in living memory. By the same token, the same is said about dragons at the dawning of Creation."

"Has anyone asked them?"

"And gone mad trying to decipher the reply."

"What do you believe, Franjean?"

She felt the ghosting echo of his grin. "If I can move it, I can steal it."

She felt Thorn's spirit brush past hers as he made his physical way to her.

"I think they've been testing me," she said, in what was meant to be a joke but came out as something harsher.

"They test everyone," he replied lightly.

"In my case, though, are they passing judgment?"

"To what end, Elora?"

"I was hoping you could tell me."

"Walk with me a ways, would you? I think we're secure enough here from prying eyes. Or spells," Thorn added with a crinkle of old mischief around the eyes.

"I thought magic didn't work in Sandeni."

"That depends on how you define the term. What you did was magic of a sort."

"*I* did nothing, Thorn, except perhaps persuade Tam's body to work a little harder and faster."

"And who sustained that body through all those trials and tribulations? The fire in you, Elora"—and he tapped a knuckle lightly on her breastbone—"comes from . . ." He was about to kneel down and tap the floor beneath them, as surrogate for the molten core of the earth itself, but then thought better of it. He wore an odd

378

expression as he looked to the floor, to Elora, to the sky, then finally back to Elora. "I was going to say the earth," he confessed, "but now I'm no longer so sure."

"That isn't comforting, Thorn."

"I'm trying my best."

"So am I!"

She was silent for a time.

"Something happened to me," she said, "in my healing trance."

"I feared as much. That's what brought me down to you. I had to be on hand to help."

She took his hand in both of hers and held him blindly, as a child might, while she told him of her two encounters with Kieron Dineer. At her story's end, she looked to him for answers, only to see him shake his head.

"I don't know."

"Dream then, maybe? Nothing to worry about, I hope?" The intentional lightness of her tone belied the anxiety that twisted her insides.

He pulled her closer to him on the bench where they sat side by side, and thought of how he used to be able to lay his arm comfortingly across her shoulders; now the best he could manage was to catch her 'round the waist.

"After all these years with those two scoundrels," he said in the same easy manner, meaning the brownies, "you'd think I'd have better learned the art and craft of dissembling."

"That serious, huh?"

"I wish I could tell you different, Elora. The linkage between spirit and body is stronger in you than in any I've ever known, myself included."

"Yet the Deceiver has his hooks deep in me, and now apparently so does Kieron Dineer. How can that be, Thorn?"

"Blood is the traditional binding element for such things."

She snorted disparagingly, "Oh, wonderful, you mean we're all related?"

"Anything I say here, child, I speak from ignorance. But the kinds of magicks the Deceiver has demonstrated, the way he acts upon the waking world—especially his need for a living, tangible host—leads me to suspect his origins are of the Circle of the Spirit. Kieron is dead, we both saw him die, but Kieron is also a dragon, and who knows what rules apply to them, if any rules at all! In both the instances you speak of, your spirit left your body. I can only assume that in some way that act left you vulnerable to Kieron's power."

"How can he have power if he's dead?" she demanded in exasperation. "And don't tell me it's because he's a damn dragon."

"That might well be the case. You know," he noted thoughtfully, "the dragon that brought me to Tir Asleen the night before the Cataclysm was named *Calan* Dineer. And his behavior was just as high-handed."

"If he knew what was coming, why didn't he warn everyone?" Her voice grew rough, thickened by grief and rage. "Why did they just let things *happen*?"

"Do you think I haven't asked? There were nights, while Rool and Franjean and the eagles and I were wandering, that I would stand beneath the endless stars and scream his name until my voice was a ghost. I would light a magical beacon brighter than any noonday sun. I tried to command his presence, I begged for the mercy of a single visitation. And came to realize that dragons come to us in their own manner, and at their own pleasure. If we would go to them, we must first find the way."

"Rool spoke of those who tried going mad."

"To wield power on that level, to have safe congress with the likes of firedrakes and demons, madness is almost a prerequisite."

"Kieron's already been killed once, Thorn. Why does he want me to do it to him again?"

"Better yet, Elora, why does your troubadour seem able to prevent it?"

"I should have listened to Khory and joined you in your citadel."

"No," Thorn told her with some emphasis. "You made the right decision. The trouble with most Kings is that they too often have no contact with the people they rule. They suffer few of the consequences of their decisions. Your task is different—to weave the strands of these separate, antagonistic Realms into a single, common thread. You can't do that without knowing them. And that's the kind of knowledge you must discover for yourself."

"Whether I like what I learn or not?"

"What do you mean?"

"I was window dressing tonight," she said, indicating the scene before them. "It was Tam those bullies were after. They hated him, Thorn."

"I can imagine."

" 'Troll-boy' was what they called him."

"I've heard the term." He didn't like it.

"And I've been inside his heart. I *know* him, Thorn, as well as I believe I know the constable over there."

"In what way?"

"Tam is Nelwyn," she said, and when Thorn turned his face to her, "as much as Renny is of the High Elves."

He had the good grace not to deny it.

"A world without the Veil Folk is a shadow of itself," the constable told her, after Thorn called him over. "Yet by the same token, the prejudice of the Veil Folk cannot keep one Realm, one race alone, from claiming its rightful place. Achieving its destiny. Any more than they can people."

As she watched his fellow constables go about their tasks, and a team of ambulance surgeons supervise Tam's evacuation on a stretcher, Elora found herself examining every face with a fierce, questing intensity for the telltale signs of difference she now knew to be there. In the main, she was disappointed. Most of the forms and faces were Daikini through and through, but every now and then, in the structure of the body, in the subtle shadings of the face, she found clear evidence of mixed blood.

"I didn't think it was possible," she said to him, "for the races to interbreed."

"And why is that?" Renny inquired in all innocence.

"Well, I just . . . I mean . . . I . . ." Flustered beyond words in the face of the constable's infuriating equanimity, Elora could only shrug her shoulders and give up.

"There's an old saying, Elora," he told her, "to the effect of, whatever the obstacles, love will find a way. You sang a rather emphatic song about it earlier this evening, don't you recall?"

"If I'd been a little more reasonable, Constable, a little less passionate—!"

"You blame yourself for this?"

"It isn't what I intended."

"You stir up folks, they don't always go the way you intend. No matter how true the message, child, not everyone will believe."

"I might love my horse," Franjean groused from his perch on Elora's shoulder, "that doesn't mean I'll wed the creature."

"Tell that to the Centaurs."

"They're Shapers, a bastard breed."

"Be careful, little master thief. In this city you smile when you say that." Renny was smiling as he spoke, but there was danger behind his eyes. In appearance and manner, he presented himself as the gentlest and most easygoing of souls, but that was only a single aspect of his nature, the public face that was of the most use in his work. There was another part of him nowhere near so pleasant and it had just drawn a line that the brownie was not to cross.

"I'm sorry you had to kill that boy, Constable." For while Khory had slain the student facing Elora, Renny had dealt with the one who held her.

"He was a man, in terms of age if not honor. Your decency does you credit, Elora, but save both tears and sympathy. He would have spared neither for you."

Another constable arrived with mugs of chocolate, and Elora noticed that before Renny handed them out, both he and Khory made a series of small passes over the tray, each checking in their own way to ensure the beverages were safe.

"Taking no chances?"

They both looked at her, with an unblinking direct-
ness she found eerily reminiscent of hunting cats.

Too damn much in common, she decided of them, then
and there, *all of it deadly.*

They made no reply. Why belabor the obvious?

"Thorn, did Khory tell you . . ." Elora began, and then
fell silent, dismayed to find that her hands were trembling. She laced her fingers together, gripping the mug so
tightly her fingers turned as pale as the sturdy china, so
determined to overcome this sudden bout of weakness
that she couldn't lift the drink to her mouth. "What I discovered along the frontier?" she continued, staring into
the dark pool of chocolate as if it was a scrying pond
where she might divine some aspect of the future. "I don't
believe the Deceiver is our only foe."

"Dear child," Thorn said with a loving tenderness
that nearly broke her heart, she'd missed it so, "whatever
made you think he was?"

Then, and only then, did proper tears come as the
shock of the night's events at last hammered its way
through the bulwarks of her pretensions.

The mug fell from nerveless fingers as once more she
accepted the embrace of the grave little man who was the
centerpiece of her life.

"It's all right," he said over and over, holding her close
with the extraordinary strength of his kind, so seemingly
out of proportion to the construction of their bodies. At
the same time he stroked her hair, while she buried her
own face in the junction of his neck and shoulder and
held on to him for dear life.

She snuffled loudly, to signal she was done, and he
provided a handkerchief. She didn't leave her knees, but
stayed with back bowed, head bent, unwilling to face her
other companions after such a display. Until a fresh mug
of steaming chocolate entered her field of vision, and she
tilted her eyes enough to see that Khory was holding it.

"What a baby," Elora muttered, disgusted with herself.

"For being human?"

"You don't cry!"

"I'm not human. I'm a demon wearing human form."

"Wouldn't make that common knowledge," Renny cautioned.

"Are people afraid of *everything?*" Leftover distress from her bout of grief gave the question a snappish quality Elora didn't intend.

"What they don't understand, of a certes," agreed the constable.

"However, like any sensible species," Thorn added, "they respect powers that have done them harm in the past. The reputations of demons is not wholly undeserved, in any of the Great Realms, on either side of the Veil."

"The fact you bonded with a demon, Drumheller," Franjean accused, "to bring *that one*"—a gesture toward Khory—"into being, that's one of the main reasons barrows the world over are closed to us now."

"That isn't fair, Franjean," Elora protested. "Simply because demons are dangerous, does that make them inherently evil? Any more than a lion, or a shark, or an eagle?"

"Or a troll?" suggested Rool.

"Or a troll," she agreed. "Strange days," she told herself as much as the others, "where a troll can be found possessing more essential humanity than a Daikini."

"Strange days indeed," Thorn agreed. "And getting more wondrous all the while."

"I am right, though," Elora said to Renny as she pushed to her feet and took the stool catty-corner to him. "About you and Tam. And you're not the only ones." She turned back to the Nelwyn. "Thorn, did you know?"

"It's not something the clans speak of easily, Elora. The Nelwyn way is to keep to ourselves, in public and private."

"But love will ever find a way," Renny repeated.

"You sound like you're making fun now."

He smiled sadly at her. "Hardly. Nelwyn and Daikini,

elf and Nelwyn, Daikini and elf, the cards have been shuffled every which way over the ages. For the best of reasons and the worst, the Realms have a lot more in common than many will care to admit."

"I don't think I've ever seen people with that kind of mixed blood before."

"Having seen so *much* of the wide world, of course, eh?"

"Go sit on a tack, Franjean."

Sputter of indignation from one brownie, amusement from the other at his comeuppance.

"Well, I *have* seen the world," Thorn said, "a goodly portion anyroad, and in the main Elora's quite right. Such folk are very few and far between. Except in Sandeni."

"Possibly, Mage, because the city makes them welcome. Our citizens are free; we're judged one and all by our deeds, not the accident of parentage."

"So how's a body to know their proper place?" demanded Franjean.

"Make your own."

"Fine." Elora nodded. "Where does a 'Sacred Princess' fit into your scheme of things?"

"Not as a ruler, Elora. But perhaps a leader . . ."

"Therein lies a key difference between you and your adversary," Thorn said. "It's also why he's so blessed hard to resist. The Deceiver offers peace, a goal which none can really argue with. He offers equality, which strikes a major chord among the Daikini, who've long felt they were anything but. If you accept the supposition that *he* knows best, it's not so bad a world he holds forth."

"Why?"

"I've never been able to shake the feeling there's something familiar about the Deceiver. Implacable a foe as he is, and dedicated as we are to his destruction, I can't think of him as evil. Wrong, that's certain, in a fundamental and absolute sense. Cruel, ruthless, despotic, pick any pejorative you care to name. But not *evil*."

"Hardly a comfort, Drumheller," Khory spoke up, "if you're on the wrong end of his spear point."

"What would you do, Elora?" Thorn asked, to her surprise.

"I beg your pardon?"

"You no longer desire to be a bystander. How would you proceed from here?"

Her first instinct was to try something that had already worked, to attempt to contact the lords of Greater Faery and achieve a rapprochement with them as she had with their counterparts of Lesser Faery.

She shook her head, passing on Thorn's question for the moment, preferring to listen to what the others had to say.

"Would they consider an alliance?" Thorn asked Renny, and the exchange wasn't at all government minister to policeman but rather one equal to another.

"Who *are* you?" Elora wondered of Renny, searching his features for a clue. His mask was far more complete than hers and hid its secrets too well.

"Why should they?" the constable demanded. "What's in it for them? Or rather, what price are you willing to pay for this alliance?"

"Freedom," she snapped.

"They already have it."

"The Deceiver's closing the World Gates, he's stripping the world of its magic."

"And how much contact do they have with this side of the Veil anyway? They can find other venues for their amusement. It's the Daikini Realm he's hell-bent to conquer, nothing to do with them. And should they decide otherwise, should these raiders of yours out along the frontier prove to be the vanguard of something more formidable, their goal will be to eliminate the Daikini altogether."

"The Realms are all of a piece, interlinked one to the other," she cried, meeting the constable's imperturbable calm with a fury as elemental as a demon's nature. "That's why they're represented by overlapping circles; what touches one ultimately touches all!"

"Figure that out all by your lonesome, did you?"

"That's *right*!"

"Well, then"—Thorn smiled lazily and in his eyes was a level of respect she hadn't noticed before—"we might have ourselves a shot after all."

"You were baiting me!"

"And quite successfully. You've a temper, Elora. It's a fair chink in your armor. Learn to control it better."

She set down her cocoa, stepped clear of Thorn, and stood to face the constable.

"This war isn't only a conflict of force of arms," she said, putting words to the feelings that had been swirling through her throughout these past weeks, from the time she left Torquil's. "But of the force of ideas, as well. Losing to the Maizan guarantees the Deceiver's victory. Our triumph over them doesn't necessarily assure us of the reverse.

"You're quite right, Constable. I have nothing tangible to offer the Lords of Greater Faery. My army's pretty much standing around me. Every monarch who would have sworn me fealty is ensorcelled in Angwyn. I have no claim on their successors, and given all that's happened since, I'll tell you flat the smart play for them is neutrality. Or an outright alliance with the Deceiver. By any objective standard, our cause has been pretty much lost from the start." She stifled a smile. "But by any objective standard, it's unlikely that Daikini and High Elf would mate."

"If you sing half so well as you speak, Lady Elora, it's no wonder you're so popular."

Renny stood up, at last to his full height, and Elora marveled at how effective a stooped back and slumped shoulders could be. He was taller than Khory, possessed of a lean, whipcord power that she suspected overmatched that of most men two or three times his bulk. He held out his right hand, and she took it in hers.

"I'll do for you what I can," he said.

"That's a start."

Winter came early that year, far harder than anyone could remember. With it came the Maizan.

The first frost was hard on the heels of the harvest, and the first snow well before the equinox. The storms themselves weren't so bad: one blizzard, plus a brace of lesser tempests that added no more than a few additional inches to what had previously fallen. Roads remained passable, disruptions to civic life lasted no longer than a day or two after the storm.

It was the cold that killed. Regardless of how brightly the sun shone, or how clear was the sky, the temperature rarely rose above freezing. All it took was a little breeze to make traveling out of doors a bitter and daunting experience, and any sort of proper wind was deadly. For the most part, the air remained as dry as a high desert, so leached of moisture that the snow crunched underfoot, and therein lay a fatal deception. In summer, under high heat and no humidity, sweat evaporated off the skin almost immediately; if a person wasn't careful, they might become dangerously dehydrated in surprisingly short order. Much the same applied now. It was easy not to notice how brutal the cold was as it sucked the heat from a body until one was already struck with bursts of frostbite or actually began to freeze.

At such a time the value of Sandeni's transit system became clearly evident, especially on the prairie, where cable cars ran through tunnels. For the most part, it was able to handle the increased traffic. As the weeks passed and the weather stayed uncommonly harsh, with the greater part of winter yet to come, there were more and more expressions of concern. Not so much about the power source, though ice upstream had lowered the water levels of the rivers. The presumption of the engineers and hydrologists was that the force of the flow over the precipice was more than sufficient to prevent the falls themselves from ever freezing.

That confidence didn't hold for the infrastructure of the municipal railway itself. Cold affected the grease that lubricated the great driving wheels about which the cables turned. The fear was that one of them might jam. Depending on which wheel it was, and how quickly the maintenance engineers responded, the effect on the system might be an inconvenience, or a catastrophe. And hard as that cold was on the driving wheels, it took a far greater toll on the cables themselves. The weather made the cable stiff, which required more grease to ease it along its roundabout track. This in turn required the brakemen to clamp their shoes more tightly, to achieve a decent enough grip to engage the car. Which began leading to failures of the gears in the cars, as they broke under the strain, and even of the cables themselves.

The upkeep was constant, the crews more and more exhausted.

While none of the rivers was likely to freeze, the same could not be said for the city's canals. By equinox they were solid, and some enterprising entrepreneurs quickly established a growing fleet of horse-drawn sleighs to replace the normally ubiquitous water taxis. The city mobilized its youth, both middle school and college age, to shovel and sweep the streets clear of snow, while at the same time taking a precise inventory of its stocks of food and fuel as it became increasingly clear that a normal winter's supplies might not last to the solstice, much less the following spring.

Elora was of two minds about the season. On the one hand, she was heartsick over the misery it caused. On the other, she couldn't remember when she'd had such fun. This was only the second true winter she'd experienced in her cloistered life and she was determined to enjoy it to the fullest. By night she and Duguay continued to fill the tavern. By day she haunted the professor's library, searching the volumes for anything that would be of help. She learned quickly to live with disappointment.

She was welcomed into Tam's home, and that in turn gave her entry to Sandeni's mixed-blood community. In Tam's case, the crossover had occurred three generations back, beginning with a Daikini great-great-grandmother and a Nelwyn sire. The paradox was that due to the considerable difference in life spans, she was actually able to meet that ancient forebear. He was an ironmonger of formidable ability, from an offshoot minor house of the Rock Nelwyns, as knowledgeable in his way as Torquil but lacking that master artisan's subtlety of craft. The talent was unmistakable as was the quality of workmanship, but sadly there was no grace to what he made. By the same token, it was no small achievement to match his skill, no mean privilege to be invited to share his forge.

The house was an eclectic blend of Daikini and Nelwyn, treating each race's traditions with respect but very little reverence.

"Like wi' metal," Raasay (for that was Tam's great-great's name) said, though at the time he was molding glass in his furnace instead of steel, "there's a place an' purpose, an' a value, no denyin' that, f'r wha's pure." Listening to him took concentration and it was easy to see where Tam came by his own broad country accent. But the timbre of the words had a life and vitality that belied the man's age and made him a pleasure to hear.

"The same while, tha' purity puts a limit on what y' c'n do with it," he continued, thriving on his attentive audience as much as Elora did on hers. "Gold has beauty, but it's malleable. F'r a proper piece o' fine jewelry, it needs be an amalgam wi' summat a bit more base, t' give it strength. Same applies t' iron; good as it is alone, it's better forged as an alloy into steel. Same f'r blood, I be thinkin'. No more shame t' bein' a mix than t' bein' pure."

"I've heard Tam called a mongrel," she said, huffing beads of sweat out of her mouth as she pumped his bellows to keep the fire glowing white-hot.

"Not t' his face, I'll wager." The old Nelwyn spat a laugh at the thought, which Elora echoed. All the while he spun the blowpipe, gripping the metal as delicately with just the tips of his fingers as he might the finest piece of crystal, using his breath down the pipe to shape the molten glass bubble growing from the opposite end. At the same time Elora, arms bare, her undershirt molded to her powerful form by sweat, stoked the furnace with heaping shovelfuls of coal.

"Never to his face," she agreed with a roguish chuckle all her own.

"Never had dog nor cat in this house wasn't a mongrel. Street saves, the lot. Some had their faults, same as two-legged folk, but most was worth the trouble. Tough wee scrappers, too. Spit in the eye of any critter what tried t' cross 'em. Pride comes from what they've made of themselves, y'see, not what's got handed 'em. Me, I got no hands f'r this." Even as he spoke the vase took shape, flashing sparkling facets of color as the radiance of the hearth refracted through bends and twists in the flowing glass. "I do it f'r a distraction, f'r fun like when I'm tired o' hammering. Me da were no better, nor his. Craft like y' would na' believe, but nothin' more. But I got a great-grandlass, Tam's aunt, looks as Daikini as they come, an' she can make pure magic wi' this fire."

"I've seen her work." In some of the finest shops in Sandeni, at prices that made even Elora swallow. She recognized the signature design immediately, and burned with silent, secret shame at the realization that she'd been served with some of that very crystal in her tower in Angwyn. And most likely smashed it.

"Summat o' me, summat o' me dear wife, some spark from who knows where. But the result, lass, the result is a beauty I could never achieve on my lonesome. Nor from any Nelwyn mate, neither, meanin' no disrespect. Not sayin' this is f'r all. I'm sayin', f'r some, it's *right*."

After the blizzard, and before the legions of civic sweepers returned the streets to vehicular traffic, the city belonged totally to its children. Young in body, young at heart, everyone took a holiday, piling snow high into blockhouses and staging snowball fights from one corner to the next, populating the parks with a whole other community of snowfolk, using anything that would slide to cascade with shrieks of mingled terror and abandon down every available slope. Vendors of hot drinks and soups and stews did a record business that splendid day, joy so thick in the air it could almost be touched.

The next snowfall was more desultory, too dry and powdery to be of any real use, the day too cold, the wind too cutting, for more than a brief outing. That proved the template for the days to follow, as though the first storm had been no more than a tease, a haunting reminder of winters that were once and might have been, but would not be.

As the trolley made its way downtown toward the Citadel, Elora hunched in on herself upon the open bench and watched the people that they passed. They trudged with shoulders down, like cart horses hauling a monstrous heavy load, almost shapeless beneath massive layers of tunics and sweaters and cloaks, heads wrapped so completely with hats and scarves that only eyes could be seen and then only when you were face-to-face. They weren't people anymore, at least out of doors, they carried themselves as beasts of burden, as worn in spirit as in body.

Elora still favored the clothes she'd taken off the Maizan sorceress, in part because they made her feel sleek and dangerous but mainly, thanks to the brownies' efforts with needle and thread, because they fit. She'd gone shopping more than once since arriving in Sandeni, delighted for the opportunity to indulge herself in some conspicuous consumption, only to grow out of those purchases within the month. It was as if her body had deliberately held itself in check during her stay among the Rock Nelwyns and was now taking its revenge. Khory still had the edge on her in height, Elora suspected she always would, but the pair of them positively loomed over every other woman she'd ever met, and Renny had commented one evening that they were a close match for the High Elves. All this growth left Elora feeling gangly and ill at ease with her body, and she'd never felt that comfortable with herself to begin with. Spoiled rotten throughout her childhood, she'd hit adolescence as a plump, round face, round form, with her vocal cords the only part of her that got any regular exercise.

Today she was stronger than she'd ever been, probably than she'd ever dreamed, but none of the disparate elements even came close to fitting properly. She looked at herself and saw someone whose legs were too long, torso too powerful, shoulders too broad. Where others had soft curves, she was sleekly muscled, modestly endowed where fashion preferred voluptuousness. She looked like a wanderer, with a body good for striding off toward distant horizons, or riding horseback if a mount was available.

She didn't know it yet, but hers was the look of a natural leader. Eyes turned to her when she passed as automatically as to a standard. That was never more obvious than when she took the stage. Good as he was, and that was *very* good indeed, Duguay could not equal the passionate intensity of her performances. When Elora sang of love, couples found their hands lacing together, reminded of the best of what had brought them together. When of loss, there were tears aplenty. And when, as she always did, she sang of freedom, they *believed*.

Gradually she and Duguay simplified her makeup while at the same time crafting a no less striking public persona for her. She kept her hair short and spiky and blue black as printer's ink because she liked the contrast and it was a style no other woman would dare. The argent color of her skin they carefully faded, to create the impression that she was just naturally pale. Kohl was used to accent the shape and depth of her eyes, blush to further enhance the sharply defined bone structure of her cheeks, a shade of lipstick found to match the color of her leathers. The result, reproduced on handbills posted throughout the city, was a face totally defined by its hair, its eyes, its mouth, as unconventional as it was entrancing, with a level gaze that inspired trust and a faint quirk to the lips that hinted with her hair at a wild twist to her soul.

No one believed she was in her middle teens, and the stories she heard told about herself while roaming the city were so outrageously implausible she couldn't wait to tell her friends and share their laughter. The best, the most rudely ribald, she worked into her repertoire.

She even found a way to meet with Thorn, though

not often, and not on any regular schedule. Their meeting place was the professor's library, because the university was so huge, its facilities so comprehensively interlinked and generally so crowded that it was virtually impossible to follow someone within its walls.

"Is the weather the key?" she asked one glorious afternoon, her attention continually distracted from the piles of documents strewn across the professor's tables by the crisp and clear sunlight splashing gloriously through the top-floor windows. They were a mix of clear and stained glass, the one primarily to provide illumination, the other to create beautiful patterns of color. The layout of this level was an open plan, the only shelves those that lined the wall. The floor itself was bare, save for desks and chairs. The ceiling had been removed as well, allowing an unobstructed view past the massive bracing beams all the way to the steeply gabled roof.

"You tell me," the Nelwyn said.

She chewed on a bit of her lower lip, flash-tapping her fingers on the table in a drumroll. "I hate it when you answer a question with a question."

"That's because you're the one who has to provide the answers."

"Meaning you already know."

"Meaning *you're* the one who *needs* to know. Understanding the why of a solution—the process of deduction—is far more important than the solution itself."

"I can't get away with intuition?"

"*You* can, Elora. But how then do you explain it to others?" Thorn leaned forward, that simple act somehow commanding all her perceptions to focus on his face, so that only his eyes were clear before her. She had never seen him more intense, or more serious. "There will come a time when you go to those who believe in you and say, do such and such a thing for no other reason than that they *trust* you. But that trust must be earned. They must know your word is good, the instincts sound. And you have to know you're right.

"You must inspire men and women to love you, and

though I pray the moment never comes to pass, you must then be prepared for the day when you send them to their deaths. And watch, as they do so willingly."

She blinked rapidly, telling herself it was the sunlight making her eyes tear, but her voice was unusually husky as she spoke.

"Then you'd have done better with Anakerie in this role," she told him.

The moment she mentioned the Princess Royal of Angwyn, she regretted it.

After the Cataclysm, and due consultation with the monarchs of the other Great Realms, Anakerie's father established an order of servitors, called Vizards, to serve as bodyguards to the Sacred Princess. There would be twelve, one for each of the Realms, and they would go masked, for the honor would be in the deed itself, not for being known for it. They would serve for a calendar year. The first selected for that first cadre was his own daughter and heir. To the King's mind, he could have bestowed no greater honor.

Anakerie didn't see it that way. Barely a teenager, she was unable to reconcile Elora's manifestation with the death of her mother and the disappearance of her beloved twin brother, for all that had happened the terrible night of Elora's arrival. She was damned if she'd serve Elora in *any* capacity. She had her father's strength of will and his lack of tact, and the pair of them butted heads as suicidally as a matched set of mountain goats dueling on the lip of a precipice. He was sure she'd yield. It never occurred to him that she'd find another way. Anakerie, by contrast, once she saw the fight was hopeless, simply ceded him the field. They had their final argument and the next day she was gone.

Within a year Anakerie had found her way to the nomadic Maizan and won herself a place of honor among them. They weren't comfortable with strangers but they respected skill and talent above all else. For all her tender years she had both in abundance. She grew from girl to young woman among them and broke the heart of any man who thought he could claim her. Those who wouldn't take no for an answer got their skulls cracked for their troubles, even their castellan, Mohdri. He desperately wanted to win her heart and had his life saved by her instead.

Though she came to love the Maizan, and look on Mohdri's advances with more charity as time went on, Anakerie remained a daughter of Angwyn. Her father never forgave her for her flight, but he was also too good a war leader to allow such a superb potential asset to go to waste. He swallowed his pride and asked her to come home, as she swallowed her own hurt and anger when she agreed.

Then came the night of Elora's Ascension, and the ensorcellment of not only Angwyn but all the monarchs who'd assembled for the celebration.

As far as anyone knew, Elora Danan was responsible for the death of Anakerie's mother, the disappearance of her brother, and ultimately the overthrow of her realm in the bargain. By rights, there should be a deathmark between the two women.

The wild card in that deck was Thorn.

"Anakerie is as fine a general as she is noble a Princess," he conceded, speaking with great care the better to mask his own powerful feelings for her.

"How noble, Thorn," Elora asked gently, "if she willingly serves the Deceiver? She knows him for what he truly is."

"The Fates grant we get the opportunity to ask her, when this foul business is concluded."

"Don't you dare go all formal on me!"

"And don't you use that tone of voice, my girl. Now answer my damn question before this lesson is totally wasted. *Is* weather the key?"

A quiet chortle floated from the shadows where Khory lurked, so still that Elora had quite forgotten her presence. Wherever Thorn went, the demon child was never far away, any more than the brownies strayed from Elora's side.

"Sandeni exists on trade," she told him. "The city is self-sufficient to a point, but its prosperity and power derive from the goods it ships and the services it provides the traders. The roads remain passable, the rivers increasingly less so. The flow of merchandise becomes as clogged as the flow of water. If storms close down the highways as well, some merchants could be in dire straits."

"That happens every winter."

"Not to the same extent, Drumheller. I checked the archives. There are maybe a handful of years since the founding of the city that ice impacted on the rivers to such an extent before solstice or New Year's. Traffic's been at a virtual standstill since equinox, near two months ahead of schedule. Stroll through the courtyard of the Mercantile Exchange sometime, even the Cascani are hurting. Everyone's hanging on, they don't see themselves as having any choice. Stretch out loans, call in favors, do whatever's necessary to survive until spring. But suppose spring comes late? Suppose the thaw is sudden and violent, and the rivers stay impassable, and the roads are flooded? Suppose next year it's just as cold for just as long?"

"You perceive a pattern in these events?"

"The cold doesn't smell right."

"Ah."

"Which you've known from the start."

"I was paying attention. And my nose is bigger."

Another soft chortle, which Elora guessed was more at her expense than Drumheller's. She shot a glare at where she thought the sound came from but wasn't surprised to find that Khory wasn't there. It was another of the warrior's exercises, to test her own abilities as much as Elora's by sneaking up on the younger woman, announcing her presence by tapping Elora on the shoulder with drawn sword. Elora's challenge, of course, was to sense her coming.

Thus far, she'd done so only in her dreams. Today was no exception.

"The air had a different taste to it in the mountains," she explained to Thorn. Actually, she hadn't given this the slightest thought until he prompted her, but once he had, all the aspects fell into place like the final pieces of a jigsaw puzzle. "Silly as it sounds, it was *cleaner* somehow. What I smell when the storms blow off the prairie reminds me of Angwyn. It's the same taste the wind had on the ocean, right before the Deceiver attacked our boat. It's like the breeze off a mudflat, there's something rotten to it."

Thorn said nothing, but merely sank deep into his comfy chair, nursing his mug of cider and urging her on with a pair of upraised eyebrows.

"I have an affinity for fire," she said. "You, for earth. From what we've seen, the Deceiver has hold of the air. Over Angwyn he's created a whirlwind that's somehow sucking every scrap of warmth from the air."

"The technical term, for what that's worth, is 'heat sink.'"

"Whatever. Who knows how powerful that whirlwind's grown since we fled the coast? The eagles haven't been past the western mountains but what they've heard from migratory species is horrible, and it dovetails with traders' gossip in the market and the taverns. The whole of Angwyn Bay, land and sea together, is ice. And it's spreading farther north and south with every day. It's as if the world's suddenly been turned on its end, to make Angwyn the new North Pole, and the Deceiver's sending forth glaciers like they were armies.

"If that's so, maybe this wind and the storms it's brought along are his heralds. These are desert winds, Thorn, of that there's no mistake. They come from a place so cold that every drop of moisture's frozen from the air long before it reaches us. The snow we've seen falls from the sky that's already here. Which means, on top of everything else, we're likely deep into a drought and don't even realize it because it's started in winter when no precipitation is considered a blessing."

She drew herself from her chair and began to pace,

strides taking her through the elongated rectangles of light and color cast by the skylights high above. She was illuminated by a succession of highlights that served to accentuate the dominant elements of her features. She looked wild and untamed, with a strength of spirit growing in tandem with her body. What she lacked was patience. So much was changing within her, each day brought some new challenge to be overcome, a harder reality to cope with. Her frustration came from the fact that she could see no end to it. Her life had been shaped from birth by forces beyond her control. Now, when she was trying to assert herself, her own body had decided to betray her, becoming a kind of Deceiver unto herself.

"The Realms are *bound*," she said, working through the problem aloud, beginning with the fundamentals she already knew. "The Circle of the World, the Circle of the Flesh, the Circle of the Spirit. Each of the three of us claims an aspect of the world, that means our actions, our use of active sorcery, must have an equivalent effect on it." She rushed to one of the tables, shunting books aside until she found the tome she needed, quickly comparing a couple of pages with the notes she'd scribbled on a separate sheet. She made a fist, pounded lightly on the desktop. "The energy that fuels magic is bound into the fabric of the world, but the genius necessary to wield it comes from the Circle of the Spirit. Mohdri casts a spell to draw all the energy of magic to himself, it finds a physical analog by stealing the warmth as well. Which in turn makes it harder for his enemies to resist him, which brings him closer, faster, to his hoped-for victory. *Damn!*" she cried, and this time there was nothing light about the blow.

"What?"

"Don't you see the trap? If we fight him the same way, the enchantments we'd have to employ to seize control of his spell and then reverse it can't help but have an equivalent collateral impact on the physical world. This isn't a case of Bavmorda waving her arms and transforming an army into pigs"—referring to the battle before the Demon Queen's fortress of Nockmaar—"and then you and Fin Raziel negating it. For you to counterattack with the Deceiver's weapons, to face him on his level, might well crack the surface of the globe loose from its foundations. And I don't dare think what might happen if I tried."

"That makes sense."

"What I don't understand are the Maizan."

"How so, Elora?"

"Can't they see what's happening? Don't they ever look over their shoulders? Are they so busy conquering the world that they haven't noticed the Deceiver's destroying it behind them?"

"Think about who the Deceiver is. To their eyes, he appears as Mohdri, their beloved castellan. Their leader, the bond between them forged by blood and sweat and steel. Anakerie rides in the place of honor at his left, but they only follow her because he wills it so. They obey, because she holds her place in his name."

"He isn't real, Thorn, not as we define it. If I had to pick, I'd say his nature was closer to demon than human. He has no physical being. From what we've seen he can't even exist among us, much less act on our world, without a living, tangible host."

"And for some reason," the Nelwyn said, "the person he most desires to play that role is you."

"Never mind that for now. If we can somehow eliminate Mohdri, we force the Deceiver to another host. Or better yet, deprive him of one altogether! At least that might deal with the threat posed by the Maizan."

"Been considered, been tried."

"You never told me!"

"Success would have spoken for itself. I saw no need to burden you with news of failure." It wasn't a happy memory. "I could almost swear he knew we were going to make the attempt. If Khory hadn't spotted the trap, if Anakerie hadn't smuggled us safely from their camp . . ."

"She saved you?"

"Don't sound so scandalized."

"Don't keep springing so many surprises."

"She isn't our enemy. She never has been."

"You sound like that worries you."

"The Deceiver knows so much about everything else. He's familiar with so many intimate aspects of our histories, our very souls, why is he blind here? Or is this yet another trap?"

"You mean, is Anakerie playing some sort of double game? Only pretending to be on our side?"

He shook his head, with a downcast turn to his eyes that struck at Elora as if she could see the vision in them of Anakerie's execution, and she knew Thorn was envisioning the same.

"No. My terror is that he knows she's betraying him, and it doesn't matter."

"That's saying everything is predestined."

"You refuse to believe that?"

"Every day I'm free."

Everyone complained about the weather. It tainted every conversation and put folks in a perpetually sour mood. In a season of celebration, all Elora heard in one form or other were complaints. "My boss is a cow." "My husband doesn't understand me." "Nobody cares." "Work rots." "I got gypped." "Did you see the way she looked at me!" "Bloody government!" "Bloody peasants!"

As the holidays approached there was little active charity in deed and even less in spirit, replaced by a prevailing undercurrent of surliness and resentment. The sharp and biting edge that characterized the best of Sandeni humor took on an element of active cruelty.

Even Elora wasn't immune to this pervasive atmosphere of bleak malaise, and not simply because she heard her full name used more and more as a profanity, the ironic counterpoint to some misfortune, as when your house burns down and someone notes that "Elora Danan must have blessed you."

As her own researches in the university library led her only to dead end after dead end, her smile came less readily and there was a growing wariness to her walk, an

air of tension to her carriage that manifested itself in a reflexive tendency to respond to the most casual and ordinary of interactions as a potential attack. She no longer
slept well. She didn't want to sleep at all. At some point
before waking, she'd find herself atop Tyrrel's tor, where
Kieron Dineer awaited. He would be the dragon sometimes, or she, or both, or neither. Regardless of the per-
mutations, the outcome was always the same. He wanted
her to kill him, and refused to accept no for an answer.

She was glad she slept alone, she didn't want anyone
seeing her when she awoke from the worst of those vi-
sions, mouth full of the same metallic taste she remembered from Torquil's foundry, skin drenched with sweat
as if she'd actually been immersed in the ghost dragon's
flames. Sometimes she was so angry that it would have
been a horror for anyone fool enough to cross her path.
Others, she was so heartsick she could hardly breathe
through the terrible, whooping sobs. Whatever the case,
on those nights when Kieron's specter came to her, the
most she dared after waking was a light doze, hardly
more than a catnap but nowhere near as refreshing.

Yet at the same time she yearned for companionship.
Someone to hold her, comfort her, fill the aching void in
her heart and soul that had been with her from the moment of her birth.

One of her songs said it best, a sad ballad of a child
ever dependent on the kindness of strangers, allowed
friends but never a family to call her own. She called it
"The Song That Never Ends" because it had no ending.
She never performed it, never did more than croon it
lightly to herself alone in the sanctity of her room. At
those moments, when the shadows gathered most deeply
about and within her, she couldn't withstand the fearful
mixture of anger and loss, aching love and betrayal she
felt for her mother.

Her emotions coiled out of her like a serpent, a foulness made almost tangible by their intensity. She hated
herself for the rage she felt. She knew her mother hadn't
abandoned her. She told herself her mother loved Elora

more than her own life, willingly sacrificing herself to give Elora a chance for survival, but part of her soul remained that of the newborn girl who'd barely begun to breathe before she was cast away, who never knew why her mother had left her alone.

There wasn't the same animus for her father as she felt for her mother. He had no being, none had seen him, none had known him. She could not hate what to her had never existed.

It made no sense, of course. The true object of her enmity should be the demon sorceress herself. It was Bavmorda who killed Elora's mother, who'd tried her best to do the same to Elora. The infernal paradox was, Elora felt sorry for her. Though she'd been only a baby, she'd come away from their encounters with a strong residual image of her foe. A sense of the woman that was in the beginning, before her bright promise had been corrupted.

That made her hurt all the more, having a greater, truer sense of the woman who'd moved heaven and earth to bring about her destruction than she did of her own mother.

When those moods were foulest, when even the brownies learned to keep their distance, her footsteps invariably took her down the stairs to the dark and deserted tavern, where Duguay waited. It wasn't for his company she came. Whatever he saw on her face when their gazes crossed brought the troubadour no satisfaction. She would move to the center of the stage, never taking the opportunity to shift tables and chairs aside to give herself more room. She accepted the space wholly as she found it.

Then she would dance.

First, she would define a rhythm. Sometimes that inspiration came from without, others were dictated by the beat of her heart. That pulse would set up a resonant response, a minor articulation of the spine, a careless flick of the fingers. One motion would inspire the next, in ever-increasing complexity, as a solo instrument might initiate a simple melody and then be gradually joined by the others in the orchestra until the tune became a symphony.

Watching Elora on those dark and terrible nights was watching a person at war with herself. There was in her a breathtaking capacity for love, made all the more powerful by an equally powerful delight, a fundamental sense of wonder that remained a part of her even now. Especially now. Yet hand in hand with it ran as primal a rage, as though on one side of her was held absolute creation, and on the other its opposite, destruction. She stood between them, forced to balance these polar forces who demanded that she choose one or the other when her true desire was to find a way to stitch them together.

She would leap for the rafters and find a way to cast the illusion of holding herself in midair, in defiance of every law of gravity. She would race through a sequence of steps so quickly the choreography could hardly be seen, much less copied. She dared spins that should be possible only on skates, on ice; then, with a sureness and precision she never displayed in public, instantly downshift her tempo from staccato to legato and embark on a sequence of slow movements that in their own way appeared equally unbelievable. She didn't seem human in those moments. To behold her was to wonder if she was indeed some statue brought to life, or some purely elemental creature somehow made flesh. How else to explain her ability to hold every pose?

Here again came the impulse that she was at war, not simply with herself but with all the laws and strictures of nature, as if she could shrug them off as readily as any spell.

Duguay sat in shadows, never touching the goblet of mulled wine poured before him on the table. He watched her with eyes like beads of jet, doll's eyes, lifeless yet deeper than any abyss. Hunting eyes. Hungry eyes.

He never once tried to join her. Not so much out of the belief that he wouldn't be welcome to her dance but from the recognition that he had no place in it.

"You know what I see in him," Franjean noted softly,

so softly to Rool from their perch in a chink among the rafters. They had no idea what they were facing on these terrible nights and so called upon all their stealth to make their way to a ceiling hidey-hole that gave them a clear view of the room, bringing with them weapons enough to turn the place into a killing field should the need arise.

"A particularly nasty varmint who's found himself on the wrong side of the glass from something tasty."

"Don't much care for him."

"Never have myself, from the start."

"What about Elora, Rool?" They didn't have to ask themselves what the troubadour wanted, that was plain with every look and gesture. Their worry was why he'd made no move thus far to take it. The first time she'd come downstairs to dance, they'd assumed him responsible—especially when they found him there before her—but it soon became clear he was as bewildered by her acts as they.

"Thank all the Blessed Powers she doesn't drink," was his laconic response.

"That isn't funny, Rool! Lummox."

"Wasn't meant to be. But the principle's the same. And mind your mouth."

"Is she mad, do you think?"

"Aren't we all?"

"Rool!" The edge of warning to Franjean's voice was as sharp as the edge of fear that underlay it.

"After all that's happened in her life, she'd have every reason."

"No less than Drumheller."

"Agreed. Which is why I'll wager she's no less mad than he. And no more."

She danced until sheer fatigue made her drop. There was no gracious end to the evening. She was wholly in control one moment, a jumbled heap on the rough wood floor the next, her lungs working harder than the bellows of a forge to draw in a succession of monstrous breaths, as though she'd just been raised from drowning.

At last Duguay took an action. With an undeniably

sensuous grace of his own, he rose from his chair to take Elora in his arms. He cradled her there a moment, with more emotion to the gesture than a child merited, yet less than would be due a lover, almost as though he found himself conflicted as to which best applied to her.

Then, with the propriety of a gentleman, he returned her to her room and to her bed. And that was that.

Elora never spoke of these nocturnal performances, and the brownies never inquired, though they made a full report to Thorn Drumheller. If exhaustion brought her the opportunity for dreamless sleep, that was evidently a price she was willing to pay. Not happiness in any measure, for anyone involved, but at least a form of contentment.

Khory had her straight sword, an old campaigner's weapon, double-edged and as keen a blade as had ever been forged, of metal so finely tempered that years of hard use had left but the smallest impressions on its bright steel. A simple cross guard protected a hilt long enough for both her hands to hold, allowing its use either as a fencing rapier or the more traditional broadsword. She could kill effectively with either a stab or a slash and her formidable strength allowed her to handle it with the ease of a weapon a fraction of its weight.

Elora held the long sword favored by the warriors of the eastern islands. In length, it was a rough match for Khory's blade, but hers was shaped along a shallow curve, with a single cutting edge. It was primarily a slashing weapon, and as such had almost no equals. Both women wore mail and padding but these weapons were intended to cut through both. Their best defense, now as always, was their own skill.

They stood perpendicular to each other. Elora offered Khory a profile view, holding her hilt a little above and behind shoulder level so that the blade sloped along a downward arc past her cheek to rest atop her leading arm. Khory faced her, legs apart, sword in one hand, point down, a disconcertingly relaxed posture.

Both were in boots and trousers and wore gauntlets to protect their hands and forearms. Bandannas were tied about forehead and throat. They were sodden, and both women were breathing heavily. This wasn't the first duel of the day, and to Elora's great delight, they both had the bruises to show for it.

She wasn't here by choice, this was a decision both Renny and Khory had made for her and enthusiastically enforced.

"I can take care of myself," she'd protested, when they made her their proposal.

With those words came movement of her own, re-flexive and blindingly fast, inspired by some cue far beyond the range of rational thought or awareness. Her hand leaped to her traveling pouch and emerged with one of the knives carried within, the shortest of the curved islander swords. As Khory's straight blade slashed toward the junction of neck and shoulder, Elora used her own much like a bar, with both hands on the hilt simply to block it. The shock of impact, one blade against the other, bounced her from her seat and she turned that to her immediate advantage by kicking out against it with both feet. Unfortunately, Khory's muscles were a match for her reflexes and she cleared the tumbling chair with a powerful leap that landed her almost on top of Elora. Elora took a desperate slash with her small sword, at the same time trying to pitch herself beneath the table to the relative safety of the other side. Khory blocked it with a foot, stomping down hard enough to make Elora cry out, though she never relinquished hold of her weapon. That didn't matter much as the demon child casually laid the tip of her sword against the younger woman's breastbone.

"Fighting with furniture." She smiled, and offered Elora a hand up. "I like that."

Elora couldn't help herself. She stuck out her tongue.

"The point is," Renny told her after she'd righted her chair and collapsed herself into it, draining the glass of water Khory gave her in a succession of monstrous gulps, "you have enemies." Before she could make any sort of snarky rejoinder, he went on, "And your cover is not as all-embracing as you believe."

"How do you mean?" She thought he was about to say one of her companions had betrayed her, and hurried to marshal every possible rebuttal.

"Your secret may be safe from the Maizan, but as you've said yourself, there are other forces at play in the world. You stood against them at Ganthem's Crossing."

"There were no survivors, Renny," she told him, and the memory gave her no comfort. "Who's to tell?"

"Don't talk foolishness, Elora. Greater Faery is the home of the Wild Hunt. There is nothing the High Elves enjoy more than a chase. The wilier their quarry, the more determined they become. You have to be prepared."

Khory opened their duel, bringing her sword up and around in a sweeping arc that sizzled the air in its wake. At the last moment she reversed her hands and the direction of her cut, pivoting on her offside leg to bring the sword around behind her back in an attack that struck at Elora's flank rather than her head. It was a magnificent feint and Elora had read it perfectly. The crystalline *tang* of steel on steel sounded through the top floor of the library, whose decent width and exceptional length made it ideal for such training. At his own desk, floors below, the professor rolled his eyes and shook his balding, unkempt head in his hands, asking yet again how he'd allowed himself to be drawn into such a chaos. Elora swung her long sword parallel to her own body, point to the floor, to block Khory's strike. In the same flow of movements, while maintaining the block, she swept the two blades up and away, continuing the pivot to use her offside leg as a scythe to cut Khory's out from under her.

She had the satisfaction of seeing the older woman fall, but fast as she tried to follow through with her sword, Khory found a way to backpedal clear. Again and again, Elora swung at her with all her strength, energized all the more by a determination not to be beaten, but she couldn't find a way past Khory's guard. Thrust, thrust, parry, reverse, slash, slash, thrust, slash, kick, parry, thrust, slash, Elora maintained the pressure on her foe with an intensity that would have left anyone else gasping, somehow managing to increase the speed of her attacks as she progressed, painfully aware from past experience that she dare not allow her opponent the slightest respite.

Seeing none offered, Khory seized her own opportunity. She let the girl disarm her, at the same time controlling the disengagement so that her sword fell where she wanted it. She slapped Elora's blade aside and followed up with a brutal sequence of blows to the body. Fists to begin with, and then with feet, as Elora tried to open some distance between them so that she could once more effectively bring her sword into play. A roundhouse kick to the solar plexus doubled Elora over, another to the upper body sent her sprawling.

Before Elora hit the floor, Khory had her sword in hand and was on her way in for the kill. Only this time the surprise was hers. Flat on her back, Elora parried Khory's hammer blows, lashing out at full extension in a series of sweeping attacks that forced Khory into a succession of frantic bunny hops, lest she lose both feet at the ankles.

From that point there was no more delicacy or art to their duel. They faced each other at an arm's length and bashed away at each other, as though with a pair of clubs, emphasis on upper-body strength and reaction time, hardly any at all in delicacy of manner. Suddenly Elora shifted gears, totally changing the dynamics of the fight to those of a fencing match as she took a step backward and lunged. It was a splendid move, until Khory snapped her own blade down in a wicked parry that turned aside the attack.

Where the swords had come together with the shock of steel bars, they now took on the aspect of crystal chimes, a succession of taps that followed one upon the other faster than a drumroll beating the call to arms.

Then, out of nowhere, a mistake. Elora pushed herself a hair too far in a desperate attempt to score against her foe. This wasn't altogether unexpected, she'd been visibly tiring as the duel progressed, though this hadn't significantly affected her speed. The thing was, the extraordinary speed of the duel had its effect on both combatants. None watching could recall seeing this level of intensity maintained for so long. At such a pace there was no time for a conscious assessment of the situation. Action prompted immediate reaction, any strategizing had to be conducted on a separate level of being. The aggressor had to have a plan, the defender had to intuit that plan and determine an appropriate counter while actively and ferociously engaged in her own defense. At the same time both combatants had to remain ever ready to capitalize on any opportunity.

That, now, was what presented itself.

Elora was vulnerable. Khory responded accordingly. Two moments, encompassing far less than a second of elapsed time, and the instant Khory committed herself, she knew she'd been suckered.

Elora spun herself along the length of Khory's outstretched blade, hissing as it sliced through padding, mail, and flesh, accepting the pain of her wound as a necessary price of victory. She struck the taller woman across the face with her elbow, then brought both hands up and together on the hilt of her long sword and used its blunt pommel as a hammer to deliver an even harder blow. In a real fight, the follow-through would have been to sever Khory's fighting arm and then, as the woman reeled in shock, either take her head or open her body from shoulder to hip. Instead Elora hooked an ankle and dropped Khory on her back, collapsing onto her sword arm to pin it down and slapping the flat of her own blade across the other's chest.

She couldn't do any more after that. She flashed a grin to proclaim her triumph and let herself topple after her sword, to land all nicely cat-curled in a ball by Khory's side, her head resting just below the warrior's breast. She was breathing so hard it hurt. Khory, damn her, hardly more than normal.

"I hate you," Elora grumbled.

"You won."

Elora pushed herself up to a quasi-sitting position, weight spread between a hip and an arm she used to brace herself in total denial of the fact that every muscle in her body felt as limp as overcooked noodles.

"You didn't fight as hard as you could."

"If I had, you'd be dead." Khory blinked at her, narrowing her gaze in a way that made the tattooed design over her left eye appear even more hawklike and creating the unnerving impression that Elora was truly in the presence of something other than human.

"I did not fight you to the best of my ability," she said matter-of-factly. "But you fought me to the best of yours. You fought on *my* level, Elora, and you found a way to win."

"Well," Ryn Taksemanyin called from a safe distance, brandishing towels and a jug of lemon-flavored water, "after that display, *I* sure as hell wouldn't challenge either of you. On dry land, anyway."

"And in the water?" Elora asked him.

His tone was flippant but the answer deadly serious. "Drag you deep and watch you drown before you reached the air again."

Elora shuddered.

"That's cold, Ryn," she said.

There was a gauntness to his form that was new to him and he carried himself with a gingerly delicacy more common to old men. The spell the Maizani had used had been a cruel one and its negative effects on him were only intensified by the determination and manic ferocity of his resistance. Thorn had worked long and hard to repair the damage, but the fact remained, he was too far from home. The wounds were to his spirit more than to his flesh and true healing would come only with his return to the blue-water ocean. There'd been discussions of sending him east, to the Chengwei coast, but his true home was off Angwyn, now ice-rimmed and as uninhabitable below the waves as above them.

411

He hunkered down beside the women and handed them each a glass.

"Wyrrn don't fight for fun," he told Elora. "We love our tussles, but there's a big difference."

She stripped off her hard leather tunic, her mail undercoat, the padding worn beneath that, all the way down to her formfitting cotton undershirt, and tossed the lot carelessly aside. She took a step away, thought better of it, turned back before Khory had the chance to cough a quiet reminder, and gathered up her leavings to place them neatly on their racks. Occasionally the habits of her mistaught youth overwhelmed the better behavior she'd learned since. Taking proper care of her gear and space was her own responsibility. She had no one to pick up after her anymore.

Then, after returning her long sword to its scabbard—a deceptively plain and unassuming piece of work, without the usual ornamentation, whose beauty lay wholly in the quality of materials and craft—she held out a hand to Khory and hauled the warrior to her feet. They exchanged a formal bow of disengagement and Elora stepped through one of the windows to the balcony beyond and some badly needed fresh air.

After the warmth within, given aspects of a steam bath by their exertions, the outside chill was a bracing shock. Elora didn't mind in the slightest, even though she was bare-armed and in a thin shirt, dressed more for the opposite end of the year. There was a steady wind from the northwest, stiff enough to make her eyes water, and a definite hardship for anyone else.

She heard the thump of a cloak being shaken open behind her and then its familiar weight across her shoulders. It needed no fastening. So long as she stayed still, the cut of its high collar would anchor it in place.

There was a fair view from the roof, over the skyline of the university to the dome of the Citadel. A glance over the edge showed the walkways mostly empty of traffic, the students all in class. Ryn stepped up behind her, taking position to block some of the wind. She appreciated the consideration but couldn't help a frown at the feel of his fur. It had lost a fair portion of softness and luster these past months and she could feel bones beneath where before had been a cushion of body fat and muscle. There was a smell to him of sickness. She'd offered to help, as she had with others, only to discover this was a healing that lay beyond her abilities. There was nothing wrong with the body, it was his spirit that needed restoration.

"It must be hard," she said, "to be so far from home for so long."

"We're a wandering kind," he replied with a dismissive shrug, as if that was all that needed being said.

"No regrets, then?"

"I'm here by free choice, Elora. It's a struggle worth the winning, with friends worth the knowing. What's to regret?"

He folded an arm about her and gathered Elora even closer so that he was right behind her. "I can't get over how you've grown," he told her.

"Sorry."

"No no no, that's not what I mean, it wasn't a criticism." He was speaking so quickly his words ran over themselves, spurting out before his thoughts could sensibly order them. He called it quits with a deep breath and a rueful groan.

"I feel like a piece of taffy," she grumped.

"Nothing fits?"

"I guess it's just because everything's happening so fast, all at once. I mean *I* can see the difference. I keep banging into things because by the time I get a decent sense awareness of my proportions, they've all changed again."

"It won't last forever, you know."

"Your word on that, Ryn Taksemanyin?"

"What do you mean?"

"Never mind." Then, suddenly: "Do you have the slightest notion what—or *who*—I am?"

He started to reply with a platitude, but realized she'd set him up for just that.

"I don't," she said flatly. "Not like the rest of you." She looked out at the far distant horizon and let out all her breath in a great huffy cloud of exhalation. "I need a place I come from, Ryn, so I can know where I want to go."

"And if that's not possible?"

"It's like trying to sail without a keel. I can't fight the wind and current."

"Bollocks," he snapped, taking her own pet expletive. "You have that place, Elora—a Nelwyn farming village, a Daikini castle, a sorceress's stronghold, a tower in a great and doomed city. We begin our lives as the gods and Fates design us, but a lot of what comes after is ours alone to determine."

"Like being turned to silver?"

"No more, no less than assuming a coat of fur. Sometimes homes have to be built. Sometimes, Elora, dynasties and epochs and sagas have to be started. Sometimes, friends have to die."

"Maybe I'm not up to the job, Ryn."

"Then you're not."

They both heard a shout from below and peeked over the parapet to see a student race the length of the yard, to disappear into the classroom building across the way.

"You don't know him," Ryn said to her, hazarding a last word. She knew full well he meant Duguay, that his concerns about the troubadour echoed those of the brownies. It was plain to her as well how afraid he was that this antagonism would sever the ties that held them close, but also how determined he was to speak his piece.

Her response was in kind. "I don't know myself," she told him with a sad smile. "Yet."

"The Citadel semaphore's busy," he said, pointing westward.

"I see."

The semaphores were big, square flags, mounted on long poles that could be swung independently through the whole arc of a circle, and together, the two worked in concert to represent all the letters of the alphabet. Certain combinations could even establish whole words. Given the view from the plateau and the distances involved, they were often the most effective means of transmitting messages to and from the cataracts.

"Are the eagles up?" Ryn asked her.

Elora craned her head toward the horizon, her eyes shifting marginally out of focus.

"Both. Anele's a couple of miles high, I think. Bastian's roaming farther out. They have a rider coming up on the last cataract, another a half day behind, yet another a half day behind that. All pushing hard."

More shouts from the yard, a gathering tumult as every door was flung wide and the entire student body rushed into view. Professors as well, their dark robes and frantic scurrying reminding Elora of an anthill under attack.

She heard footsteps behind, the uneven tread and strained breaths of the professor as he clambered up the last flight of stairs, the still and silent glide of Khory's boots.

"What do you think?" Ryn asked one and all.

It was Khory who answered, as though this was a moment she'd long been waiting for.

"The Maizan."

Chapter
13

I꜀ᴛ WAS ALL THE NEWS BY BREAKFAST.

"A delegation," Duguay reported as he and Elora shared the morning meal with Susan and the rest of the staff around the biggest table in the tavern. When she arrived, Elora remembered this as being as bountiful as any feast, platters laden with fruits and cheese, crackers and breads and jams, porridge and raisins and honey, plus whatever was available from the stove. The variety remained, but less so the quantity. Wholesale prices were rising on a weekly basis but everyone knew that even a fortune wouldn't matter much if there was no food to be bought.

"To discuss issues of bilateral trade and mutual benefit to both parties."

"Go easy on the coffee," Susan cautioned as Pilar topped off her cup.

"Oh, that's not fair," the other woman groaned. For her it was as necessary a start to the day as breathing, often far more welcome than opening her eyes.

Susan shrugged. There were evident signs of strain around her eyes, Elora saw, and her mouth as well.

"Nothing I can do. As far as the highgrove blend is concerned . . ."

"Of course," Pilar groused, "my favorite."

". . . what we've got is what we've got. And that appears to be the end of it."

"I thought the roads were still clear to the south," Elora said.

"Roads are clear every which way, for the most part," Susan told them. "Provided you can keep self and stock from freezing along the way. Wagon train's in, they just don't have the freight we need. No crop this year from highgrove. Frost caught 'em by surprise, sounds like they lost everything."

"The Chancellor's office issued a statement," Duguay announced, a trifle exasperated by the interruptions and lack of attention, "to the council and parliament noting that the diplomatic initiatives of past months appear to have born fruit and that they look forward both to a positive exchange of views and a speedy resolution of any outstanding differences."

"Such as," Elora suggested as she savored the last of an orange, "are you and yours still hell-bent on conquering the world?"

"That's a bit cynical."

"In the case of the Maizan, perfectly justified."

"You don't like them, Elora?"

"Susan," Pilar asked, her voice touched with apprehension, "if the crops don't come in this harvest season, if the weather's so lousy that the plants themselves are crippled, what happens next year? What does the city do for food?"

"What's to like, Duguay?" Elora challenged. "We

417

came, we saw, we killed, we conquered, who's next? The Maizan credo and life story, in a nutshell. They're perfectly prepared to share with others, provided it's their sandbox, their toys, and only their children allowed."

"Is that what you hear, Elora," the troubadour responded, "on all those peregrinations to the cataracts down on the prairie, or out beyond the tableland suburbs? Or," he finished pointedly, "on your frequent sojourns to the university, hmnh? Learning a lot, are we? Bettering ourselves every day, in every way?"

"What I hear is that people are frightened." For emphasis, she tilted her head toward Pilar. "What I know is that they have fair reason."

"Only two choices available, pet." She bridled at the intentional diminutive and shot him a glare to remind him so. His answer was a slow smile. "Do you sanction a slaughter of the embassy the moment they dismount?"

"What would that accomplish?"

"Says here, the Maizan delegation will be led by their warlord."

"Anakerie?"

"The same. Strike off her head, you'll no doubt do the body some considerable harm. Take time presumably to choose a replacement, and who knows, they might not be as good."

"I assume they're here under a safe conduct, not to mention the fact there's been no official declaration of war."

"Technicalities"—Duguay sighed dramatically, as if the entire exchange was no more than a running joke—"always technicalities. I assume then that assassination is quite out of the question."

"Why are you doing this?"

"Merely dancing the steps you've choreographed, pet. You outlined the structure, I'm putting it together. You can't ignore them, they won't go away, or be wished away. If you won't kill them, there's but a sole alternative. Make a deal."

"Here endeth the lesson."

"Hardly. But you brought it on yourself."

"What could Mohdri offer that the Sandeni would accept?"

"Survival's always a good place to start."

"The Republic's been threatened before, Duguay, it's never yielded."

"Suppose it came down to a choice: the city's survival or that of the Sacred Princess?"

"What?"

"She yields of her own free will, or if the city gives her up, all is well. But if she flees, annihilation. Tell me, Elora, as a concerned citizen, would you consider that a fair exchange? One life for a multitude? Or a fair price, the multitude slain for that one to escape?"

"This isn't funny, Duguay."

"Perhaps not. But amusing. And definitely relevant."

She couldn't believe what she was hearing, she didn't know how to respond, with humor or silence or her fists. She was saved from the choice by a summons to the door, where she found an official ministerial messenger. A thick envelope of heavy vellum was delivered, bearing the official seal of the Chancellor, its very appearance reeking of importance.

With a twist of her fingers, she broke the seal.

"We have a commission," she announced after reading the contents. "An invitation to perform at the gala state banquet welcoming the Maizan delegation."

Immediately there was applause from Susan and the others, plus cheers and whistles and a toast that clinked mugs with juice tumblers. Duguay looked indecently pleased with himself, as though this was something he alone had brought about.

"Where is it?" he asked her, acknowledging the congratulations and pats on the back and a kiss from one of the women.

"The Cascani Factor's house, in Kinshire, the borough at the foot of Lake Morar."

"Will we attend, pet?"

"Hellsteeth, Duguay, I wouldn't miss this for the world."

Anakerie rode off the plains with less of an escort than Elora remembered Mohdri bringing with him to Angwyn. A company of cavalry, numbering an even hundred, and that included their baggage train. They wore armor, she wore none, though she had adopted the gleaming jet hues of their own apparel. She rode her horse like they were as one and commanded her men with equal assurance.

The years had scarcely touched her, Elora saw through Bastian's eyes. The eagle kept a respectful distance from the Maizan, describing lazy circles through the sky well beyond their bowshot. There was death between these two races and a hatred even Elora knew better than to try to assuage. Among the Maizan it was considered a badge of honor for their young men to claim the feathers of a golden eagle. The means by which they did so involved the ritual slaughter of their captive, in a spell that bound the anima of the eagle's soul to that of its killer. The eagles in turn considered the Maizan their mortal enemies and took any opportunity to exact swift and bloody vengeance for their dead.

Anakerie had rarely smiled when Elora knew her. Now she looked like she'd forgotten how and the soul behind her eyes was deeply shrouded, keeping both thoughts and secrets to itself. Her height wasn't outstanding, it was carriage and demeanor that made her appear far taller. Her form was slim, but possessed a whipcord power far out of proportion to her actual size. Far more important was a phenomenal speed that allowed her to evade the attacks of men two and three times her bulk. True, they could crush her with a single blow, but by the time they got around to delivering it, they'd already be dead.

Black wasn't the color for her, Elora noted critically. There was too much warmth in the faintly bronzed cast of her skin, too much life represented by hair the color of polished mahogany, shot through with strands and flashes of fiery auburn. The shade reminded Elora of Ryn, of all people, especially since his fur was touched by the same autumnal hues. There was no slack to the skin over her cheekbones and the lines trailing off the eyes and around the mouth were deeply etched. They were calculating eyes, never at rest, gauging every situation, seeking out her opponent's every weakness, warily anticipating a surprise attack or deciding how best to make one of her own.

"Is there something perhaps *I* might help with?" asked the professor.

Elora let out a yelp of startlement that burst forth from Bastian's beak as a piercing cry. She floundered in her chair, he in the air, and with a tremendous wrench she severed the mental ties between them, apologizing profusely as the contact faded for the headaches such shock would bring to both.

She blinked over and over again, her eyes so wide and staring that she looked like someone in a fit of panic when in fact she was only seeing through them the way the eagles did through theirs. For those few moments her body seemed to be composed of cast metal. Her hands had clamped tight on the arms of the chair as though for fear that if she released her hold she'd fall straight up into the sky, off the world entire and all the way to the end of Creation. The only part of her that moved was the surface of her chest, and that only a little as her breath came in staccato *huhf* sounds, one inhalation after the other.

Gradually her pulse slowed and she found time to take a decent breath. Her eyes were closed and she wanted to keep them that way, the better to deny the pounding in her temples as yet another field of phantom spikeblossoms bloomed beneath her skull. She flexed her hands, one after the other, as though this was some new experience. Watching her, the professor could have sworn he beheld someone who didn't remember how to move.

"Please don't do that," she said at last, creasing her

eyes open and giving the professor a small smile of reassurance.

"I," he repeated a number of times, clearly flustered and concerned by what had happened, chastising himself for not knowing better and desperately afraid he'd done her harm, "I'm terribly *terribly* sorry!"

"It's all right. Could I . . ." Now it was her turn to pause and swallow and cough as she tried to speak through a larynx laced as thickly with spikeblossoms as her head. She cleared her throat but the best she could manage was a croak. "Some water, please?"

"Of course, my dear, right away, right away."

There was a carafe on a nearby table, the water flavored with mint the way she loved it. She polished off a tumblerful right away, then slumped into the depths of her chair in hopes that a few minutes' relaxation would restore her enough to deal with her ailments.

Banishing the headache took more effort than she anticipated. She wasn't aware she'd dozed until the clink of china and silverware heralded the professor's return. More blinking as she dragged herself out of the chair and to a semblance of wakefulness. As the table came into focus she couldn't help breaking into a smile.

"What's this?" she asked incredulously.

"You were kind enough to treat me to tea," the professor explained, "when we first met. I thought it was past time to return the favor."

There was a chased silver pot of some antiquity, mismatched with a tall stoneware jug filled with steaming water. A pitcher of milk, a bowl of sugar, a pair of mugs completed the service. On a serving plate was a fruitcake with marzipan icing that she knew was his favorite, and one of hers besides. The scones were fresh and were presented with a selection of butter, clotted cream, and jam preserves. There were sandwiches as well, nicely stuffed, although nowhere near as elegant in presentation as she'd seen in downtown tea shops.

He took his tea with milk, she preferred it black with sugar. They both reached as one for the same piece of fruitcake, shared a chuckle, then shared the cake, Elora making sure when they broke it that the professor got the larger piece.

"Was it impressive," he asked, "the Maizan procession?"

She cocked an inquiring eyebrow but said nothing, preferring to savor the rich taste of her cake and wash it down with a swallow of tea. She had decided from the first to take the scholar into her confidence, and Thorn had agreed without the slightest argument. It turned out that he and the professor were old acquaintances, who regularly whiled away an afternoon or evening, when duties permitted, over tea or brandy and a game of chess. Elora's rationale was that the more the professor knew of her, the more help he could be.

"It wasn't so hard a deduction, my dear," he said, though he was proud of himself for having made it. "You're not the only one who watches the Citadel semaphore, which is how I knew when they arrived. I've seen how you withdraw your concentration from time to time, evidently to merge it with some other person or creature. When I saw you here, I assumed that's what you were doing. I"—and here he looked shamefaced— "didn't realize what effect my interruption would have. After all the time we've spent together these past weeks, especially considering all that I'm supposed to know about you and the Veil Folk, such a presumption is inexcusable."

"It's all right. No harm done, to Bastian or me. My own fault really, I have better things to do. In a couple of nights we'll be face-to-face, Anakerie and I."

"Is that wise?"

Elora shrugged. "How much do you know?" she wondered.

His turn to make the same gesture. "As much as can be read, or asked, or divined. Within these walls is one of the greatest storehouses of raw intelligence about the Great Realms on the continent. I'll wager, even the world. The labor of my lifetime, and a goodly score before me, collecting, collating, codifying—all of which is utterly worthless if we cannot find a way to put it to use."

As he spoke then, something altogether unexpected occurred. Without warning, her eyes brimmed heavy with tears. While her face was working fiercely to deny their presence, the professor gently pulled her into his arms and enfolded her in a rough and fatherly embrace.

"It's all right," he said over and over, useless as the words sounded to his own ears. He knew she was crying and in a way these were far worse than hearty sobs, the grief and sorrow as naked in her as any bared blade, and able to cut just as deeply.

"All I want are answers." She snuffled but made no move to disengage.

He nodded sympathetically. "To questions as yet unknown."

"It's as if the Deceiver knows everything. He has a plan. All we're doing is making things up as we go along."

"Reactive, not proactive."

"Huh?"

"Consider police work, my dear. You can either wait until the crime has been committed and then track down the malefactors. Or, not so easily accomplished, determine what inspires those crimes and find a way to head them off before they happen."

"Learn their plans, you mean?"

"No, my dear, it's not quite so simple. If a man steals because he's hungry, find a way to help him earn that bread. Provide a legitimate means of winning self-respect, or providing for yourself and your family. Let the community know your purpose is to be their defender, win their regard, earn their trust. Help them, that they may better help you."

"I have a dozen such communities to preach to, Professor," she said wearily, pushing away from him and fishing in her pockets for a handkerchief. All those tears had made her nose run as well, while her face looked so wet and puffy she might just have been slapped by a sodden cloth. She waved her hands helplessly. "I don't even know what some of them *are,* much less what they want."

"Elora." He looked her in the eyes; she met his searching gaze as he used his thumbs as a pair of impromptu towels to wipe her cheeks dry.

"Yes?"

"Is there anyone else to do the job?"

She shook her head, suddenly feeling more six than sixteen.

"I'm truly sorry," he said, with meaning.

"What I want sometimes, more than anything, is to run away and hide under my bedcovers and tell all the Great Realms to go hang themselves."

"I like that. Those Maizan, are they as impressive as their reputation?"

"Breed 'em big, dress 'em bigger. The armor and the horses help. You see them coming, it's like the whole of the Wall is tumbling down on top of you. But that's only part of what they do."

"This you've seen or this you've learned?"

"Both. Up-country, when Duguay and I were at the fort up by the Cascadel headwaters, the Colonel commanding held court with his staff every night at dinner, almost like a seminar in tactics." She smiled shyly. "I like to listen. I remember what I hear. There are three divisions of Maizan horse: heavy brigade, light brigade, and flankers. Those who rode in with Anakerie, they're the heavy mob. Think of them as a sledgehammer, used to smash the opposition in a mass head-on attack. Light brigade focuses on speed, they wear mail instead of plate armor, quicker horses, lighter spears, to exploit the holes in the enemy line opened up by the heavy attack. The flankers are harriers. Favorite weapon's the bow. Use them to scout, to hit-and-run. They make you so crazy with distractions that you miss what's happening right in front until it's too late, or maybe goad you into some stupid, ill-considered response.

"Now, that's ideal for open country warfare. And that's all folks assumed the Maizan were good at. Like looking at a master bowman and never imagining he knows how to use a sword. Or better yet"—she smiled inside and out at the thought of Luc-Jon—"a country boy with country manners; would you think of such a lad as a licensed scribe?"

"Most wouldn't, no," he replied.

"There you have it. The supreme advantage of the Maizan is not that they move so fast and hit so hard, but that they do everything else required of an army. They have engineers, they understand siegecraft, they fight as well on foot. But since that doesn't fit the preconception, nobody thinks of them in those terms."

She scarcely touched her mug after she sat down, silent for so long a time with her knees folded snug to her body, her heels resting on the lip of her chair, that her tea went cold. The professor took it to pour her a refill.

As he did so Elora's gaze was caught by the shape its condensation had left on the table. Without a conscious decision or the slightest hesitation, she reached out a finger to repeat the circle once, then twice.

"What do you see?" the professor asked her.

"Earth, Air, Fire, Water," she repeated, as she had to herself countless times before, labeling the image on the table as she had so often in her thoughts, tapping her finger at each of the cardinal points of the topmost circle. "The Great Realms of the Circle of the World. Beside it, the Circle of the Flesh: Daikini, Lesser Faery, Greater Faery, I'm not sure. And beyond, the Circle of the Spirit, about which I know nothing, save that that's where the dragons live."

"What do you remember from your Ascension?"

"A big blur." She shook her head. "Been down that road too many times, searching my memory on my own and with Thorn to help me. If the images are there, he couldn't find a way to pull them loose by spells." She snorted in rueful dismay. "My immunity to magic proving itself a two-edged sword.

"But I don't think the images are there, at least not in any way that makes sense like normal memories. The

426

Deceiver hit me pretty hard"—she held out her hands to indicate herself—"as you could see if it weren't for Duguay's disguise. In the process he chewed up my memories pretty thoroughly. I was under his glamour most of the time anyway, I had eyes pretty much only for him. I remember Anakerie's father but I couldn't describe the man to save my life. Same with Cherlindrea. The only face that's firm is the dragon." Her own face suddenly twisted, and she took a quick, convulsive swallow of tea, gasping as the raw heat scorched her throat. "Kieron Dineer.

"And the Deceiver killed him," she finished.

"Is such a thing possible?"

"Take my word. I was there."

"To be honest, I don't much credit their existence."

"In a world that's chockablock with all the denizens of Greater and Lesser Faery, not to mention sorcerers of all sizes, shapes, and natures, how can you doubt it?

"Trust me, Professor. Dragons are real. And mortal, at least in body. I can't seem to get Kieron's spirit—strange." She took a more restrained sip as she considered this new thought. "I never considered it before but we were never introduced, so how do I come to know his name? Anyway"—having no answer, she decided to move on—"he haunts my dreams. We're always on Tyrrel's tor and he always wants me to kill him again." Another thought, another longer pause that turned her mouth downward into a frown. "And Duguay's always there to interfere."

"Your partner, the troubadour?"

"You don't like him either?"

"I like looking people in the eye, my dear. It makes me nervous when I can't."

She tapped the tabletop again, taking refuge in a return to an earlier stage of their conversation by marking the cardinal points of the circle she'd drawn below and to the left. "I remember animals at the Ascension. No, wait, they were people, robed as avatars to represent them. Makes sense. After all, one circle is the world, the next ought to represent what lives *on* the world. The flesh.

Daikini are a Realm, they get their place on the Second Circle. Or should the animals go first? Do they fill in this missing slot then?"

"You don't sound convinced."

"I'm not. It's like, all of a sudden, I have too *many* pieces for the puzzle. Daikini is right. Lesser Faery— brownies, fairies, Nelwyns, trolls, boggarts, and the like. Greater Faery, encompassing the Domains of Elfland and Faery. They all belong."

"Your animals complete the circle."

"No, they don't." With each thought, as they cascaded from her lips as fiercely as water down the cataracts, her tone grew more firm, her manner more certain. She was onto something. "Animals are *of* the world, just as Daikini are wholly *of* the world. They're a Domain of a Realm, a lesser aspect of a greater whole, the same as brownies and fairies and Nelwyns are Domains of the Realm of Lesser Faery. I said as much to Rool once but never made the connection. They had no business being represented like that at my Ascension, but there was a perceived need to fill all twelve slots in the Great Circle and no one knew the true order—or *nature*—of things.

"See, Professor?" Again she indicated the circle, excitement energizing both voice and manner. "Start with the World. Move on to the Flesh: Daikini, wholly of the world; Lesser Faery, mainly of the world but with a step beyond the Veil; Greater Faery, of the Veil but with a step still in the world. The final stage has to be something, someone wholly *beyond* the Veil, the jumping-off point for the next circle entirely, whose only connection to the flesh and the world has to be the spirit, as its name says."

"Which is?"

"An altogether total mystery, except that at some point we find the dragons."

"Could they represent your missing link?"

She shook her head. "No. Dragons and demons, they're outside all the realities, they transcend all the rules. That's why they're only supposed to come to you in dreams. . . ." Her voice trailed off and she sagged back in her chair, indicating herself in wry humor. "Case in point.

"Circles are a great image," she said. "All I seem to be doing is going 'round and 'round in them."

"Have another piece of cake, you'll feel better."

She did, in both regards, and then she thought some more. She got to her feet, drew her sword from its scabbard, and while the professor watched with eyes almost as saucer-wide as hers had been she battled shadows from one end of the floor to the other.

When she was done, he applauded until she quickly shook her head for him to stop.

"That was magnificent," he protested.

"Khory is magnificent," she told him. "I'm competent. A modicum of skill, but no art." A memory touched her. "Like the grandfather of a friend of mine. He was saying . . ."

"Yes," the professor prompted.

"I'm sorry," she said hurriedly, setting aside the sword and walking stiff-legged with eagerness along the line of shelves she had appropriated for her own use, to hold the books she was using. "Something," she told him over her shoulder, "another friend told me. About a legend, of a race called the Malevoiy."

"Umm. Black leather cover," the professor called out, "almost big as you. Silver chasing, three straps, somewhat the worse for wear, a little further toward the corner there."

"*Got it!*" she cried exultantly, and then grunted with the effort needed to carry the book to a table.

"What's this leather wrapped around, anyway," she demanded of no one in particular, "lead?"

"I'm surprised you've no one to help."

"They're all working for Thorn tonight, even the brownies. Duguay's down in Kinshire, talking to the Factor about our show."

"Those old scribes had their ways of keeping their work from being stolen. Were I some thief, I'd choose booty I could carry, not something that weighed as much as me."

The cover, once unbuckled, made an audible thump when she heaved it open. Here, Elora had to sigh, and not with exertion. The writing was indecipherable.

The professor adjusted his spectacles, which left them perched precariously at the end of his nose, and slipped the middle pair of his fingers down what she assumed was a table of contents, making comments whose ambiguity nearly drove her crazy before he let out a squeak of accomplishment and folded over a thick sheaf of pages.

"Here we are," he announced, and then asked Elora, "What did your friend say, about the Malevoiy?"

She had to think a moment to get it right. "That they could speak firsthand of the dawning of the world, but that no one's knocked on their door in living memory."

"Interesting turn of phrase, that."

"Why?"

"They were, so it says here, the first of the races to step wholly beyond the Veil."

"What do you mean, 'step'? As in from the world?"

"Could that be why the Realms are linked by circles? To imply that their status can change? Oh, that would be delicious, to find the High Elves of Greater Faery suddenly banished to this side of the Veil. Serve them right, in their arrogance."

"Professor, do you know what's happening along the frontier? Greater Faery's been raiding the outland settlements. Suppose banishment isn't the change of status they contemplate, but conquest?"

"Well that wouldn't be at all pleasant, for either side. The Malevoiy are the oldest of Faery," he said flatly, and then his eyebrows rose. "And they are apparently as feared on their side of the Veil as some of the Veil Folk are on ours. Could they be the progenitors of demons?"

"You tell me, you read the language."

And so he did, to the best of his ability, long into the night as their tea turned cold and their cakes stale. With reading came inspiration, which sent him to another floor in search of some title to pursue a phrase that had popped out of nowhere in his thoughts, while Elora scrambled through a pile of notes and pages of her journal to satisfy a notion of her own. She wasn't sure which was more daunting, that for all her work there was still so much that remained unknown even within these walls, or that in these past weeks of effort she'd managed to discover so much.

When the professor returned, he found her dancing, an elegant skitter-step routine that was accompanied by the hum of a random tune interspersed with phrases he recognized from her researches. This time he didn't interrupt.

She looked fearfully embarrassed when she caught him out of the corner of her eye. "As a kid," she explained in a great rush, "I wasn't allowed to do *anything*. I like being physical, I like moving, it establishes a bond between my mind and my own body, the same way I use my In-Sight to merge with Bastian. Sometimes I can dance my way to an inspiration."

"Any luck?"

"I'm still working on it. And you?"

"The Malevoiy texts make reference to a World Gate, and you'll never guess where."

"Don't, please don't say it's somewhere in this building."

"It would be useful."

"You mean it *is*?"

"Good gracious no, whatever gave you that idea? No, it's somewhere within the environs of Sandeni, up here on the plateau. But of course that was ages upon ages ago, when the Malevoiy were manifest on both sides of the Veil."

"The ley lines have moved, the Gate won't be active. Will it?"

He huffed a sigh. "I honestly don't know. But there's something else I've found."

This volume wasn't nearly as impressive as the

Malevoiy chronicle. The binding was torn, as were a number of pages, and there was water damage throughout.

"There was a flood," the professor told her apologetically. "Basement storage, below water level, a weakness in one of the retaining walls, an unholy mess. See here, though"—and he pointed to an illustration—"what do you make of this?"

"A Daikini country dance, what of it?"

"Look at the border illuminations, Elora. I know the ink's faded but I also know what I see. Is that not the frame of a World Gate?"

The breath went out of her, all at once, so suddenly she had to grip the edge of the table to keep from swaying. The professor sensed her distress, took her with an arm across her shoulder, and held her close, which is when she noticed they were very nearly of a height together.

Without slipping loose from his grip, she stretched arm and torso along the table to pluck up the "bestiary" Luc-Jon had sent her. There was no hesitation about which page to turn to and she slapped the open book beneath the illustration the professor had set before her.

The sigil in her volume and the one atop the illumination were the same. As they were for the image seared in Elora's memory from Carig's rogue Gate.

"Is there a name, a reference to any being?" she asked.

"This is a story of some kind, an entertainment." The professor clearly disapproved. "There is reference to an otherworldly being, but not a hostile one. His role is benevolent, one might almost consider him a force for creation."

"A *name*," she prodded further.

"He is called the Lord of the Dance. Wait." The professor's voice tightened with concern as he flipped further through the book. "I may have spoken too soon."

"How do you mean?"

The framing illumination was the same, though significantly more damaged than its counterpart. A tremendous amount of detail had been lost from the illustration as well, but what could be seen conveyed totally the opposite impression of the one before. That had been a celebration of joy, this was one of transcendent horror, as far removed from the other as could be conceived.

"Which is it?" Elora demanded. "When I first saw this sigil, the entity it represented was being Summoned as an agent of destruction, yet you've just been telling me something completely different, that it works for creation."

"Can't it be both?"

"I don't know!" she cried, and was immediately sorry for her outburst.

"Realms exist within the circles, and Domains within the Realms, that is the structure of things."

"Try telling that to a demon, they hate structure of any kind."

"Chaos is a state of nature. Is it merely a Domain or a Realm unto itself?"

"We know the dragons are a Realm," she said. "Else why would Kieron have been at my Ascension?"

"The references aren't to a single entity."

"Hmnh?"

"To do his work, the Lord of the Dance needs a partner."

"There you are," Duguay called in hearty greeting from the top of the circular stairs. "I have been looking for you so *hard,* my pet."

His smile was as glorious as a spring sunrise, filling the room with a warmth and radiance Sandeni hadn't seen since snowfall and might not ever again.

Elora didn't notice. At long last she had eyes only for his.

Cascani House, as it was called, was chosen for both banquet and discussions because it was recognized by all the parties concerned as both neutral territory and safe ground. Not only did their reputation for scrupulous honesty and fairness in business dealings make the Cascani ideal hosts, but more important their Rules of Hospitality applied to all their guests. For so long as company remained beneath their roof and in no way transgressed that hospitality, no harm would come to them. To that cause, Factors pledged their honor, their fortunes, and if necessary their lives.

Sandeni troops ringed the wall that surrounded the large, comfortable mansion and the square that opened off the main gate. The house itself stood atop a crookback bluff that jutted out into the Morar like a solitary tooth, providing a magnificent view eastward of the Wall and the falls, as well as an equally impressive panorama of the first cataract. That meant, unlike most residences, which were oriented parallel to their main courtyard, this house was designed perpendicular to it. Instead of the formal rooms branching off on either side of the reception areas, guests proceeded to them along a straight line. The layout, with its towering windows, played to the visual strengths of the scene. Regrettably, it also made the building a devilish pain to heat and in this harsh a winter that proved no small task. Two huge hearths blazed away in the formal dining hall, combining their efforts with a succession of vents along the baseboards that admitted hot air pumped out from a pair of holocausts in the basement.

Officers of the Sandeni Constabulary manned the gate itself, complemented by Cascani Household Guards, who in turn were complemented by Maizan at the entrance to the house itself. The mood overall was wholly professional, and if an undue amount of attention was focused on the Maizan, with hands ever so casually close to the hilts of swords or knives or cudgels, everyone was tactful enough to take no overt notice or make a comment. As the saying went, "The lion may be housebroken, but those are still a damn fine set of jaws." No one wanted to be bitten, even by accident.

Elora wore her leathers, her tartan warcloak flung diagonally across her chest and over the opposite shoulder and down her back in the highland fashion. With

Duguay by her side she crossed the square in long, leonine strides as if the land itself were hers. When she blossomed from the shadows and the massed torchères of the gate caught the hues and shadings of her painted features, she claimed the instant and absolute attention of every figure present.

It was a superb meal and Anakerie had proved to be an utterly charming guest of honor. She sat at the high table with the Chancellor and the Cascani Factor, her ranking officers interspersed at a dozen other tables among representatives of the council, the parliament, the business community, the trading and banking community, the diplomatic corps, and anyone else with influence enough to wangle an invitation.

As severe as she'd appeared during the procession through town, she was utterly resplendent this evening. She normally wore her hair, for convenience in battle, in a thick, single plait that touched the base of her spine. Tonight it hung undone, swept sharply back from the right side of her face, then over and around the crown of her head into a glossy fall of color that draped across the opposite shoulder and breast. On her forehead was a circlet of pure silver that had been handed down from mother to daughter in her family for countless generations, whose only ornamentation was a sigil of woven knotwork marked with four precious stones. Ruby, emerald, sapphire in a triangle surrounding the dominant element, a delicately faceted, perfectly cut diamond. The knotwork itself was difficult to see because of the modest size of the sigil itself, but close examination would reveal an interlocking arrangement of circles.

Only Anakerie knew it was the most artful of forgeries. The original she'd given to Thorn as a keepsake, a pledge of feelings neither of them dared admit, much less name.

About her throat was gold, a torque of Maizan workmanship that proclaimed both her rank and her relationship to their castellan. It was said that once donned, this collar could never be removed, symbolizing an eternal bond of fealty and devotion. At each end were set a pair of exquisitely carved fire chips, a rare form of ruby that used the warmth of living bodies to generate a radiance all its own. The effect wasn't terribly apparent in a room with ambient light, but in shadow they gave the disconcerting impression of two sets of glaring predatory eyes.

Her gown was off the shoulders, a shallow scoop neck that hinted at the hollow of her breasts, long-sleeved and cut as much for comfort as for style. It was a gown that moved easily on her, but that left no confusion as to Anakerie's status. Its color was a blue so rich it shimmered in the light as though its threads were actually spun crystal. Every so often a wayward beam struck one like a prism and found itself shattered into a myriad of component colors.

The entire assemblage was on their best behavior, true feelings locked away in the recesses behind tightly shuttered eyes or masked by ready smiles and glib exchanges. The laughter was genuine, because many of those present knew how to work a room, and which jokes were appropriate for the occasion. Among the direst of enemies there were always topics of common ground: the best way to train a horse, or hunt wild boar, or that most hoary and venerable of standbys, the weather. Here, the Maizan even found themselves the object of some expressions of genuine sympathy; for hard as the winter was proving in Sandeni, the general presumption was that it must be far more brutal on the open range.

Dinner was served, and eaten. Toasts were made, and returned. Light conversation, especially at the high table, marked the beginning of forthcoming negotiation as Anakerie and the Sandeni Chancellor tried for a better sense of the other. They weren't talking positions, or terms, nothing of any substance pertaining to the conference to come. This was far more important. They had never met, they knew of each other solely by reputation, their goal tonight was to divine some insight into how the other thought. Was it an intuitive mind or a linear one, given to rational deduction or leaps of flash and fancy, calmly imperturbable or prone to excess? Did he play a deliberative game of chess, did she prefer a timed game? Did they prefer chess at all, or poker?

There were discreet questions about Mohdri. He had actively led the Maizan until the fall of Angwyn, in the forefront of every major battle as well as every negotiation. He'd been seen rarely since.

Anakerie smiled, a surface expression honed and perfected by long practice, that gave not the slightest hint of her true thoughts or feelings. Three years ago she had seen Mohdri fall, impaled on the horns of a stag, crushed beneath the body of his fallen, dying horse. The wounds were mortal, yet within the hour of that moment she saw him on his feet, directing his troops, apparently fully recovered. When she first met Thorn Drumheller in the dungeons below her father's palace, he had told her of a deadly threat to the life of Elora Danan and the safety of her kingdom. She hadn't believed him. Looking into Mohdri's eyes after that final battle, when Thorn and Elora had made their escape, she realized that she was looking at a masquerade. The body was Mohdri's, every gesture and word identical with the man she had once almost loved, but the soul was something else. She understood then why Thorn called his adversary the Deceiver.

Although he had a body and the temporal power it commanded, the Deceiver made little use of it. He gave the governance of the Maizan to Anakerie, but although she'd earned a place among them as a child, the only girl ever to do so, and distinguished herself in a score of campaigns, she had to prove herself to them all over again. She was glad to do so. Those duels proved the ideal outlet for the rage and grief over the loss of her city and her father that threatened even now to consume her.

This was none of her making but she swore to make sure as few would suffer from it as was humanly possible. In the past the Maizan had been excellent conquerors but poor rulers. They were forever losing through ignorance and plain stupidity what they had fought so valiantly to take. She set out to change that. She established a code of justice that was fair to all, and found the warriors to enforce it honestly. Again and again she pounded through the thick skulls of her generals that there was more honor and glory, and ultimately profit, in taking a city whole rather than in ruins. The farther they expanded, the harder it would become to control the land they already held. To succeed, to *survive,* the Maizan needed loyal allies at their back. It was a hard lesson for a people whose paramount precept had always been to trust no one outside their own.

Through all the work, the battles with those foes determined to fight, the deadlier struggles within her own ranks, one face comforted her. Not the one she would have expected to strike a flame in her heart, not in a million years. She could number the times they'd met on the fingers of a single hand, yet she knew his face, the gentle radiance of his soul, would be a comfort to her till she died. His was the face she searched for as she rode into Kinshire, as she had made her entrance past the guests. She knew he was in Sandeni, she had a volume of comprehensive reports from field agents as testament to that. At the same time she was glad he wasn't here.

As Anakerie, she loved him. As Warlord of the Maizan, she was his sworn enemy. By direct order of the Castellan himself, he was to be slain on sight, he and all his companions. Only Elora Danan was to be taken alive and unharmed.

Despite the best efforts of her spies, however, and her cadre of Black Rose assassins, the Sacred Princess was apparently nowhere to be found.

Then the Household Chamberlain appeared and with the third rap of his seven-foot staff of office on the polished floor, conversation quickly faded, ushered away by a hurried flash of whispers as those who knew what was to come gleefully alerted those who did not.

Duguay led the way, gloriously colored, a rainbow walking, so bedecked in bows and tassels and ribbons that one clueless wag likened him to a drapery shop. He took large steps, confident of his feet's ability to take him anywhere he wanted to go, and the broad smile he gave the audience along with a languorous bow of greeting made women swoon and even the pulses of a few gentlemen beat a hair faster. Then, a reverse of position and a second bow, to the patrons of the night's entertainment at the high table. The Chancellor and the Factor acknowledged with nods of the head, but Anakerie had eyes only for the cloaked and silent figure that seemed to glide in behind Duguay.

At the sight of her, Anakerie went very silent, very still, so small and subtle a change in her demeanor that only one other figure in the hall noticed.

As if on cue, or in answer to a call that only she could hear, Anakerie's eyes lifted from Elora and fixed on that other.

In that gaze was a message meant for him alone. It was a smile, and from where he stood well hidden against the farthest wall, Thorn Drumheller replied in kind and in full measure.

Duguay and Elora had been working with the household musicians since receiving the invitation. From their station in the corner the fast-paced beat of a dumbbell mallet on the stretched leather head of a tiompan burst forth, calling on Elora to dance the reel. For the next few seconds, while the beat of the drum established itself, she remained still as a piece of carved stone, every aspect of her hidden beneath her hooded cloak.

With the closing of that introductory measure, the drum was joined by uilleann pipes and a bagpipe as well, to cheers and applause from various Cascani scattered through the assemblage who recognized the tune. From stance and manner it seemed to Anakerie, as to everyone else, that Duguay would lead off the performance, but that sudden crescendo of music ignited a like explosion of movement from Elora. In a single, sweeping motion that sent her into a leaping full circle, she cast the cloak from her shoulders into Duguay's arms and claimed the dance for herself.

Her gown was the same shade as her leathers, the night-washed scarlet of the Black Rose, the color of blood spilled in passion. It was in two parts, hung low on her hips with a bandeau top to cover her breasts. It had body and weight, draping itself artfully along the line of her body when she moved against it, and flowing outward as well in graceful circles. As with Anakerie's gown, Elora's was stitched with crystalline thread, giving it the same capacity to refract the light that struck it, the difference being that in Anakerie's case the effect made her appear all the more regal. For Elora, she appeared to be shot through with either blood or flame.

The patterns on the cloth had been replicated on her body paint. To those who'd seen her before, she had never looked more elemental. For the others, they beheld the vision of some otherworldly being, no doubt from far beyond the Veil, who had joined them for the evening. If appearance alone wasn't enough to convince them, the dazzling athleticism, the terrifying audacity of her dance more than did the trick. To watch Elora Danan that fateful night was to behold music made flesh. Each separate note struck its resonance in her body and called forth an equivalent response. There was no lag between inspiration and execution. She and the musicians were more in sync than the figures on an automaton, and shot through with a passion as fiercely beautiful as life itself.

But she was merely the prelude. Seemingly without warning, where the dance had been a solo, suddenly it was a duet. If anything, the movements became more daring, more intense, more passionate, the two figures playing off each other as well as the music. Gasps were heard, some cheers, rounds of spontaneous applause. Many a breath was held and not an eye left the two partners.

Except for Anakerie's, which found Thorn again and shared with him the unspoken realization that what they were witnessing was more than mere dance. The Maizan Warlord had known her destiny since she could walk.

She'd learned long ago to recognize a duel when she saw one.

Duguay led, then Elora, then he again, then with a playful whoop of laughter that found an enthusiastic echo in the audience, she seized the role back. When next he claimed ascendancy, however, it was plain that it would not be easily relinquished. This time there was no contest between them. He cast her in the subservient role and she accepted, and when he spun her to the side so that he might finish the dance as she'd begun it, solo, she let him.

If there was any tension, no hint of it showed when they stepped forward to take their bows. The moment the music struck its final chord most of the house was on its feet, raising hands and cheers to the rafters and clamoring for more, a request the performers were only too happy to oblige.

Duguay held center stage and had the audience entranced. His jests made them laugh, his music was a delight, he'd never been better. All the while Elora remained off to the side, sitting on her ankles in the eastern fashion with her feet folded under her, her guitar held upright at her side in a manner that reminded Anakerie of a warrior sitting sentry with a blade.

At Duguay's conclusion, the applause was generous, meriting a brace of encores.

Elora didn't move from her place.

Then, in her husky, broken voice, she began to sing. A cappella, unaccompanied, about two lovers. Two lives, rich with promise, that would ever remain unfulfilled because of one woman's twisted ambition. Her voice alone provided the frame and foundation of the ballad, she wanted nothing to distract from the images she was crafting. With the opening refrain, somehow all unnoticed, she slipped the guitar into her lap, plucking single strings, then chords, then striking an impatient percussive beat on the body of the instrument with her fingers.

She painted a vivid picture of a land and a time

where life had become warped and twisted: under the rule of the Demon Queen, pleasure came no more from joy in the wonders of the world but in the delight of another's pain. Power abjured responsibility, became an end unto itself, the purpose of achieving it was to achieve more. The goal was to triumph, to become the absolute zenith of all things, and any hindrance to that end was to be destroyed. So fell the father, so fell the mother, so would have fallen their only gift to the world, their daughter, had a midwife not spirited her away.

The Demon Queen was not so easily deterred, and the song began to increase its tempo ever so slightly. The gentle midwife, too, made the supreme sacrifice. But the child found another rescuer, the unlikeliest of heroes, whose heart and courage bore no relation to his stature. Through his efforts, with the help of dearest friends, the shape of their part of the world, mayhap the world entire, was changed for the better.

As for the Demon Queen, she met the end she'd planned for the baby, ultimate obliteration.

Someone began to clap, only to belatedly realize that the song wasn't done. The tiompan drummer was beating out a complementary rhythm, taking his cue from the pattern of Elora's own handslaps on the guitar face.

She continued her theme, singing of another time and of two sets of lovers where before there'd been but one. Here again, Anakerie sought out Thorn, because when he had been her prisoner she had bonded briefly with his mind and soul, and she knew from that brief union that one of the pairs of lovers was Thorn and his Nelwyn beloved. They had won the good fight and looked forward to the joys such victories bring. So full of dreams, so rich with promise.

A jangling chord, a moment of stillness, a harshly spoken sentence from Elora.

"The world split asunder, and they died."

She forged ahead with a driving, relentless pace, painting the picture of that lost and lonely child, once more cast adrift, pursued by a foe even more implacably ruthless than Bavmorda, centerpiece of a struggle that appeared just as hopeless.

Only there was a difference. The child was not a child, and her champions no longer had to fight alone. If destiny, through whim or cruel design, had chosen to set its mark on her, she would seize destiny by its throat and teach it she was not to be trifled with. Too many had suffered, too many had died. She might be defeated but their sacrifice had stripped from her forever the right of giving up.

This was not a war about placing any Sacred Princess on a throne. It was about the freedom to choose your own path, and take responsibility for all that followed.

She stopped again, in mid-phrase, but no one dared utter a sound. She hadn't left her knees, yet it seemed as though she could fix her gaze on every other eye in the room and take their full measure.

She sung once more of lovers, and then the refrain, *"We will be free."*

She sung of dreams, and then the refrain, *"We will be free."*

She sung of dragons, and then the refrain, *"We will be free."*

She sung of hope, and then the refrain, *"We will be free."*

With each repetition, the tempo increased, the passion and the intensity. When she sang the fourth refrain, another voice from deep within the crowd joined her. With the fifth, she had a chorus. By the sixth, every voice in the room that wasn't Maizani.

The one she heard best was the one she'd hoped for all along, even though she knew that given the opportunity in battle, Anakerie would try her level best to kill her. The Warlord's lips barely moved and she sang so quietly that neither figure flanking her heard a word, but Elora heard it all.

"We will be free."

She built to a last crescendo and with the final refrain rose with effortless grace to her feet, holding her guitar high as though brandishing it like a standard before an army, letting those four words pound at walls and windows like thunderstones before a final crashing chord brought her song to its end.

"We will be free," she sang with full voice and with all her heart, even as the force of that singing tore at her throat like claws, *"and we shall!"*

The cheers before were nothing. People were on their feet, applauding, whistling, stomping, hollering, the front rank of Cascani surging forward to engulf both Elora and Duguay, chanting the refrain to her song like a chant as they hoisted them up on communal shoulders, the better for the rest of the crowd to see. Among the Maizan were a couple of glum faces, not because they were displeased by the song but, contrary folk as they often were, because they, too, had found themselves caught up in it, bellowing that fateful refrain as heartily as the citizens of Sandeni they'd come to conquer.

At the high table the Cascani Factor was on his feet, slamming his big hands together. The Chancellor stood more deliberately, to offend his guest. Anakerie sat a long moment, then allowed herself a regal smile that acknowledged the singer's skill and her incredible audacity. Then, the last in all the room, she, too, rose from her chair and offered up a proper and polite round of applause.

"My lords," the Chancellor cried, using the voice he turned to whenever debate in parliament got a bit too rambunctious, "ladies and gentlemen, I crave your indulgence a small while longer. There is something"—and this he directed more to Anakerie—"I should like you to see before we end this night's festivities. I hope it will put our forthcoming discussions in their proper context."

"There's no need to show me the Wall," she said with relaxed charm as he led her among the crowd to the eastward-facing bank of windows. "It's been in my face for far too long."

"I don't doubt it."

The Chancellor beckoned to an aide, who proceeded to summon Duguay and Elora over. "A magnificent per-

444

formance," he told them. "I especially liked your final song."

"The Chancellor is too kind," Elora said with a shallow curtsy.

Anakerie took a slow measure of the girl. Her eyes were on a level with Elora's nose, which wasn't so terribly bothersome unless the girl wasn't done growing.

"Allow me to present Anakerie, Warlord of the Maizan."

Another curtsy, deeper and more formal, a gesture of authentic respect.

"Your Royal Highness," Elora said.

"That's a title I don't use anymore." The unspoken conclusion lay between them: *for a realm that no longer exists.*

The aide returned and whispered in the Chancellor's ear.

"Ah. Splendid. We're ready."

"For what, may I ask?"

"You may well, my lady. You know, my founding great helped lay the first foundations of this city. He was a bricklayer, charter member of the guild."

"How nice."

"But he knew the great truth about this place. . . ."

"Which my founding great—a quaint phrase that, Chancellor—also recognized about Angwyn the instant he saw the Bay and the King's Gate. What of it?"

"It's true, our location plays a major role in our prosperity. But there's another leg we stand on, and I thought this would be the ideal opportunity to present it to you."

Anakerie's officers stirred nervously, drawing a bit together and slipping through the crowd to vantage points where they could better defend their warlord in case of trouble. They had no obvious weapons on them but they were prepared and more than ready to improvise. Most likely a futile effort, they knew, but they planned to go down swinging and not alone.

The Chancellor made a hand gesture to his aide. "Alert the semaphores, Nerys."

Despite the cold, the windows, which also served as towering doorways, opened to allow those who wished out onto the lawn. Elora led the small charge, and wasn't surprised to find Anakerie close behind, though the Angwyn Princess was gathering a heavy cloak across her shoulders while Elora herself remained bare and unprotected.

"You'll catch your death like that, girl," Anakerie cautioned.

"Your Highness is too kind."

"There's room to share."

Anakerie held the cloak open.

For a moment the two women faced each other, tension plain between them. Then Elora repeated the shallow curtsy she'd made inside.

"I am in your debt, Anakerie," she said lightly as she stepped beside the Warlord, into the comforting shelter of her cloak.

"Good. Someday I'll hold you to it. Tell me, Elora, what's the big surprise?"

"Blessed if I know. *Oh!*" The exclamation came in response to the lighting of giant torches, mounted on the end of the semaphore arms. The two women couldn't see the signal tower directly, since it stood on another headland closer to the cataracts, but its fires burned intensely enough to shine right through the wide-open rooms of Cascani House.

That cry of surprise and wonder proved but the first of many, as people scurried hither and yon across the yard, mindless of the cold as they rushed to catch sight of the line of torches which were lighting in sequence along both shores of Lake Morar, all the way from the cataract to the falls.

In the distance, the spectacular waterfalls were defined at night by the phosphorescence of the water itself, cascading off rocks during their descent or when they crashed into the lake below. Either way, the trails appeared as haunted, pale silver on blackest indigo.

The double line of torches reached the base of the

towering cliffs and there Elora, suitably impressed, assumed would be the end of it.

Then was heard a collective gasp, from a score and more of watching mouths, with pointing, outstretched arms to match, as a second line of torches appeared atop the Wall itself, stretching south toward the Shados and north beyond the point of easy sight.

It has to be miles, Elora thought, and marveled at the logistics of the enterprise, to get so great a number of Sandeni's pugnaciously opinionated citizenry to volunteer for *anything,* especially when it involved standing in freezing cold on a bleak winter's night.

The Chancellor wasn't done yet, for in the far distance out across the prairie, colossal bonfires burst simultaneously into flame atop each of the Three Maidens.

From the darkness Elora heard a voice begin the closing verses of her song, followed by the refrain. Another voice joined, and then another and another, until the entire lawn was filled with her music. The next refrain, though, was taken up by voices outside the wall and it quickly spread down onto the beach, where soldiers stood at relaxed attention. They sang, too, as did the torch holders on the shore, and in a surprisingly short time, those atop the cliff as well.

It was a memorable sight, one every person present knew they'd carry as a treasured memory to their grave, thousands upon thousands of people, holding lit torches in the chill winter darkness, until even more amazingly they all broke into song. The final refrain of Elora's anthem. She didn't know if they could see her from on high, she didn't rightly care as she strode to the tip of the promontory and threw up her hands as an exhortation for more joyous noise.

The wind was against her but still she heard laughter and good cheer and the crescendoing lyrics of her song.

"My people have spoken, milady," the Chancellor said, leaning close to Anakerie so he could make himself heard. "We are a free people, this is a free and independent land. And will remain so evermore. Tell that to your castellan."

The smile she returned to him was just as diplomatic. In her eyes, though, was a terrible sadness.

"We all have dreams, Chancellor," she replied as she looked toward the small, deceptively slight figure of Elora Danan. "Come the dawn, however, we must deal with the world as it *is*."

CHAPTER
14

ELORA DIDN'T WANT TO LEAVE.

The official guests departed in good time and smart order, though there was some agitation among the Maizan when Anakerie decided to stay awhile longer. They considered every town that wasn't theirs hostile territory and preferred their visits kept as short as possible. They kept to themselves and stayed mainly inside Cascani House.

Someone had lit a fire on the promontory and a small group gathered to share some wine and watch the lights sparkle atop the cliff. Quite a number had planted their burning torches on the Wall and despite the occasional gaps the sight remained impressive.

"How many you think?" wondered Ryn, who'd snuggled himself so close to the flames that his fur was actually steaming. In all the excitement earlier, no one noticed him clamber out of the lake and hide himself onshore. It was the first time she'd ever heard him complain of being cold and Elora was concerned he might set himself alight in his desire for warmth.

"Up there?" She shook her head. She still wore her costume, wanting to prolong the sense of power and grace she'd achieved during her performance. Duguay had produced the carryall satchels with their belongings and, most thankfully, her own tartan cloak, which was slung over her shoulders and under her backside both to keep her warm and to provide somewhere dry to sit upon the ground.

She tried to count but quickly gave up in favor of a single, spoken "Lots."

Someone offered a beer, but it took only the merest sip to remind herself why she didn't drink the stuff. She preferred her bread baked, sometimes toasted, never brewed. She was content with water, with the company, with the view.

Morar was the first lake below the falls, and the greatest, larger than the five that followed put together, better than three miles wide and near a dozen long. According to local legend, it was formed when a promontory rock calved off the face of the Wall to strike the earth with such terrible force that it opened a huge fissure that in turn became the basin floor of the lake. The land rose at the western end to form a headland to the cataracts, and those same tales claimed that the rocks jumbled there were the leftover summit of the original fallen pillar. Which was a neat trick, when one considered that the length of the lake was better than ten times the height of the rock that supposedly made it.

That was the nature and delight of legends. Truth was quickly relegated to the status of an afterthought, if not forgotten altogether.

Hearing that, and thinking of her own life, Elora had to chuckle.

The lake district was as thickly settled as atop the plateau, in a scattering of separate villages and townships. This close to the Wall there were no great farms, but every house had a plot of land sufficient for a garden, some even for an orchard. The earth was rich and water abundant. The only real drawback was the lack of fresh game, as the ever-encroaching settlements drove local animal life farther away.

The moon had just cleared the Wall, looking for those briefest of instants as though it rested precisely atop the two topmost spires of the Citadel. Its light lay across the surface of the water like a swath of silver paint, in a shade that matched Elora's skin. From this distance, and in this light, Elora could only make out three streams of water, and two of them came together halfway down the crag. The third she recognized as the Paschal, dropping straight and true as a plumb line to Morar below.

"It sounds like thunder," she said, with the same still reverence she'd use in a church.

"You get used to it." Ryn nodded.

There was a mild explosion of talk, thickly laced with profanities, from around the far side of the bonfire, which turned out to be a group of ministerial aides enthusiastically lampooning the talks their superiors would begin on the morrow.

The opening Maizan position (absolute surrender) would be rejected as wholly unacceptable by the Sandeni, nor in all likelihood would the Maizan think much of the initial Sandeni response (Go to hell, dog robbers!). For the week following, the trained and motivated professionals on both staffs would bustle back and forth, presenting appropriate position papers, trading on nuances, seeking out the slightest room to maneuver, looking for someone to bribe or better yet blackmail, angling all the while for a resolution both sides might be able to live with. In the meanwhile many intemperate and highly provocative remarks would be exchanged (*off* the record, thank you very much) by both sides regarding each other's ancestry and/or amorous proclivities.

Then a deal would be struck.

"Or," someone said casually, managing with one phrase to kill all the laughter and good humor the comedic tirade had generated, "there'll be war."

"I'd call the Maizan demented," Ryn said with a lazy stretch, "if I didn't know what drives 'em."

"We *don't* know what drives them, Ryn," Elora retorted quietly, though given the roar of the crackling fire and the noise opposite from the drinking party it was doubtful even normal tones could be overheard. "That's the trouble."

They heard laughter, inspired by a series of not terribly inventive japes that under the circumstances were accepted by one and all as screamingly funny.

"How do you tell a generous Maizani offer from a nasty one?"

"You can have your severed head served on a plate, my good man, or set on a pike before the city gate as food for crows."

"How utterly charming," Elora said with a sour expression.

"The jest or the commentary? What did you mean before, 'We don't know'?"

"Plain words, Ryn, plainly spoken."

"Humor me, I'm sick."

"Don't say that!" she snapped.

He hunched himself around, his expression serious, and she yearned to see him as she had during that madcap flight from Angwyn. She'd never met anyone so instantly comfortable, never told him that she often thought of him as her stuffed bear made flesh.

"I've been a churl and a swine lately," he said. "I owe you my life, Elora, and I never made the time to offer a proper thank-you."

"That's all right."

"I was raised better than that."

"I only wish I could have found a way to set things right."

"You can't save everyone." Her eyes began to flash

and he held up a temporizing hand. "Rather, not everyone can be saved. Is that better?"

"Not much. Not really. And you'd better not number yourself among them, do you hear?"

"And obey!" Unspoken, amusedly, went the addition *most dread and royal high-and-mighty-ness!*

"Why hasn't he found me, Ryn?"

He knew full well she meant the Deceiver. "Count your blessings, if you please."

"Was I that well hidden among the Rock Nelwyns? I mean, if you listen to him I'm the ultimate object of his desire. Here's a creature possessing such power he can ensorcell Angwyn *and* the monarchs of the Twelve Great Realms. He slew a dragon, he set Cherlindrea's sacred forest ablaze, why does he come after me with surrogates? He posted a *reward,* for goodness' sakes!"

"Perhaps he's not so impressive as you think. Or perhaps he needs his power to keep Cherlindrea and the others enchained?"

"Interesting supposition. And that's my point. After all this time what do we truly know? He's not Bavmorda, of that I'm sure. This war is not about the acquisition of power for its own sake or for personal self-aggrandizement. He has a goal and a purpose and we can't fight him effectively until we know what it is."

"Ask Keri, why don't you?" He gestured toward the house with his chin. "She's standing over there on the veranda." His smile broadened, as if in acknowledgment of a private joke. "She sits on one side of the bench, Thorn on the other, trying to make the world think they're simply sharing a common space. She's Mohdri's warlord, remember, bet she's privy to all his secrets."

"Don't talk silly. That's as dumb a notion as the jokes they're telling. And stop using that name, she hates that, she used to box my ears in Angwyn whenever I did."

"The Princess Royal struck the Sacred Princess?" He sounded delightfully scandalized.

"I think it was a matter of defiance of her father, and of putting me in my place. I was pretty unbearable."

"You're looking thoughtful again."

"What are you staring at, rude boy?"

"You, actually. That's a becoming costume."

"Duguay's design." Ryn's feelings about that name were plain and immediate, as was her response. "Oh, don't start, Ryn," she pleaded, taking him by the hand, "please, not tonight, it's too lovely a night, don't spoil things."

"Very becoming," he conceded. "A compliment to the woman who wears it."

She flushed so fast, so intensely her skin felt like it was glowing.

"Tell me more," he said, "about the Deceiver."

"I'd like to," she said. "I've got to tell it to Thorn and I'm pretty nervous about it. Sometimes I wonder if I'm the only one who understands, but then I think, these past months, maybe I'm the only one who's had time to look. The rest of you were too busy doing.

"The Deceiver is the catalyst, the preeminent *current* threat, but he is *not* what this is all about. It's the *Realms,* you see, twelve component aspects of a single whole— like parts of a body—trying to pull themselves apart in different directions. If the Deceiver hadn't kicked them all in the teeth by lopping off their titular heads in Angwyn, I'd stake my title that most of them would probably be at war by now."

"I thought your Ascension was supposed to stop all that."

"Ryn, you saw me then. Would one word from my mouth have the slightest credibility? Would I have even cared? I looked around that hall and the first thought that came to mind was, now at last I get my own back!

"The Deceiver is an opportunistic infection, the disease is the Realms' refusal to live together."

"You can't force them to, Elora."

"Then we have to close the World Gates, just like the Deceiver's doing, and sacrifice those Realms as a doctor might a gangrenous limb to save the patient. There may be battles by armies, but the war itself is for the hearts and minds and souls of the people."

"Good luck winning them over, my girl."

"I'm not Anakerie, I can't run an army. But I can make people *listen,* Ryn. I can make them think and feel, and possibly even *learn.*"

"One soul at a time?"

"If I have to. That's the other difference between us, the Deceiver and me. He's a monarch, as much as any of those he's ensorcelled. He orders, others obey. The change he brings the world crashes down from above. I'm starting at the bottom, with ordinary people. His way is faster, my hope is that mine will last."

"Until the world freezes, anyroad."

His ears quirked, ever so slightly, and he went completely still.

"Do you hear that?" Elora wondered to him softly.

"Hard to distinguish over the competition."

"It sounded like a hunting horn."

Ryn was about to scoff when a piercing cry of alarm brought them both around to behold Rool running flat out toward them across the lawn.

"Elora!" he called. And then, impossibly, louder still, *"Elora Danan!"*

The hubbub around the fire vanished as if a switch had been thrown or a door slammed shut, until one querulous voice inquired, "The Sacred Princess? *Here?*"

"Rool," she cried, "what have you *done?*"

"Someone answered him?" they heard. And then: "Who's over there?" And then, the words all tumbling one upon the other, too many voices speaking at once, "No one but that ragmop of a Wyr." "Isn't that the singer, what's-her-name?" "Her name's Elora." "Her name's *Elora!*" That last was a shout, followed by the clatter and thump of too many bodies trying to untangle themselves into coherent motion at once, with no thought and less coordination.

In the meanwhile Rool had reached Elora and hurled himself to her shoulder.

"Go!" he roared to them both. "Don't question, don't argue, just *go!* Can't you hear that bloody bedamned horn, now *go!*"

They were on their feet and moving in mid-harangue, faster with every step. The Ryn Elora remembered would have been to the house like a shot. Instead she had to hurry him along.

The horn sounded again, far louder than before, and underlying it was the sound of hoofbeats.

"What the hell is that?"

She would have stopped and turned for a look in the direction of the sound, many others did, but Rool started shrieking in her ear and she hardly slackened her pace.

"You remember Ganthem's?" he told her.

"I'll never forget," was her reply.

"You aren't the only one. The difference is, High Elves never forgive."

The first horses of the Wild Hunt cleared the boundary wall of the estate as Elora and Ryn reached the steps of the veranda. She labeled them horses because that is what they most closely resembled, but these were no horses, any more than the riders could be mistaken for human. The animals gibbered with rage and hunger and she thought for an awful moment that she was being chased once more by Bavmorda's Death Dogs. In that moment it was clear to her where the Demon Queen had acquired that damnable strain of hunting hound.

The horses struck the earth with hooves composed of three huge, hooked claws, each step gouging terrible wounds in the ground as a foretaste of what they would do to prey. Realizing their peril, far too late, those still on the lawn began to run.

None survived more than a couple of steps.

They fell beneath those awful hooves, or the fangs that filled these animals' mouths instead of a ruminant's flat teeth, or the gleaming crystal blades of the riders. There was blood as they fell and screams strangely after, as though the souls of the slain were being dragged to some hideous fate.

A sword was leveled in Elora's direction and a squad wheeled with such precision, making a right-angle turn without losing a single step, they might have been mounted on turntables. Ryn took her in his arms, and before she could protest, much less struggle, he hurled her across the patio and through the nearest open doorway.

Then he turned to face the onrushing charge.

He thrust a bench into the path of one, hoping to trip the beast, but its unearthly agility allowed it to spring over with ease. He didn't stop to think, events were happening so quickly, the battle erupting with such sudden and extreme ferocity, that by the time he'd done so he'd be dead. The Wyr ducked under a second beast and unhorsed its rider, whose neck made a satisfying and final *krak* when he landed.

Sadly, numbers and his own debilitated state worked against him. Even as Elora clambered to her feet inside, a horse delivered a fearsome body blow, ramming its chest into him. He went flying, another rider drawing blood with a sweeping slash of his blade, another mount finishing the job with a rake of its claws as Ryn crashed unmoving to the steps.

A whole host of voices screamed their protest at that sight. Elora's was one, but her outcry was nothing compared with the one uttered by Anakerie as she charged down a flight of stairs.

"A sword," she bellowed, as she would on any battlefield.

"The Danan," one of the riders called out in a glorious tenor. "Where lies the Danan?"

Elora had already been seen. As she pitched herself clear of its path a horse burst through the glass doorway, filling the air with a shower of glittering and deadly shards. Neither horse nor rider appeared affected by the impact, and any hope Elora entertained that the animal might have a harder time on the polished floor were instantly dashed as its claws punched through the gleaming tile as if it were rice paper.

Duguay had brought her traveling pouches with the cloak and she'd automatically strapped them on. Now, scrambling to find footing of her own and keep track of the attackers, she thrust a hand inside, to come up with her long sword.

"Anakerie," she called, in a fair approximation of the

Warlord's combat tones, and threw the weapon to her, while drawing its companion mid-length blade for herself.

With a wild grin and a war cry to match, Anakerie leaped into the air for the sword. She was spinning as she caught it, completing a full revolution by the time she touched down again, using the momentum of that movement and the speed she built up to add to the force of her first blow.

It took the nearest horse across the neck and without pause sliced deep into the rider as well. Shock made him jerk the reins, so that both he and his mount collapsed into a sideways crash that sent them skidding across the floor, the rushing torrents of their lives staining it scarlet behind them.

Elora stood staring, a little bit of shock, far more disbelief, at the sight. It wasn't the brutality of the moment that startled her but the sheer beauty of the slain elf knight. As a race, they were at least a head taller than the tallest Daikini, attenuated creatures whose general resemblance to Daikini served to make them even more unreal to the eye. His armor was hide sandwiched between a lacquer laminate, the pieces fastened together by an intricate array of brocade ties. Somehow, though the armor was as hard to the touch as steel plate, it followed the specifics of the wearer's form so that it appeared almost skin-snug. Underneath, for padding, was a quilted jacket, with baggy trousers to match. The fundamental elegance of the being itself was sustained through every aspect of its being, whether clothes or weapons. Form was wedded to function on every level, to create an appearance of consummate loveliness.

To look at these warriors, it was hard to see them as a threat. They were too beautiful.

For many, that was a fatal mistake.

Elora was still for all of a matter of seconds, and that was nearly her last mistake as well. A warrior aimed his sword at her back, the young woman sensing his presence a fraction too late, turning to face him too slowly to save herself.

Rool's arrow struck at the elf knight from Elora's shoulder, Franjean's from the upstairs landing, striking him one after the other with all the fierce life energy the brownies could imbue them with, fueled by their rage at this attack and their even more desperate concern for Elora's safety. The elf flew off his saddle as though he'd been lasso'd from behind, hammered backward onto the wall with such force that he cracked his armor if not his bones. He was hurt but far from finished, and struggled up from where he fell, his face twisting with rage and pain and exertion.

Rool nocked another shaft and let fly, but he'd used too much of his life force in that first reflexive response. The arrow he fired had hardly more energy than an ordinary flight, and even though the parry was ugly, the elf was able to bat it aside with his sword. He swung for Elora and just as she had done in her training duels with Khory, her own curved blade rose to check him. He was faster than any Daikini, even bashed and battered as he was, but Elora had honed her skills against the demon child, whose speed was beyond belief. There were none of the harsh sounds of contact between steel blades, this engagement like the others raging throughout the room and yard beyond was marked by a succession of sweet chimes as metal struck crystal.

Before this exchange was done, Elora knew she had him.

"Yield," she called to him. "Lay down your weapon."

He nodded shallowly, curtly, let his sword fall. Elora didn't want to take her eyes off him or lower her guard, so she called on Rool to tell her what was happening behind her back.

That was what the elf was waiting for. He had no respect for Elora's abilities, even though they were proving better than his own, it was the brownie he regarded as the only legitimate threat. As soon as Rool looked away, knives appeared in both his hands as if by magic, though in fact they'd come from spring-loaded sheathes strapped against his forearms. With a sideward sweep of the leg, he struck at Elora's wrist to slap her sword aside. That done, he meant to bury both his daggers in her unprotected back.

Except that she was turning even as he was, reacting only the barest instant behind him. A kick intended to break bones and possibly disarm her made only the most marginal contact as she folded at the knees, dropping at the same time into a crouch.

Here, the elf's height worked against him. He couldn't bend quite as fast and his own momentum made it that much harder to reverse direction. Suddenly he was the one who was vulnerable, Elora spinning through a single revolution like a top.

There was no time. For hesitation, for second thoughts, for anything. Both combatants were committed to a course of action that could not be recalled.

The elf began to mouth a curse, but in Sandeni they were little more than words. The last thing he saw was Elora's face. There was no rage in her, only a great sorrow.

Her aim was as true as Anakerie's as she stabbed upward through the side seam of his breastplates, beneath his ribs, into his heart.

There was no time to react to his death, a sweep of her gaze across the room conveyed the whole of the situation.

Anakerie stood alone on the veranda, straddling Ryn's body, her gown ruined by dark stains on the glorious blue fabric, the sword Elora gave her whipping through the air faster than any eye could follow, her body moving only slightly slower as she stood her ground against every warrior that came against her.

Within the ballroom was an ever-more-chaotic melee, a mad mix of struggling bodies, shouts and screams, the clash of blades and fists.

"Where's Franjean," she demanded of Rool, "where's Thorn?"

She didn't dare use her InSight to find them, she needed all her wits to stay alive.

"Maizan!" she heard, and saw Anakerie's escort,

armed and armored, charging on foot into the room like a cresting wave, shoulder to shoulder. They had no shields, but they wore steel head to toe and accepted no foe from either side of the Veil as their equal.

Warriors came together with an audible crash and the form of battle dissolved instantly into a myriad of individual combats. The Daikini would seem to have the key advantage, since the very substance of their weapons was anathema to their opponents and in this crowded and relatively confined space the elves would not be able to utilize their extraordinary speed. The Maizan assumed as well that the elven armor would be no defense against their scimitars.

To their surprise, and very quickly their horror, that proved not to be the case. Faery armor could be broken, but only with a tremendous effort, and while that blow might prove successful, it left the warrior who delivered it exposed to other attacks. The enemy in front was not the paramount threat, but the two who struck from either side.

The opposing forces could not be more different, in appearance and in style. With the entrance of the Maizan, the Daikini appeared as dark, brutish shapes, workmanlike and graceless, stamped from a single mold. By contrast, though the elves fought in concert they never lost their individuality, or the phenomenal grace that made this appear more like a performance than a pitched and bloody battle. No striking cobra could hope to match their speed, and their strength beggared description. Blows from the Maizan that would have slain any other foe too often spent themselves on empty air. Before that luckless warrior could recover himself his life was done. Or a pair of hands would close on some poor man's head, with long, elegant fingers you'd think would have trouble cracking an eggshell. There would be a moment of dread realization, when the Daikini so caught might mistakenly believe he'd just been clamped between the jaws of some vise, and then a twist of those delicate wrists would break his neck.

The Maizan were valiant, they were skilled, they were doomed.

Khory Bannefin saved them.

She wore no armor, save a shirt of fine mail beneath her leather tunic. She faced the elves with a sword in either hand and a look of wild joy on her face. Fast as the elven warriors were, she proved faster, her thrusts and parries an ongoing masterpiece of precision. Not a move was wasted, nor an opportunity missed. She killed for herself, she drove her foes onto the swords of others, she took so great a toll in so short a time that the elves had to fall back a few steps to try to regroup.

She gave them no chance, but lunged forward to bury the point of one blade in a naked throat, pivoting sideways to stroke her edge across another's shoulder to nearly sever his arm, backhanding her second blade to parry an attack, following through and completing her turn with the first blade to open her foe across the hips. The elf dropped, yowling in agony, ravaged as much by the touch of her steel as the actual damage she'd inflicted with that dreadful wound until a following Maizani finished him. By then, Khory had moved ahead, to another duel, another victory.

Thorn used no blade, but fought with a quarterstaff twice his height that reminded Elora of the rod the Lord Regent of Lower Faery had carried on Tyrrel's Tor. He was hard to reach with swords, though short enough to be stomped on, but he never let his adversaries come close enough to try. With a fair speed of his own, and an uncanny accuracy, he stabbed out with the point of his staff as though it was a lance, at ankles and knees and groin, blows meant to harry and possibly cripple, and if his attacks doubled that unlucky warrior over so that his head came in range, Thorn would shift his grip on the polished ironwood and slap the elf down with a sharp clout to jaw or skull. At the same time Franjean kept up a harassing fire of his own, conserving his energies after that initial burst to save Elora, intent not so much on inflicting mortal harm as on distracting as many of the elves as possible so that other hands might finish the job.

One set of those hands belonged to Renny Garedo,

and Elora saw at once that he was being especially hard-pressed amidst a pile of still forms who were more Daikini in Sandeni and Cascani livery than they were warriors of Greater Faery. He'd led his men as well as they had fought, which was with all the courage any leader could hope for, but his very presence seemed to inspire the elves to a manic ferocity, as though his existence was an insult that couldn't be borne.

Renny made no attempt to escape, or join forces with other defenders. Quite the opposite. He used the elves' focus on him to draw them away from more valuable targets, making plain that he considered his life fair exchange for those of Thorn and Elora.

Elora thought differently.

There were only a few Maizan left, but they were advancing steadily on to the veranda. The flow of battle had swirled Khory to the side, placing her closer to Thorn and Renny.

She didn't attempt to use her speaking voice. After her performance, there was precious little of it left. Even in top-notch condition, she wasn't sure she could make herself heard over this din. She didn't like using mindspeech with Khory. Each contact brought with it a reminder that the human structure of her thoughts was only a surface construct. Beneath it, like an ocean beneath an ice field, was something deep and dark and wholly unfathomable, whose essence was the deadliest entity known to the Twelve Realms. That was why, in this battle, Khory proved as much a lightning rod as Renny. The elves sensed the dual nature of the demon child and saw this as an opportunity to revenge themselves on a race they hated almost as much as they hated the Daikini.

There was no time for doubts, or hesitation. Thoughts had to give birth instantly to action or they were of no use.

"Khory," Elora called in mindspeech. "Bring Renny to Thorn, stay with them both."

There was no entreaty to what she said. As before

with Rool, these were royal commands, and meant to be obeyed.

She heard no acknowledgment from Khory, expected none. Trusting the warrior woman to do what was right, Elora turned her attention the other way.

Rool had heard her instructions. He had his own thoughts about them.

"Best you join 'em, Elora, safety in those swords."

She kept her silence and let her body answer for her. She'd taken hardly a step before Rool realized her intent and hullabaloo'd a protest.

"Are you *demented,* girl? Stop this foolishness, this instant, before we're both of us for the high jump!"

"I won't let you die today, Rool."

"What about *you?*"

"Anakerie's fighting on her own! I can't leave her!"

"She's a trained professional, you silly nit, this is what she was *born* to do!" In his agitation, the brownie cast aside all sense of propriety and tact, saying whatever came to mind and contemplating worse in a vain attempt to deflect Elora from her headstrong course.

Franjean heard the outcry. In this close a proximity, what one of them saw the other instantly knew, and he wasted no time in telling Thorn. They all recognized the danger but there was nothing to be done about it. The press of bodies arrayed against them was too great, they had to secure their own position first.

Elora sent a chair skidding across the veranda, catching one elven warrior in time to turn a fatal stab into a nasty slash that glanced messily off the bones of Anakerie's back. As though the move had been intended all along, she reversed her grip on her sword and stroked its tip across the elf's throat. Blood fountained, life fled, and she brought the curved blade around and up to parry the thrust of another foe. Their weapons crossed only twice more before Elora was on him from the side in a tackle that pitched him into a tangle of bushes. Again without missing a beat, Anakerie scooped up one of the elven knives and hurled it at him with a sideways flick of the wrist.

"What are you doing here?" she snarled at the younger woman as they stood shoulder to shoulder over Ryn's still form, their blades weaving a daunting, deadly pattern before them while Rool did what he could from his perch atop Elora's shoulder.

"I thought you needed help."

"*Your* help, singer? That'll be the day."

"We stay long enough, Highness, that day may yet dawn."

How long they fought, neither could tell. A clock might tell them minutes and they would say it lied, because to them it seemed like hours passing. They were hard-pressed from every side, even after they were joined by the two or three Maizan to fight their way to the veranda. The sights and sounds and smells, every physical sensation, blurred and distorted in Elora's perceptions into a ravening pandemonium that stripped the moments of their consequence. She lost all sense of herself as a being, and worse, of those she fought as well. They became objects, as did she, and the fact that flesh opened when she cut it and blood spilled and eyes turned glassy lost its meaning. She fought as fiercely as she was able because her life was at stake, and that of friends and comrades, but that was a truth her body knew far better than her mind.

Then, from nowhere, disaster.

An elf, already cut to the quick by Anakerie, deliberately impaled himself on Elora's shorter blade. His hands closed about her, one on an arm, the other to her crotch, and with a tremendous heave he threw her to the lawn. Too late, Anakerie brought her own blade across his body in a blow of equal power that separated head and one shoulder from the rest of him.

Elora landed badly but forced herself to her hands and knees, taking a quick bearing so she'd know the best way to scuttle, first thoughts not for herself but for Rool. She called aloud with mindspeech and felt her heart contract when he didn't reply.

She heard an outcry from the veranda, saw Anakerie's charge to her side blocked by a mounted elf whose animal quickly gutted one of the Maizan with its foreclaws. She heard the approach of other horses but had hardly begun to move before she felt something light as gossamer fall across her lower legs. An instant later a scream of real pain was torn from her as those nigh-weightless strands cinched themselves so tight she thought her bones would splinter.

She tried to move but the best that could be managed was to flop about like a landed fish as she caught sight of bands of glittering energy burning on the surface of her flesh.

"I have the Danan," she heard, and saw an elf dismount.

"Kill the bitch," shrieked another, still on horseback.

"That is not the plan, nor was it the task set before us."

"A pox on both. We've lost too many this hunt, she's not worth the price!"

"And what is a Wild Hunt, my friend, if the quarry proves us easy prey? You are more than wrong, her courage this night is proof of that. The Danan is beyond all price. And soon she will be ours."

From a pouch, the elf withdrew a ring big enough to fit Elora's neck as a collar. It was gold, four fingers broad by half a finger width deep, etched with runes and sigils that flashed a sickly lime fire from some impossible depth and made her nauseous as she tried to gain a proper sense of them.

It broke in half in his grip, like any ordinary piece of jewelry, but to Elora it registered like some dreadful predator baring its fangs before its prey. She struggled against the bonds that held her, cast about frantically for something to use as a weapon. She caught sight of Rool, sprawled unmoving on a shattered flagstone, and as quickly looked away for fear her eyes would lead the elves to him while he was helpless. The elf thrust the collar forward to ring her neck with it, and looked down on her pityingly as she blocked him with her hands. She didn't try to hold him by the arms, but instead put both hands against the collar itself, trying with all her might to push both it and elf away.

The stalemate didn't last.

To her horror, Elora felt the metal beneath her fingers soften. It was too close for her to see, but desperation cast forth her InSight, giving her a fragmented, kaleidoscopic vision of the scene through the eyes of both her attackers. The collar began to flow like putty, sending forth questing tendrils—all suffused with that sickly radiance—around her gloved hands, through the spaces between her fingers, to reach almost languidly toward the exposed column of her throat. Without any knowledge why, the certainty came to Elora that the moment one of those strands touched her, encircled her, her fate was sealed.

A brace of brownie arrows bludgeoned the elf on horseback with the force of a battery of thunderstones, his lacquer breastplate shattering from the irresistible blows, as did the heart and bones beneath.

At the same time Elora heard a bellow of raw rage together with the whistle of something solid through the air, saw from the topmost tilt of her eyes the looming shape of Thorn Drumheller as he swung his quarterstaff like a bat with all the strength in his compact Nelwyn form. The elf's skull broke from that monstrous impact as readily as his companion's armor, and then another figure crossed Elora's vision as Khory's blade passed before her in a blur of motion to sever the dead man's hands from his falling corpse. With a cry of her own, Elora pitched the collar as far from her as possible.

"It's all right," Thorn told her as she scrabbled for purchase on the slick and trampled grass. "It's all right," he repeated over and over, gentling her as he would any panicked child, as he had his own when they were frightened.

Yelling for Khory's assistance, for once making no mention of her antecedents, Franjean made his way down Thorn's sleeve until he could leap to the nearest level of steps and race to his comrade's side.

"The elves?" Elora asked, the best she could manage a raw and husky whisper.

"They're done," Anakerie replied, where she stood alone.

They were all of them a sight, scored with blood, and some of that their own. Their clothes were a ruin, stained with sweat and filth and torn in the bargain. About them all was the stench of death, an awareness of the lives they'd taken, but more of the fact of their own survival. None could quite believe it.

"What," Elora tried again, "happened here?"

"What better way to win a war," Thorn noted idly, as if they were having a discussion over dinner at Black-Eyed Susan's, "than to strike off your enemy's head and possibly claim their greatest talisman, their true hope, for your own?"

"Murder me, you mean?" Anakerie asked him, taking a moment to see for herself that he was whole and relatively unharmed. Their glance lingered only moments on one another, and the touch of his fingers to hers as she passed was even briefer, but both spoke volumes.

"You, and the Chancellor, the Factor, as many of the notables as could be put to the sword. It worked at Angwyn for the Deceiver, why not here as well?"

"There are those who learn from history," she said in grim appreciation of the stratagem, "solely in order to repeat it."

With a terrific wrench of the legs, baring her teeth in a howl to match, before any of the others could make a further move to help, Elora broke the bonds that held her. The effort left her panting, in a spasm of shuddering sobs that she buried along with her face in the folds of Thorn's robe.

"That was a tanglefoot web," Renny noted to no one in particular. "Those can't be broken."

"It's magic," Khory told him. "Can't hold her."

Renny held up the collar they'd tried to affix about Elora's neck. "This is magic, too. It's a Slave Ring. It binds the wearer, body and soul. They're said to be worth a King's ransom."

"Keep it away from me," Elora cried out, as did Thorn, with a different pronoun.

"If this has been keyed to you, Elora," the constable said, "it's a danger for as long as you live. Unless you find the Mage who made it and have him release the binding spell."

"Destroy it, then." She hunkered herself closer to Thorn, gathering her sore legs snug beneath her for their protection.

"To be honest, I don't know if that's possible."

"What's the danger, if she's immune?" Anakerie asked.

"This is *old,* milady," Renny told her, and the others as well. "None can relate its origins, all that is known is how to bring it into being—by means so foul I will not relate them—and then make use of it. You saw how she fought, her soul knew full well what it faced here. She'd have accepted death before this collar. The Slave Ring is an abomination, as is the fiend who commissioned it. Neither is to be trifled with."

Elora turned tear-streaked cheeks to Thorn. "The wheels have no hub to anchor them."

He nodded. "And so begin to spin ever more fiercely out of control."

"And that's your role, little Sacred Princess," Anakerie mocked from up by Ryn as she tended as best she could to his wounds and tried to make him more comfortable, "to hold things all together?"

"There's a *pattern* to all things, damn it," Elora flared, Anakerie's gibe bringing her to her feet. "A structure."

"An order, I know. You talk like Mohdri, and make about as much sense. Listen to him long enough, you find yourself wanting to believe he really does mean best. A little present pain, to balance against a future of prosperity."

"Except he's wrong."

"And you're right?"

"The circles interlink because the world is *one.* Actions and reactions, each affect the other throughout the

469

whole. The air turns cold and Daikini suffer. But so does Lesser Faery, and who knows, perhaps the dragons do as well. In every tale, every history, they're spoken of as the source of genius, of inspiration. Theirs is the Realm we visit in our dreams. But if there are none of us to dream, what becomes of them? If there are no dragons to inspire our dreams, what ultimately of us?

"The Wall exists, that's a plain fact, and the Daikini of Sandeni had learned to live with it. As the Cascani have learned to live with the Wyrrn. As an elf and a Daikini did so Renny could be born. It's not so hard." She looked across the garden, eyes brightening with tears she would not shed at the sight of so much carnage before they finally came to rest on the collar in Renny's hand. "If you give yourself a chance."

She blinked her eyes clear and fixed them back on Anakerie. In three quick steps, she stood before the Warlord and all took note that when she scooped up her long sword and held it at the ready, Anakerie made no move to stop her. It was strange then, to think that their aspects had suddenly reversed, the Warlord, who was twice Elora's age, becoming more the child.

"What's happening?" Elora asked in a quiet, measured tone that Anakerie knew well, having used it often herself. It had nothing to do with being royal, but everything to do with leadership. "What have you done?"

"What I'm supposed to," Anakerie replied with a wan smile. "Find a way to win. That's why I have spies. So I would know the Chancellor's 'surprise'—that little demonstration on the lakeshore and the cliff—almost as soon as the idea was presented to him."

She didn't move, as though she herself had suddenly become enmeshed in a tanglefoot web, and while she spoke in a military monotone, her eyes grew ever more haunted with the realization that she had committed an offense that was unforgivable.

"With so many people on the Wall, and every eye on us out here, who's to notice what's going on behind their backs?"

"You're talking of the populace, not the military," scoffed Renny. "You can distract them as much as you like, the army will still be prepared."

"We have our own sources, Anakerie," Thorn agreed. "We'd know of any mass troop movements."

"Who said anything about 'mass,' peck?" The word was normally an insult, one that Thorn did not tolerate. From her lips, it was an endearment and an old joke between them. "And who says this has anything to do with Sandeni?" That was to Renny. "Elora understands better than I, I wish I'd realized that sooner. Sandeni is a battle, Mohdri wants to win the war."

"How?" Elora demanded of her.

"He's been drawing all the magic of the world into himself. If he becomes preeminent, if all power derives from him, then so will absolute control. He can define the relationships between the Realms, establish a peace, and then enforce it. The best way to do that, he believes . . ."

"No," Elora breathed, thunderstruck, as comprehension came to her.

". . . is by claiming the power of the dragons. At the very least, there won't be a sorcerer in any of the Realms—maybe the lot of them combined—who can actively defy him."

"What's that to do with Sandeni?" Renny asked.

"There's a *World Gate*," Elora said. "More ancient than the city, some believe one of the most ancient in the world, a portal to the Realm of the Malevoiy. The lords of ancient Faery who do not come to earth, as we Daikini who are wholly of the earth do not go to Faery. Who have to be the gatekeepers to the Circle of the Spirit. Where is it?" The question came in a rush of words as she grasped Anakerie by the shoulders. "Where's the damned Gate? *Tell* me!"

"*I don't know!* Truth, I didn't want to know. I want the war to end, I want no more blood and no more suffering, on *either* side of the Veil." She broke Elora's hold on her to sweep her arm around, encompassing the battle site. "Mohdri is a horror, something twisted and unnamable,

471

for all his shadow plays at benevolence. He may mean well, I believe he's forgotten how. There's an anguish in him that undercuts his every goal." She looked suddenly from Elora to Thorn, then down at Ryn. "He has no faith, in himself least of all. But for all of that, the Elora Danan I thought I knew was no match for him, even with Thorn Drumheller by her side.

"I was raised to wear a crown," she said at last, proudly for all her sorrow. "I have a people to care for. I don't have the luxury of fighting a lost cause. Except that may be precisely what I've done.

"I'm sorry," she said, meeting Elora's eyes. "I should have had faith."

"I had none," Elora said as gently in return. "But I learned."

She faced the others. "Whatever madness Mohdri has planned, we have to stop it."

"The problem is," Renny commented, "the Castellan's forces know where they're going."

"They may not be the only ones, but we have to get up to the tableland."

"The cable car—!"

"Too slow! Horses," Elora cried, "where are horses, we need horses!"

"Our mounts are in the stable," Anakerie said. "Take them."

"And what of you?" Thorn asked, taking her hand in both of his. She was sitting on the topmost step, Ryn's shaggy head resting on a pillow improvised from the cloak of one of her slain escort. She'd bundled the Wyr snugly in her own.

"I'm not a free agent."

"Nor is this a hopeless cause."

She smiled. "Oddly enough, I wasn't speaking of the responsibilities of state. I mean those of blood."

Ryn tightened his grip on her other hand, though a baby's would have been stronger.

"Keri," he husked, his voice a ghost of itself, as he very nearly was, "don't do this!"

"Hush," she told him, flashing her eyes back and forth between him and Thorn. "And don't call me that, only the one I love can call me that."

"Dissembler," Thorn said. "As I recall, only your *brother* could."

"Mixed blood," Ryn said weakly, "don't only live in Sandeni. Shamans among the Wyrrn read prophecy as well as anyone; they knew the coming of Elora Danan would herald a time of change, and great danger. They had an indication of the role Angwyn was to play in those events. Our mother was Wyr, and though she loved our father from the moment she first saw him, she believed it a hopeless love because of the difference between the two races. A shaper spell was used to cast her in the semblance of a Daikini, and she set forth to win the heart of Angwyn's king. He never knew that his firstborn was pledged to the service of the Wyrrn. Should prophecy come to pass, one twin would remain on land, while the other would be spirited away to sea, in hopes that whatever fate the Cataclysm presaged, one of them might survive to unite and lead both kingdoms."

"You never knew?" Thorn asked of Anakerie.

She shook her head. "When the Black Rose captured him and enchained his soul, that was my revelation. Wounds to the flesh we don't share, but our spirits . . .

"I have to take him home, Thorn. I have to *find* our home. Then I'll see about our destiny."

"We're all of us lost souls in that regard, Anakerie. Cut loose from all we've known, the better to build anew."

"You'd better go."

"I'll find you again, Keri."

"In better days, I pray."

They said no farewells, save for a kiss that started small and quickly blazed with a passion fierce as any signal bonfire.

Already mounted, Elora met Thorn at the front, and reached down to take him by the arms and set him on the saddle before her.

"Hold on," she warned as she kicked the animal into motion, "this won't be a fun ride."

Seven of them departed Cascani House at a gallop on a quartet of horses—Thorn and the brownies riding with Elora, while Khory Bannefin, Duguay, and Renny Garedo rode alone—past a host of folk rushing in the other direction to offer what belated assistance they could to those within the grounds. More than once they were challenged as they made their way as best they could out of Kinshire, but Renny's badge of office cleared the road. Elora wasn't surprised to find Duguay waiting, utterly unscathed. She would have sent the others to find him if he hadn't been there.

The road was clear and straight along the shoreline, and these were horses bred to eat the miles. They quickly settled into a steady lope that wasn't as fast as an outright gallop but which could be maintained for hours, and raced through the chill night toward the Wall.

"I need your help, Thorn."

"Asked and done, child."

"The horse is yours, I need to cut loose."

He understood her shorthand, and as she cast her In-Sight up and over the crest of the plateau, he applied his own to the thought processes of their mount, offering reassurance more than guidance as they sped along their way.

Elora shot faster than any arrow, closing her mental eyes on horseback, opening them miles farther ahead to find herself staring at a paper-strewn tabletop, badly lit by a scattering of candles amongst the detritus of too many meals taken at the work space.

The professor had dozed off. Having no time to wake him and explain, she quietly usurped control of his body, first by puffing out every light so he wouldn't inadvertently set the library afire, not to mention himself. One flame had been a little too close to a sleeve for comfort. Darkness was no impediment for her, MageSight worked quite effectively even through another's eyes.

She found his notes about the Malevoiy, and smiled

with his lips to discover a current map of the city in their midst. He'd laid out a grid system, charting the change in aspects over the centuries, to determine the likely position of the Gate when the Malevoiy were active and then relate it to the present day.

The answer made perfect sense.

There were other things she wanted to check as well, which took longer than she expected. From the desk where she preferred to work, she found the worn old storybook the professor had discovered. She had no access to her journal—that hung from her waist within the apparently boundless confines of her traveling pouch—so she had to make do with memory and whatever rough scribbles she'd made at the table. Luc-Jon's "bestiary," though, she'd left behind with the professor and she quickly flipped through one book, then the other. The last illustration in the storybook was of a wedding, a bright and joyous affair so well delineated she could easily imagine all the figures coming to life before her. As with the others, a World Gate formed the ornamental frame of the picture. A handsome man and a lovely woman danced with riotous abandon on its threshold.

She pursed the professor's lips and sighed as she turned to the earlier images. The final sigil was incomplete, but sufficient remained for her to determine a significant difference between it and the ones that preceded it.

Elora felt the tug of Thorn's awareness on her own. The riders were approaching the funicular terminus.

Page by page, resisting the Nelwyn's summons, she leafed through the bestiary, until she found what she'd been after. The match for the sigil in the storybook, save that it was complete in every detail, on the page directly following the symbol for the Lord of the Dance, the one that Carig had etched into his own Gate to summon that entity.

Before she left the professor, she walked him over to the couch that was tucked against one wall. It had seen its share of years and the embroidery was a touch threadbare, but the down pillows were still plush and the stuffing intact. To sit on it was to discover an irresistible desire to rest and many's the drowsy afternoon, with the sun illuminating dust motes in the air and warming the room as toasty as any solarium, when a momentary catnap had turned into a proper sleep. She stretched the old man's body out full-length, and used his hands to arrange a wool throw as best she could around him. Then she let him rest . . .

. . . and returned to the chase.

There was quite a commotion at the station, soldiers everywhere, constabulary as well, every defense fully manned. No one had expected an attack by the elves, and no one wanted to be caught by surprise again. As before, Renny's badge got them through, with some help as necessary from a judicious presentation of Thorn's own chain of office. They learned that the Chancellor and his party had been evacuated to the plateau, only that now reports were coming down of trouble there as well.

"We have to get up top," Renny urgently told one of the officers. "When's the next car?"

"Regular service has been suspended," was the reply. "We're running as needed."

Under escort, because Thorn was connected with the Chancellor's office and someone had just attempted a blanket assassination of the government, they made their way across the bustling promenade.

A shout rang out, echoing in the cavernous space, and they found themselves met by Tam and Rico.

"Wha's all this, then?" Tam inquired, figuring that since they were mostly familiar faces he might actually get some proper news. "We in a war?"

"They won't let us up top to go to work," Rico explained.

"We don't have time to explain, I'm afraid," said Elora. "We have to get up top ourselves."

"Mebbe we c'n hitch a ride," Tam suggested.

"No point," the sergeant commanding their escort told them. "Trolley service is suspended as well until we get this situation properly sorted out."

"That could take a while," Rico noted sardonically.

"It'll take," the sergeant said heavily, as sergeants do, "as long as it takes."

Suddenly Elora spoke up. "How familiar are either of you two with the layout beneath the plaza?"

"Me, not so much," Rico confessed, "but Tam did a stretch in maintenance and repair, working on the big wheels."

"They're with us," she said, and no one questioned her decision.

"Lookin' not so bad," she told Tam as they boarded one of the huge freight elevators. The clutch was engaged, and with a sharp jerk they began their ascent.

"Damn th' man's hands, don't he know *nothin'* 'bout his proper work?"

"Leave off, lad. Not everyone's good as you," Rico cautioned with a smile.

"I'm not tha' good, Rico, but he should be better!" He finished with his voice in a moderate shout, pitched so the funicular brakeman could hear, one professional to another. Then, to Elora, in a calmer tone: "Wha'cha need o' me, then, eh?"

A simple enough request—was there any underground access to what was called the "enchanted isle."

Rico whistled. "Don't ask much of a man, do y', 'lora. Supposedly worth a body's life to even set foot on that place, much less stage an outright break-in."

"Does that mean no?"

"Na' quite," said Tam, to the amazement of his friend. "There's a tunnel."

"You're sure?" Elora had to know. Otherwise their only way in was over the bridge.

"There's catacombs, y'see, deep under," Tam explained. "A proper rat's nest if y' don't know the way."

"And you do," Renny asked of him.

Tam shrugged. "I was young. I was curious."

"What about all the protections that place is supposed to have?"

"Give over, Rico," Tam told him, with a collegial

thump. "Them's what applies only to pure-blood Daikini, not mongrel mixed-bloods like me. Passage got found when they built the plateau terminus. Did it the hard way, too, some poor yob or other stickin' his head where it weren't allowed an' catchin' the chop for't. Architects figured pretty quick what had to be overhead, so Raasay volunteered to go walkabout through there, make sure nothin' nasty weren't hidden."

"As opposed to things that decapitate you?" Elora wondered.

"Gargoyles, they do make proper watchdogs."

"No one's ever crossed one twice," Renny agreed.

"So Raasay did the lookin' an' made the story part o' the family hist'ry."

"You know the story?"

"How else you figure I satisfied my curiosity, eh?"

"The gargoyles weren't too pleased to see Elora when she crossed the bridge up top," Rool said as Tam fished a set of keys from his kit bag and threw the bolts on an otherwise nondescript iron-banded doorway.

"Got more than a mite twitchy, they did," echoed Franjean as the door swung wide.

"There could be trouble!" they chorused in unison.

"There won't be," Khory said as she stepped over the threshold, sword in hand.

"Khory, wait," Thorn called out, hurrying after her, with Elora, Duguay, Renny, and the two others close behind. "*No!* You can't slaughter them for doing their duty!"

"I won't have to, Drumheller," she said. "Someone's done it for me."

The tunnel led them beneath the moat that surrounded the island. It was braced and shored by massive timbers, like any excavation but none of the surfaces had been lined. Walls and floor and ceiling were a mix of rock and earth, which left a perpetual dampness to the air as moisture leached down from the river. At the far end, after making their way a moderate distance, the tunnel opened into a chamber that might once have been a storage cellar of some house or other. The change in atmosphere was marked, the dank environment of the tunnel giving way instantly to air that was both warm and dry.

The gargoyles, the two Elora had marked on the cenotaphs at the bridge plus others from the gables of the various houses on the island, all lay shattered on the dusty floor, their remains strewn about with a vengeance that suggested this hadn't been an easy victory.

This was as far as Rico decided to go, as he had no Veil blood in him and less skill with any weapon, and family waiting besides. Renny would have preferred sending Tam with him but he was needed as their guide.

Elora expected to find something upright, in the manner of the Gate that Carig tried to form. Instead they came upon the largest chamber of the lot, whose walls formed a circle twenty feet across. They stood above it on a balcony, midway up the wall, from which a line of steps etched into the wall itself wound around the circle to touch bottom directly beneath them. The floor looked utterly normal, big inset blocks of paving stones coated by the dust of ages.

"No footprints," Renny said. "No sign that anyone's been here before us."

"Got lost, maybe?" Franjean interjected hopefully.

"He's been and gone," Thorn said, going to one knee right at the edge of the balcony and gazing over the edge with an intensity that would put the eagles to shame. Tam stretched his torch past him to illuminate the chamber as much as possible for the Nelwyn, unaware that MageSight rendered such solicitude unnecessary.

" 'He'?" Elora inquired.

"The Deceiver. I suppose we should be flattered. He thinks so much of this enterprise that he's come on it himself."

"How could this be?" Tam wondered. "There isn't any magic in Sandeni, tha's fact, sir."

"There's some," Thorn told him. "Sufficient to sustain the gargoyles and make comfortable any of the Veil Folk who choose to visit here, but otherwise you're right.

There's nowhere near the power required to open so ancient a Gate."

"Unless you've spent three years amassing the energies of half a continent," Elora said.

"There is that," Thorn agreed. "And brought the necessary catalysts with you."

"What do you mean?"

"See those alcoves." He pointed. "There are twelve in all."

"With statues standing watch." She nodded. "They look like they've been here as long as the Gate itself, they're worn away to almost nothing."

Thorn shook his head. "Dust they may appear, Elora, but an hour ago I'll wager they were as alive as any of us. A dozen sorcerers to act as proxy for the Realms themselves, with himself as surrogate for you."

"Has he taken everything from them?" She spoke in barely a whisper, not wanting to comprehend the enormity of what had been done to these twelve souls.

"All they are, all they were, all they ever hoped to be, in every aspect of their being. Only those shells remain, formless, featureless. This is the end result of the Rite of Ultimate Oblivion."

"How could he do such a thing? How could *any-one—*?"

"For the right prize," Renny said softly, closing his hand on her shoulder in comfort, "some men have no limit. To courage, or depravity."

"We have to follow," she said.

"Is that possible?" Renny asked.

"We shall have to see," Thorn said. "But this is as far as you can go, Constable, and you as well, Tam."

"I'm game f'r more, master, if y'll have me."

"Hold that hope, Tam," Elora told him as she gave him a hearty embrace of parting. "We're bound to need it somewhile."

"What about this one?" Renny asked, gesturing to Duguay, who was lounging patiently against the wall.

"He's with me," she said.

"We're together," was Duguay's reply, and if his words didn't make plain what that meant between him and Elora, his glance left them no illusions.

Renny didn't think much of that notion, nor did Tam, but there was nothing either could say on the matter, especially considering the circumstances.

"You've been quiet," Khory mentioned to the troubadour.

"You're quiet all the time."

"That's my nature, master jongleur."

"I have what I want. I'm where I want to be. What more is there to say?"

"Didn't see you make much of an effort at Cascani House," called one of the brownies, the first time either had addressed him directly.

"I sing and I dance, little friend," and he executed a modest but lovely step-turn, step-turn that closed with an arm outstretched to Elora. She swept her offside leg around in a shallow arc that billowed out her skirt, as lovely a move herself, but made no attempt to take his hand. In fact, her move seemed more along the lines of a parry and disengagement. As the energy of his gesture crested toward her like a wave, she simply slipped to the side and watched it pass her by.

"I'm ready," Thorn announced. "Elora, stand by me, please."

"In a moment," she told him, and turned to Renny Garedo. "Rool, Franjean, you're to stay with the constable."

"The devil you say," snapped one.

"The devil we will," echoed the other.

"This isn't a request," she said, with a quiet steel to her voice that would have impressed Anakerie. "You're both hurt, and where we go . . ."

"Our place, Elora Danan . . ." Rool began.

"Is on your shoulder," Franjean finished.

"Not this time."

"We stay . . ."

". . . but *that* one." A dagger look toward Duguay.

"Yes," she said simply, and with that word brought all discussion to an end.

Rool kept his eyes locked on Elora's, searching her gaze with his own as if to determine whether she was speaking her own mind, or some thought planted there by Duguay. At the same time Franjean rounded on Khory and bared his teeth at her in an expression that was dauntingly fierce for one so small.

"You!" he snapped at the demon child. "Keep her safe, I charge you."

"Her and him both," she replied, indicating Thorn as well. "You see me again, warriors, you'll see them."

Elora clasped her hand about the constable's forearm, in a warrior's salutation. With heads as high and backs as straight as their wounds would allow, the brownies made their way across to Renny, one staying tucked in the crook of his elbow while the other clambered all the way to his shoulder.

She took up her position by Thorn's right hand, Duguay stepping immediately to Thorn's left, with Khory a full stride behind Thorn, sufficient clearance to draw her sword while she remained close enough to actually do some good with it.

Thorn held together the fore- and middle finger of his right hand and began a tracing in the air, the symbol Elora had showed him from her research, that of the Malevoiy. In their wake a trail of autumnal fire, energies of scarlet and gold, traced the air as though he was leaving a path of burning oil on a field. The strokes were sure and clean, executed with an uncanny precision, and from the start a shape was discernible. With each additional stroke of the foundation sigil, the room began to vibrate as power was awakened and coalesced within the sleeping stones.

Even as Thorn hurried to complete the pattern that initial burst of fire began to fade.

"I was afraid of this," he muttered, "I can't sustain the manifestation."

Unbidden, Elora slid right behind him and set her hand on his with her own fingers extended as his had been. With an ease of long familiarity, InSight merged them into one, allowing his skill access to her strength, and she felt her blood burn as he began again. His hand was larger than hers, though he was a bit more than half her height, his fingers longer and more delicate, though they possessed the strength to heft boulders. Not so long ago, her skin was far smoother, unmarked by any toil. Now she wore nicks and tiny scars, calluses and scored nails, all testifying to the strength she possessed and the work she'd done to earn it.

Together they repeated the pattern, with an occasional flash of teeth from Elora as the requisite power was drawn swiftly and suddenly from her in tidal surges that announced their presence with painful cramps. This time the sigil lasted until Thorn was finished, and blazed brightly afterward.

"Well," he said, surveying his handiwork with not a little pride. "That's done."

"Nothing's happening," Elora noted.

"A key's no good unless you fit it to its lock," Thorn said.

He grasped the sigil by its outer edge and Elora raised her eyebrows to see that it remained solid to the touch as he plucked it from the air and held it in one hand. The fire didn't have the power to burn him, which seemed strange to her because she could feel its intense heat on her bare face and shoulders and belly.

Thorn took the sigil and tossed it lightly like a plate, to the precise center of the room below.

"Shall we go?" he invited them all, and led the way to the circular steps.

Chapter
15

ELORA WATCHED THE SIGIL AS THEY DESCENDED. INI-
tially it rested on the ground without having
the slightest effect on the dust and stone beneath it, making not even the slightest indentation, which made her wonder if a thing could
exist yet have no physical substance.

Then things began to happen on both sides
of her. At specific intervals along the stairway,
Thorn would describe a new set of sigils on the
wall. He needed no assistance from Elora for
this, the manifestation of the key sigil apparently generated sufficient power to sustain the
secondary symbols by itself. At the same time
the texture of the floor gradually began to alter
as well. A darkness spread outward from
where the key sigil lay, the way ink might
through water from a startled squid. The floor

turned black, and then shifted beyond that color to something altogether more intense, which reminded her of the obsidian pillars that flanked the bridge to this Faery isle.

The last step was more like a small jetty, providing room for them all to stand. Above them, in a rising spiral around the whole circumference of the room, the secondary sigils seemed to glow from someplace within the walls, as though the energies Thorn had called forth radiated from the essential fabric of the stone. The same held true for the key sigil. Viewed from the balcony before they started their descent, it appeared to float on the floor as something distinct and separate. Now, having reached what they thought was its level, it had sunk beneath the surface, its radiance suffusing the whole of the obsidian pool.

There was no movement to the substance of the pool, but it gleamed with a luster to rival the polished lacquer armor of the High Elves. Elora didn't resist the impulse to peer into its depths in search of a reflection. Disturbingly she found one, but it wasn't at all like gazing into a mirror or any other kind of reflector. There was a quality of three-dimensionality to the face that gazed back at her, and more intriguing, a solidity that almost convinced her she was looking at a vision of Elora that was just as tangible and real as she was herself.

She saw another step, shimmering at ankle depth beyond the jetty platform, which she realized would place it below the level of the real floor. Before Thorn or the others could voice any opposition, she took that step, and then the one beyond, and so forth, in a steady gait . . .

. . . only to find herself ascending a circular stairway to emerge from a pool identical to the one she thought she was immersing herself in. She looked about herself in sudden startlement, catching a glimpse of her reflection looking up from the steps below, and wondered if the pair of them had simply switched places, in violation of every natural law she knew.

She waited what she hoped was a decent interval but none of the others emerged to follow her. She considered going back but desired first to see what stood atop the steps.

There was quite a difference. Where Daikini worked in wood and stone, the architects of this most ancient of physical Realms used crystal in their construction. As drab as the other side of the Gate had been, these walls were composed of the most gloriously intricate mosaic, a multitude of tiles, none larger than a fingernail, as meticulously cut as they must have been richly colored when first emplaced. There was a quality to the air that made all her physical senses register things far more intensely. She beheld more shades to every hue than she had names for, yet she could perceive each with a clarity that was almost painful. Sadly, that only made the diminution of the tiles all the more poignant. Time had worked on them as it does on all things, weathering them away, stealing their intensity, until they remained as no more than shadows of the splendor that once had been.

This chamber was open to the air, though she wasn't sure if that was the original intention as she beheld fluted crystalline columns rising in graceful arches to form a twelve-paneled dome above her head. She assumed the pillars were carved, as they would be in a Daikini construction, but as she drew closer she wondered if they had grown instead, to be shaped and pruned into this shape as an arborist might design a tree.

Most, she saw from the first, were broken, leaving chunks of stone in jumbled heaps around the pool.

Elora emerged from the top of the spiral staircase into a realm of perpetual twilight, a ghostly radiance that struck her as light that was gradually losing the ability to glow, forgetting this fundamental essence of its nature as people of a certain age begin to misplace the details of their lives. The landscape thus illuminated was barren in the same disturbing way, chockablock with the shapes and forms of existence yet marked everywhere she looked by a transcendent weariness, as if the very act of maintaining physical coherence was more trouble than it was worth.

Once upon a time this might have been a site of angular cliffs and dynamic vistas, but weather and sheer age had worn away most of the sharp edges. Daunting it may have been, but now the dominant impression was surprisingly tame. There wasn't much in the way of open ground, either, as though someone had swept through here long ago and smashed every imaginable promontory, natural or otherwise, wholly to rubble. Or perhaps they'd simply collapsed of their own accord.

There was age here, in the stones and earth and air, a quietude that had existed for longer than any of the races they had known could possibly remember.

"My-oh-my," she said as softly as she dared, comforted by the sound of her own voice, disturbed by the fact that it had no resonance. Sound traveled as weakly through this ancient air as did light, and she suspected a full-throated roar would go unheard beyond a handspan's distance.

"Ancient beyond our comprehension," she murmured to herself, "and incredibly weary of all that history, but not yet done. Dreamers seeking the source of dreams. Is this the world that's forgotten how, or simply run out?" Her voice was tinged with a gentle sadness. "Have they nothing more *to* dream?"

Hardly.

The new voice made her jump, her startlement coming from the eerie flat quality of those tonalities as much as from the fact of them being here at all.

At first she feared she might have imagined this, because none of her senses, not MageSight nor InSight, revealed a sign of the speaker. Then, in a way that trickled rime ice the length of her spine, a form seemed to disengage itself from a standing stone. Without apparent motion of any kind it glided from stone to stone toward her.

Thou ask't too much of senses.

"What else have I to go on?"

What, indeed? Thou art the Danan.

Statement, not question.

"I'm Elora Danan."

The Danan, yes. Thou hast come.

"I'm here, yes. Tell me, is this the fourth station on the Circle of the Flesh? Are you the firstborn race of elves that have gone wholly beyond the Veil?"

We are Malevoiy.

"In honor and, I hope, friendship, I bid you greeting." She meant what she said, every word, yet something about the moment, something about the man, wouldn't allow her to relax her guard.

The shape ghosted a smile, revealing a gleaming flash of predatory teeth that set her heart to pounding.

"I've come to ask your help."

That is known to Us.

"So you're not as far from the world as people believe."

We care little for such belief. That We exist is sufficient.

Only it wasn't, that she saw plain as daylight, and sensed as well that dreams in this realm might not be as tired and lackluster as she had presumed.

Thou art the first to find the way to Us, in an age.

"You use the royal plural, have I the honor of addressing the liege of this Realm?"

We are Malevoiy.

"Is that—"

We are. We were. We shall ever be. Thou art the Danan. Thou dost come before Us as supplicant, beseeching Our aid.

"The Realms are in danger."

How can the pieces hold fast, without a center to anchor them?

"I was hoping you could tell me."

Ah. And for this boon, what price? Wilt set thy kind, the Daikini, beneath Our yoke, to do with as We will and serve Us as We please, in perpetuity?

She rose, in no way matching the ethereal stillness of the Malevoiy's movements but with a grace and power uniquely her own.

"That's the bargain I'd expect from a minor Domain

of elves," she said, sensing that the creature had been serious about his terms, and yet at the same time the whole exchange was a source of considerable amusement.

Such were We, once, though Our Domain was in no way minor.

This, she decided, *is going bloody nowhere.* In that same thought, she decided to call it quits.

"I thank thee for thy hospitality, dread lord," she said. "I'll find my own way home."

Twelve rings affixed on three, to be bound entire by one, that is the scheme and riddle of things, Danan. To thee falls that task of binding, if thou hast heart and skill and daring. To tame the world is nothing, for We have done so. To tame the flesh, the same, for We have done that also. But to transcend, to reach to the Realm of spirit and beyond . . .

"You've done that, too."

When the world began, We were. When the rock of Creation split asunder to cast forth its multitudes, We were. Much have We seen, much more *would* We see.

"Then why don't you?"

There must be a balance. It must be restored. Thou art the key.

"So I gather."

We hold forth thy destiny, Danan. Wouldst claim it? Wouldst embrace Us?

There was ice throughout her body, in every particle of her being, as though her nerves had just been sluiced down with a bucket from an arctic mountain stream. She didn't understand how her heart could manage such a beat and not explode from the effort, or how one portion of her being could be so terribly cold while her blood generated such heat that her entire body was sheened with perspiration. She felt stretched, worse than on any rack, each tendon articulated, yet in absolute paradox she had never felt more at one with a place or a moment.

She would die here. She would kill.

It would be good.

Elora descended to the pool and, once again, without the slightest quirk of dislocation found herself climbing an identical set of steps, as if she and her mirror image had instantly exchanged places to continue on their way.

Thorn and Khory and Duguay were waiting.

"Elora Danan," Thorn called as he reached out to snatch her to clear of the pool and onto the jetty, "what have you done? Thank the blessed you were only gone an instant."

"It was longer than that, Thorn."

"Drumheller," Khory noted, "look at the pool. Your sigil's changed."

"A gift," Elora told them all. "A token. Of . . . respect. A favor granted, against a future favor in return." She took a deep breath and was a little surprised to find she didn't tremble. Quite the opposite, in fact, she felt unnaturally calm. "I've met the Malevoiy."

Duguay, she noted, had no overt reaction to her news.

"You asked their aid?" Thorn demanded of her.

Khory kept her distance, quietly gauging Elora's stance, as though she alone knew what had been offered and was waiting to learn Elora's response.

She shook her head. "It assumed I would. It offered me my destiny. I got the impression I was as important to its survival as to the other Realms."

"Of a Realm, of a circle, all are bound, little Princess."

She nodded to Khory. "So it said."

"Was there a reply?" from Thorn.

"It made none. Yet." She didn't like the Nelwyn's tone.

"And his price?"

"If it was serious, the price is too high."

"We may need that help, Elora, to fight the Deceiver and Greater Faery both."

She shook her head and let that slightest of movements stir her into a modest pirouette on the ball of one foot.

"All the stories—the tales and the legends used to terrify the children of every known race—they're all true," she told them. "The Malevoiy are predators, in the fullest sense of that word. The Wild Hunt we faced tonight, my friends, that's but the palest echo of what the Malevoiy did. Hard as it may be to see now, in their prime they were the embodiment of passion, driven by a hunger as red and raw as the world they made their home."

She looked from Khory to Thorn to Duguay, to see in their eyes a pale reflection of the part of her soul the Malevoiy had touched.

"They want those days again," she said. From Khory, she drew a steady, assessing gaze that carried with it a resonance of what she'd felt from the Malevoiy. Strangely, it reminded Elora of Luc-Jon's wolfhound, and with a start she realized that she was perceiving a vestige of the woman whose body Khory's spirit inhabited. Like the wolfhounds, this ancient warrior had been a foe of the Malevoiy, as implacable, as dedicated, as formidable. She had fought them, she had shed their blood and brought an end to lives that otherwise were immortal. And herself been betrayed and murdered for it, by one she loved.

"They want me to bring them to pass," she said. From Thorn, a sense of shock and horror that was almost physical as the moral center of his being caught up with the moment and he came to realize all that had transpired. *So easy,* she thought wryly, *to mark a set of circles on a tabletop and check off each of the Realms in turn, like running down a shopping list. We imagined physical risks and physical dangers galore, old duffer, we never took the leap, to consider the consequences of our encounters with the Realms of the Spirit. Or the price.*

And this is only the gateway! Who knows what we'll find beyond?

Without warning, Duguay snapped out his hand to catch Elora's by the wrist and draw her into a pair of sweeping circles.

"This place is death, pet," he told her. "You don't belong."

"Where would you prefer?" she responded with a sultry smile, her manner suddenly a match for his, as though a spark had just been struck to bone-dry tinder.

"Master Faralorn," snapped Thorn, "release Elora, at once!"

Lazily, with supreme self-confidence, Duguay swung her through a last pirouette and looked over his shoulder toward Thorn with a gesture and expression of studied disrespect.

"You don't get it, do you, peck?" For the first time he used the insulting diminutive for Nelwyns, and he meant it to hurt. "Malevoiy have no claim on her, nor do you. She's *mine*. Always has been, always will. This is *destiny*."

He never released his hold on Elora, though the grip was no more than fingertip to fingertip, and continued to guide her through those empty turns, a piece of vacuous choreography meant solely to demonstrate his control of her.

"I lead, she follows, we dance. There's the end of it."

"You can't do this," Thorn cried out.

"It's done."

"Wrong," she said, the quiet strength of her voice leaving the troubadour suddenly dumbstruck.

They faced each other, unmoving, and then, with a discreet shimmy of the hips and no sense whatsoever of how she accomplished it, Elora's belt and traveling pouches plopped to the stone. A similar flick of the shoulders divested her of her tartan cloak, leaving her dressed as she'd been for her performance in Kinshire. She flashed a hint of teeth in a predator's smile that brought an answer in kind from her partner.

"It's barely begun," Elora said.

With a snap of the wrist, she spun herself into his arms, her body pressed against his, and it was plain right then and there how much difference half a year had made. When they'd first met, for all her hardiness, she was small and a lot more tentative than she would ever admit. Height had come to her since, and breadth of spirit to match that of her powerful shoulders. She had a swimmer's build, but her strength was disguised by the sleek and elegant line of her body.

The girl had been no match for him, she took her lead from him.

In Duguay's arms, she was a woman, who faced him as an equal.

She set the dance and in a twinkling the pair of them had spun down the steps to disappear into the pool.

With a cry of mingled grief and rage the like of which he hadn't uttered since he beheld the shattered, scarred landscape that had once held the proud fortress of Tir Asleen and more beloved friends than he could easily number, Thorn snatched up belt and pouches and plunged after her, uncaring of risk or destination. Khory followed a quickstep behind, and her sword was ready.

They came too late—the Princess, the Mage, the Demon, the Dancer—to the summit of Creation, the Realm of the Dragons.

In size, the caldera of this ancient mountain dwarfed even the Wall, and small wonder, considering the bulk and dimensions of the beings who called it home. The four of them emerged from the line of steps to find themselves facing a veritable ocean of soft sand that would have stretched farther than the eye could see were it not for the jagged escarpments that loomed on every side, as though all the world you could see on a normal day was in truth but a minor part of some other world that was unimaginably greater.

In this place of wonder, they beheld desolation.

All was ice. The sand glittered with shiny crystals of frozen water, the rock was coated with hoarfrost, the air so cold each breath seared the lungs. The assault had come so suddenly, so savagely, the dragons had no chance to defend themselves or even to escape. About the four of them loomed the most monstrous statues, the entire community of these great and noble creatures, caught asleep or awake, in moments of relaxation or activity, hurled in that awful instant from vibrant life to frozen oblivion.

Thorn didn't need to ask who was responsible. This sacred place had been defiled by the same foul enchantment that had claimed Angwyn and destroyed Tir Asleen.

Elora didn't seem to care.

She was off the rock in a wild leap, Duguay following, the pair of them swirling like dervishes across the trackless miles of sand without a care as to how inappropriate they looked. They danced to music none but they could hear, and while Thorn had to acknowledge the evident passion of their performance, it was as nothing compared with the abyssal cold that had claimed the dragons.

Whatever Duguay had done, whatever choice Elora had made, he had to take a stand.

He called Elora's name, but the young woman ignored him as she and her partner joyously described apparently random patterns together across the sand.

There was poetry to their motion, for anyone with wit to look and grace to care. She would lead, then yield to him. He would cast her like a spinning blade into the air and use the momentum of the catch to send them off in a totally new direction. She would twist in and out of his grasp with the unbridled sinuosity of an eel.

While Thorn watched, appalled, these two unleashed the fullest measure of passion. They were fast, they were slow, they took pleasure in the abundance of a touch and the total absence of it. In this single dance, they held forth to one another the cherished intimacy of a lifetime together.

They found a fulfillment.

"I *know* you," Elora cried wildly to Duguay, using his title for the first time, "my Lord of the Dance."

"I know *you*," was his reply, "as I have from the beginning, my lady."

"I want to dance, Duguay, as we never have before."

"To what end, pet?"

"I want to burn. I want to find the firedrake in my soul and turn it loose. I want to light a furnace in this crater that no cold can stand against. I want them to be free! I want Mohdri dead!"

"It can't be done."

"Don't tell me that!"

"I tell you what is true."

"No! We can end this madness, here and now."

"Will you slay hope as well, Elora?"

She lost a beat, her feet snagging in the sand, and nearly fell, to find Duguay no longer in her arms but Kieron Dineer, the dragon who had died for her, once more wearing his human aspect.

"Kieron?" she stammered.

"Don't look so shocked," he said with a merry laugh. "Magic place, magic race, whose province is the Realm of Wonder. For us, especially here, all things are possible."

"Then save yourselves."

"We're doing our best."

"I don't understand. Where's Duguay, what's happening?"

"He's in your arms, as you are in his. But you have thoughts besides, and memories—and dreams. They are part of this as well."

"You shouldn't have died, Kieron." Her voice broke as he gathered her into his arms. "You shouldn't have died for me."

All things die, little dancer, change of voice, change of figure, taller than she and broader in every dimension with a thick shock of hair the color of jet and eyes that sparkled. He had a light dusting of beard, as much salt as pepper, and the shape of his bones marked him instantly as Kieron's sire. There was a crinkling about his eyes that spoke of a man who loved to laugh, and a gentleness to their depths that spoke of a kindly nature. His strength was self-evident and, she guessed, was matched by courage. She must have thought too loudly then, because she made him laugh.

A brave catalog of merits, my child, I am flattered.

"You're Calan," she said softly, respectfully, remembering his name from Thorn's tales of their sole encounter.

I am Calan.

495

"I want to stop the Deceiver."

And so you must, for much depends on it. Broad shoulders, but a young heart to bear such a burden. Fate does not always choose kindly.

There was a flash of sadness across his eyes, a remembrance that brought him pain, and she wanted to stop a moment, to tell him everything would be all right. Instead she put a surge of joy into her dance, whirling him after her in a circular four-four pattern that had just become all the rage in Sandeni. The elder dragon seemed much amused by her inspiration.

The circles turn, Elora, like wheels, he told her. *That is the way of things. Eternal and immutable. That cannot be stopped. But the direction can be changed.*

"That sounds like something Mohdri would say."

You are more alike than you know.

"Don't be so cruel. You're supposed to know everything, *be* everything—how could you let that monster take you by surprise?"

Is that what happened here? Truly?

"Always questions," she exploded in fury, "*always* riddles!"

Some things are best earned. What comes too easily is too often taken for granted, as a right. To bear the title of Sacred Princess is not necessarily to deserve it. Look about you, my child, tell me what you see.

"Desolation."

In that moment it was as though she'd been cleaved by a splitting wedge. Elora splintered, a part of her continuing gaily along with Duguay in her arms while a separate aspect stood stock-still upon the sand, her mouth forming an O of astonishment as she turned herself in a slow revolve, her eyes searching the magnificent forms entombed in ice about her. She'd been so caught up in the dance, and in her fury at what had been done here, she hadn't noticed an underlying sense of tremendous age, almost a weariness of spirit beside which the ennui of the Malevoiy was as nothing.

The spirit form of Calan stood beside her, to all appearances a Daikini in the prime of middle age. It was his eyes that gave the lie to that illusion, for within them was a depth that had no bottom, the accumulation of wisdom and folly, of sheer experience that Elora found wholly beyond her comprehension. These were eyes that could have seen the first dawn of Creation, this was the dragon whose fires could have ignited stars across the whole of the celestial firmament.

"No," she breathed, as a sense came to her of what transpired here.

You cannot save what is already doomed, Elora.

"No!" A keening wail that mingled denial with a terrible sense of loss.

All things have their allotted span. The struggle is not for the lives that are, but for the hopes and dreams that yet will be. You and Duguay are Lady and Lord of the Dance; you have a purpose. Now that purpose must be chosen.

"Mohdri!" Thorn bellowed again, even louder than before, in a voice and with a passion that would have done a dragon proud.

"I'm here, peck," said the Deceiver.

In form and feature he remained perfection. A sculpted body, whose face was defined by a succession of sharp and savage planes. Dark hair and darker eyes, every aspect of his being complemented by the abyssal hues of his armor. It was said in battle that Castellan Mohdri always emerged with his armor unscathed and pristine because any drop of blood that fell upon his person was instantly consumed. To face him in battle was to cast away all ties to life, because in single combat the lord of the Maizan could not be beaten. To try was death, not only of the body but of the soul as well.

Thorn had no knowledge of what the man had been like before the Deceiver claimed his form, but as far as the years since were concerned, he was prepared to believe every story. Like all Maizan, Mohdri carried a multitude of weapons, though the only ones in plain and constant view were the swords and assorted lesser blades he wore on his belt. As for the rest, chances are they would never be seen until the moment they took your life.

"Bastard," Thorn cried. "What have you *done?*"

"What I swore from the start. I am not the enemy, peck." The words were evenly, clearly spaced, as though to a backward child. "I am salvation."

"Not from what I see." The Nelwyn swept his staff around to show the frozen figures about them.

"Your vision was always limited. The Realms are at each other's throats, someone must teach them all their proper place."

"You, is it?"

"My destiny, Drumheller. My *curse!* I have fought my whole life to bring about this moment, I have beheld suffering the like of which you cannot comprehend, much less endure, I have *sacrificed*—!" He never told Thorn what was sacrificed. It didn't matter. Mohdri's eyes were wide, the expression in them so achingly familiar to the Nelwyn that Thorn was a full step forward in a reflexive gesture of comfort before Khory's hand upon his shoulder restored him to a semblance of his senses.

"And I will not be denied," the Deceiver said.

"*I* deny you," Thorn said.

"So you've said. What of it?"

"I am Thorn Drumheller," he said, drawing himself up proudly to his full height and letting his voice ring out as if it alone would prove sufficient to wake these ensorcelled creatures.

"I remember you with a kinder name."

"How can you remember what you've never known?"

"Let that be my mystery. Leave," the Deceiver said with such resignation in his voice that Thorn thought he saw this as a scene he'd played before, "and live."

The Nelwyn didn't move, save to hand Elora's belt over to Khory together with an injunction that she clear away.

She didn't listen, of course.

The demon child let fly a pair of knives and drew her

498

sword to follow. Mohdri slapped them aside and met her with a bared blade of his own. Steel rang over the ancient sands and Thorn had a sudden surge of hope as he saw that, for all Mohdri's considerable reputation, Khory was better. This was no duel of finesse and elegance; the two warriors hammered at each other with both hands, blades flashing faster in the crystalline light with every exchange of blows. Neither gave the slightest ground, the one found wanting would be the one to fall.

It should have been Mohdri.

With a terrific sequence of thrust and parry, Khory brought her weapon around a hair faster than his could follow. The swords snagged at the hilt and with a fierce twist and yank, the Castellan's hands were empty. Then, as if bored by the whole encounter, he struck with a casual sideswipe of his arm that sent her crashing to a pile of rocks nearby with the terrible sick sound of impact that spoke of bones breaking.

Thorn lashed out with all the sorcery at his command and for a while thought he, too, had a chance. He clapped fire from his hands. Mohdri shunted it aside, but only just. He brought the sand to life to entomb the Deceiver, only to watch that prison crumble to nothingness. He called lightning, he used all the raw elements of nature, he mixed spells with a madcap invention that defied sanity and, because they were in a place where no boundaries existed to divide dream from reality, watched them explode to bilious life.

He found no limit to his sorcery and summoned forth his talent in ways he'd only dreamed. He gave full vent to rage, to grief, to hatred. He made lances of solid air and laced their cores with poison. He conjured creatures of such magnitude and horror that the sight of them alone was enough to shrivel heart and soul. He hunted out the darkest parts of himself and cast them forth to battle, without restraint, without mercy. He used every aspect of his imagination in the only place there was where dreams could be manifested as the most deadly and destructive reality.

When he was done, shaking from the effects of so violent and thorough a purging, on his knees because his legs wouldn't hold him, clutching desperately to his staff to keep himself at least a little upright, he felt a strange sort of peace, like a house too long sealed, where all the windows have been suddenly thrown wide to admit the first sweet-scented breeze of spring.

He knew he hadn't won. He suspected he hadn't done the Deceiver the slightest lasting harm. He'd used all the weapons of his adversary, realizing as he did so that his adversary had to know them better. He found the Drumheller who lived without any form of constraint, who had no moral center, who was more a demon than any creature so named. He went to the place within himself where no sane man would dare to go and let loose the part of him that could do evil.

If he lived a thousand lifetimes, or found a way to walk from time's beginning to its end, he would never do so again.

There was no fear in Thorn's eyes as he watched the Deceiver emerge from the smoke and flame of his—Thorn's—conflagration. It might have been a trick of the eye, but it seemed to the Nelwyn that all those elements of foulness torn so brutally from his own soul swooped and eddied around Mohdri like boon companions.

To his surprise, he felt sorry for the man. Bavmorda was evil, that was plain fact, like the morning sunrise. Here, though, was someone who spoke of doing good, who yearned with all his heart for a better world, yet to accomplish it had embraced the most hideous of powers.

He wanted to tell Mohdri but knew it would be a waste of breath. Hearing, the Castellan most likely would not believe. And worse, believing, he would not care.

He cast about for Elora, wishing there was some way to spare her what was to come, and shook his head in wonderment to see her and Duguay dancing still.

"I knew about the skin, of course," said the fiend, referring to Elora with a pleasantness Thorn found disconcerting, as though they were old, dear chums having a teatime chat, "but what has she done to her hair? Elora Danan, I am *so* disappointed. No matter," he finished with that same companionable air. "When I have what I require from the girl, no more than is mine by right, all this nonsense will be speedily remedied."

"Do not do this," Thorn begged.

"I take no pleasure in it, believe me."

"Then find another way. If your goals are noble, why not use noble means to achieve them?"

"I tried. They failed. I'm sorry."

"Elora!" cried the Deceiver then, and if the tone of voice wasn't enough to stop the dancers in their tracks, the sight of his sword upraised over Thorn's bare neck was.

"I am the Danan," Elora replied, as though she was introducing herself to some stranger. Slowly, proudly, every inch a monarch in her own right, she turned from Duguay to face her nemesis.

Thorn's breath caught in his throat at the sight of her, because it suddenly seemed to him that he was looking at a stranger. The wildest elements of Duguay's paints had faded, allowing her natural argent tones to reassert themselves, interrupted by the violent colors of her skirt and top, equally dramatic slashes of color to accent lips and eyes and the blue-black tangle of her hair.

She looked savage but that wasn't the wonder of it. Seeing her standing in the heart of the caldera, for the first time since he'd found her in the bullrushes, he had the sense that she had found her home.

Mohdri didn't see it, or refused to understand. He chose to relate to her still as a pesky child.

"Will you *never* learn?" he hissed, giving way to an anger that bordered on the irrational as he strode toward her. Neither's gaze was still, each of them searching the other's face for something neither had a proper name for.

"I'm stubborn," Elora told him as he approached.

"I am Salvation."

"Go to hell!"

"This is my chance to set things right," Mohdri cried.

"How?"

"The dragons are the dream. Take it away—or rather, place it under proper control—and the Realms become manageable. Nothing will change, because all within them will have lost the capacity to conceive of such a thing. A balance will be achieved and, once achieved, maintained. When the time is right, growth will be apportioned as needed. Society will have order. The future will be preserved."

"What future?" cried Elora, aghast by what she'd just heard. "You're talking about another kind of death!"

"I've seen death, girl. Believe me, this is better. And wherein am I cruel here? What you condemn as slavery, others might label peace. None will resent their place in the scheme of things because none will have the slightest inkling that something better is possible. Because that judgment requires a leap of faith, of logic, of *imagination*—that my control of the dragons will deny them. It requires the capacity to *dream*."

"That's obscene."

"Don't you judge me, Elora Danan, you haven't the right."

"I am the Danan. I will fight you."

The Deceiver lashed out to catch her by the throat.

"You are nothing. You are a memory, soon to be expunged as I would cauterize a rotting wound."

Elora heard the opening stanza of the Spell of Dissolution, felt those silver moonglow tendrils reach out from the Deceiver's consciousness to hers. There was fear at their touch, but not the terror she'd felt the night of her Ascension. The image came to her of Khory in their duels together and most important of that last confrontation, when skill and talent and above all desire had coalesced to allow her, for those minutes, to stretch herself to the demon child's level.

She remembered the firedrakes, of how gloriously they slipped through the warp and woof of reality, without a care for any of the boundaries imposed on them by subjective or objective reality. They went where they pleased, and if something barred their way, they found a different path that either led them around the obstacle or to somewhere wholly different.

So it was here. The spell reached out for her but she wasn't there to be ensnared. She made the substance of her soul molten, as impossible to grasp as quicksilver, able in the process to confound the leading elements of Mohdri's spell, to tangle them and disrupt the cohesive patterning so integral to the proper dissolution of her personality.

It wasn't salvation. For a confrontation on this magus level, Thorn's power and his resources weren't sufficient to win the day, as his duel with Mohdri had most cruelly demonstrated. She wasn't even that good yet, or truly that strong.

She didn't need to be.

She reached her arms past Mohdri, felt the electric tingle of Duguay's touch.

Music swelled in both of them, he led, she followed, with the Castellan between them. The problem with casting a spell is the amount of concentration it takes. Casting one of Dissolution requires a tremendous amount, so much so that Mohdri was forced to withdraw deep inside himself to properly wield the necessary powers. He had to take especial care with Elora, far more than Bavmorda did when she attempted the same rite. She wanted the child annihilated, body and soul. Mohdri needed the body intact. That required precision.

He in no way left himself vulnerable. Any overt threat, physical or mystic, would snap him from his trance in an instant and be dealt with almost as quickly. But this was a dance. There was no danger here, how could there possibly be?

Together, the three of them retraced the steps already laid out by Elora and Duguay. Seemingly, it was a random pattern of movements, with nothing special about them. Only from a dragon's perspective could the truth be seen. They had marked the floor of the caldera with the sigil Elora had found at the end of the storybook, in effect crafting for themselves a monstrous World Gate. As Carig had etched one symbol as a Summons, so was this in turn a Banishment. The Dancer comes to the world alone, he claims a partner, and on the rarest of occasions, the pair of them return to his domain together. For Elora, once she realized the Deceiver's ultimate destination and intent, this seemed the only choice and a sacrifice she was more than willing to make.

As Elora and Duguay repeated their dance, with the Deceiver between them, they left a trail of power behind, as volatile as oil. Its climax would be the spark that set it alight, and the energy of that blaze would pop the Gate open wide. Mohdri would be carried with Duguay and Elora to Duguay's domain, there to remain forever. He might find a way out, but she doubted it, since she would remain to bar his path. For all the Deceiver's power, her senses told her that he was still fundamentally human, grounded on too many basic levels to the Circles of the World and the Flesh to long endure that of the Spirit. That the same applied to her, that the same dissolution of self would ultimately claim her, was a fact she chose to ignore. Was this her purpose? She didn't know, she didn't care, what mattered was the victory. Ending the threat of the Deceiver. For whatever followed, the Realms could settle their own affairs.

Why is Duguay smiling? she thought, and said, softly, so as not to break the seductive rhythm of their dance and disturb Mohdri. "Why are you smiling?"

"At you, pet, who dare so much and know so little."

"Some of the bravest deeds spring from rank ignorance."

"See to your friends. I will finish here."

She didn't comprehend for a moment and stumbled over a toe. No lasting harm done, Mohdri appeared well and truly caught up in the flow of their movements, responding to Duguay's cues as readily as Elora.

"What?" she stammered. "What?"

"You have a destiny. And I an obligation. I would have died at Ganthem's Crossing but for you."

"Does corporeal death have meaning for such as you?"

"The spells those High Elves meant to cast would have held me for a time. That time would have been unpleasant. Now that debt is paid. In truth, I hold in my arms what was desired from the start."

"The Spell of Dissolution—!"

"Has no power over the likes of me. You are much desired, my pet, but needed more elsewhere. Go now. Quickly."

He released his hold on her hands and, in that same blink of time, gracefully brought Mohdri around to face him so that they were arm in arm as he and Elora had been. The young woman stood stock-still, uncomprehending, and watched them twirl away, moving faster than they had before.

She turned back to Thorn and crossed the distance to him at a dead run to find him ministering to Khory.

"Get to our World Gate," she told them.

Duguay and Mohdri were dancing faster still, a waltz fit more for demons than for human beings, and Elora felt a pang of loss at the thought of the glory she was missing. The climax of both dance and spell was near.

Elora took a step toward them.

Something wasn't right.

Another step, ignoring Thorn's call, shaking her head at a stabbing discontinuity of vision as InSight yanked her to another place rich with a giddy excitement unfelt for too long a time. Elora staggered, wondering if this is what it was like to be one of those daredevils who go off the Wall in a tub, determined to make the plunge into Morar and live to tell the tale. Her breath went out of her as though she'd been punched. She looked around frantically, seeing not the caldera of the dragon's volcano but another vision overlaying it, some grand and royal celebration with music and dancing and she, as always, the belle of the ball.

She put one foot before the other, faster with every step, wishing for wings to cover the distance to Duguay and Mohdri more quickly.

The dance was interacting with Mohdri's spell to strip away illusions, it wasn't what he intended, Duguay couldn't help himself.

To her horror, Elora realized, *He's dancing with Mohdri the way he would with me!*

They stopped, all of a sudden, Duguay taking a step back in reflexive surprise, Mohdri staggering himself, wrapped in confusion, part of him screaming of danger while another yearned plaintively for the waltz to start again.

Mohdri raised his head, only it wasn't *his* head any longer. The Deceiver's mask had been torn away.

What Elora beheld was her own face.

Older, so much older, skin touched with gold instead of gleaming silver, hair the vaguely remembered shade of strawberry blond. Not so ready a smile anymore, and lines etched deep wherever lines could go. It was a face that had never known physical hardship or privation, whose fiercest struggles had always been on the battle-field of the soul. Win or lose, she had paid a terrible price.

It's a lie, Elora wanted to say, desiring more than any-thing to shout it to the highest point of the heavens. *What else to expect from a creature called the Deceiver?*

Yet it explained so much. Knowledge that no one else could have, and the power over Elora herself that came with it. The ability to anticipate events: small surprise if they had already happened to her at some point in the past.

Their eyes met, across an expanse of sand.

"You're not me," was what finally emerged.

"If I fail," her older self replied, "I am."

The horror to Elora was that the other woman be-lieved it, with a certainty as irrefutable as the turning of the world.

"I can't let you do this," she said, sure of neither thoughts nor emotions any longer but willing to trust her instincts all the same.

"You can't stop me. The power is already mine, the

dragons are little more than ghosts." Her smile was cruel, made worse by the fact that Elora could see in it a portion of her own. "They were little more than ghosts when I arrived. Their day is done, their lives but shadows, for me to claim as my own. I am the Sacred Princess, such is my right!"

Elora searched for Duguay but the Deceiver struck first, with a force and ruthlessness that made Elora gasp. She lashed out at him with a veritable forest of energy waves that drained the Dancer dry at the touch. In that twinkling, Duguay's corporeal host was reduced to a husk, but the Deceiver didn't allow the cord of his existence to snap. She held him prisoner, spirit lashed tight inside that casement of dust while she drew his power to her.

Instinct sent Elora into a leaping backward spin, a sudden movement that caught her by surprise as much as the Deceiver. She arched over her back in midair to come down straight as any spear into the core of the sigil she and Duguay had so carefully wrought. As she landed she called forth all the fire in her soul, the passions she had barely begun to tap, the dreams she would not allow the Deceiver to steal away, and shot them into the ground like a bolt from heaven.

She thought the sigil would ignite like something set afire, with flames racing helter-skelter outward from the center. All its elements, though, flared to life as one, filling the crater with a soft, golden radiance.

At the same time Elora hurled herself at the Deceiver, colliding with a tackle hard enough to bounce that armored figure to the ground. She straddled the villain's chest, calling on all the hours she spent at Torquil's forge, all the emotional intensity she'd learned by Duguay's side, and she heaved. Up and over the Deceiver went, bouncing once as she landed within the boundary of the sigil.

Little fool, she heard in her own mind, in her own voice, as though she was talking to herself, *would you doom us all?*

Elora had no answer, only determination, and an acknowledgment that this was a price she was prepared to pay.

The face might have been hers but the body remained as strong and vital as Mohdri's. The Deceiver lunged for her, Elora pitching herself aside in a frantic crab scuttle, only to be brought up short by a collision with a glowing ribbon of energy thrown up by the sigil. As Elora watched, the ground began to melt away along the pathways she and Duguay had made, the radiance rapidly arcing from gold to silver to a blue-white glare so penetrating that it made the flesh of her arms transparent as she held them over her eyes.

You think you've won, the Deceiver snarled, *but you have not. You would match yourself against* me, *Elora Danan?*

The radiance was eating away steadily at all the plots of ground within the sigil, yet the Deceiver didn't appear to mind. She stood as she might on a set of battlements, surveying the approach of some enemy she was about to destroy. The thought amused her, the battle meant nothing to her. She had no doubt of the outcome.

Learn now, the Deceiver proclaimed, *how futile is that enterprise.*

The Deceiver cupped her hands one over the other and a ball of energy popped into being. From it curled snakelike tendrils, painfully reminiscent of the ones Elora had seen wrapped tight around Ryn Taksemanyin's soul by the Maizani sorceress, only these were far more foul in origin and far more deadly in effect. It had a stench to it, this spell, and Elora's hand went to her throat as the image of the Slave Ring came to mind.

There was one tendril for every dragon, and the young woman knew that the slightest touch would mean their doom. They had been encased in ice to hold them, to sap their physical vitality and weaken their will to resist, as the Deceiver had done to all the assembled monarchs in Angwyn years before. This was to finish them, to steal away their souls, the essence of their being as a race, to some secret place of the Deceiver's, to be doled out in portions as she saw fit. Or most likely, never to be seen again.

No more laughter, no delight, no dreams of things that never were.

One dragon stood paramount among their number, on a crag that loomed above the head of the caldera, and when Elora's eyes sought his, she knew this was the true form of Calan Dineer.

"I don't know what to do," she cried, despairing that he would hear. *"I don't know what to do!"*

She remembered the Malevoiy, how it stretched its sibilants the way people think a snake might talk, of how for all its age it found delight in the thought of killing.

She would kill, it told her gleefully.

It would be good.

"No," she wept, and took no notice of the fact that one of the Deceiver's spell strands was reaching for her, and more back toward where Thorn and Khory lay watching.

In her mind Elora forged a spear. It was a work of wondrous beauty, with an edge that could cut spirit from flesh, for that was its purpose. It came from the forge of imagination white-hot, a shapeless blob of incandescence, to be taken in her tongs and hammered and pounded and honed, the metal folded again and again and again until there wasn't a substance in creation that was proof against it.

Elora worked quickly because there was no time, but she remained true to the craft that she'd been taught. In every way, when she was done, this was a creation to be proud of.

A vision of her stood tall within her mind, bouncing the spear a few times to gauge the heft of it.

She looked at each of the dragons in turn, knowing their peril, but determined to fix each and every visage indelibly in her memory.

While she lived they would not be forgotten.

In her imagination, that vision of herself reared back and let fly the spear.

And because this was the Realm where imagination could be made flesh, that spear took tangible form that selfsame instant. She and Calan were separated by miles, but that didn't matter. It wasn't the strength of her arm that propelled the shaft, but of her will.

Calan lifted his great head to the sky, as did the others in kind, and in a voice that made Elora's heart leap to her throat, the dragons cried their defiance here as they did in the story she told back at the fort, a whole lifetime ago it seemed.

As one, they called out, *Freedom!*

And like that ancient hero, they died.

There was a light too impossible to be endured. There was the heat of all creation being born. There was sensation that could not be described, as an entire generation of dragons was returned in that terrible instant to the celestial fires that gave them birth.

Elora saw it all, heard it all, felt it all. She stood at the heart of the holocaust, but was not consumed. She felt the substance of the Deceiver melt away, but knew that meant nothing. Her adversary would not be beaten so easily. In this place the Deceiver was spirit made flesh, an animate projection of her will, brought to life in part by the sacrifice of the twelve Maizani sorcerers who'd opened the Sandeni Gate. The corporeal form of Castellan Mohdri was no doubt safely bunkered deep within Maizani territory.

With measured tread, Elora crossed the whole of that great caldera, now hollow and empty for the first time in living memory.

Unsure of what they'd find, or what to do, Thorn and Khory followed, giving wide berth to that portion of ground where the sigil had been drawn and the World Gate opened. It appeared solid enough but neither was of a mind to test it.

They too had beheld the Deceiver's true face. To Thorn the sight was a stab through his heart, made worse by what Elora had done right afterward.

The dragons were the soul of the world, they stood

at the summit of the Third Circle of Creation. Now they were gone.

Elora Danan met them halfway, a vision in silver with robes the color of blood, as wild and elemental as the first spring of a newborn world.

She walked proudly, happily, and on her face was a smile that spoke of a whole world of possibilities. In each arm, she carried a dragon's egg.

The past was done. In her charge, as freely accepted as given, was the promise of the bright, new future yet to be.

CHRIS CLAREMONT is best known for his seventeen-year stint on Marvel Comics' *The Uncanny X-Men,* during which it was the bestselling comic in the Western Hemisphere for a decade; he has sold more than 100 million comic books to date. His novels *First Flight, Grounded!* and *Sundowner* were science fiction bestsellers. Recent projects include the dark fantasy novel *Dragon Moon* and *Sovereign Seven*™, a comic book series published by DC Comics. He lives in Brooklyn, New York.

GEORGE LUCAS is the founder of Lucasfilm Ltd., one of the world's leading entertainment companies. He created the *Star Wars* and *Indiana Jones* film series, each film among the all-time leading box-office hits. Among his story credits are *THX 1138, American Graffiti,* and the *Star Wars* and *Indiana Jones* films. He lives in Marin County, California.

REALMS OF FANTASY

The biggest, brightest stars from Bantam Spectra

Maggie Furey

A fiery-haired Mage with an equally incendiary temper must save her world and her friends from a pernicious evil, with the aid of four forgotten magical Artefacts.

AURIAN ___56525-7 $5.99
HARP OF WINDS ___56526-5 $5.99
SWORD OF FLAME ___56527-3 $5.99
DHIAMMARA ___57557-0 $6.50

Katharine Kerr

The mistress of Celtic fantasy presents her ever-popular Deverry series. Most recent titles:

DAYS OF BLOOD AND FIRE ___29012-6 $5.99/$7.50
DAYS OF AIR AND DARKNESS ___57262-8 $6.50/$8.99
THE RED WYVERN ___37290-4 $12.95/$17.95

REALMS OF
FANTASY

The biggest, brightest stars from Bantam Spectra

Paula Volsky

Rich tapestries of magic and revolution, romance and forbidden desires.

THE WHITE TRIBUNAL___37846-5 $13.95/$19.95
THE GATES OF TWILIGHT ___57269-5 $6.50/$8.99

Angus Wells

Epic fantasy in the grandest tradition of magic, dragons, and heroic quests. Most recent titles:

EXILE'S CHILDREN: Book One of the Exiles Saga
___29903-4 $5.99/$7.99
EXILE'S CHALLENGE: Book Two of the Exiles Saga
___37812-0 $12.95/$17.95
LORDS OF THE SKY
___57266-0 $5.99/$7.99

- -

REALMS OF FANTASY

The biggest, brightest stars from Bantam Spectra

Robin Hobb

One of our newest and most exciting talents presents a tale of honor and subterfuge, loyalty and betrayal.

ASSASSIN'S APPRENTICE: Book One of the Farseer

___57339-X $6.50/$8.99 Canada

ROYAL ASSASSIN: Book Two of the Farseer

___57341-1 $6.50/$8.99 Canada

ASSASSIN'S QUEST: Book Three of the Farseer

___56569-9 $6.50/$8.99 Canada

Michael A. Stackpole

High fantasy from the *New York Times* bestselling author:

ONCE A HERO ___56112-X $5.99/$7.99

TALION: REVENANT ___57656-9 $5.99/$7.99